BRIAN AZZARELLO
writer

EDUARDO RISSO
art & colors

MOONSHINE

VOL. 1

JARED K. FLETCHER
letters & design

CRISTIAN ROSSI
color assistant

WILL DENNIS
editor

IMAGE COMICS, INC.

Robert Kirkman - Chief Operating Officer
Erik Larsen - Chief Financial Officer
Todd McFarlane - President
Marc Silvestri - Chief Executive Officer
Jim Valentino - Vice-President
Eric Stephenson - Publisher
Corey Murphy - Director of Sales
Jeff Boison - Director of Publishing Planning & Book Trade Sales
Chris Ross - Director of Digital Sales
Jeff Stang - Director of Specialty Sales
Kat Salazar - Director of PR & Marketing
Branwyn Bigglestone - Controller
Sue Korpela - Accounts Manager
Drew Gill - Art Director
Brett Warnock - Production Manager
Meredith Wallace - Print Manager
Tricia Ramos - Traffic Manager
Briah Skelly - Publicist
Ally Hoffman - Conventions & Events Coordinator
Sasha Head - Sales & Marketing Production Designer
David Brothers - Branding Manager
Melissa Gifford - Content Manager
Drew Fitzgerald - Publicity Assistant
Vincent Kukua - Production Artist
Erika Schnatz - Production Artist
Ryan Brewer - Production Artist
Shanna Matuszak - Production Artist
Carey Hall - Production Artist
Esther Kim - Direct Market Sales Representative
Emilio Bautista - Digital Sales Associate
Leanna Caunter - Accounting Assistant
Chloe Ramos-Peterson - Library Market Sales Representative
Marla Eizik - Administrative Assistant

IMAGECOMICS.COM

ISBN: 978-1-5343-0064-4.
ISBN DCBS: 978-1-5343-0396-6.
ISBN NEWBURY EXCLUSIVE: 978-1-5343-0397-3.
ISBN FORBIDDEN PLANET/BIG BANG EXCLUSIVE: 978-1-5343-0398-0.

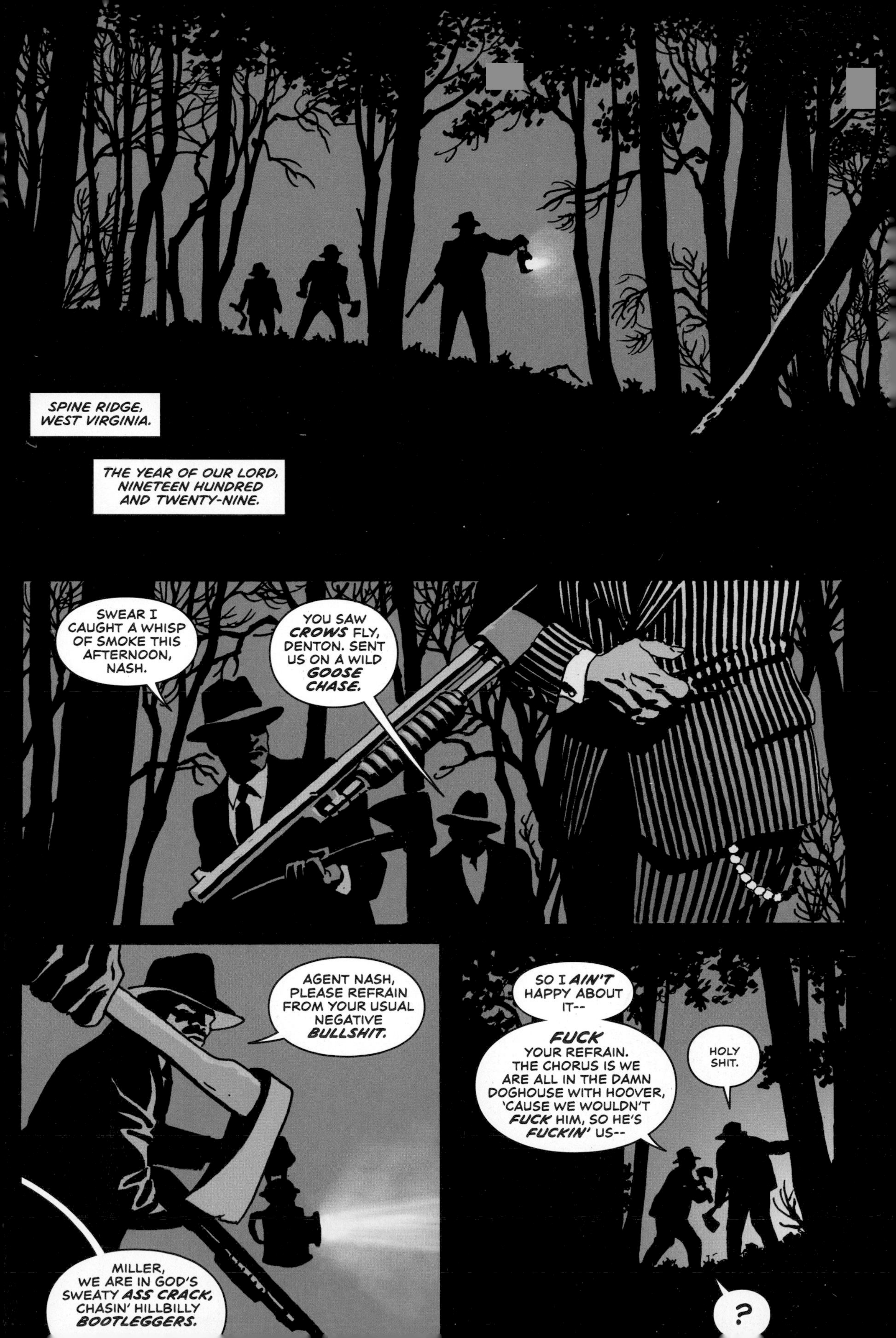
SPINE RIDGE, WEST VIRGINIA.
THE YEAR OF OUR LORD, NINETEEN HUNDRED AND TWENTY-NINE.
SWEAR I CAUGHT A WHISP OF SMOKE THIS AFTERNOON, NASH.
YOU SAW CROWS FLY, DENTON. SENT US ON A WILD GOOSE CHASE.
AGENT NASH, PLEASE REFRAIN FROM YOUR USUAL NEGATIVE BULLSHIT.
MILLER, WE ARE IN GOD'S SWEATY ASS CRACK, CHASIN' HILLBILLY BOOTLEGGERS.
SO I AIN'T HAPPY ABOUT IT--
FUCK YOUR REFRAIN. THE CHORUS IS WE ARE ALL IN THE DAMN DOGHOUSE WITH HOOVER, 'CAUSE WE WOULDN'T FUCK HIM, SO HE'S FUCKIN' US--
HOLY SHIT.
?

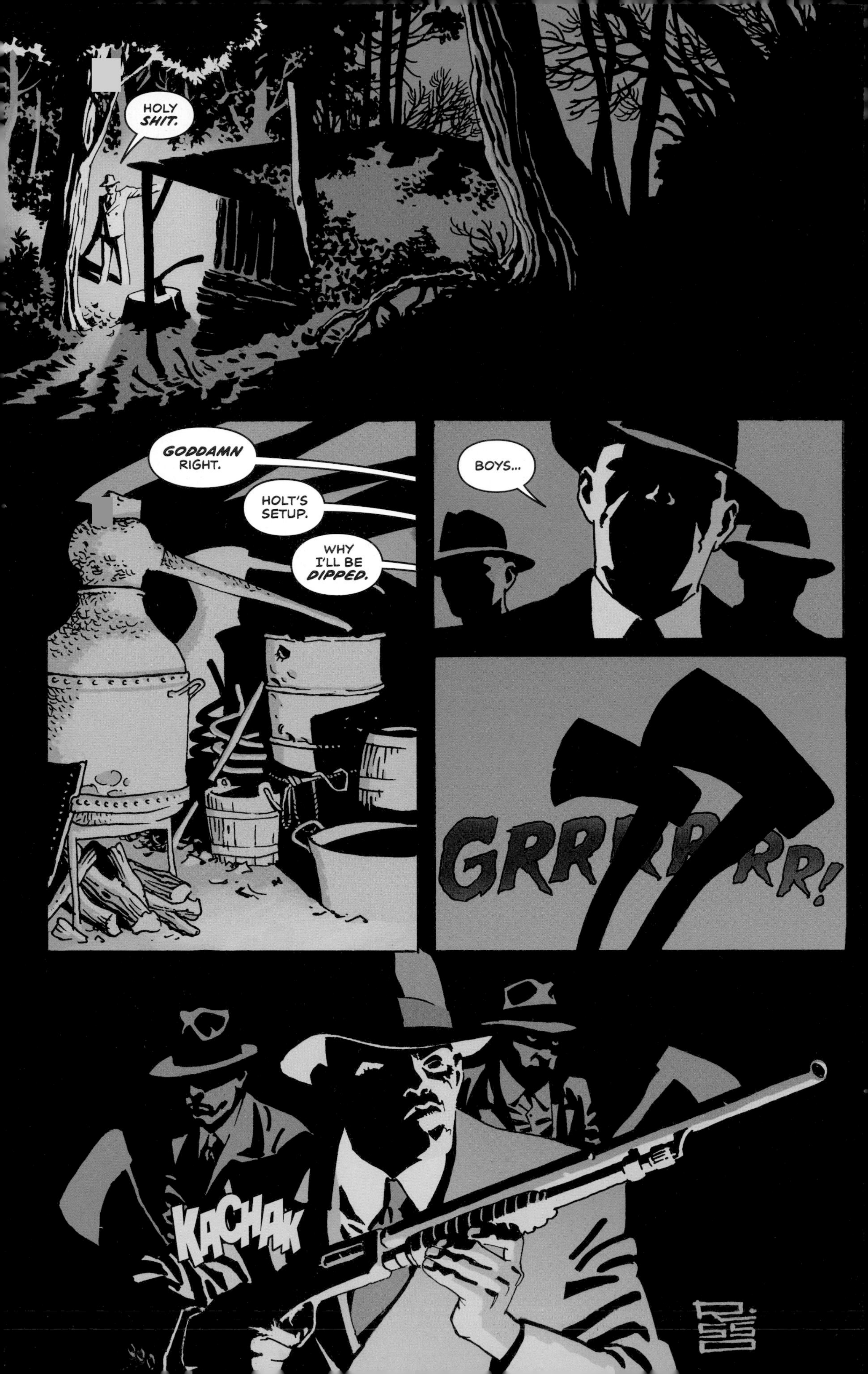
HOLY SHIT.
GODDAMN RIGHT.
HOLT'S SETUP.
WHY I'LL BE DIPPED.
BOYS...
GRRRRRRR!
KACHAK

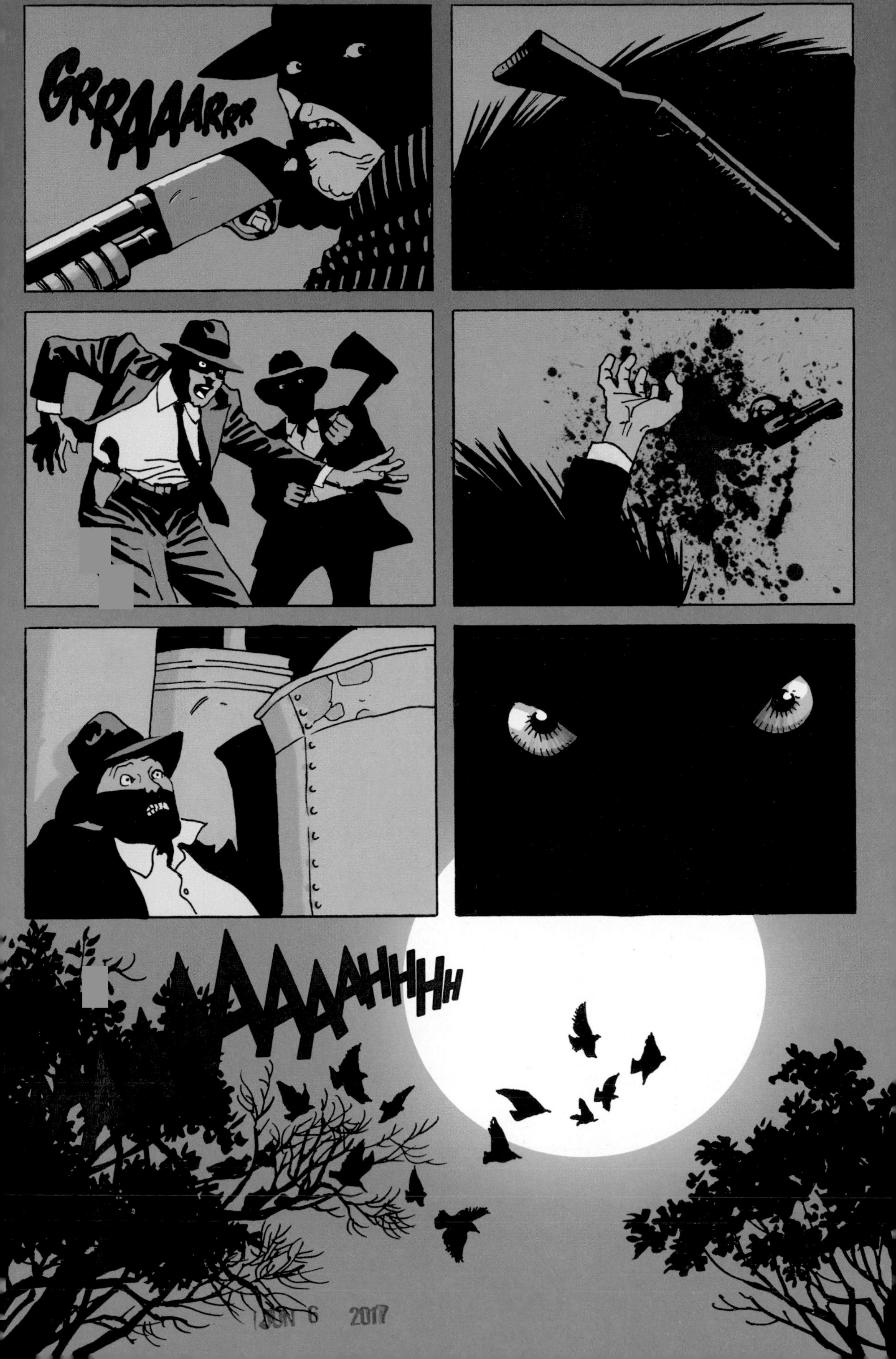
GRRAAAARRRR
AAAAAHHHH

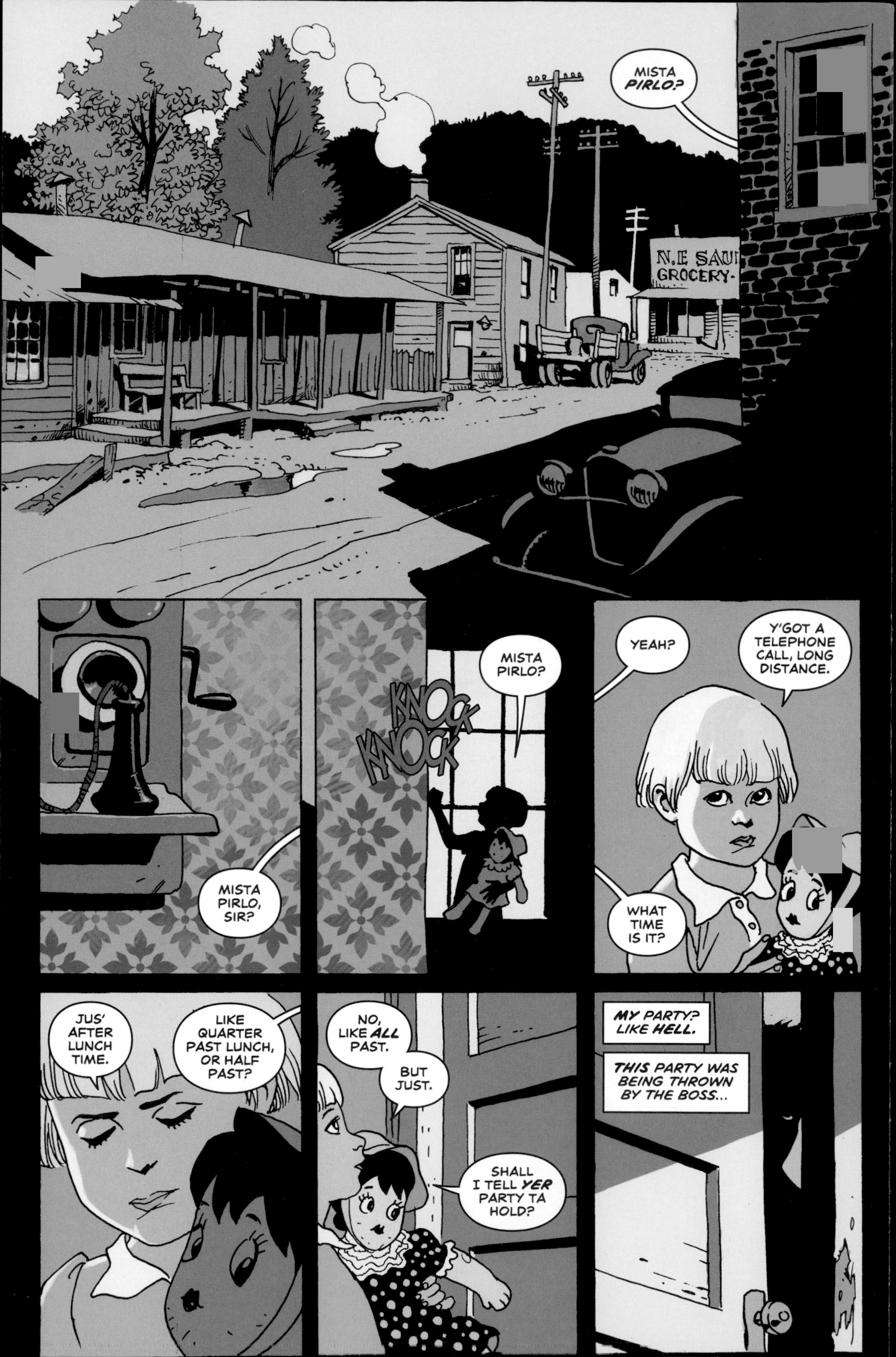
N.E SAU
GROCERY
MISTA *PIRLO?*
MISTA PIRLO, SIR?
KNOCK KNOCK
MISTA PIRLO?
YEAH?
Y'GOT A TELEPHONE CALL, LONG DISTANCE.
WHAT TIME IS IT?
JUS' AFTER LUNCH TIME.
LIKE QUARTER PAST LUNCH, OR HALF PAST?
NO, LIKE *ALL* PAST.
BUT JUST.
SHALL I TELL *YER* PARTY TA HOLD?
MY PARTY? LIKE *HELL.*
THIS PARTY WAS BEING THROWN BY THE BOSS...

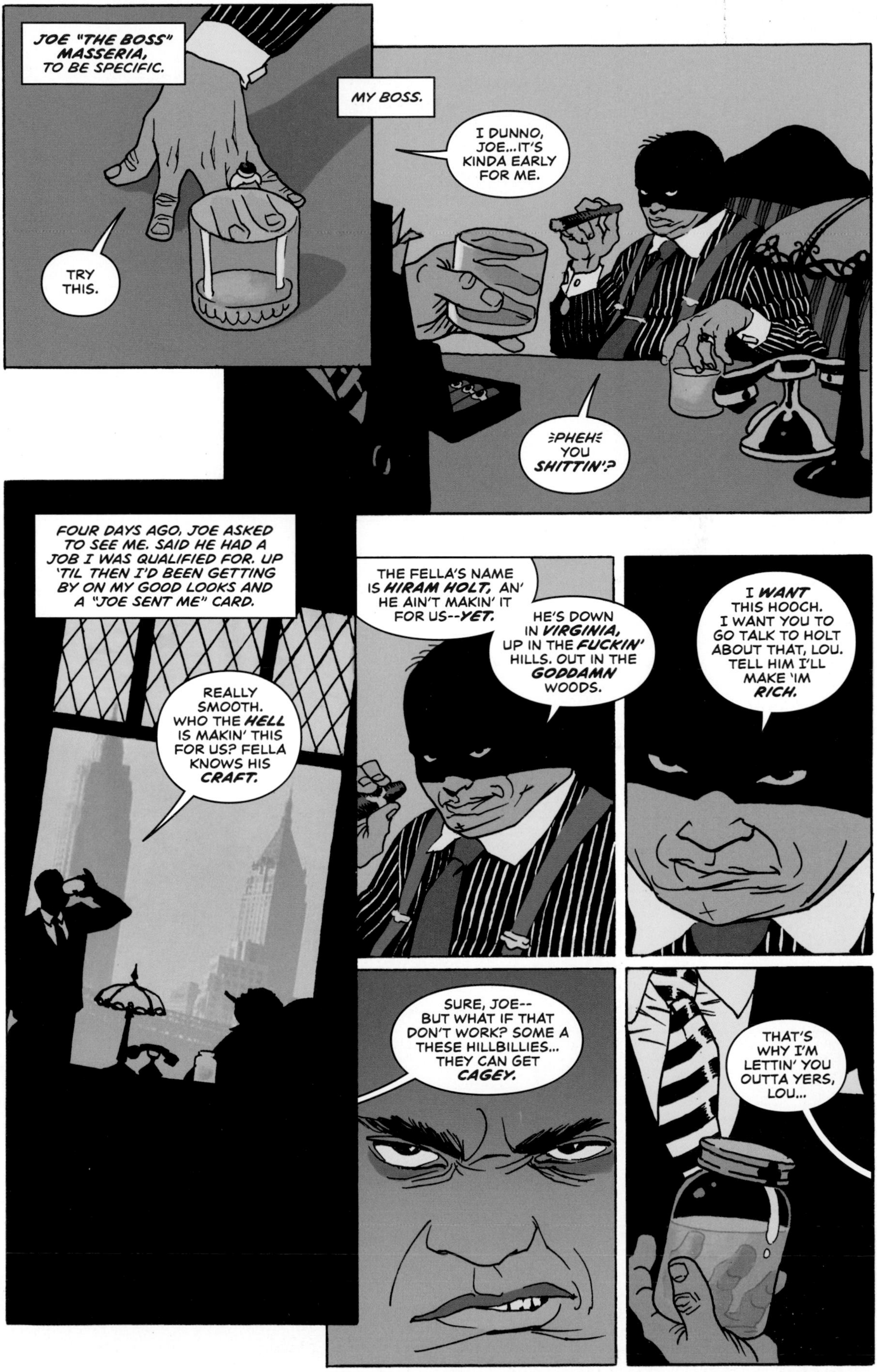

JOE "THE BOSS" MASSERIA, TO BE SPECIFIC.
TRY THIS.
MY BOSS.
I DUNNO, JOE...IT'S KINDA EARLY FOR ME.
PHEH YOU SHITTIN'?
FOUR DAYS AGO, JOE ASKED TO SEE ME. SAID HE HAD A JOB I WAS QUALIFIED FOR. UP 'TIL THEN I'D BEEN GETTING BY ON MY GOOD LOOKS AND A "JOE SENT ME" CARD.
REALLY SMOOTH. WHO THE HELL IS MAKIN' THIS FOR US? FELLA KNOWS HIS CRAFT.
THE FELLA'S NAME IS HIRAM HOLT, AN' HE AIN'T MAKIN' IT FOR US--YET.
HE'S DOWN IN VIRGINIA, UP IN THE FUCKIN' HILLS. OUT IN THE GODDAMN WOODS.
I WANT THIS HOOCH. I WANT YOU TO GO TALK TO HOLT ABOUT THAT, LOU. TELL HIM I'LL MAKE 'IM RICH.
SURE, JOE-- BUT WHAT IF THAT DON'T WORK? SOME A THESE HILLBILLIES... THEY CAN GET CAGEY.
THAT'S WHY I'M LETTIN' YOU OUTTA YERS, LOU...

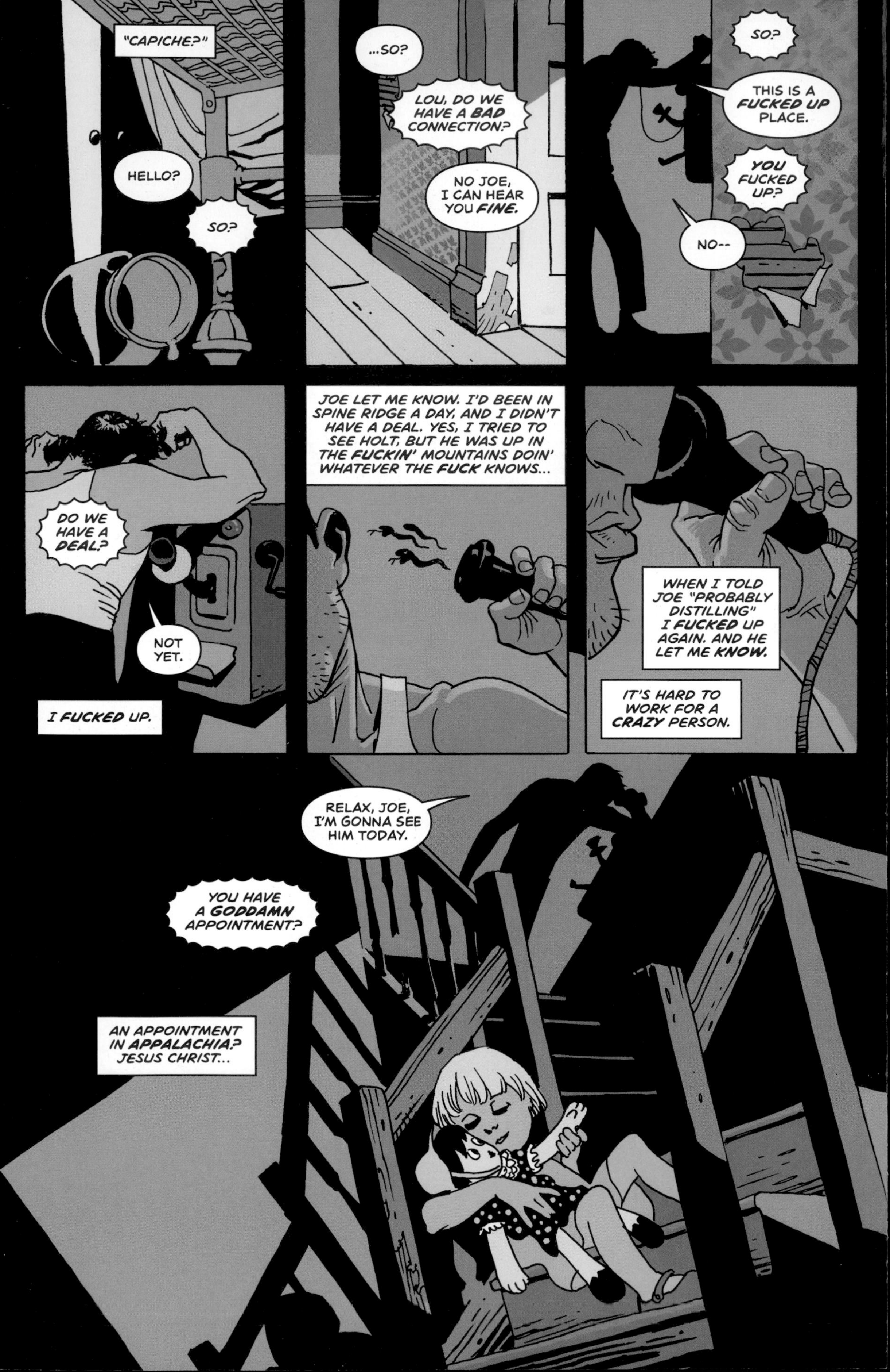
"CAPICHE?"
HELLO?
SO?
...SO?
LOU, DO WE HAVE A BAD CONNECTION?
NO JOE, I CAN HEAR YOU FINE.
SO?
THIS IS A FUCKED UP PLACE.
YOU FUCKED UP?
NO--
DO WE HAVE A DEAL?
NOT YET.
I FUCKED UP.
JOE LET ME KNOW. I'D BEEN IN SPINE RIDGE A DAY, AND I DIDN'T HAVE A DEAL. YES, I TRIED TO SEE HOLT, BUT HE WAS UP IN THE FUCKIN' MOUNTAINS DOIN' WHATEVER THE FUCK KNOWS...
WHEN I TOLD JOE "PROBABLY DISTILLING" I FUCKED UP AGAIN. AND HE LET ME KNOW.
IT'S HARD TO WORK FOR A CRAZY PERSON.
RELAX, JOE, I'M GONNA SEE HIM TODAY.
YOU HAVE A GODDAMN APPOINTMENT?
AN APPOINTMENT IN APPALACHIA? JESUS CHRIST...

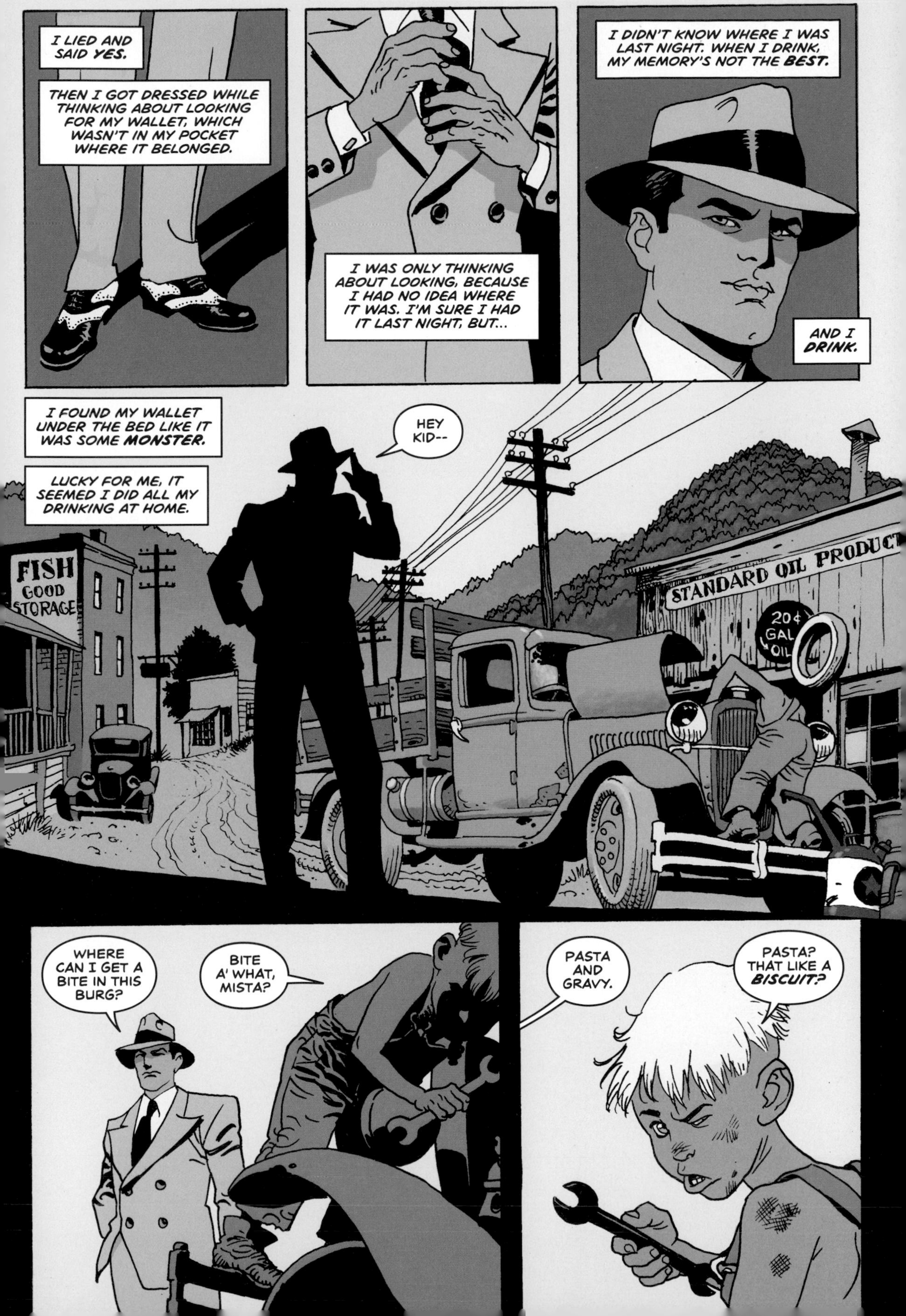
I LIED AND SAID YES.
THEN I GOT DRESSED WHILE THINKING ABOUT LOOKING FOR MY WALLET, WHICH WASN'T IN MY POCKET WHERE IT BELONGED.
I WAS ONLY THINKING ABOUT LOOKING, BECAUSE I HAD NO IDEA WHERE IT WAS. I'M SURE I HAD IT LAST NIGHT, BUT...
I DIDN'T KNOW WHERE I WAS LAST NIGHT. WHEN I DRINK, MY MEMORY'S NOT THE BEST.
AND I DRINK.
I FOUND MY WALLET UNDER THE BED LIKE IT WAS SOME MONSTER.
LUCKY FOR ME, IT SEEMED I DID ALL MY DRINKING AT HOME.
HEY KID--
FISH GOOD STORAGE
STANDARD OIL PRODUCT
20¢ GAL OIL
WHERE CAN I GET A BITE IN THIS BURG?
BITE A' WHAT, MISTA?
PASTA AND GRAVY.
PASTA? THAT LIKE A BISCUIT?

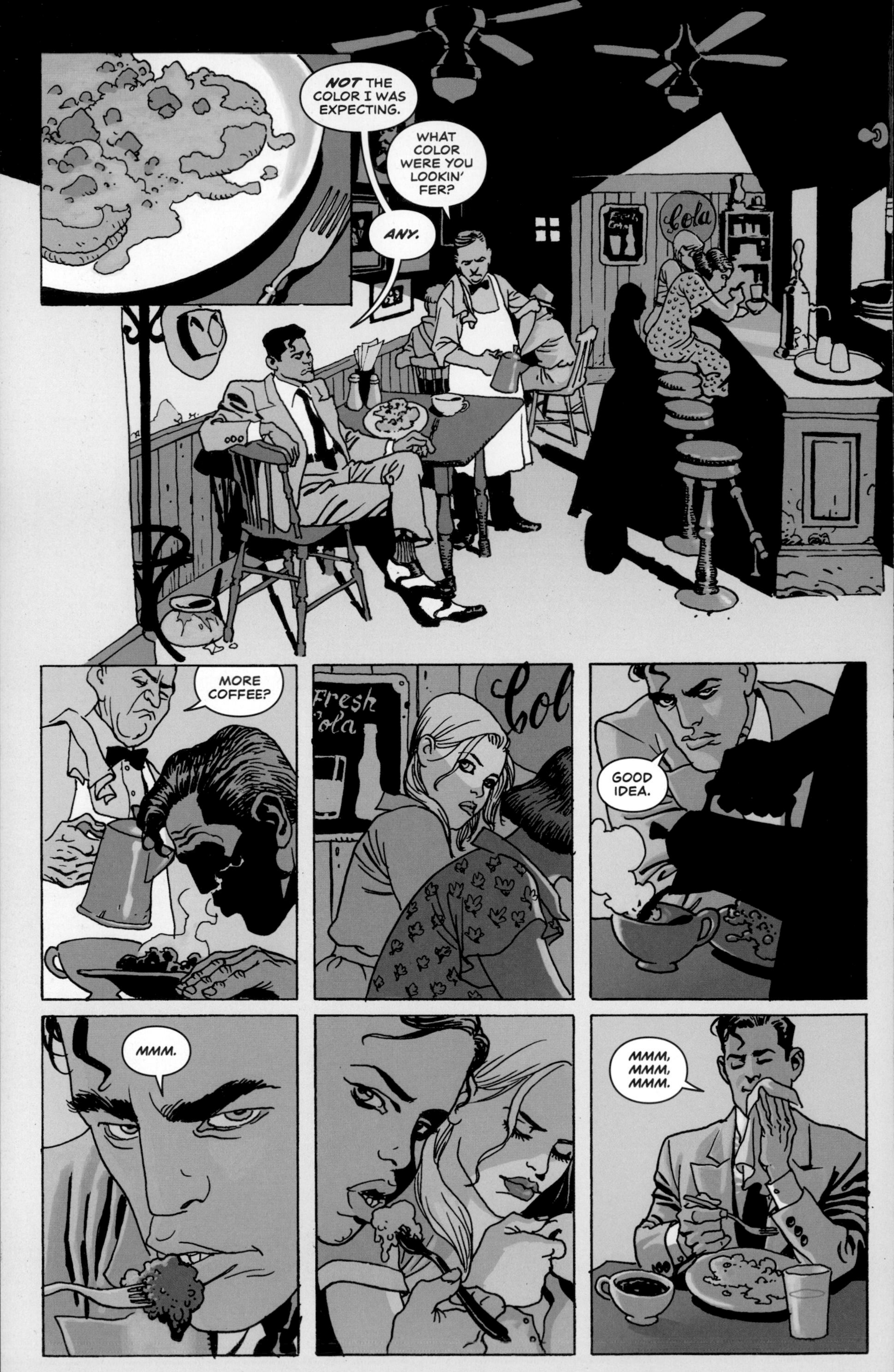
NOT THE COLOR I WAS EXPECTING.
WHAT COLOR WERE YOU LOOKIN' FER?
ANY.
Cola
MORE COFFEE?
Fresh Cola
Col
GOOD IDEA.
MMM.
MMM, MMM, MMM.

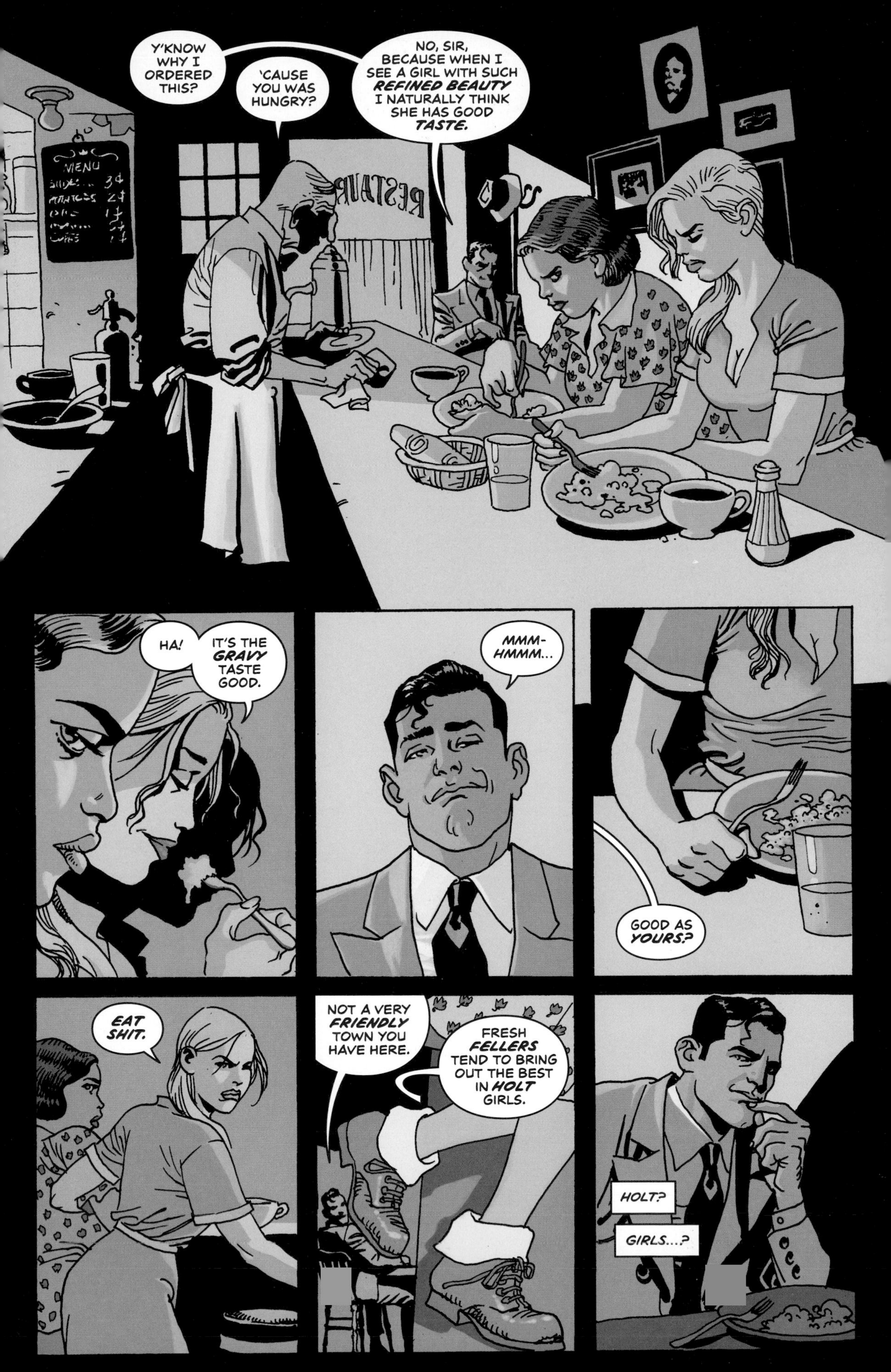

Y'KNOW WHY I ORDERED THIS?
'CAUSE YOU WAS HUNGRY?
NO, SIR, BECAUSE WHEN I SEE A GIRL WITH SUCH *REFINED BEAUTY* I NATURALLY THINK SHE HAS GOOD *TASTE.*
MENU
HA!
IT'S THE *GRAVY* TASTE GOOD.
MMM-HMMM...
GOOD AS *YOURS?*
EAT SHIT.
NOT A VERY *FRIENDLY* TOWN YOU HAVE HERE.
FRESH *FELLERS* TEND TO BRING OUT THE BEST IN *HOLT* GIRLS.
HOLT?
GIRLS...?

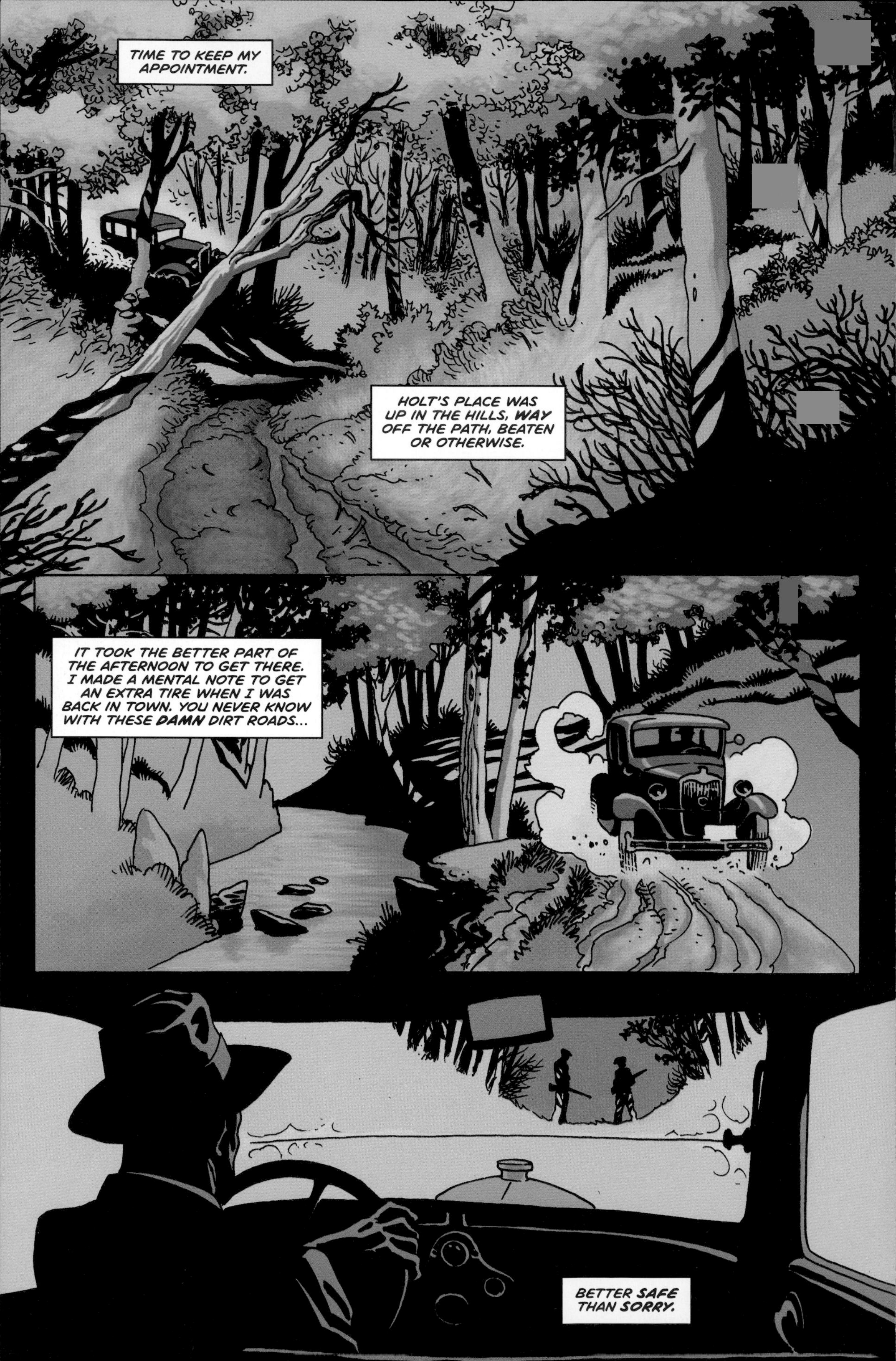
TIME TO KEEP MY APPOINTMENT.
HOLT'S PLACE WAS UP IN THE HILLS, WAY OFF THE PATH, BEATEN OR OTHERWISE.
IT TOOK THE BETTER PART OF THE AFTERNOON TO GET THERE. I MADE A MENTAL NOTE TO GET AN EXTRA TIRE WHEN I WAS BACK IN TOWN. YOU NEVER KNOW WITH THESE DAMN DIRT ROADS...
BETTER SAFE THAN SORRY.

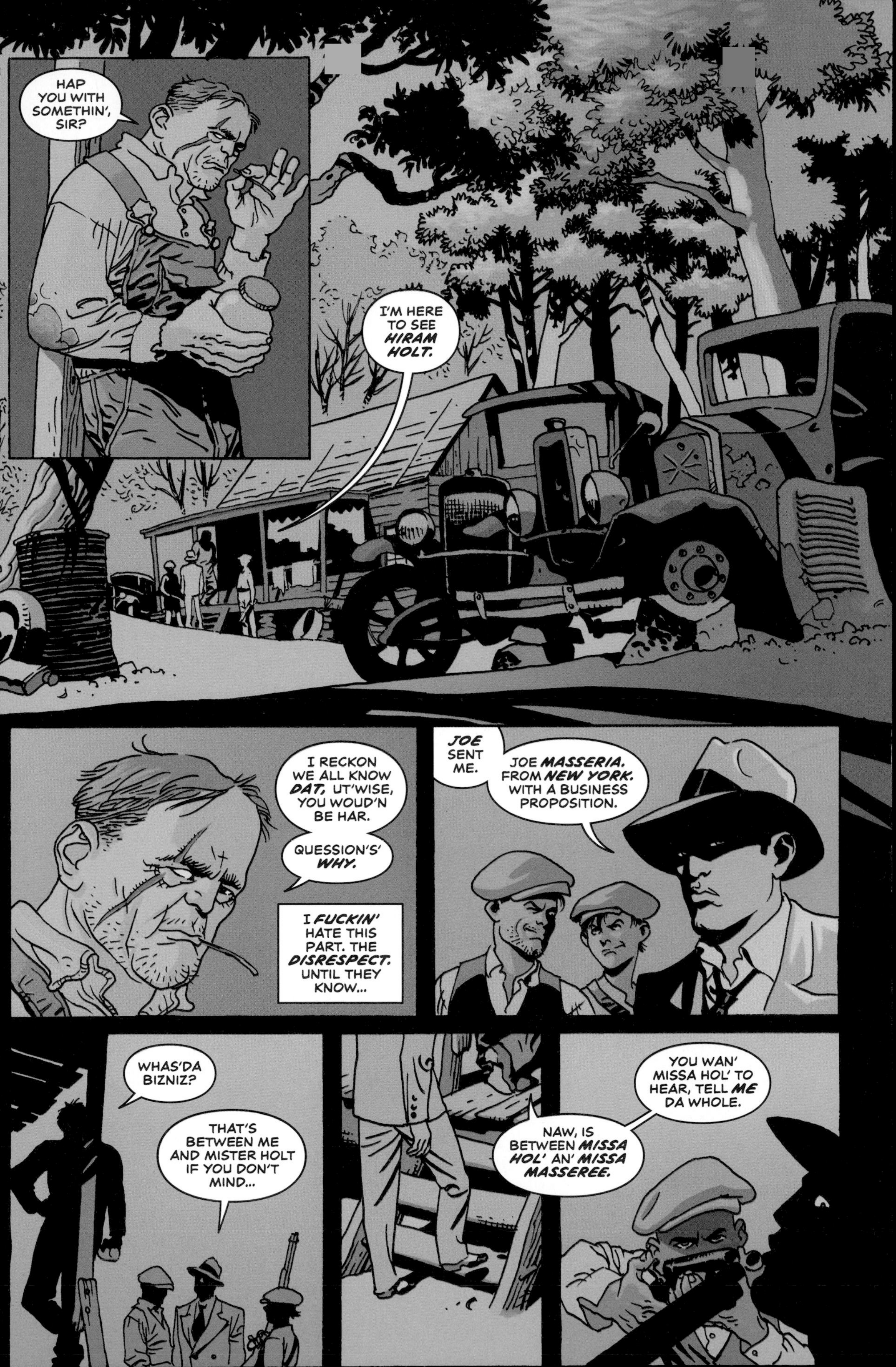
HAP YOU WITH SOMETHIN', SIR?
I'M HERE TO SEE HIRAM HOLT.
I RECKON WE ALL KNOW DAT, UT'WISE, YOU WOUD'N BE HAR.
QUESSION'S' WHY.
I FUCKIN' HATE THIS PART. THE DISRESPECT. UNTIL THEY KNOW...
JOE SENT ME.
JOE MASSERIA. FROM NEW YORK. WITH A BUSINESS PROPOSITION.
WHAS'DA BIZNIZ?
THAT'S BETWEEN ME AND MISTER HOLT IF YOU DON'T MIND...
YOU WAN' MISSA HOL' TO HEAR, TELL ME DA WHOLE.
NAW, IS BETWEEN MISSA HOL' AN' MISSA MASSEREE.

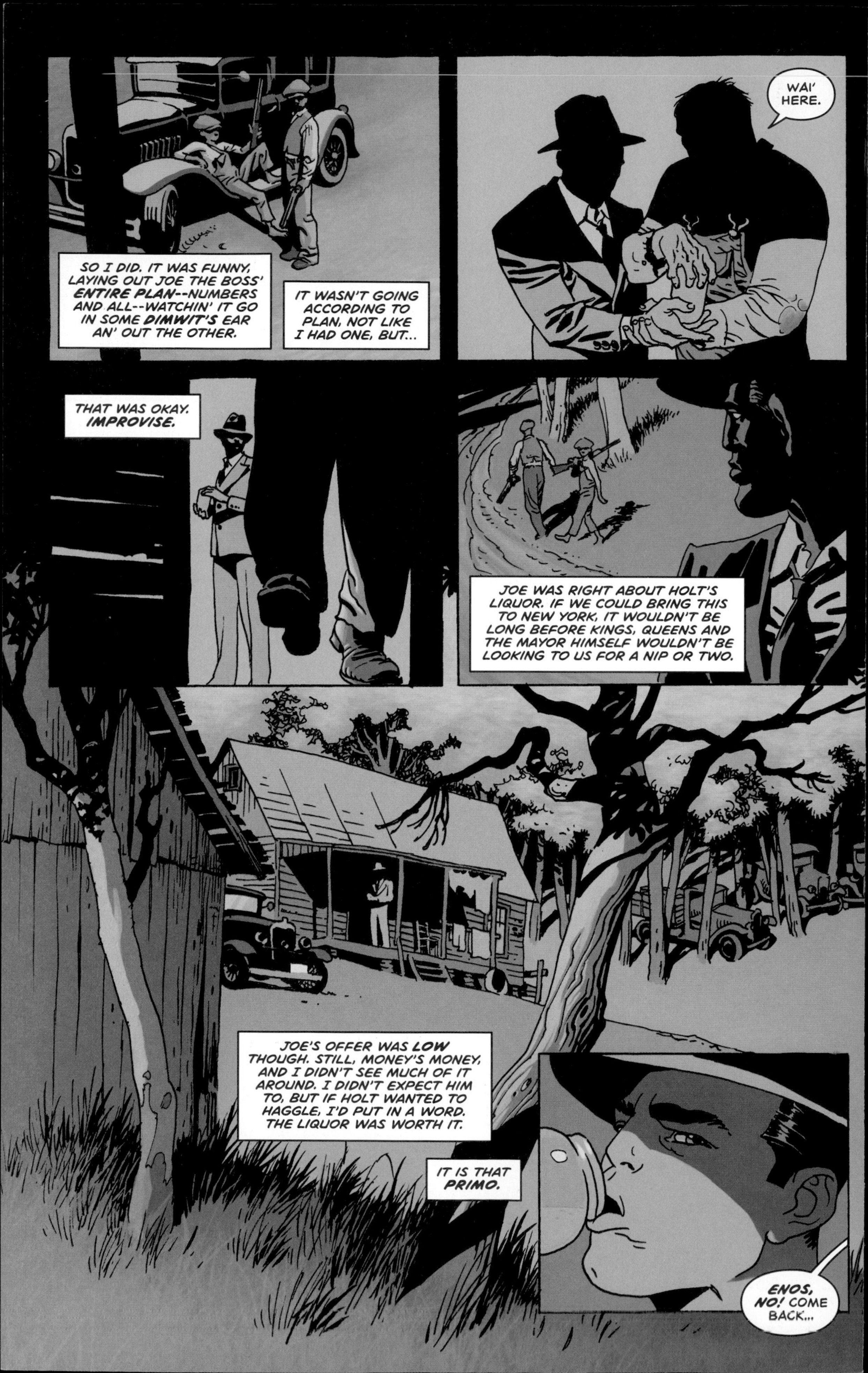

SO I DID. IT WAS FUNNY, LAYING OUT JOE THE BOSS' ENTIRE PLAN--NUMBERS AND ALL--WATCHIN' IT GO IN SOME DIMWIT'S EAR AN' OUT THE OTHER.
IT WASN'T GOING ACCORDING TO PLAN, NOT LIKE I HAD ONE, BUT...
WAI' HERE.
THAT WAS OKAY. IMPROVISE.
JOE WAS RIGHT ABOUT HOLT'S LIQUOR. IF WE COULD BRING THIS TO NEW YORK, IT WOULDN'T BE LONG BEFORE KINGS, QUEENS AND THE MAYOR HIMSELF WOULDN'T BE LOOKING TO US FOR A NIP OR TWO.
JOE'S OFFER WAS LOW THOUGH. STILL, MONEY'S MONEY, AND I DIDN'T SEE MUCH OF IT AROUND. I DIDN'T EXPECT HIM TO, BUT IF HOLT WANTED TO HAGGLE, I'D PUT IN A WORD. THE LIQUOR WAS WORTH IT.
IT IS THAT PRIMO.
ENOS, NO! COME BACK...

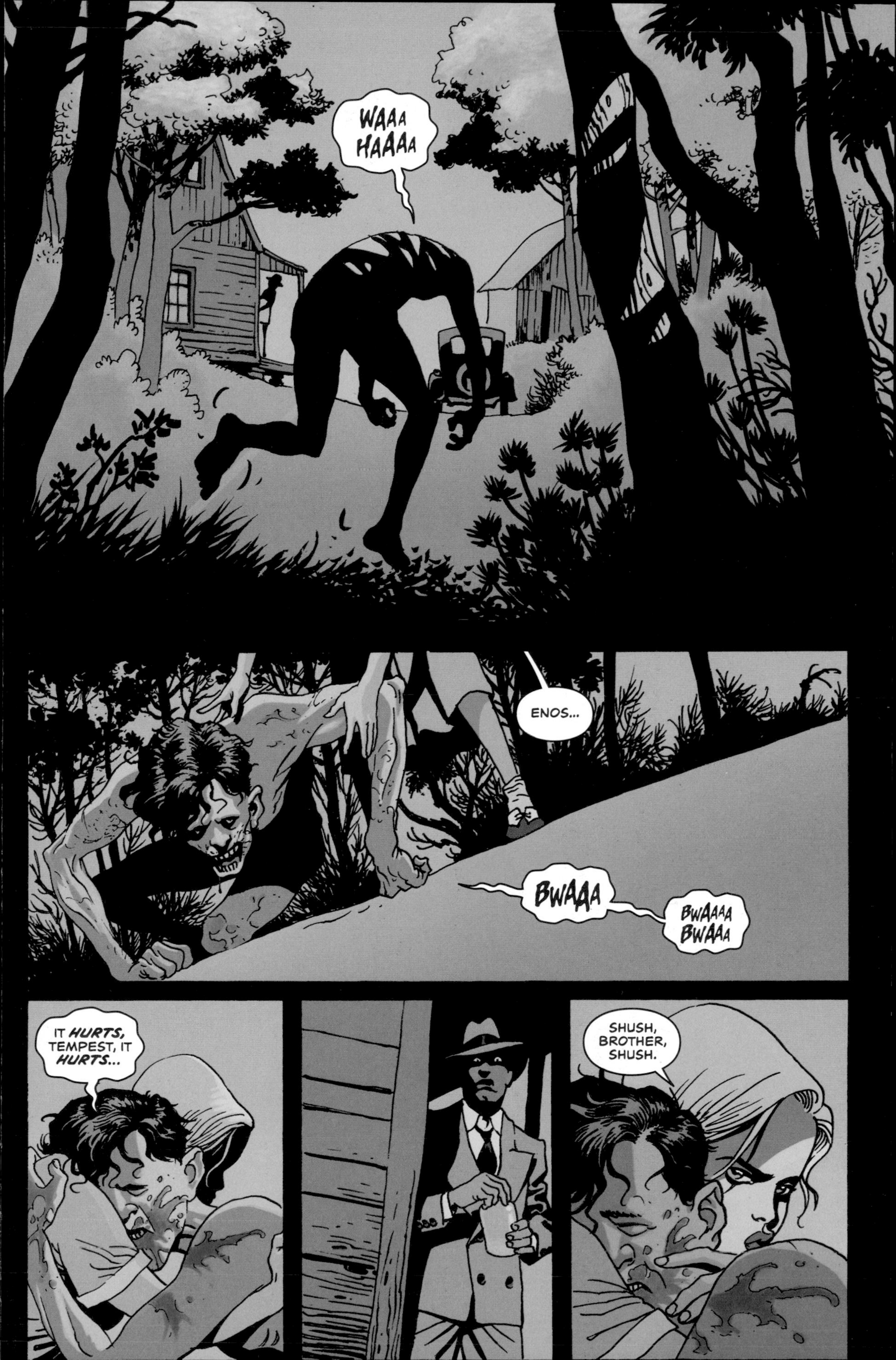
WAAA HAAAA
ENOS...
BWAAA
BWAAAA BWAAA
IT *HURTS*, TEMPEST, IT *HURTS*...
SHUSH, BROTHER, SHUSH.

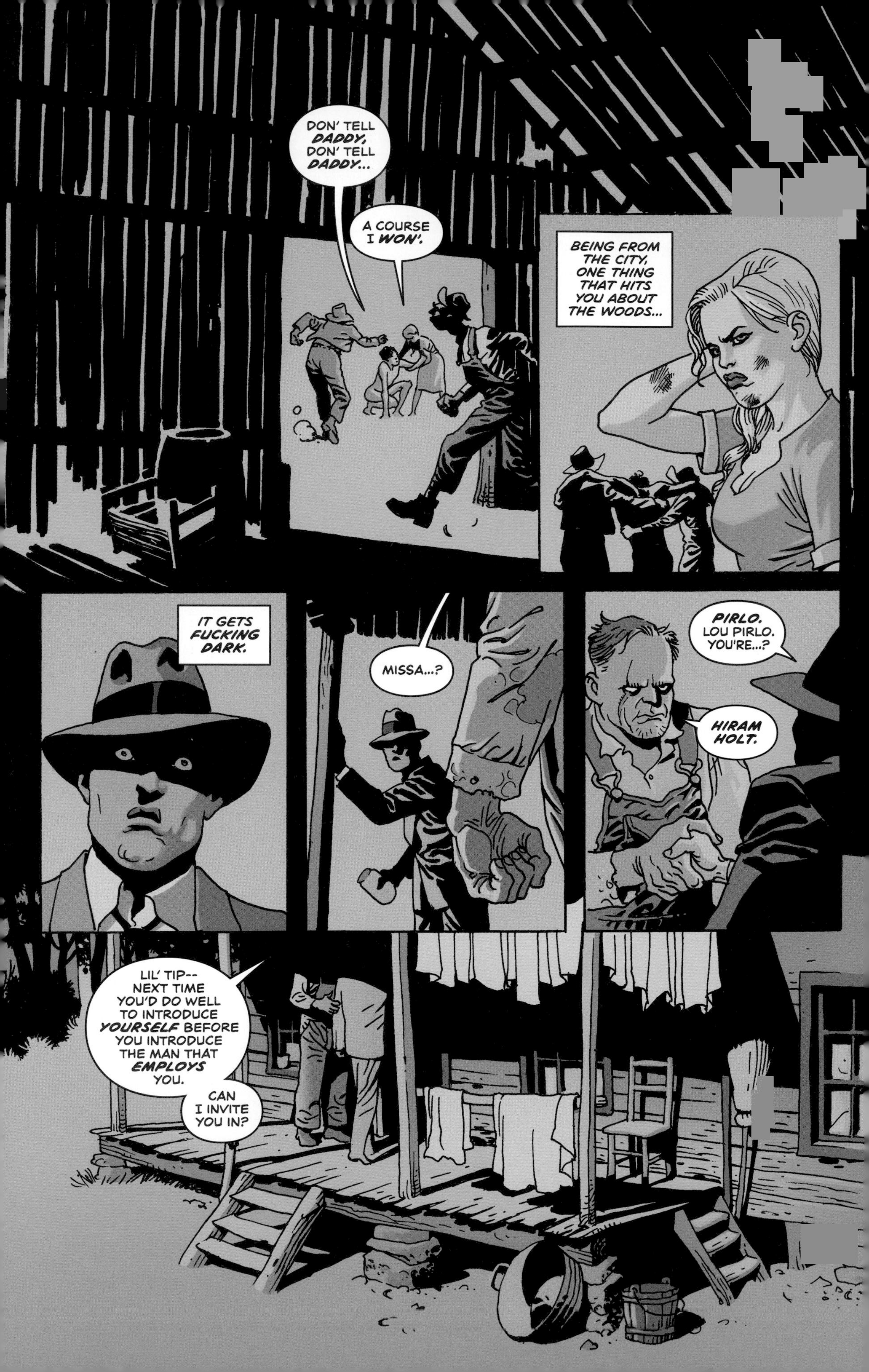
DON' TELL DADDY, DON' TELL DADDY...
A COURSE I WON'.
BEING FROM THE CITY, ONE THING THAT HITS YOU ABOUT THE WOODS...
IT GETS FUCKING DARK.
MISSA...?
PIRLO. LOU PIRLO. YOU'RE...?
HIRAM HOLT.
LIL' TIP-- NEXT TIME YOU'D DO WELL TO INTRODUCE YOURSELF BEFORE YOU INTRODUCE THE MAN THAT EMPLOYS YOU.
CAN I INVITE YOU IN?

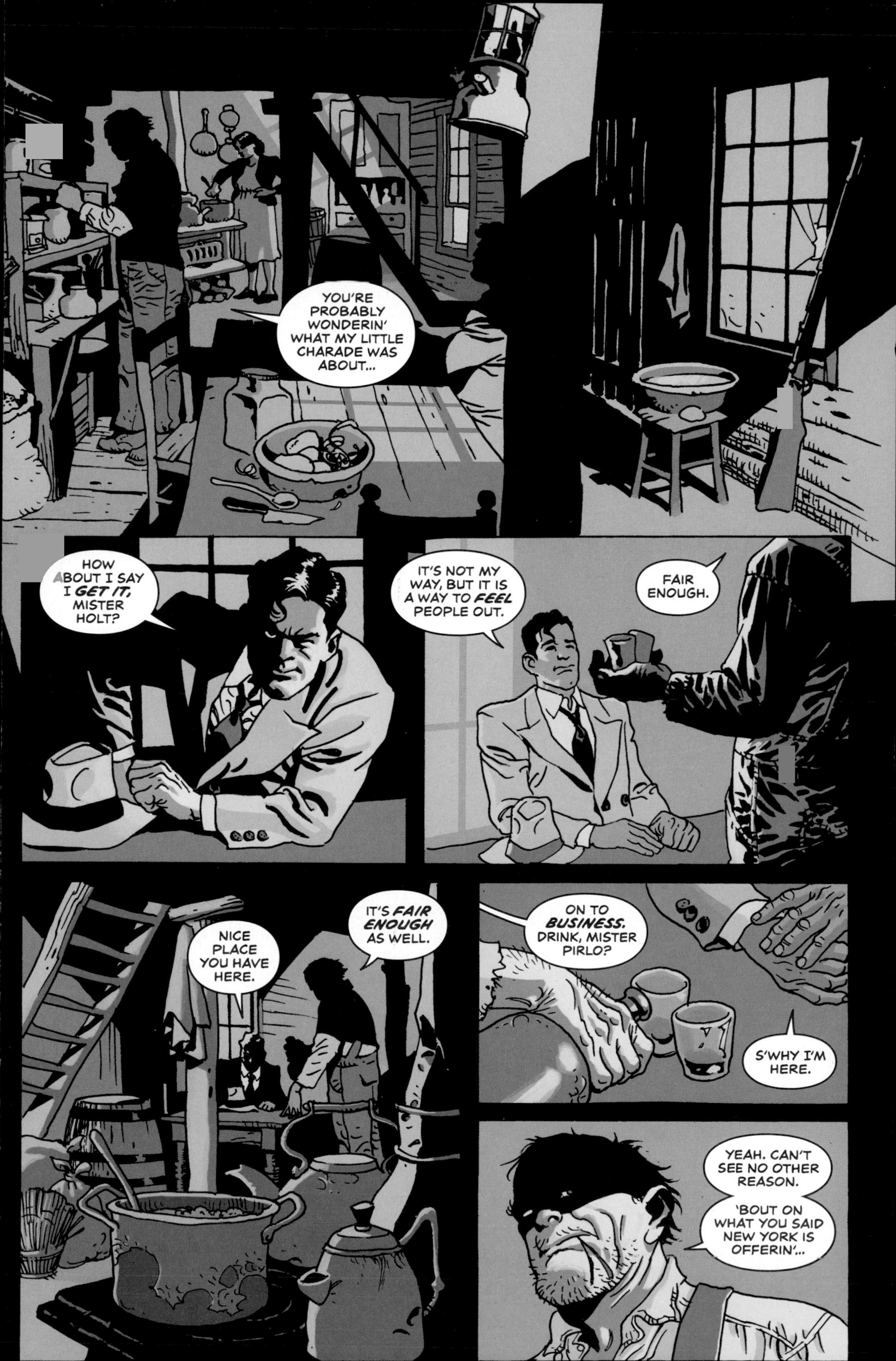
YOU'RE PROBABLY WONDERIN' WHAT MY LITTLE CHARADE WAS ABOUT...
HOW ABOUT I SAY I GET IT, MISTER HOLT?
IT'S NOT MY WAY, BUT IT IS A WAY TO FEEL PEOPLE OUT.
FAIR ENOUGH.
NICE PLACE YOU HAVE HERE.
IT'S FAIR ENOUGH AS WELL.
ON TO BUSINESS. DRINK, MISTER PIRLO?
S'WHY I'M HERE.
YEAH. CAN'T SEE NO OTHER REASON.
'BOUT ON WHAT YOU SAID NEW YORK IS OFFERIN'...

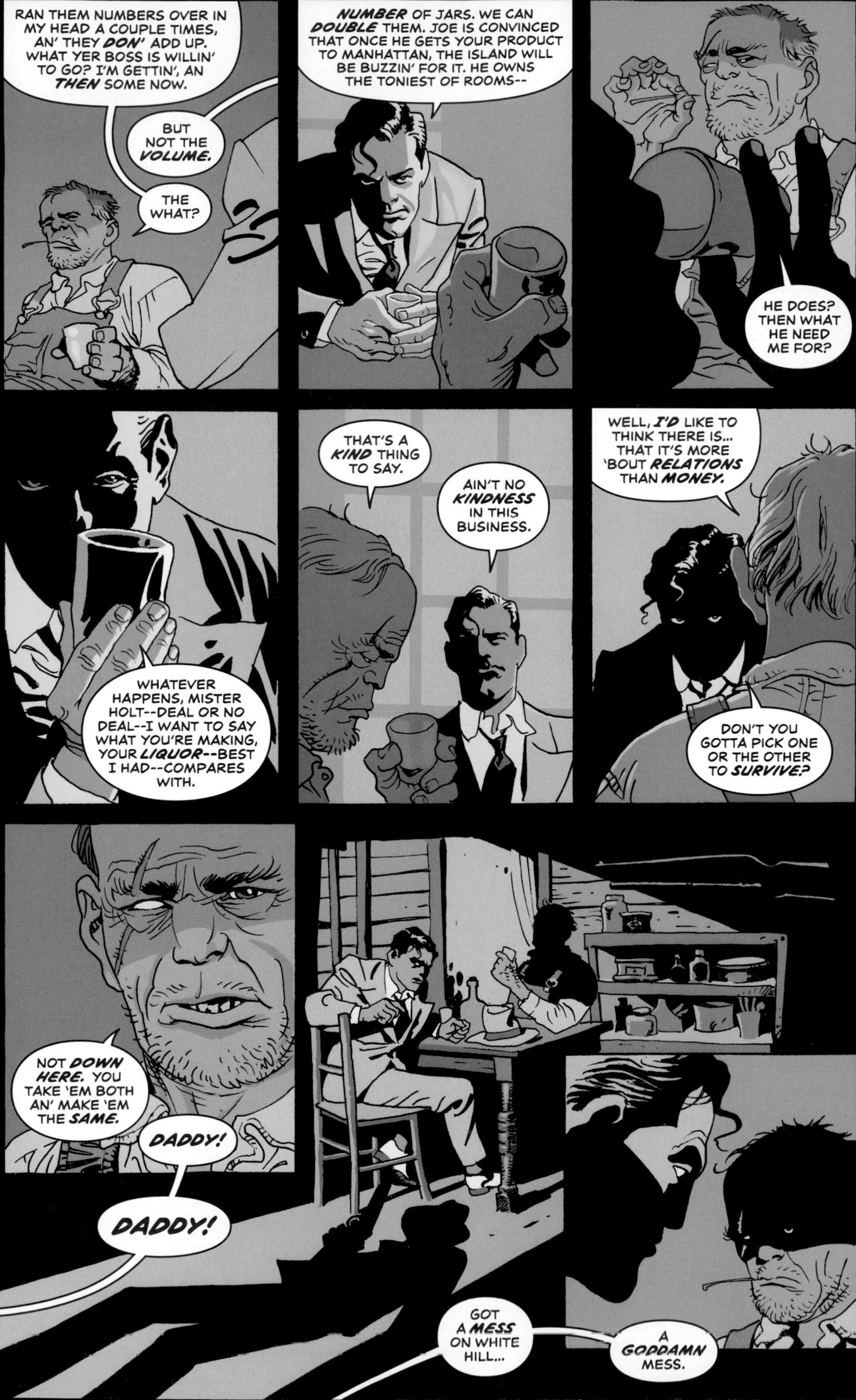

RAN THEM NUMBERS OVER IN MY HEAD A COUPLE TIMES, AN' THEY *DON'* ADD UP. WHAT YER BOSS IS WILLIN' TO GO? I'M GETTIN', AN *THEN* SOME NOW.
BUT NOT THE *VOLUME.*
THE WHAT?
NUMBER OF JARS. WE CAN *DOUBLE* THEM. JOE IS CONVINCED THAT ONCE HE GETS YOUR PRODUCT TO MANHATTAN, THE ISLAND WILL BE BUZZIN' FOR IT. HE OWNS THE TONIEST OF ROOMS--
HE DOES? THEN WHAT HE NEED ME FOR?
WHATEVER HAPPENS, MISTER HOLT--DEAL OR NO DEAL--I WANT TO SAY WHAT YOU'RE MAKING, YOUR *LIQUOR*--BEST I HAD--COMPARES WITH.
THAT'S A *KIND* THING TO SAY.
AIN'T NO *KINDNESS* IN THIS BUSINESS.
WELL, *I'D* LIKE TO THINK THERE IS... THAT IT'S MORE 'BOUT *RELATIONS* THAN *MONEY.*
DON'T YOU GOTTA PICK ONE OR THE OTHER TO *SURVIVE?*
NOT *DOWN HERE.* YOU TAKE 'EM BOTH AN' MAKE 'EM THE *SAME.*
DADDY!
DADDY!
GOT A *MESS* ON WHITE HILL...
A *GODDAMN* MESS.

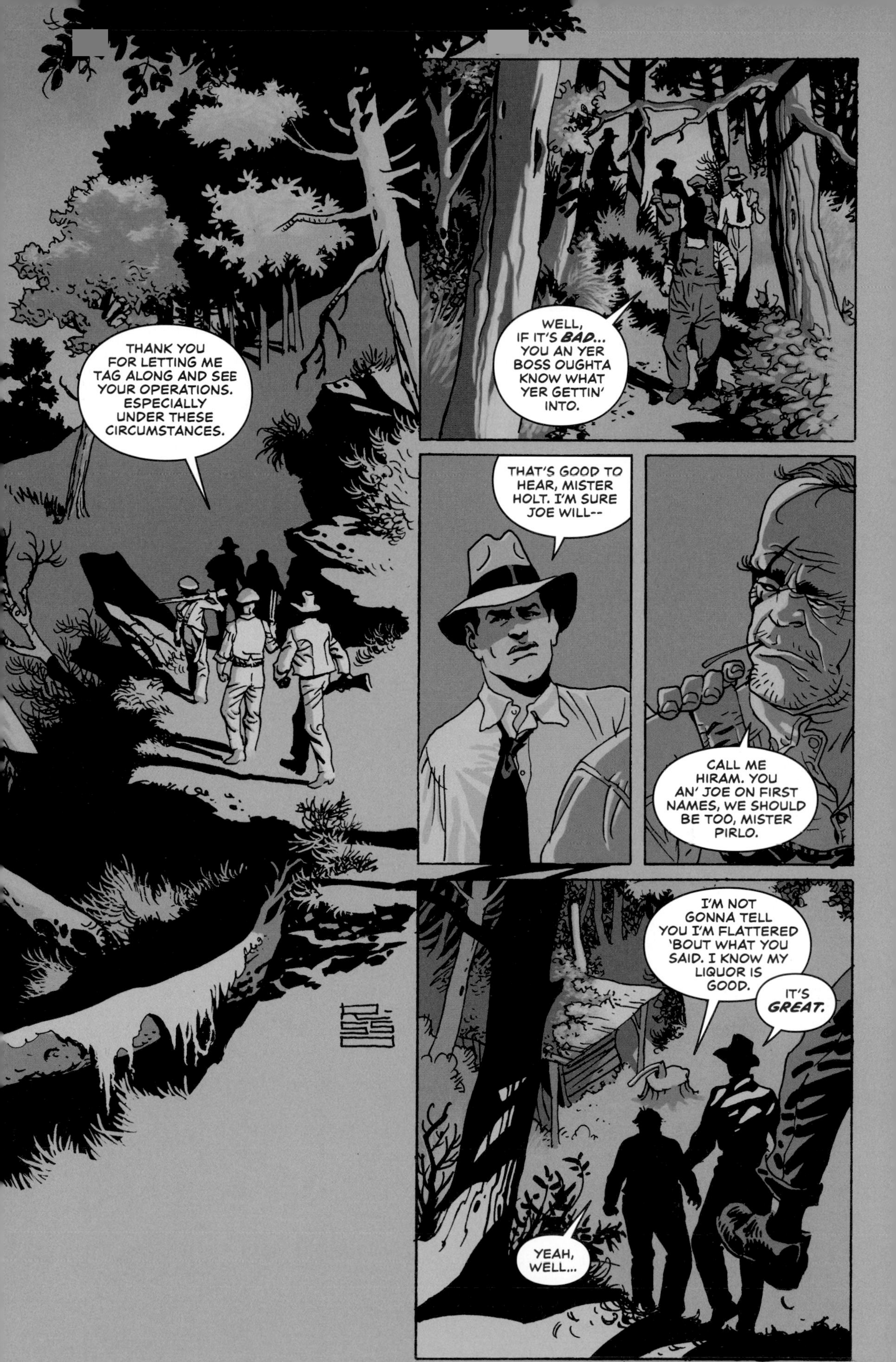
THANK YOU FOR LETTING ME TAG ALONG AND SEE YOUR OPERATIONS. ESPECIALLY UNDER THESE CIRCUMSTANCES.
WELL, IF IT'S BAD... YOU AN YER BOSS OUGHTA KNOW WHAT YER GETTIN' INTO.
THAT'S GOOD TO HEAR, MISTER HOLT. I'M SURE JOE WILL--
CALL ME HIRAM. YOU AN' JOE ON FIRST NAMES, WE SHOULD BE TOO, MISTER PIRLO.
I'M NOT GONNA TELL YOU I'M FLATTERED 'BOUT WHAT YOU SAID. I KNOW MY LIQUOR IS GOOD.
IT'S GREAT.
YEAH, WELL...

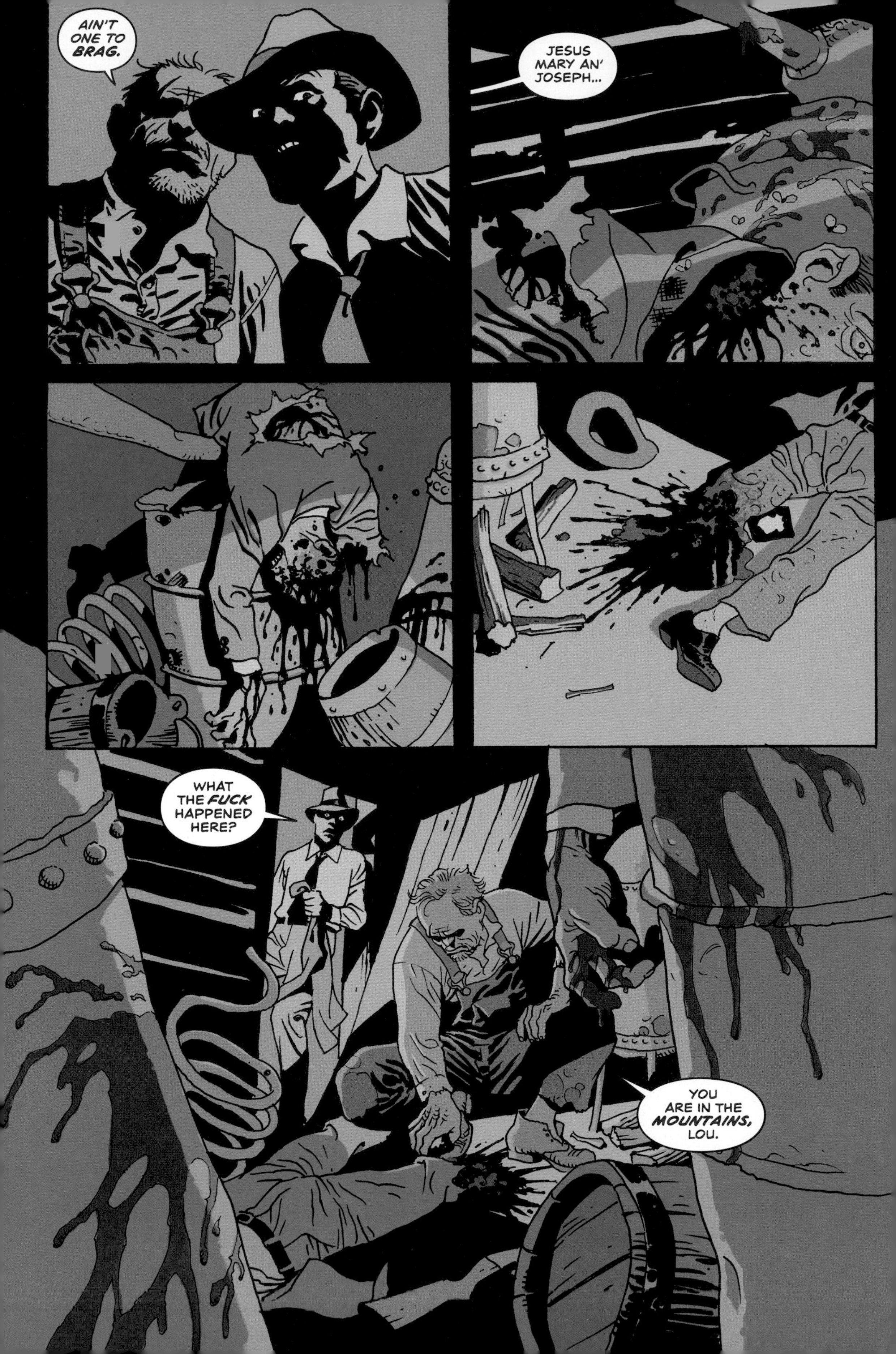
AIN'T ONE TO BRAG.
JESUS MARY AN' JOSEPH...
WHAT THE FUCK HAPPENED HERE?
YOU ARE IN THE MOUNTAINS, LOU.

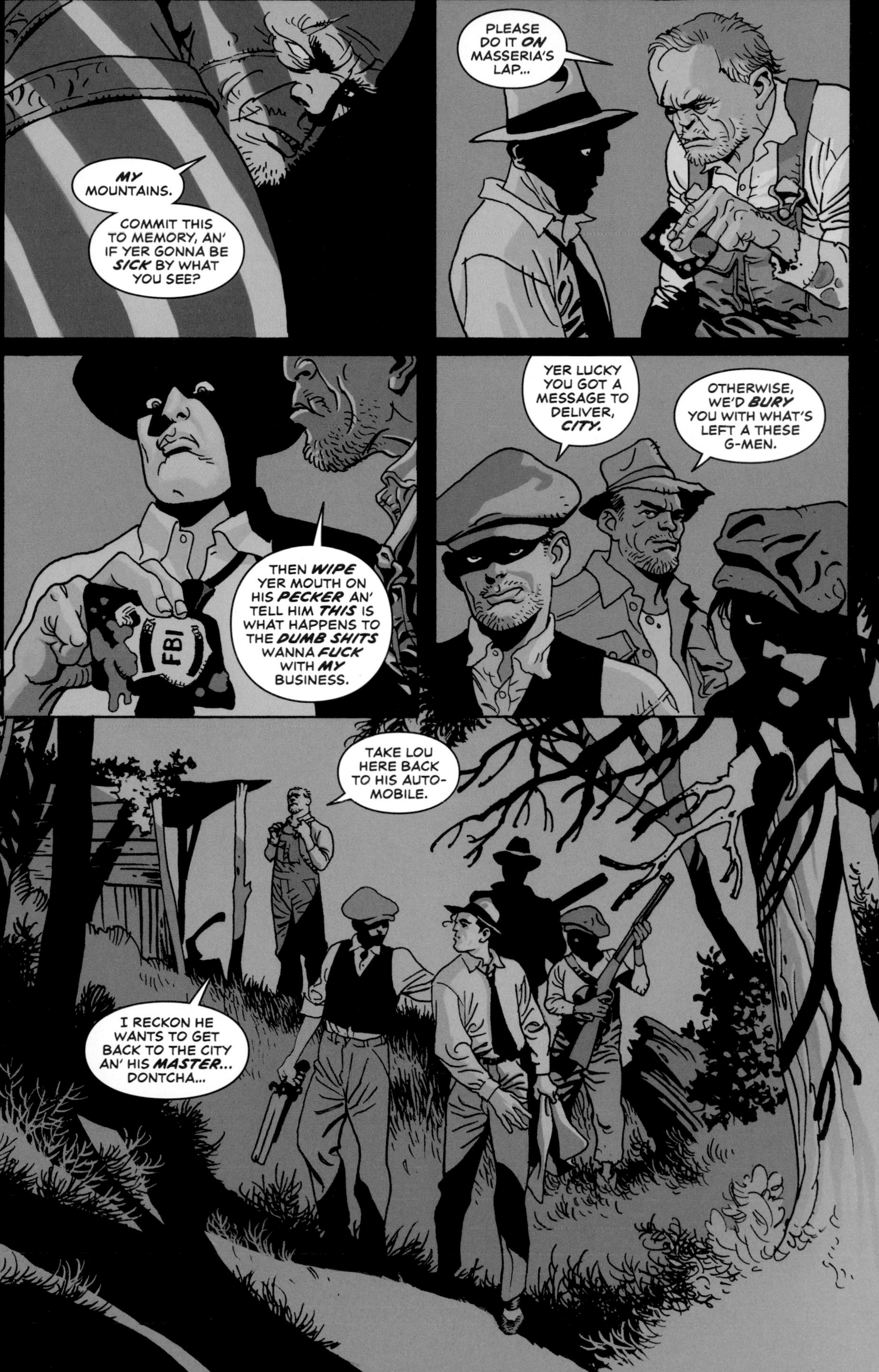
MY MOUNTAINS.
COMMIT THIS TO MEMORY, AN' IF YER GONNA BE SICK BY WHAT YOU SEE?
PLEASE DO IT ON MASSERIA'S LAP...
FBI
THEN WIPE YER MOUTH ON HIS PECKER AN' TELL HIM THIS IS WHAT HAPPENS TO THE DUMB SHITS WANNA FUCK WITH MY BUSINESS.
YER LUCKY YOU GOT A MESSAGE TO DELIVER, CITY.
OTHERWISE, WE'D BURY YOU WITH WHAT'S LEFT A THESE G-MEN.
TAKE LOU HERE BACK TO HIS AUTO-MOBILE.
I RECKON HE WANTS TO GET BACK TO THE CITY AN' HIS MASTER... DONTCHA...

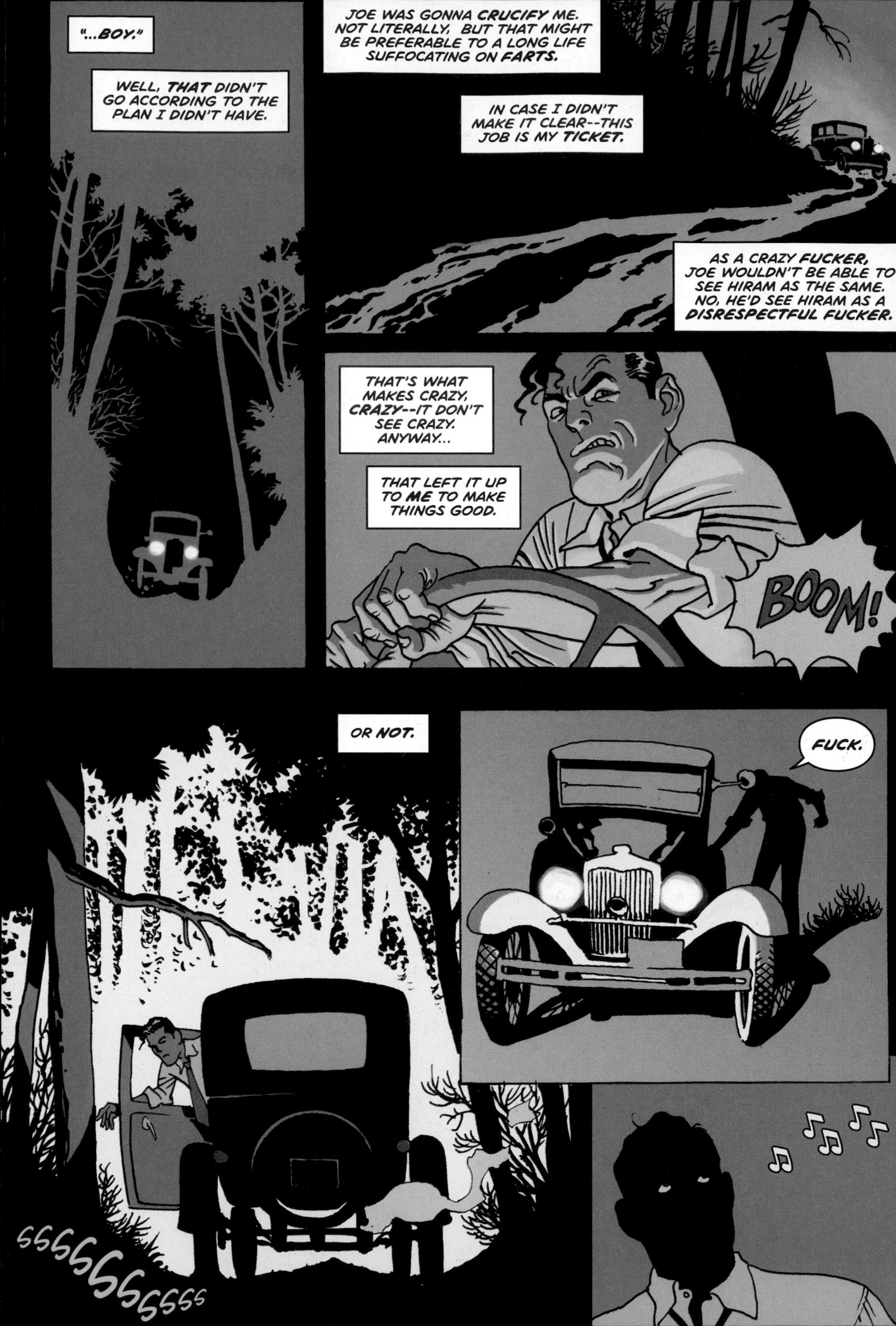
"...BOY."
WELL, THAT DIDN'T GO ACCORDING TO THE PLAN I DIDN'T HAVE.
JOE WAS GONNA CRUCIFY ME. NOT LITERALLY, BUT THAT MIGHT BE PREFERABLE TO A LONG LIFE SUFFOCATING ON FARTS.
IN CASE I DIDN'T MAKE IT CLEAR--THIS JOB IS MY TICKET.
AS A CRAZY FUCKER, JOE WOULDN'T BE ABLE TO SEE HIRAM AS THE SAME. NO, HE'D SEE HIRAM AS A DISRESPECTFUL FUCKER.
THAT'S WHAT MAKES CRAZY, CRAZY--IT DON'T SEE CRAZY. ANYWAY...
THAT LEFT IT UP TO ME TO MAKE THINGS GOOD.
BOOM!
OR NOT.
SSSSSSSSSSSSS
FUCK.

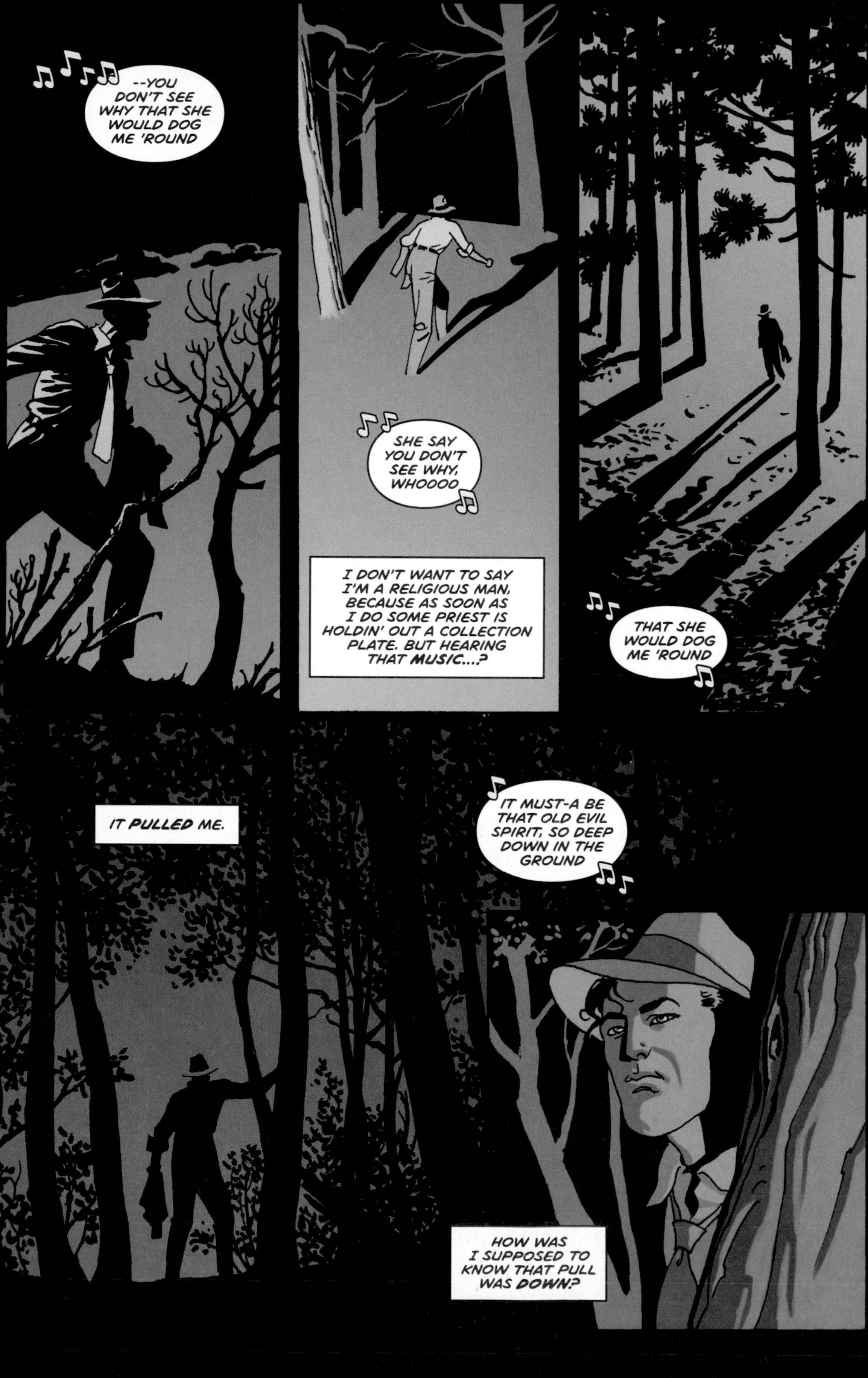
--YOU DON'T SEE WHY THAT SHE WOULD DOG ME 'ROUND
SHE SAY YOU DON'T SEE WHY, WHOOOO
I DON'T WANT TO SAY I'M A RELIGIOUS MAN, BECAUSE AS SOON AS I DO SOME PRIEST IS HOLDIN' OUT A COLLECTION PLATE. BUT HEARING THAT MUSIC...?
THAT SHE WOULD DOG ME 'ROUND
IT PULLED ME.
IT MUST-A BE THAT OLD EVIL SPIRIT, SO DEEP DOWN IN THE GROUND
HOW WAS I SUPPOSED TO KNOW THAT PULL WAS DOWN?

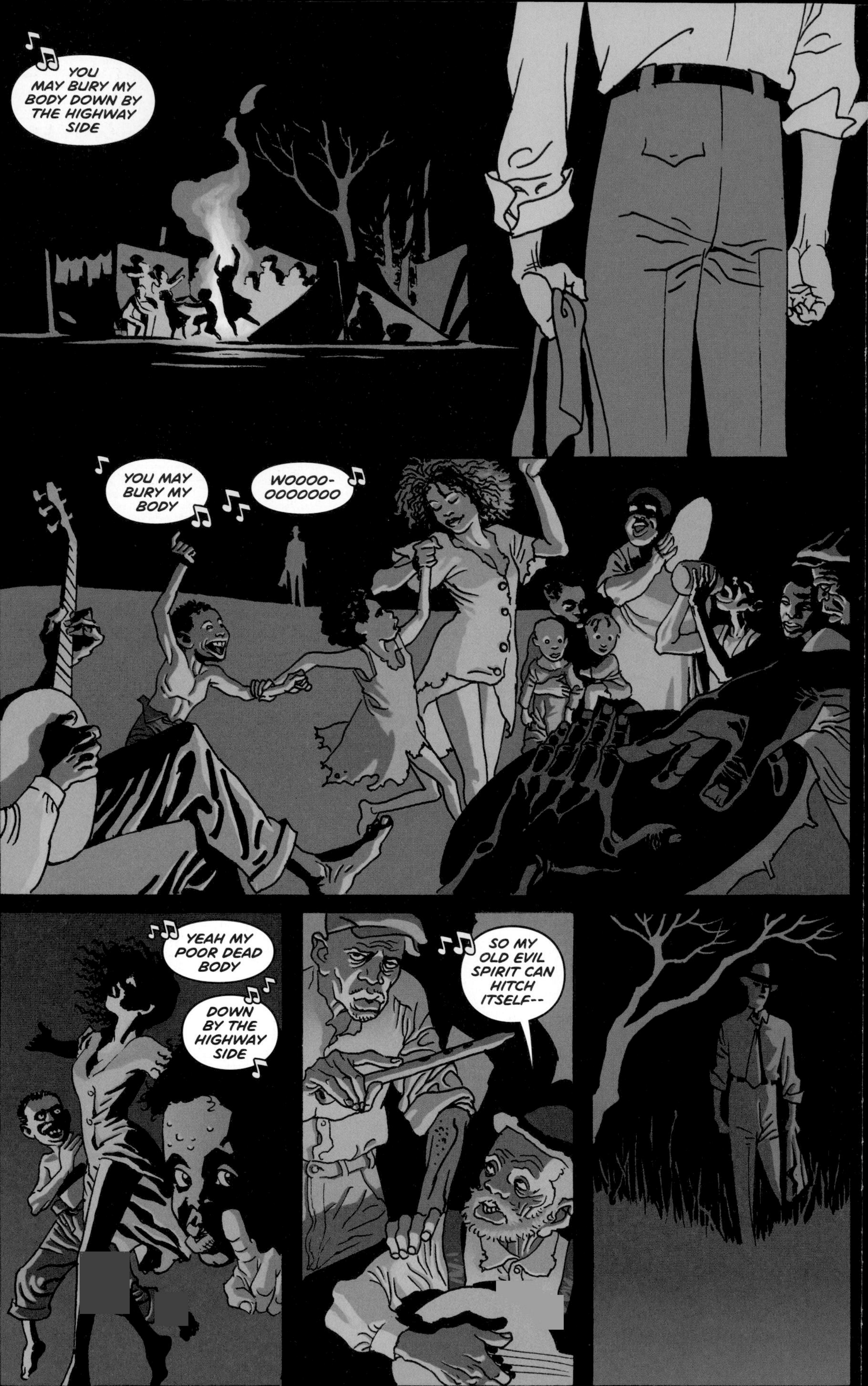
YOU MAY BURY MY BODY DOWN BY THE HIGHWAY SIDE
YOU MAY BURY MY BODY
WOOOO-OOOOOOO
YEAH MY POOR DEAD BODY
DOWN BY THE HIGHWAY SIDE
SO MY OLD EVIL SPIRIT CAN HITCH ITSELF--

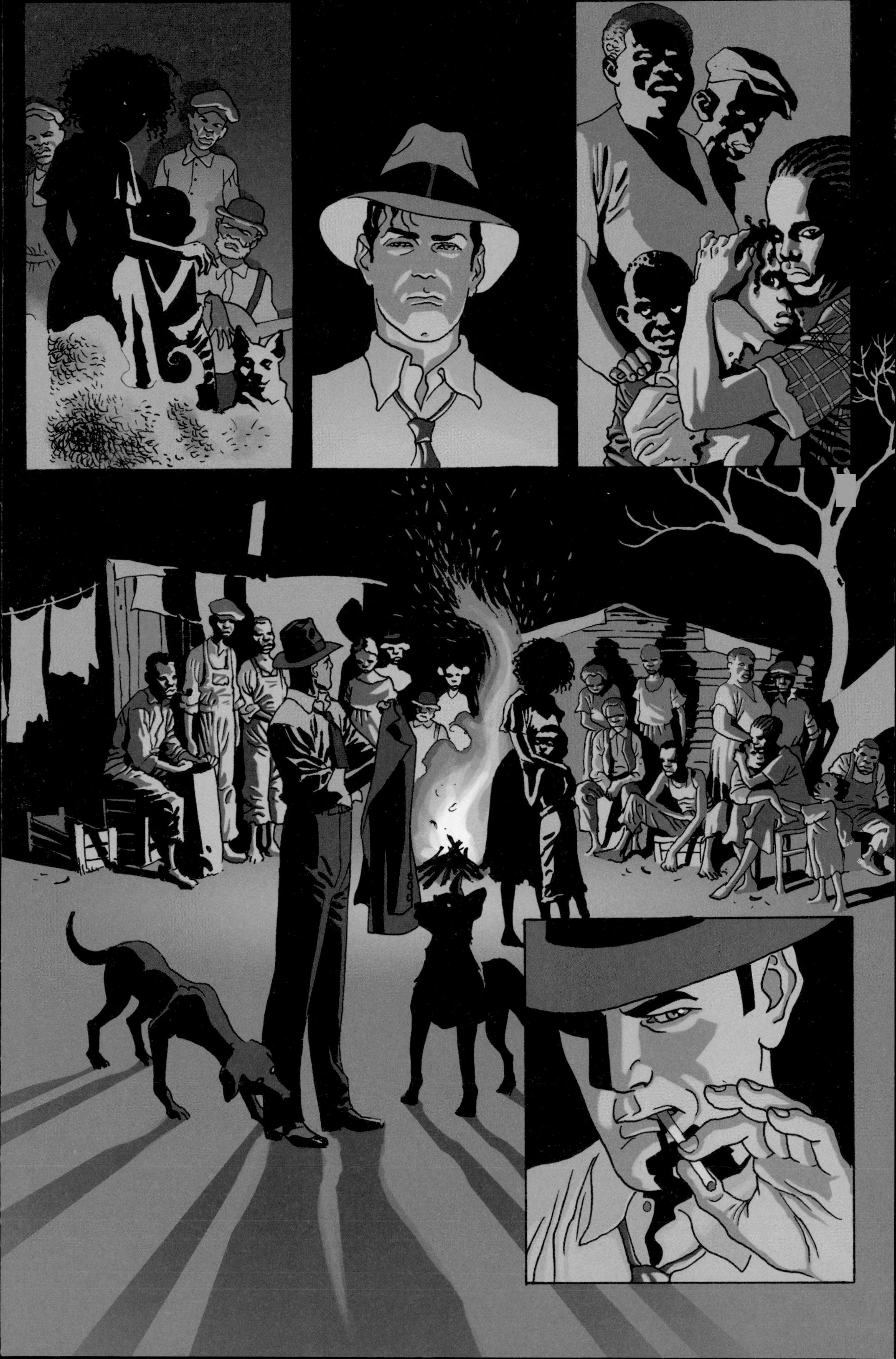

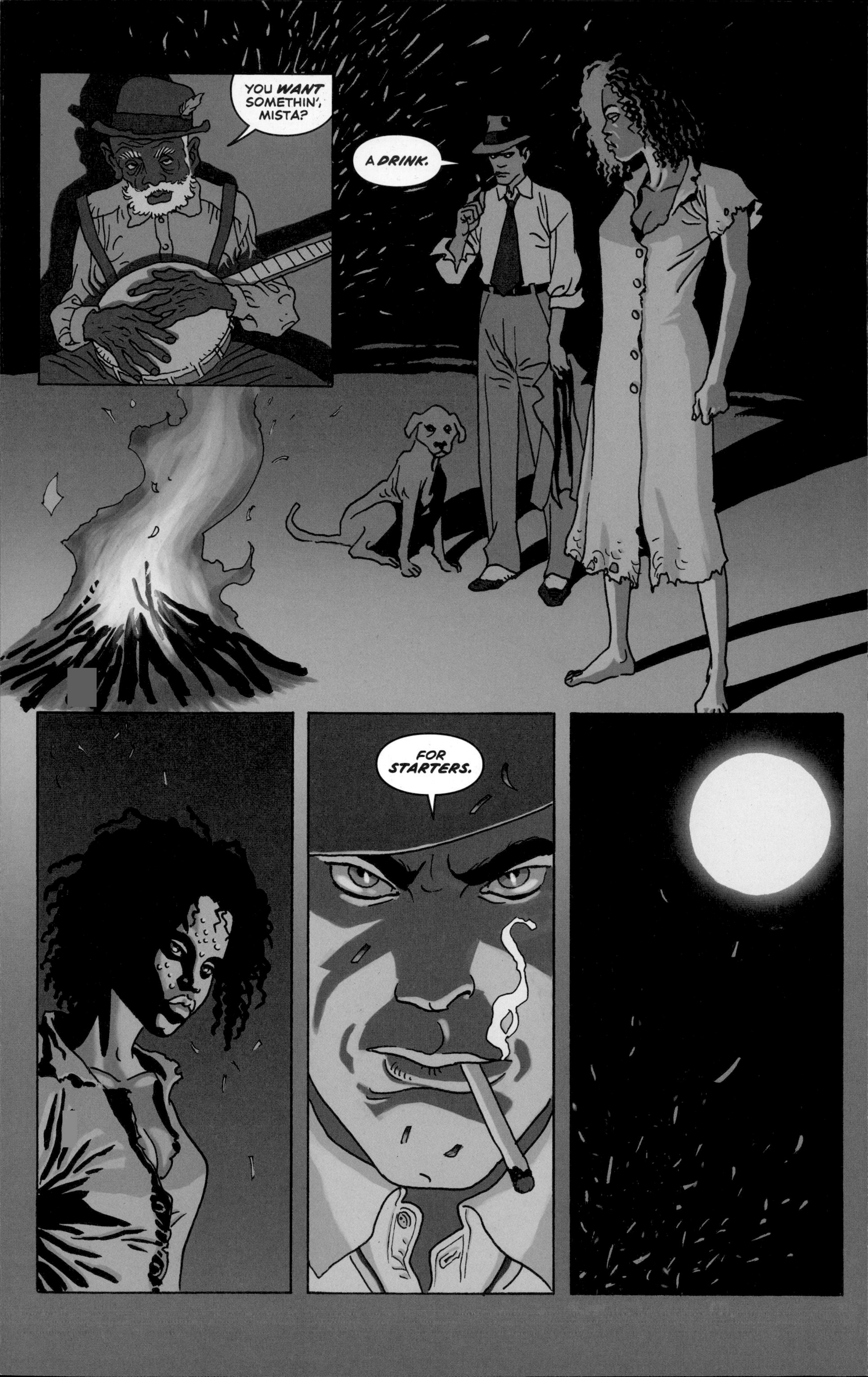
YOU WANT SOMETHIN', MISTA?
A DRINK.
FOR STARTERS.

Chapter
TWO

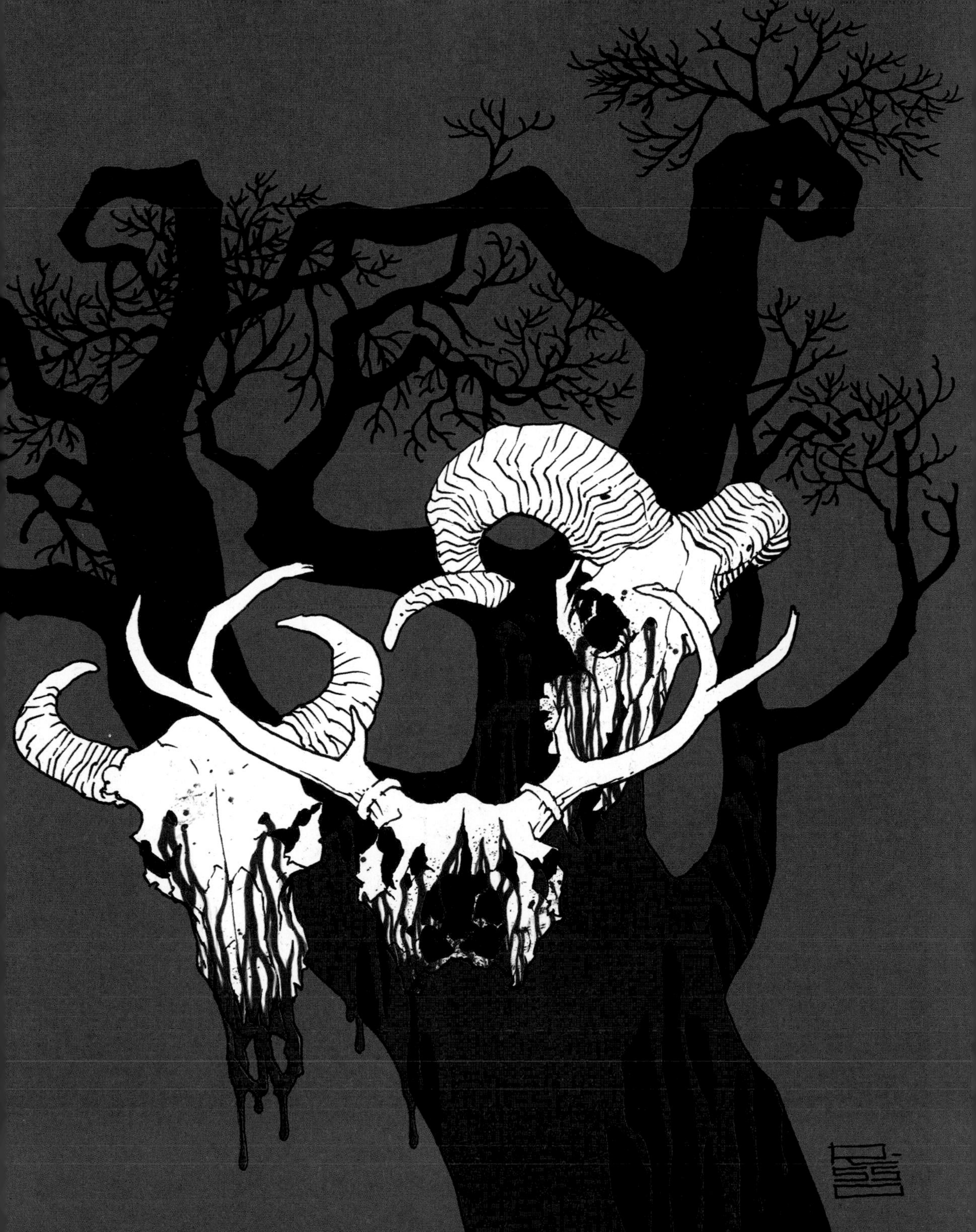

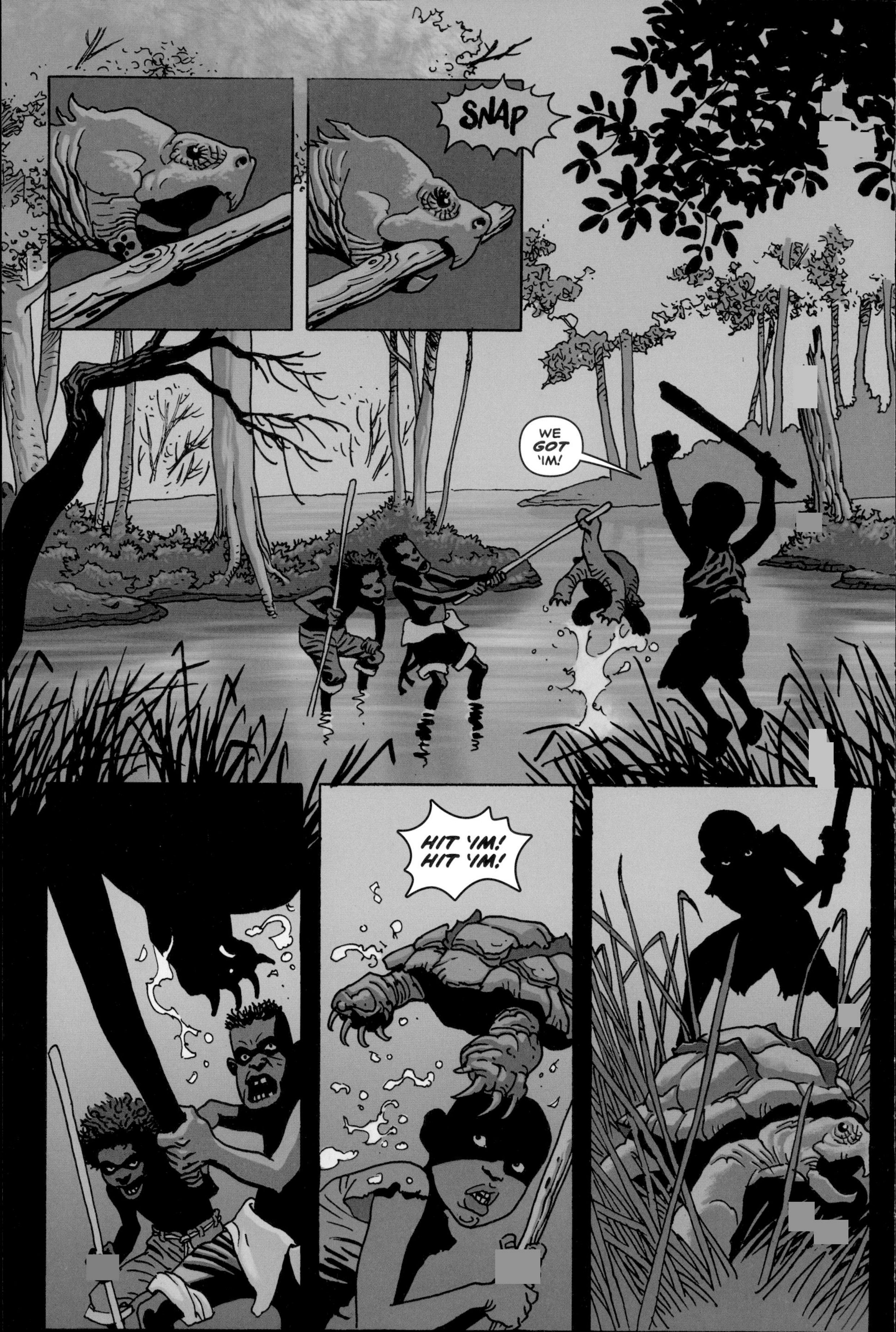
SNAP
WE GOT 'IM!
HIT 'IM! HIT 'IM!

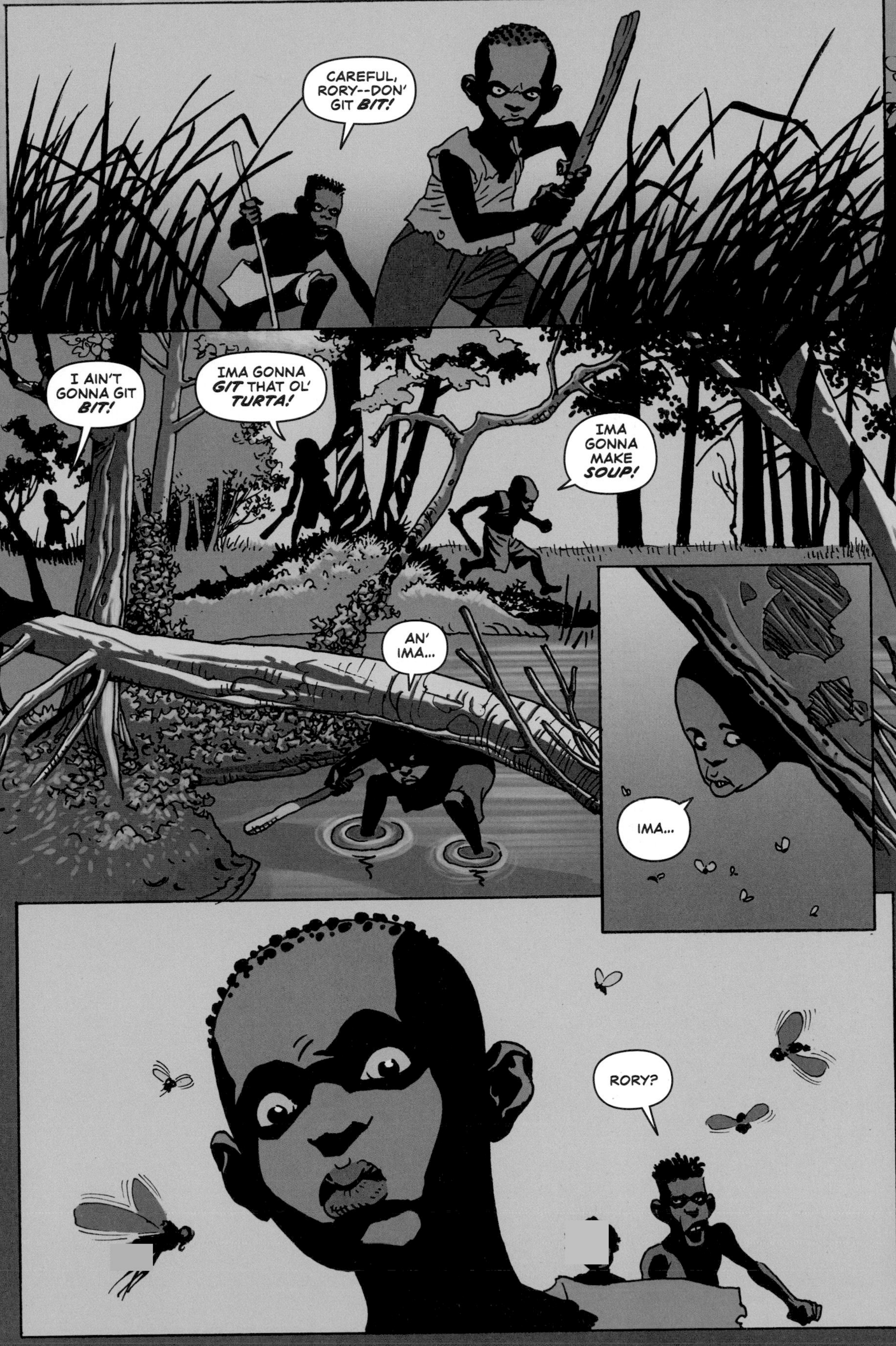
CAREFUL, RORY--DON' GIT BIT!
I AIN'T GONNA GIT BIT!
IMA GONNA GIT THAT OL' TURTA!
IMA GONNA MAKE SOUP!
AN' IMA...
IMA...
RORY?

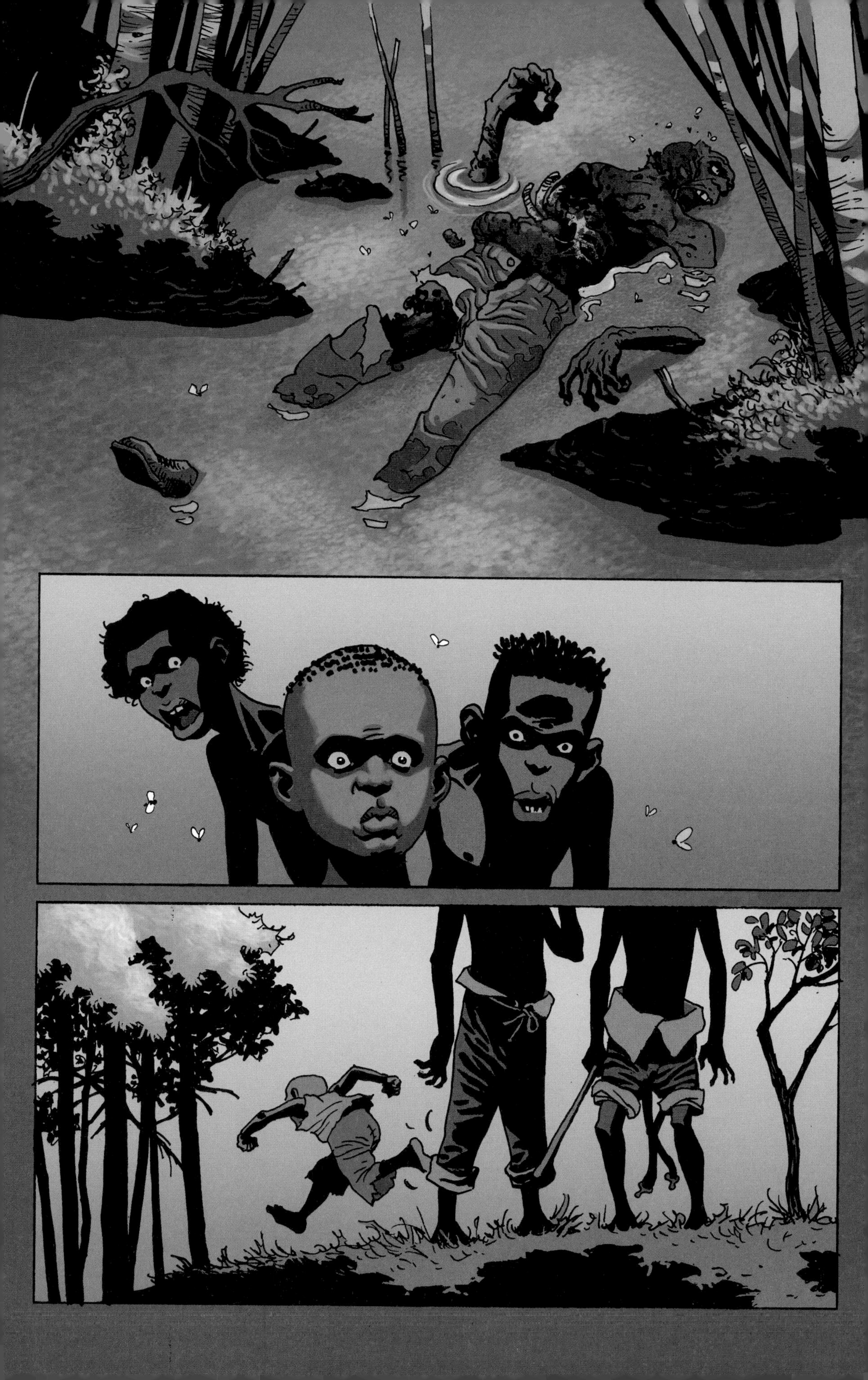

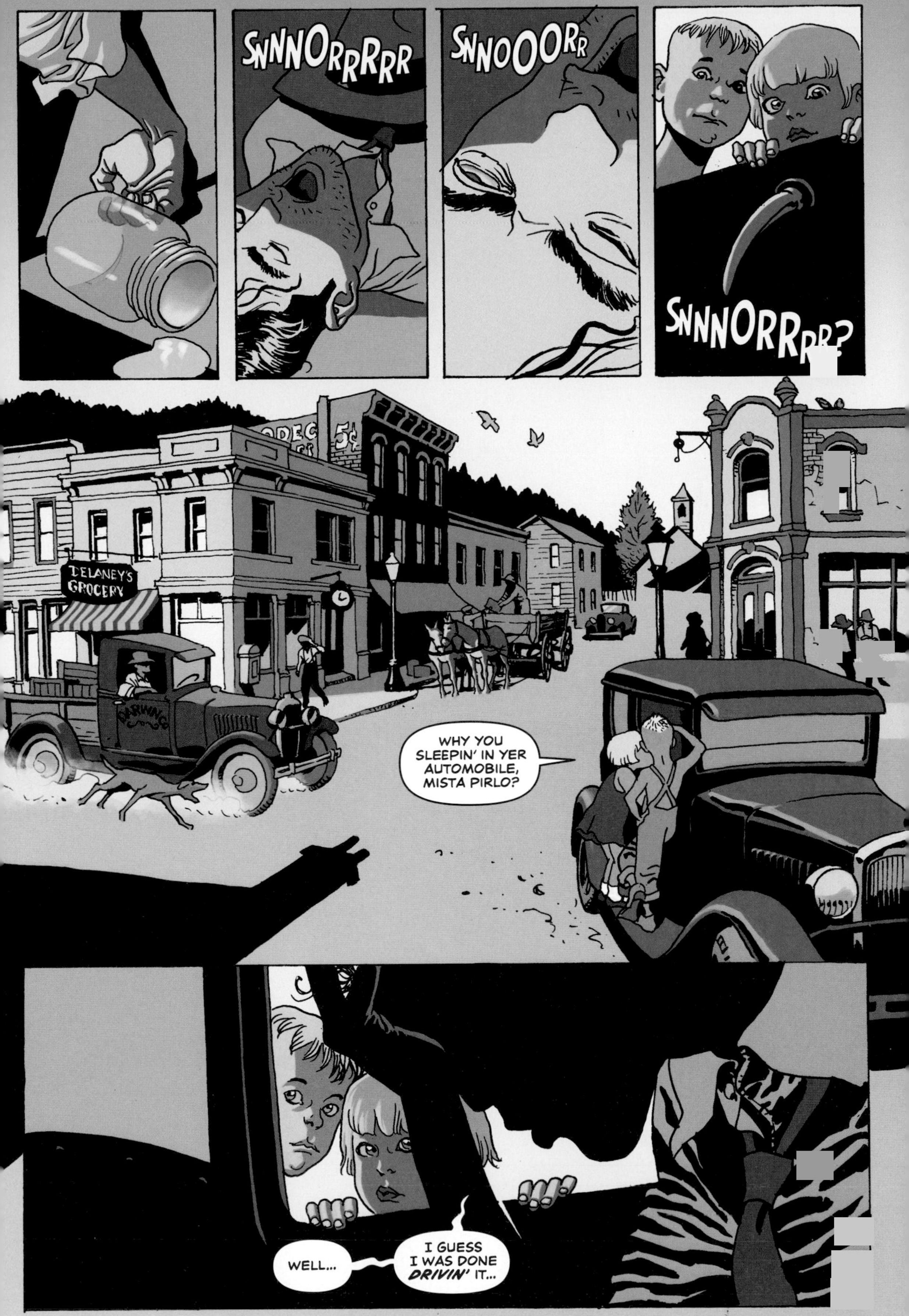
SNNORRRRR
SNNOOORR
SNNORRRR?
DELANEY'S GROCERY
WHY YOU SLEEPIN' IN YER AUTOMOBILE, MISTA PIRLO?
WELL...
I GUESS I WAS DONE *DRIVIN'* IT...

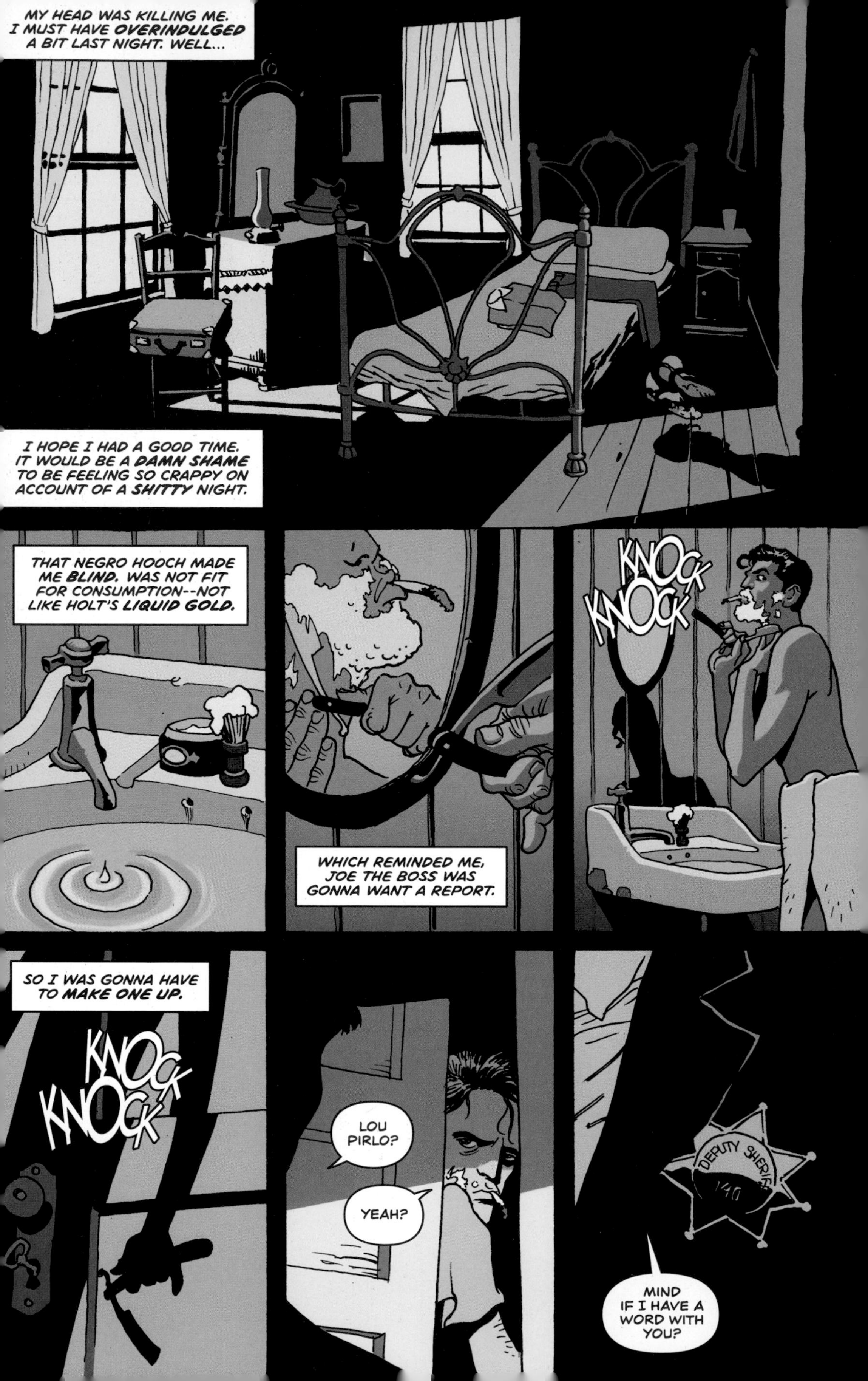
MY HEAD WAS KILLING ME. I MUST HAVE OVERINDULGED A BIT LAST NIGHT. WELL...
I HOPE I HAD A GOOD TIME. IT WOULD BE A DAMN SHAME TO BE FEELING SO CRAPPY ON ACCOUNT OF A SHITTY NIGHT.
THAT NEGRO HOOCH MADE ME BLIND. WAS NOT FIT FOR CONSUMPTION--NOT LIKE HOLT'S LIQUID GOLD.
WHICH REMINDED ME, JOE THE BOSS WAS GONNA WANT A REPORT.
KNOCK KNOCK
SO I WAS GONNA HAVE TO MAKE ONE UP.
KNOCK KNOCK
LOU PIRLO?
YEAH?
DEPUTY SHERIFF
140
MIND IF I HAVE A WORD WITH YOU?

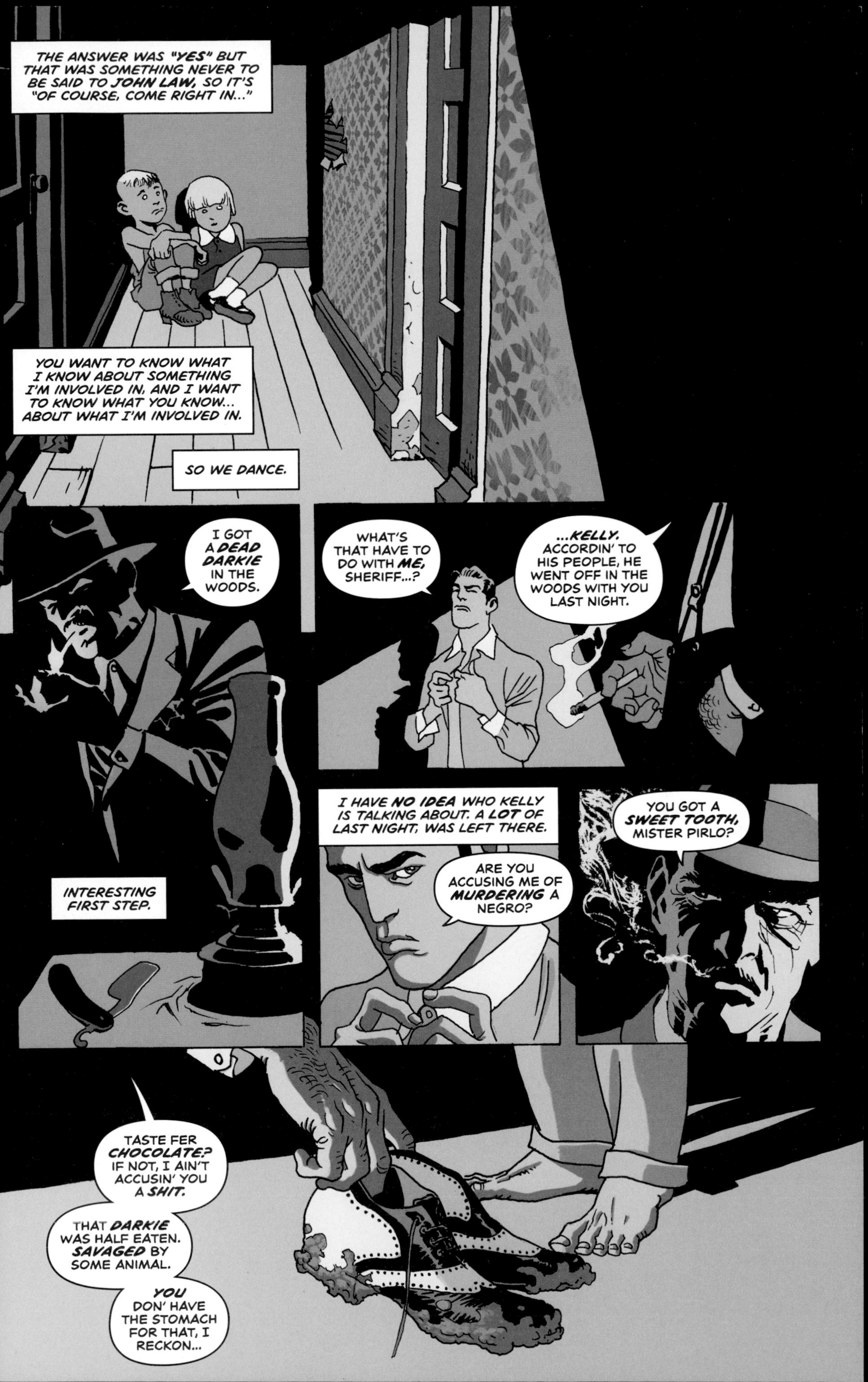
THE ANSWER WAS "YES" BUT THAT WAS SOMETHING NEVER TO BE SAID TO JOHN LAW, SO IT'S "OF COURSE, COME RIGHT IN..."
YOU WANT TO KNOW WHAT I KNOW ABOUT SOMETHING I'M INVOLVED IN; AND I WANT TO KNOW WHAT YOU KNOW... ABOUT WHAT I'M INVOLVED IN.
SO WE DANCE.
I GOT A DEAD DARKIE IN THE WOODS.
INTERESTING FIRST STEP.
WHAT'S THAT HAVE TO DO WITH ME, SHERIFF...?
...KELLY. ACCORDIN' TO HIS PEOPLE, HE WENT OFF IN THE WOODS WITH YOU LAST NIGHT.
I HAVE NO IDEA WHO KELLY IS TALKING ABOUT. A LOT OF LAST NIGHT, WAS LEFT THERE.
ARE YOU ACCUSING ME OF MURDERING A NEGRO?
YOU GOT A SWEET TOOTH, MISTER PIRLO?
TASTE FER CHOCOLATE? IF NOT, I AIN'T ACCUSIN' YOU A SHIT.
THAT DARKIE WAS HALF EATEN. SAVAGED BY SOME ANIMAL.
YOU DON' HAVE THE STOMACH FOR THAT, I RECKON...

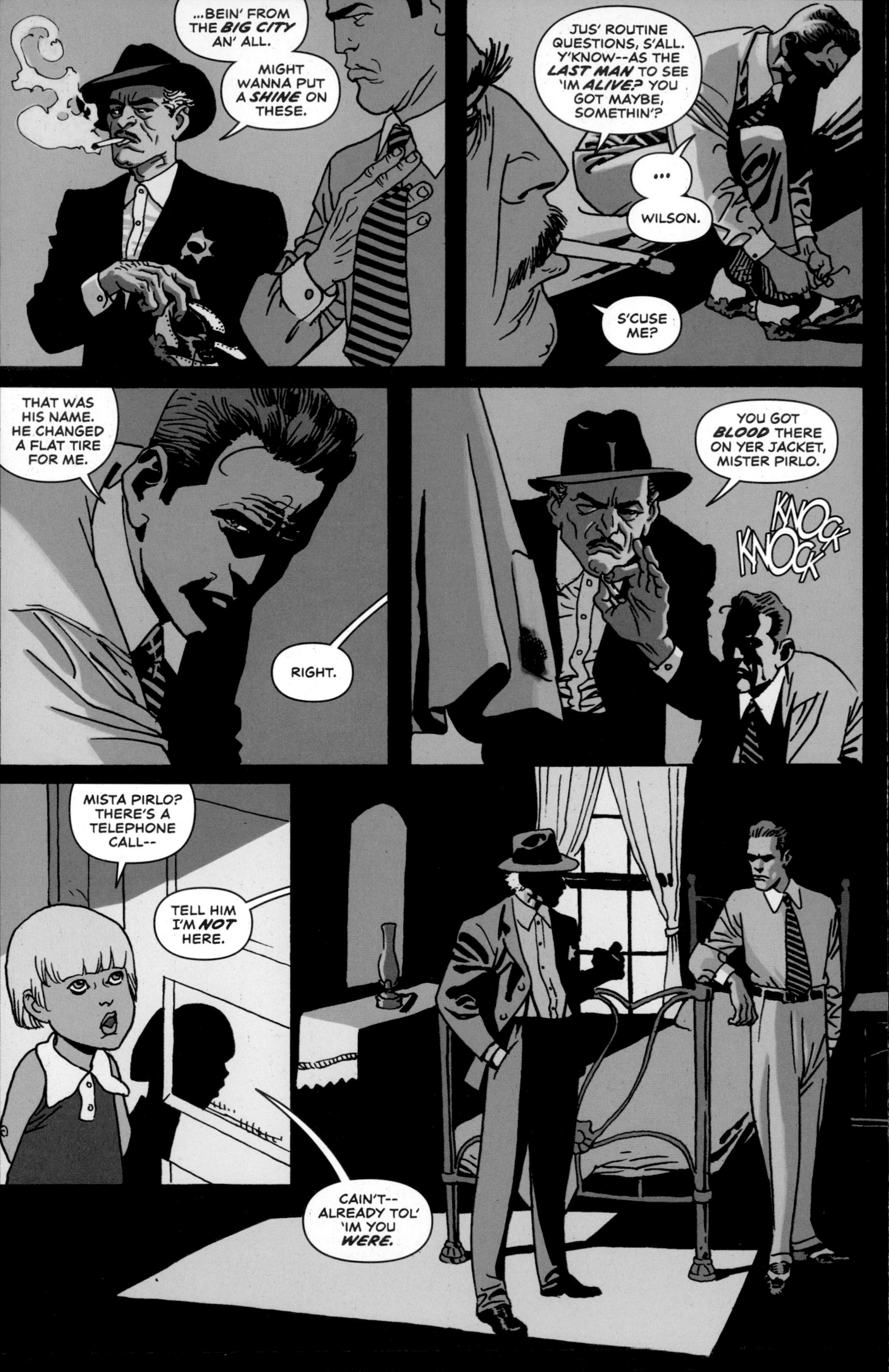
...BEIN' FROM THE BIG CITY AN' ALL.
MIGHT WANNA PUT A SHINE ON THESE.
JUS' ROUTINE QUESTIONS, S'ALL. Y'KNOW--AS THE LAST MAN TO SEE 'IM ALIVE? YOU GOT MAYBE, SOMETHIN'?
...
WILSON.
S'CUSE ME?
THAT WAS HIS NAME. HE CHANGED A FLAT TIRE FOR ME.
RIGHT.
YOU GOT BLOOD THERE ON YER JACKET, MISTER PIRLO.
KNOCK KNOCK
MISTA PIRLO? THERE'S A TELEPHONE CALL--
TELL HIM I'M NOT HERE.
CAIN'T--ALREADY TOL' 'IM YOU WERE.

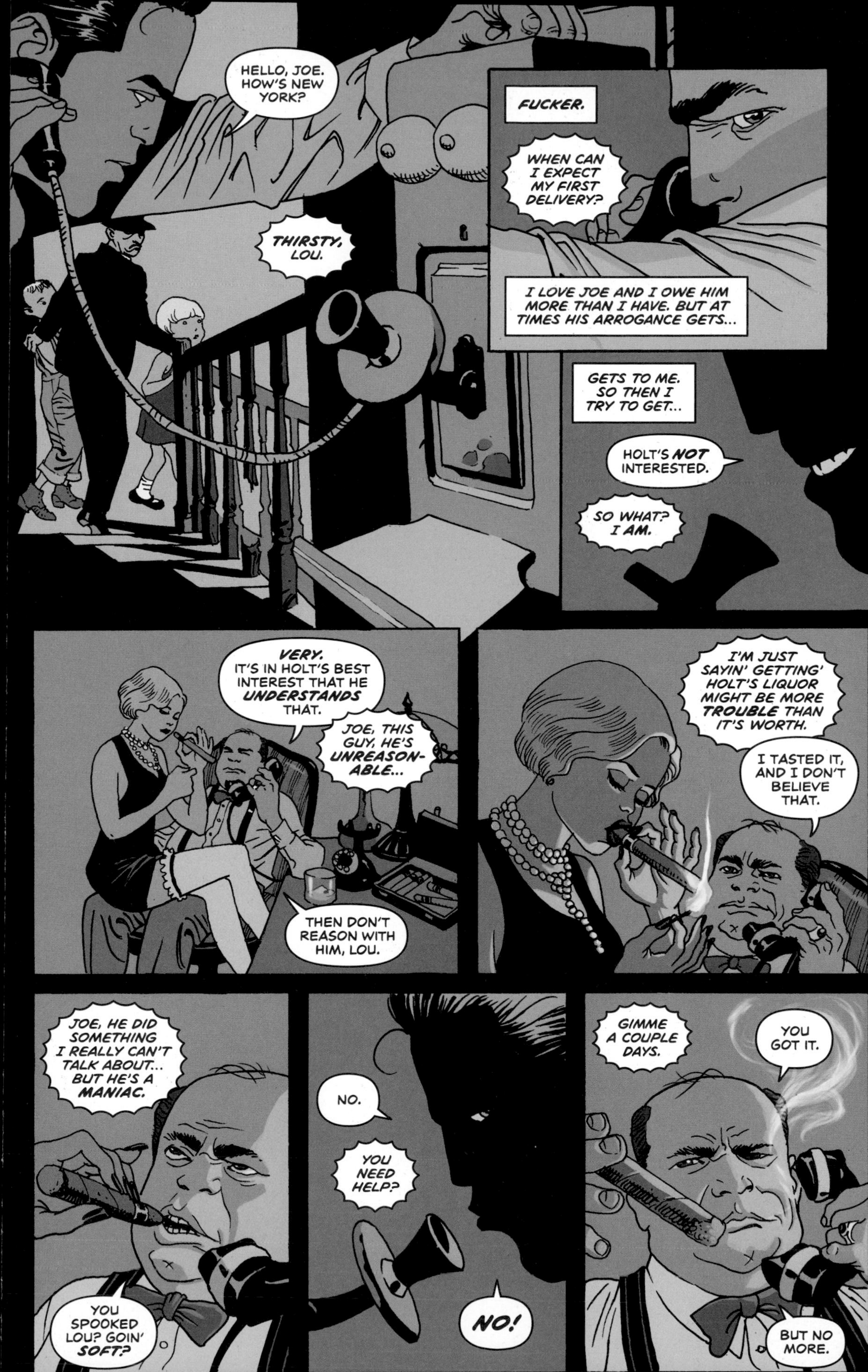
HELLO, JOE. HOW'S NEW YORK?
THIRSTY, LOU.
FUCKER.
WHEN CAN I EXPECT MY FIRST DELIVERY?
I LOVE JOE AND I OWE HIM MORE THAN I HAVE. BUT AT TIMES HIS ARROGANCE GETS...
GETS TO ME. SO THEN I TRY TO GET...
HOLT'S NOT INTERESTED.
SO WHAT? I AM.
VERY. IT'S IN HOLT'S BEST INTEREST THAT HE UNDERSTANDS THAT.
JOE, THIS GUY, HE'S UNREASON-ABLE...
THEN DON'T REASON WITH HIM, LOU.
I'M JUST SAYIN' GETTING' HOLT'S LIQUOR MIGHT BE MORE TROUBLE THAN IT'S WORTH.
I TASTED IT, AND I DON'T BELIEVE THAT.
JOE, HE DID SOMETHING I REALLY CAN'T TALK ABOUT... BUT HE'S A MANIAC.
YOU SPOOKED LOU? GOIN' SOFT?
NO.
YOU NEED HELP?
NO!
GIMME A COUPLE DAYS.
YOU GOT IT.
BUT NO MORE.

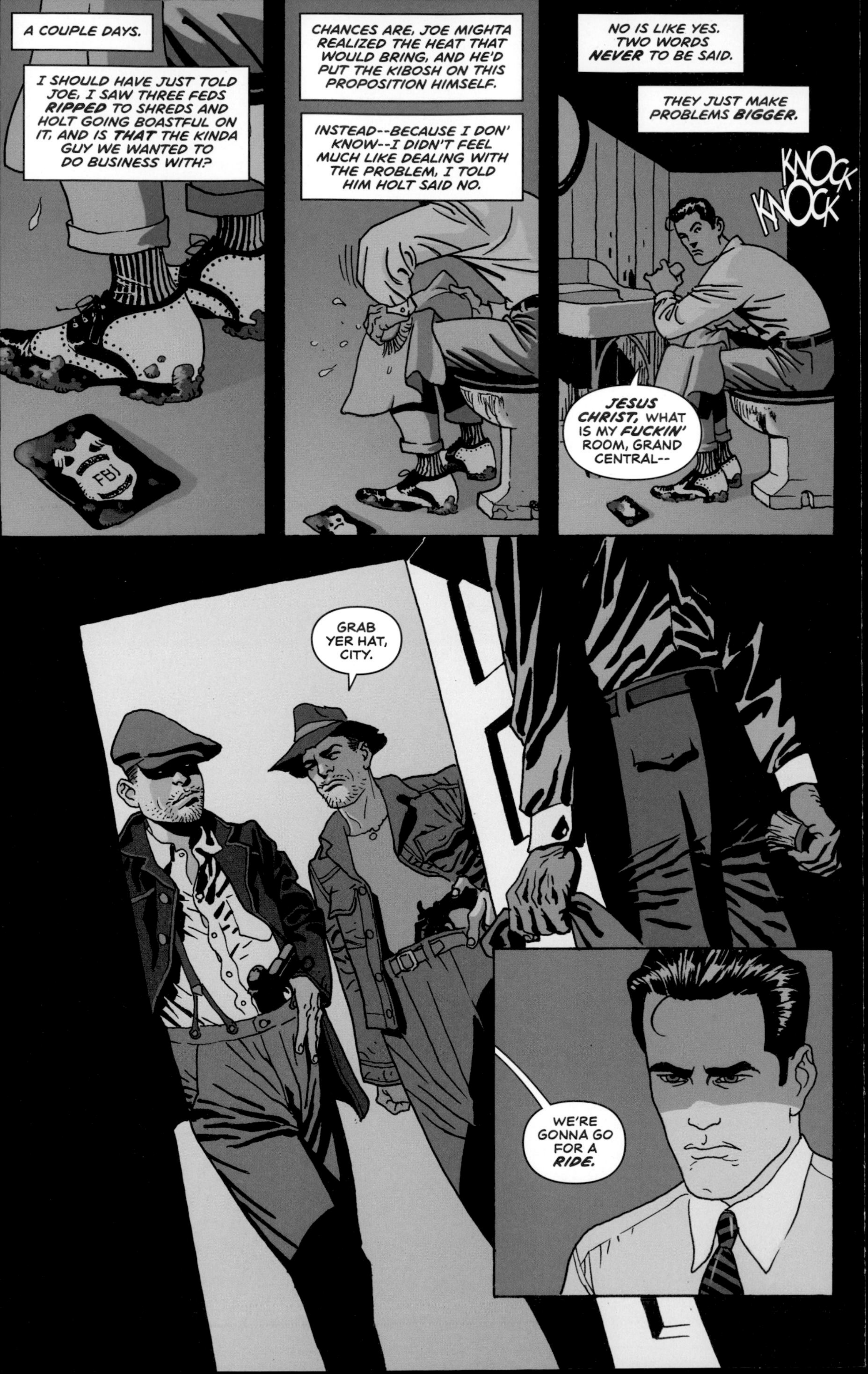
A COUPLE DAYS.
I SHOULD HAVE JUST TOLD JOE, I SAW THREE FEDS RIPPED TO SHREDS AND HOLT GOING BOASTFUL ON IT, AND IS THAT THE KINDA GUY WE WANTED TO DO BUSINESS WITH?
FBI
CHANCES ARE, JOE MIGHTA REALIZED THE HEAT THAT WOULD BRING, AND HE'D PUT THE KIBOSH ON THIS PROPOSITION HIMSELF.
INSTEAD--BECAUSE I DON' KNOW--I DIDN'T FEEL MUCH LIKE DEALING WITH THE PROBLEM, I TOLD HIM HOLT SAID NO.
NO IS LIKE YES. TWO WORDS NEVER TO BE SAID.
THEY JUST MAKE PROBLEMS BIGGER.
KNOCK KNOCK
JESUS CHRIST, WHAT IS MY FUCKIN' ROOM, GRAND CENTRAL--
GRAB YER HAT, CITY.
WE'RE GONNA GO FOR A RIDE.

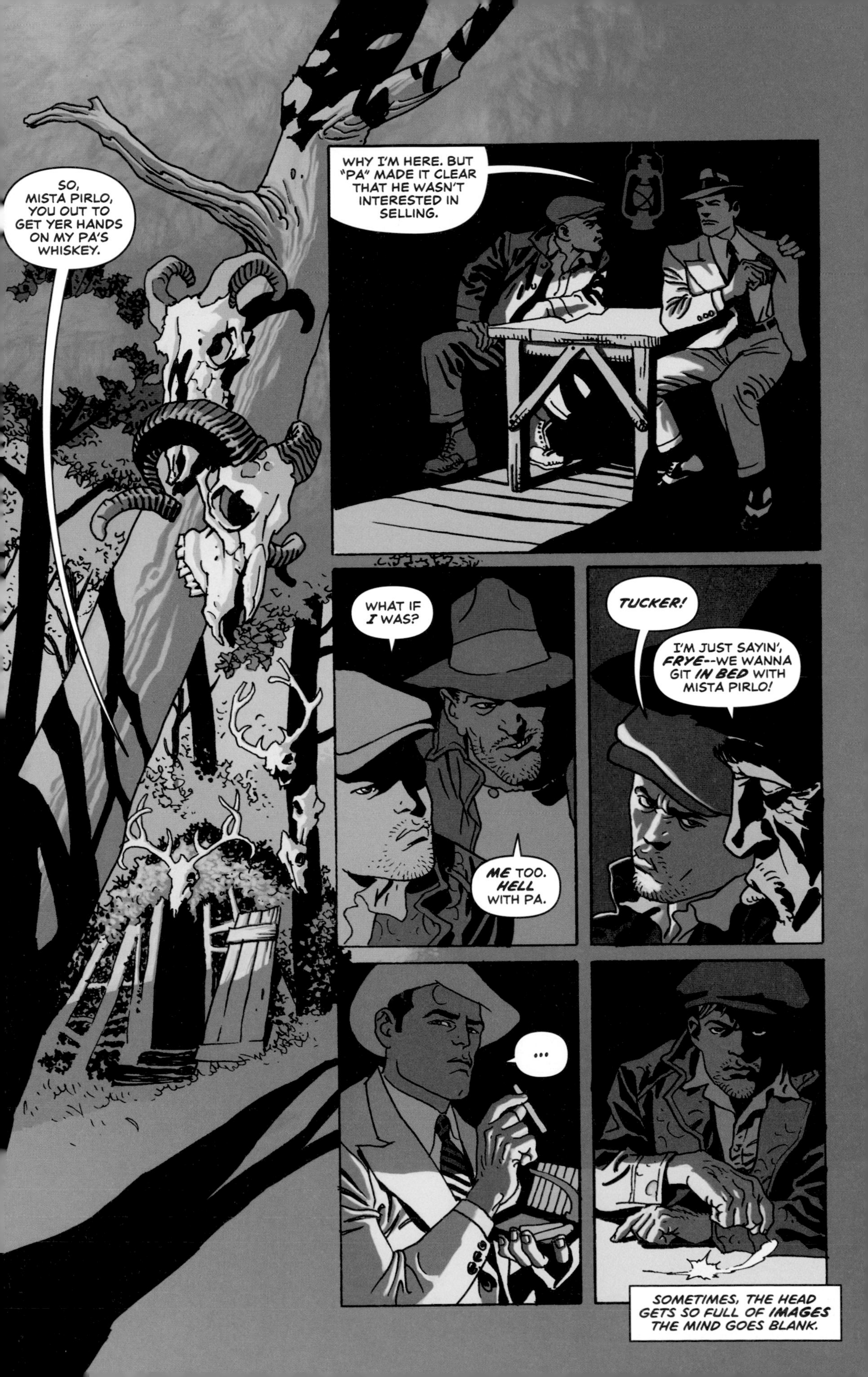
SO, MISTA PIRLO, YOU OUT TO GET YER HANDS ON MY PA'S WHISKEY.
WHY I'M HERE. BUT "PA" MADE IT CLEAR THAT HE WASN'T INTERESTED IN SELLING.
WHAT IF I WAS?
ME TOO. HELL WITH PA.
TUCKER!
I'M JUST SAYIN', FRYE--WE WANNA GIT IN BED WITH MISTA PIRLO!
...
SOMETIMES, THE HEAD GETS SO FULL OF IMAGES THE MIND GOES BLANK.

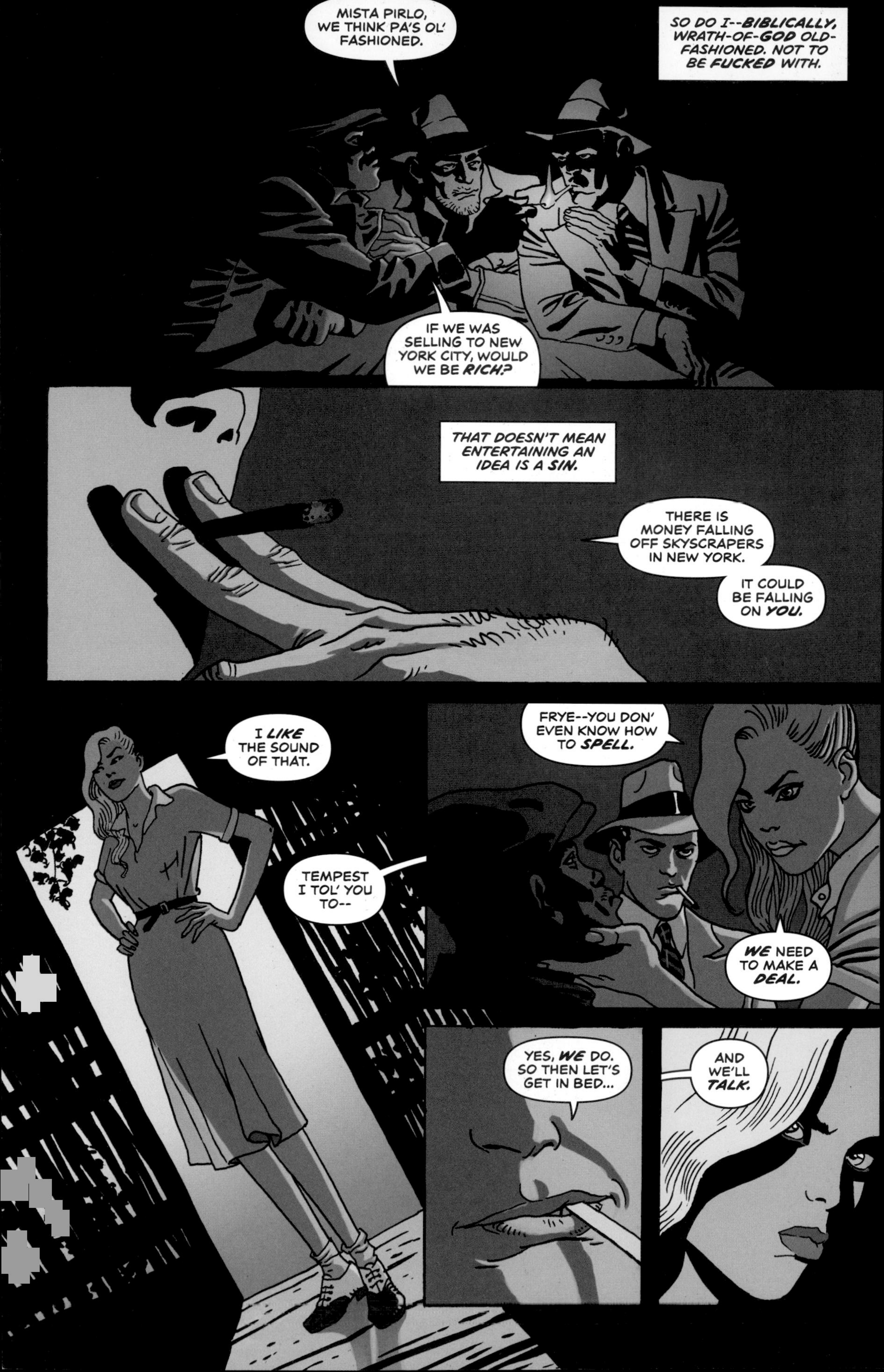
MISTA PIRLO, WE THINK PA'S OL' FASHIONED.
SO DO I--BIBLICALLY, WRATH-OF-GOD OLD-FASHIONED. NOT TO BE FUCKED WITH.
IF WE WAS SELLING TO NEW YORK CITY, WOULD WE BE RICH?
THAT DOESN'T MEAN ENTERTAINING AN IDEA IS A SIN.
THERE IS MONEY FALLING OFF SKYSCRAPERS IN NEW YORK.
IT COULD BE FALLING ON YOU.
I LIKE THE SOUND OF THAT.
TEMPEST I TOL' YOU TO--
FRYE--YOU DON' EVEN KNOW HOW TO SPELL.
WE NEED TO MAKE A DEAL.
YES, WE DO. SO THEN LET'S GET IN BED...
AND WE'LL TALK.

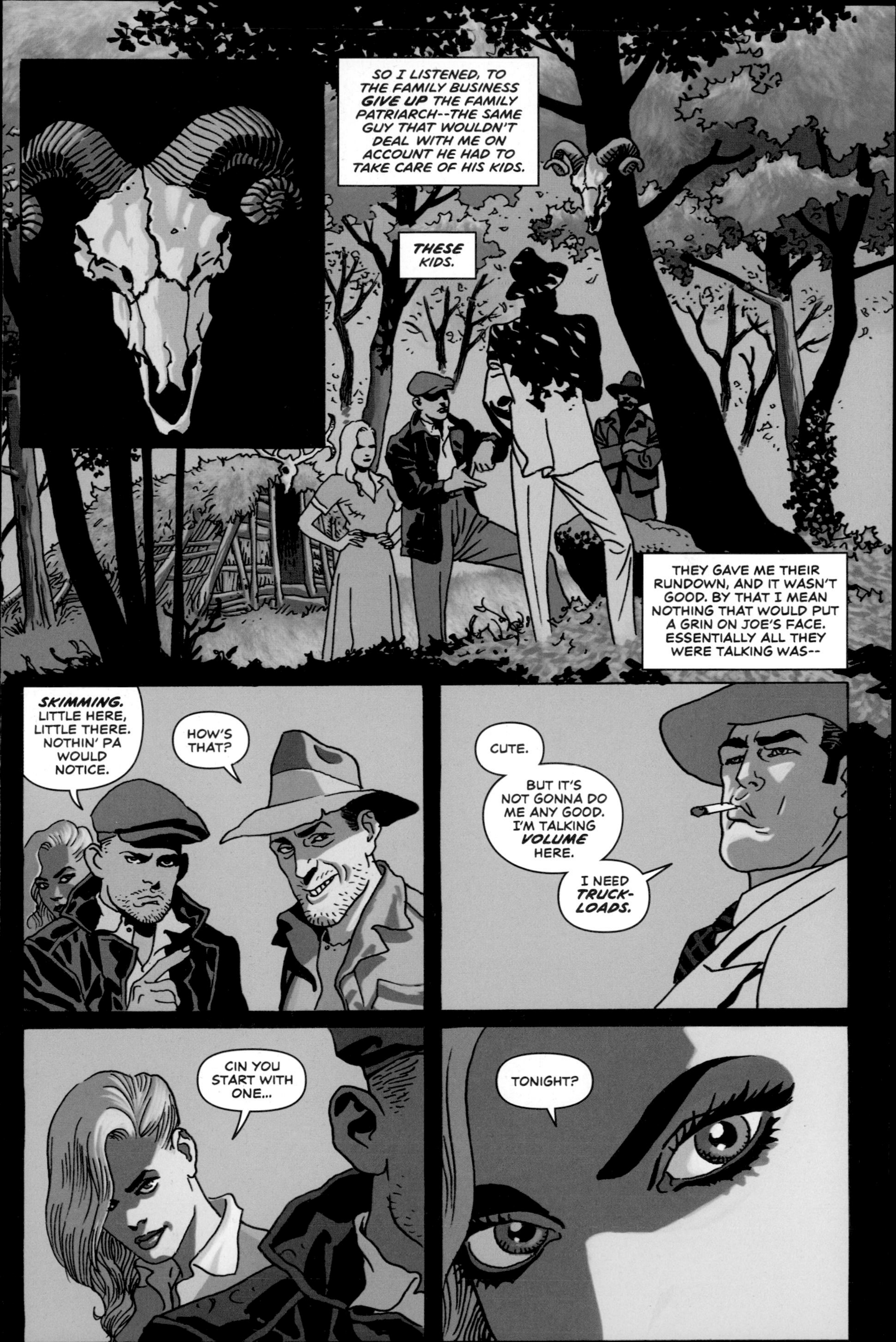
SO I LISTENED, TO THE FAMILY BUSINESS GIVE UP THE FAMILY PATRIARCH--THE SAME GUY THAT WOULDN'T DEAL WITH ME ON ACCOUNT HE HAD TO TAKE CARE OF HIS KIDS.
THESE KIDS.
THEY GAVE ME THEIR RUNDOWN, AND IT WASN'T GOOD. BY THAT I MEAN NOTHING THAT WOULD PUT A GRIN ON JOE'S FACE. ESSENTIALLY ALL THEY WERE TALKING WAS--
SKIMMING. LITTLE HERE, LITTLE THERE. NOTHIN' PA WOULD NOTICE.
HOW'S THAT?
CUTE.
BUT IT'S NOT GONNA DO ME ANY GOOD. I'M TALKING VOLUME HERE.
I NEED TRUCK-LOADS.
CIN YOU START WITH ONE...
TONIGHT?

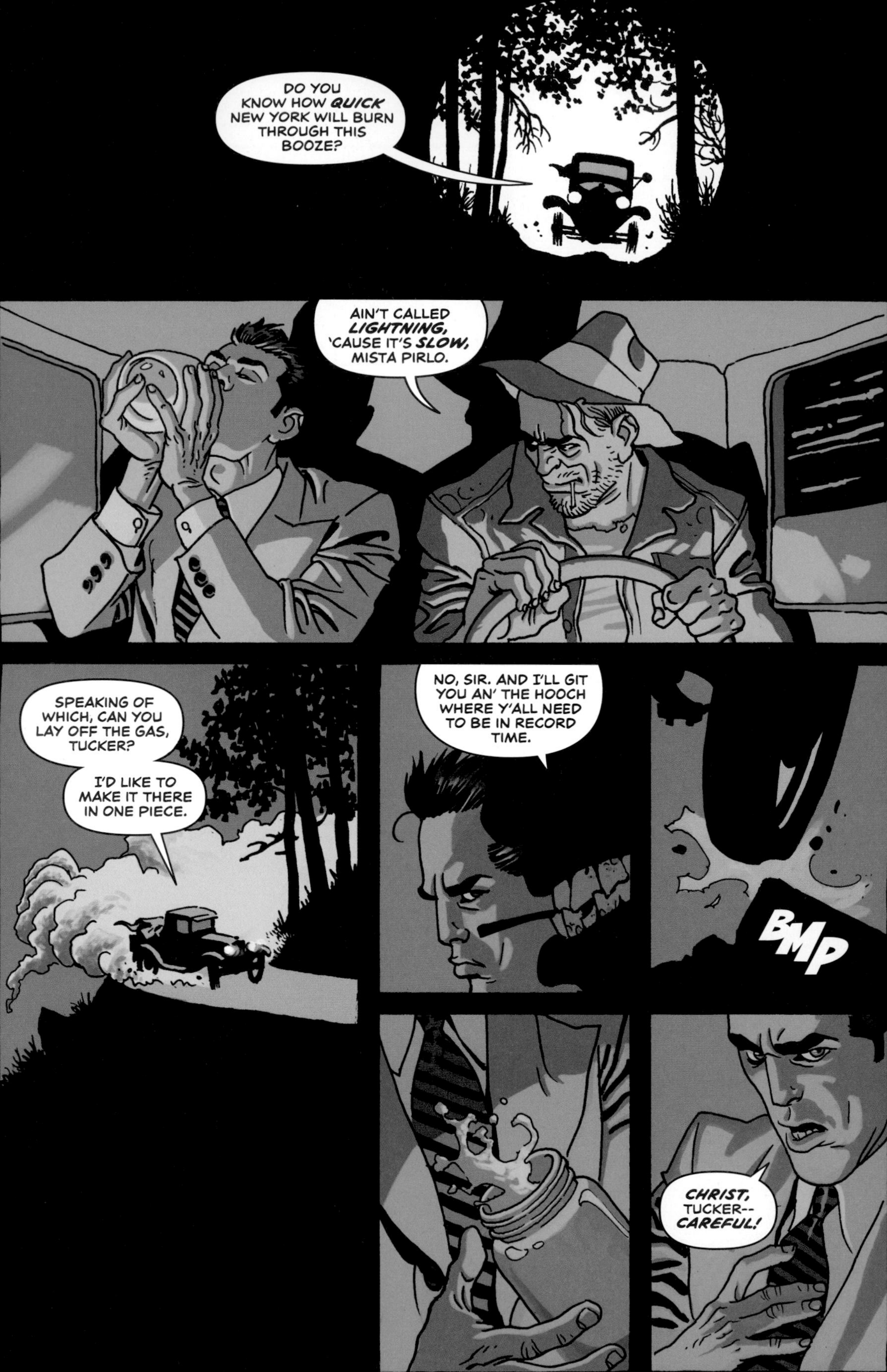
DO YOU KNOW HOW QUICK NEW YORK WILL BURN THROUGH THIS BOOZE?
AIN'T CALLED LIGHTNING, 'CAUSE IT'S SLOW, MISTA PIRLO.
SPEAKING OF WHICH, CAN YOU LAY OFF THE GAS, TUCKER?
I'D LIKE TO MAKE IT THERE IN ONE PIECE.
NO, SIR. AND I'LL GIT YOU AN' THE HOOCH WHERE Y'ALL NEED TO BE IN RECORD TIME.
BMP
CHRIST, TUCKER-- CAREFUL!

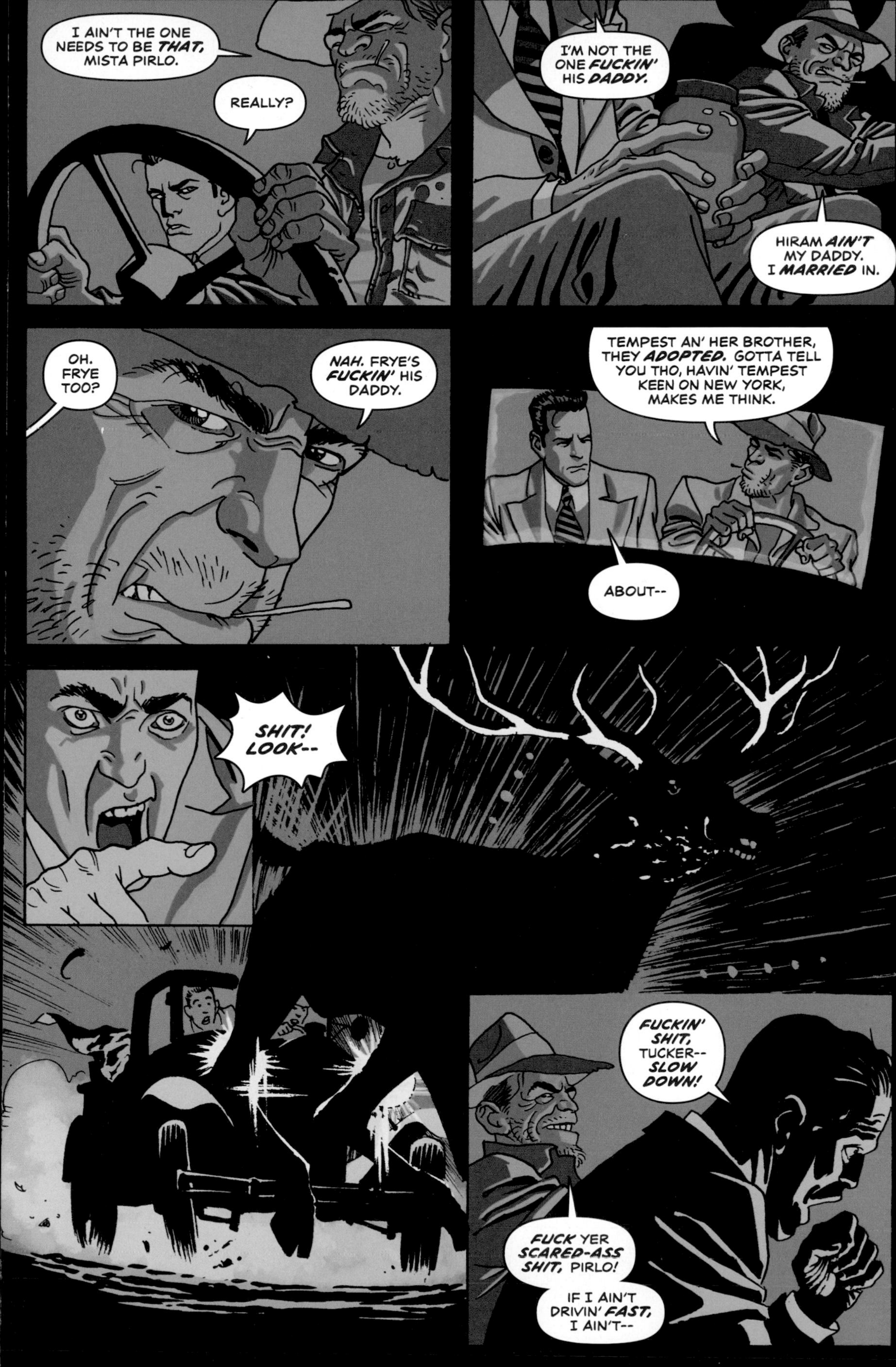
I AIN'T THE ONE NEEDS TO BE THAT, MISTA PIRLO.
REALLY?
I'M NOT THE ONE FUCKIN' HIS DADDY.
HIRAM AIN'T MY DADDY. I MARRIED IN.
OH. FRYE TOO?
NAH. FRYE'S FUCKIN' HIS DADDY.
TEMPEST AN' HER BROTHER, THEY ADOPTED. GOTTA TELL YOU THO, HAVIN' TEMPEST KEEN ON NEW YORK, MAKES ME THINK.
ABOUT--
SHIT! LOOK--
FUCKIN' SHIT, TUCKER-- SLOW DOWN!
FUCK YER SCARED-ASS SHIT, PIRLO!
IF I AIN'T DRIVIN' FAST, I AIN'T--

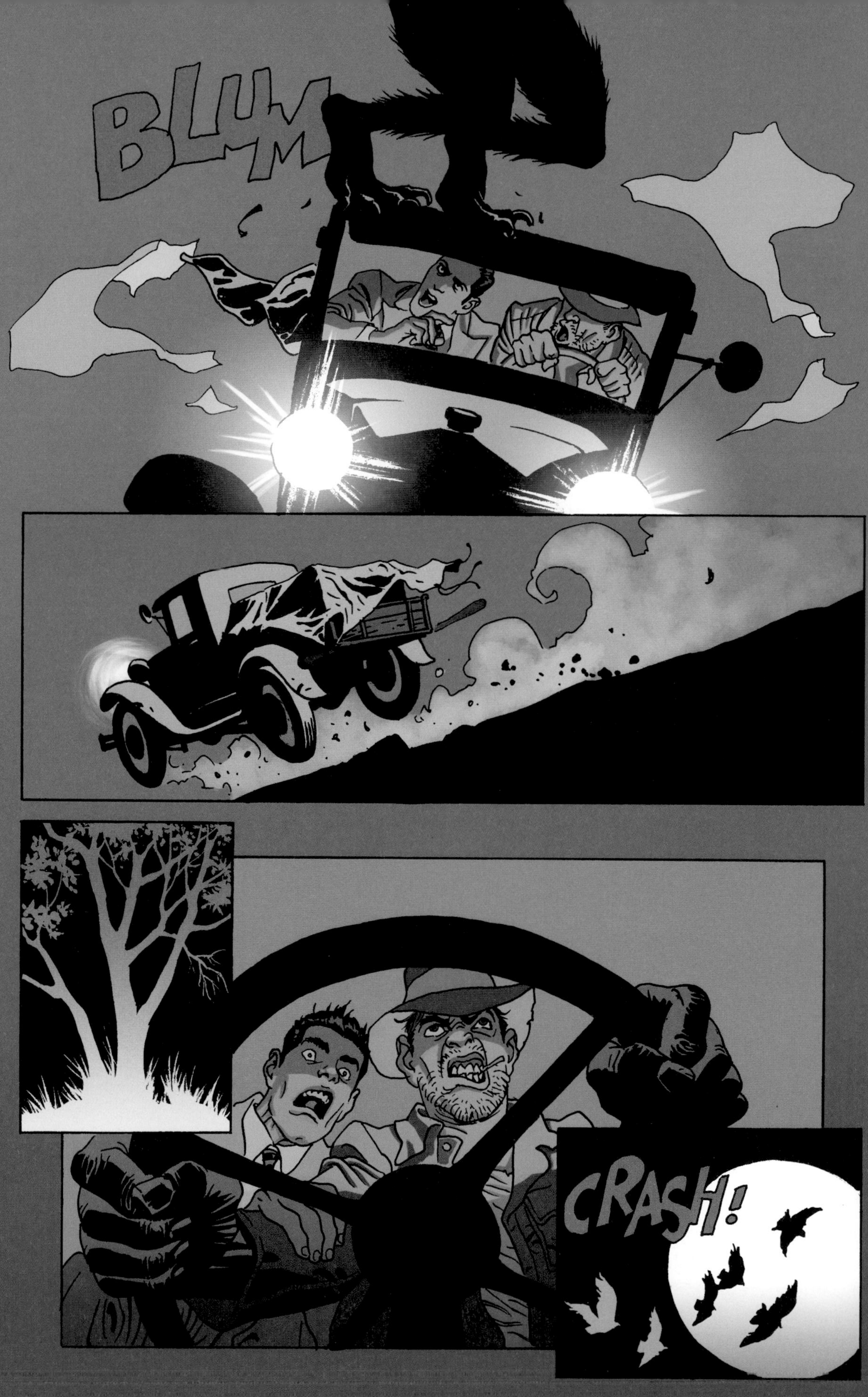
BLUM
CRASH!

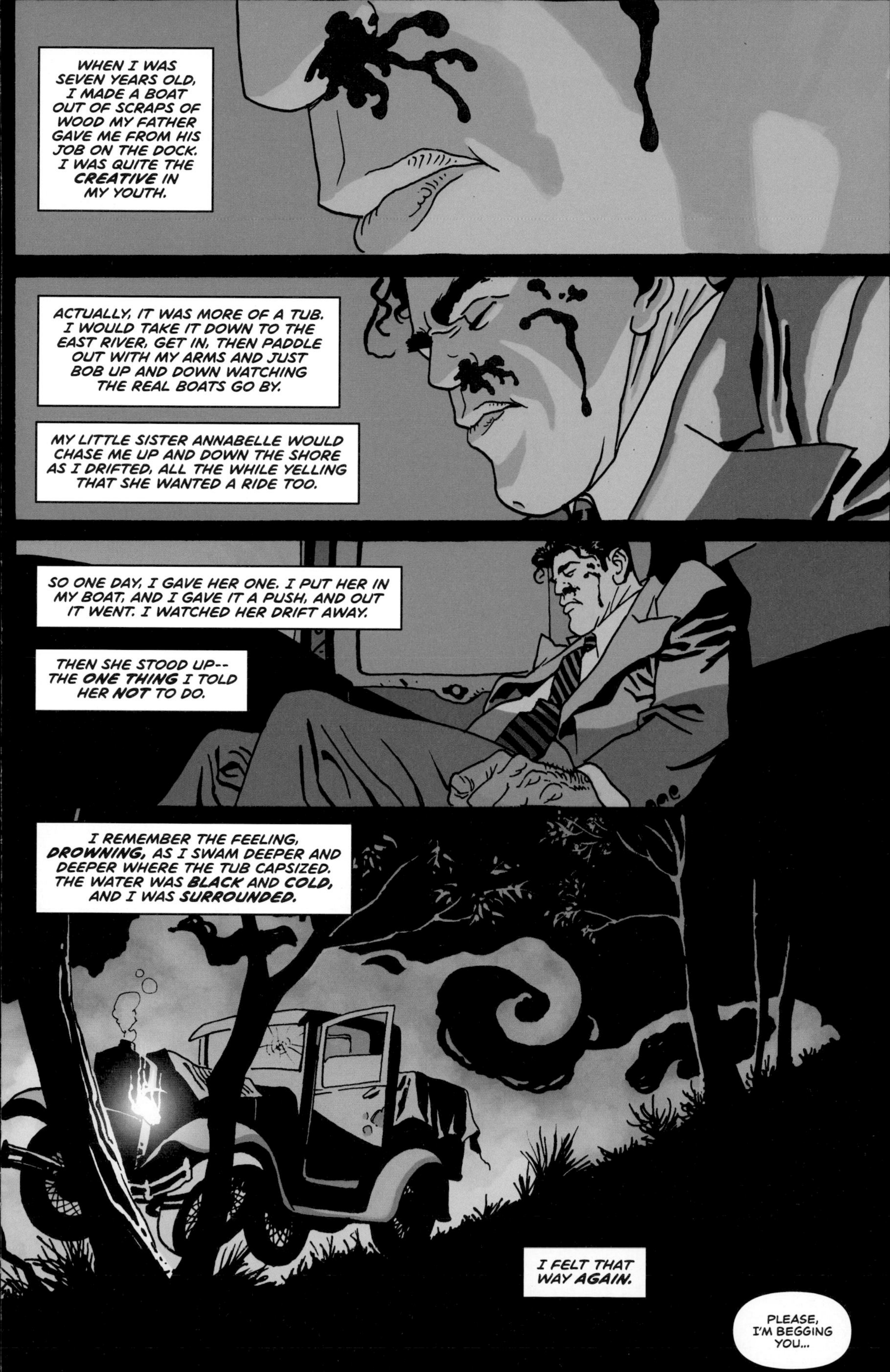

WHEN I WAS SEVEN YEARS OLD, I MADE A BOAT OUT OF SCRAPS OF WOOD MY FATHER GAVE ME FROM HIS JOB ON THE DOCK. I WAS QUITE THE CREATIVE IN MY YOUTH.
ACTUALLY, IT WAS MORE OF A TUB. I WOULD TAKE IT DOWN TO THE EAST RIVER, GET IN, THEN PADDLE OUT WITH MY ARMS AND JUST BOB UP AND DOWN WATCHING THE REAL BOATS GO BY.
MY LITTLE SISTER ANNABELLE WOULD CHASE ME UP AND DOWN THE SHORE AS I DRIFTED, ALL THE WHILE YELLING THAT SHE WANTED A RIDE TOO.
SO ONE DAY, I GAVE HER ONE. I PUT HER IN MY BOAT, AND I GAVE IT A PUSH, AND OUT IT WENT. I WATCHED HER DRIFT AWAY.
THEN SHE STOOD UP-- THE ONE THING I TOLD HER NOT TO DO.
I REMEMBER THE FEELING, DROWNING, AS I SWAM DEEPER AND DEEPER WHERE THE TUB CAPSIZED. THE WATER WAS BLACK AND COLD, AND I WAS SURROUNDED.
I FELT THAT WAY AGAIN.
PLEASE, I'M BEGGING YOU...

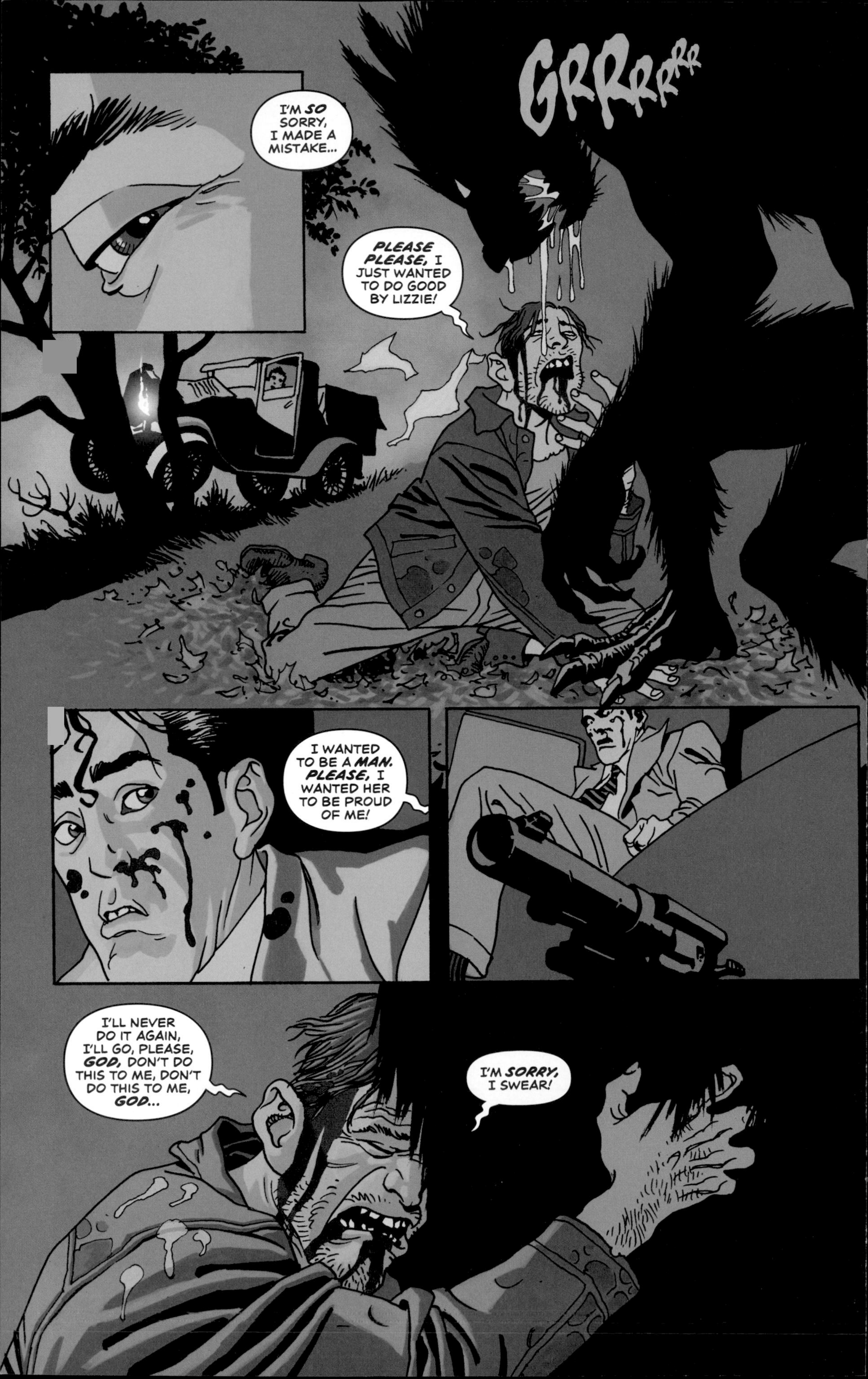
GRRrrrr
I'M SO SORRY, I MADE A MISTAKE...
PLEASE PLEASE, I JUST WANTED TO DO GOOD BY LIZZIE!
I WANTED TO BE A MAN. PLEASE, I WANTED HER TO BE PROUD OF ME!
I'LL NEVER DO IT AGAIN, I'LL GO, PLEASE, GOD, DON'T DO THIS TO ME, DON'T DO THIS TO ME, GOD...
I'M SORRY, I SWEAR!

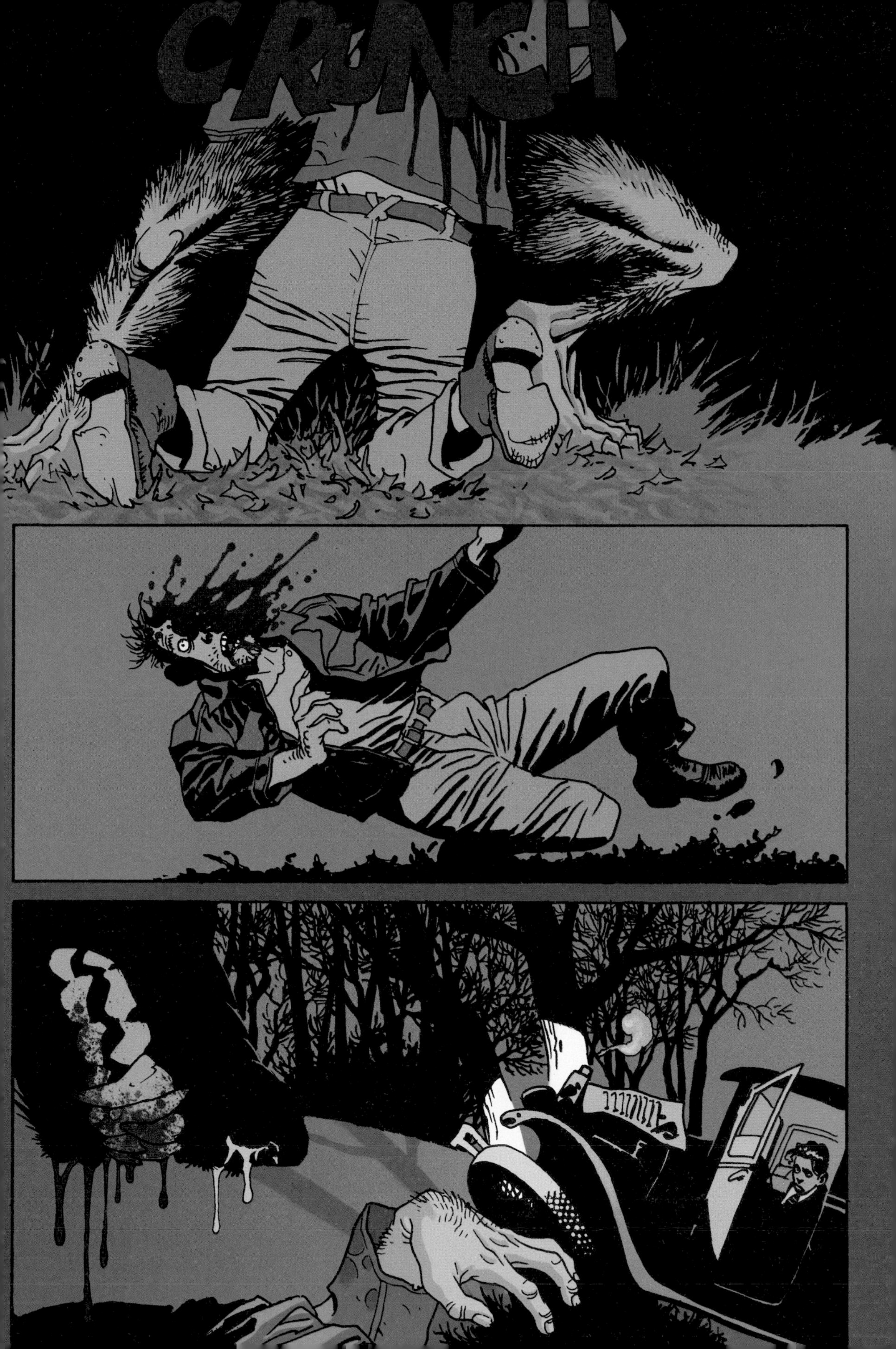
CRUNCH

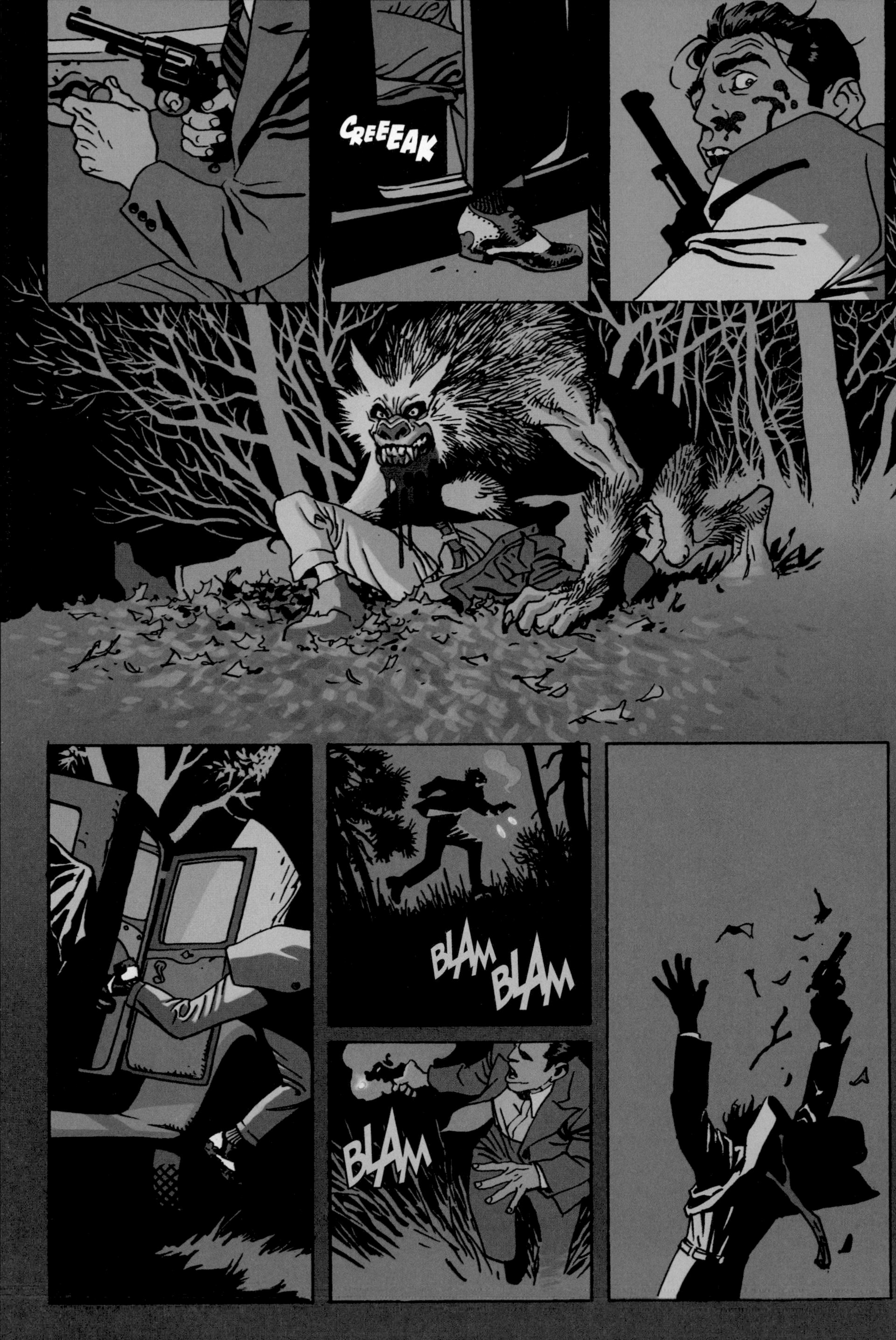
CREEEAK
BLAM BLAM
BLAM

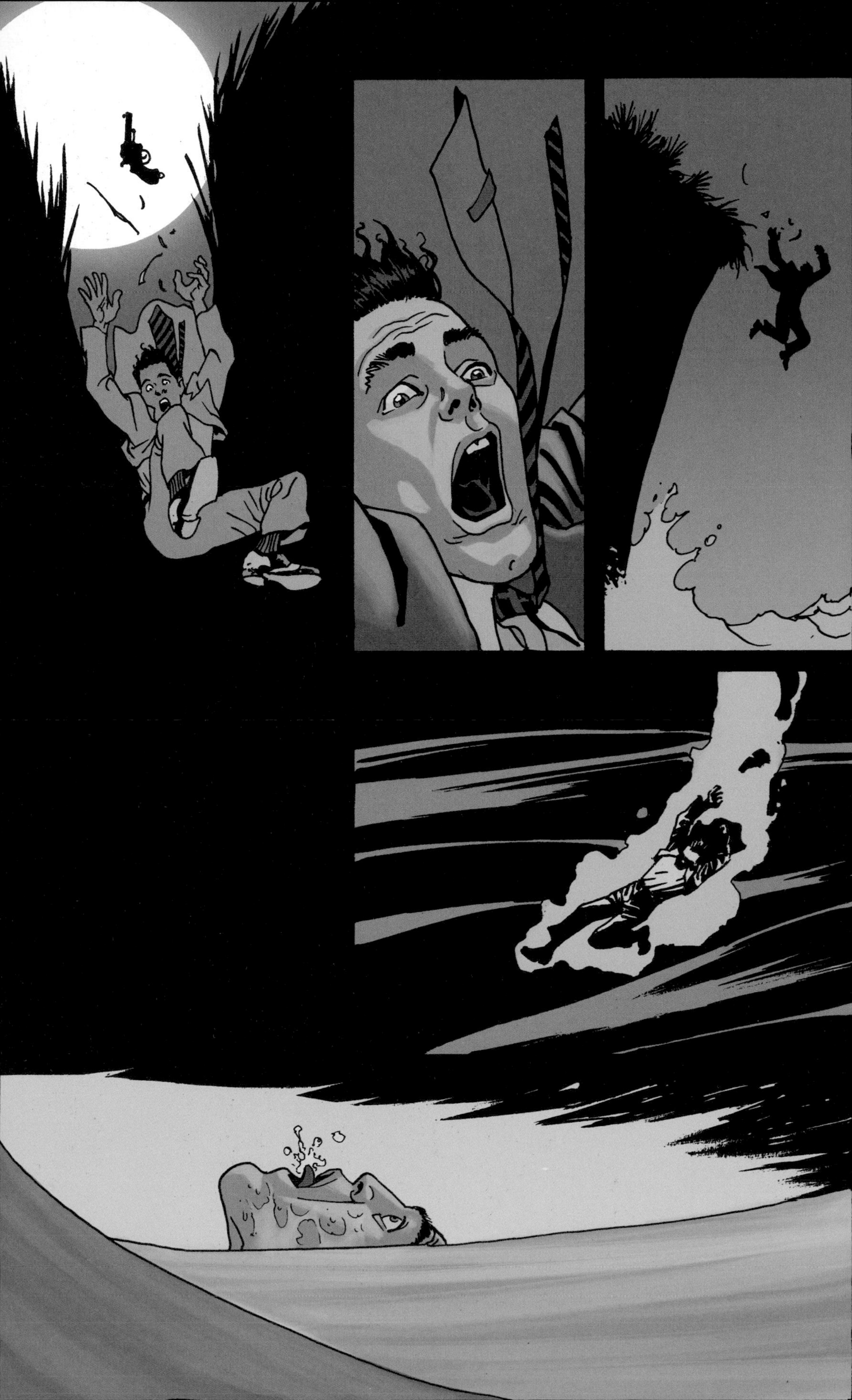

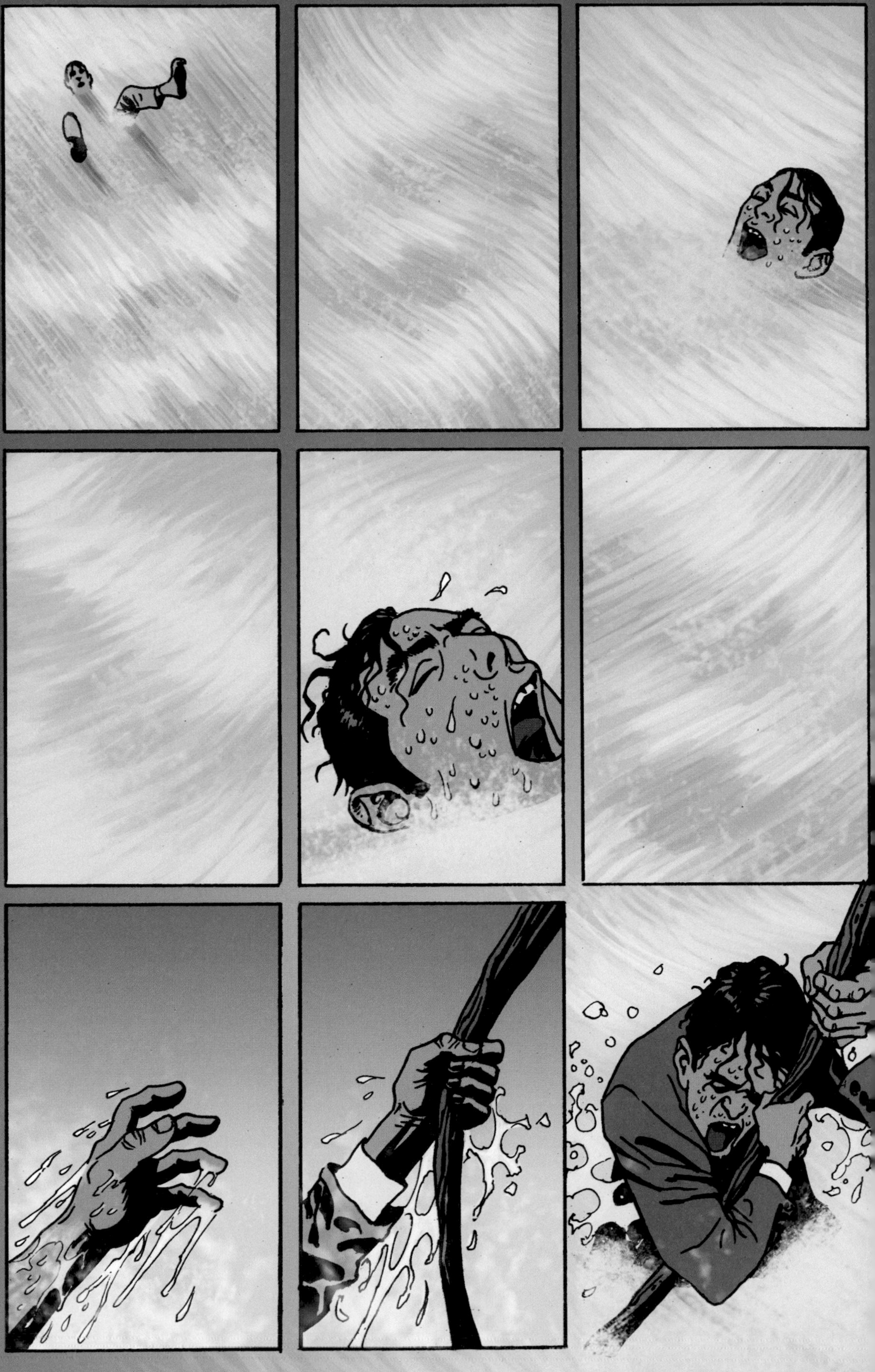

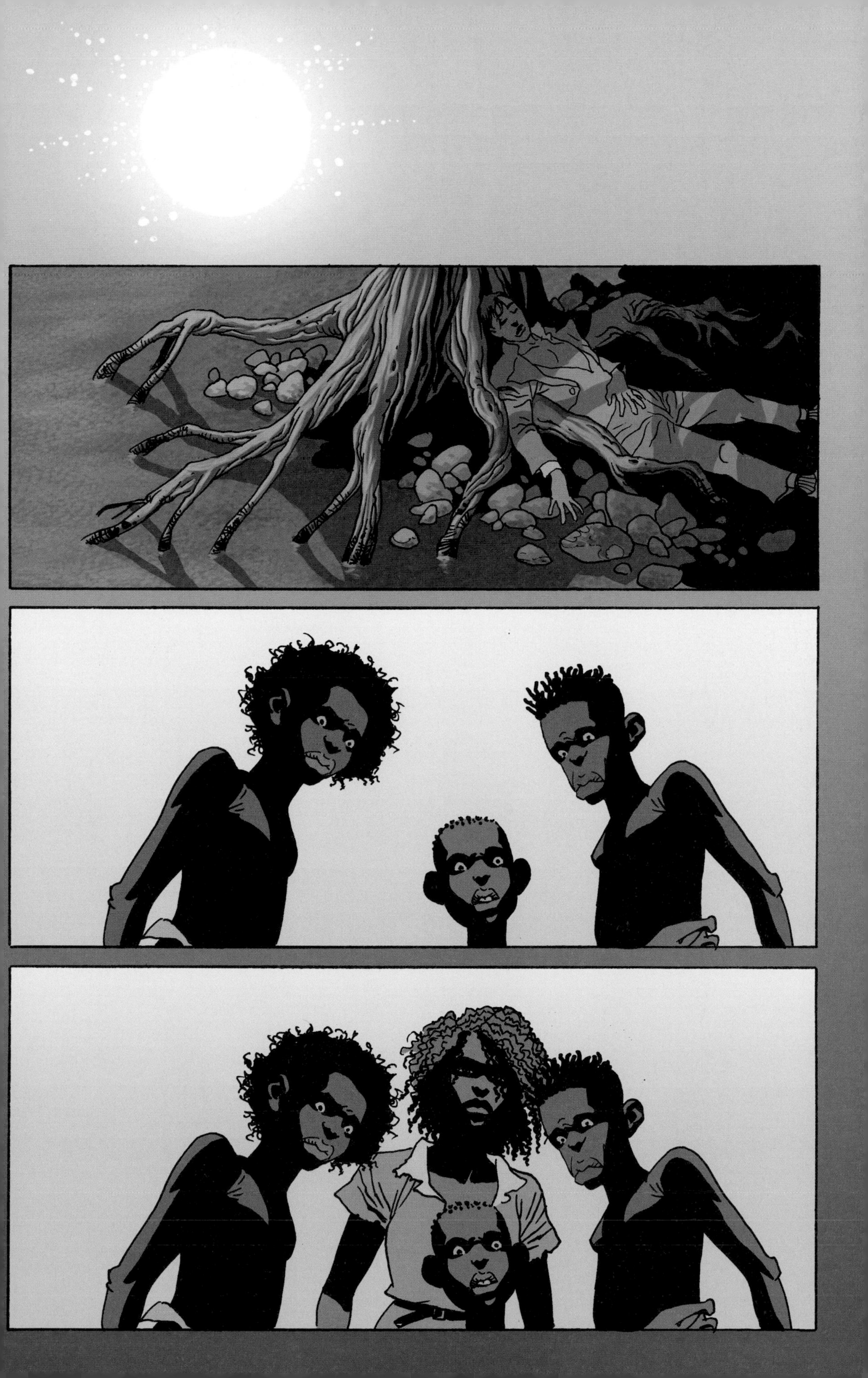

Chapter
THREE

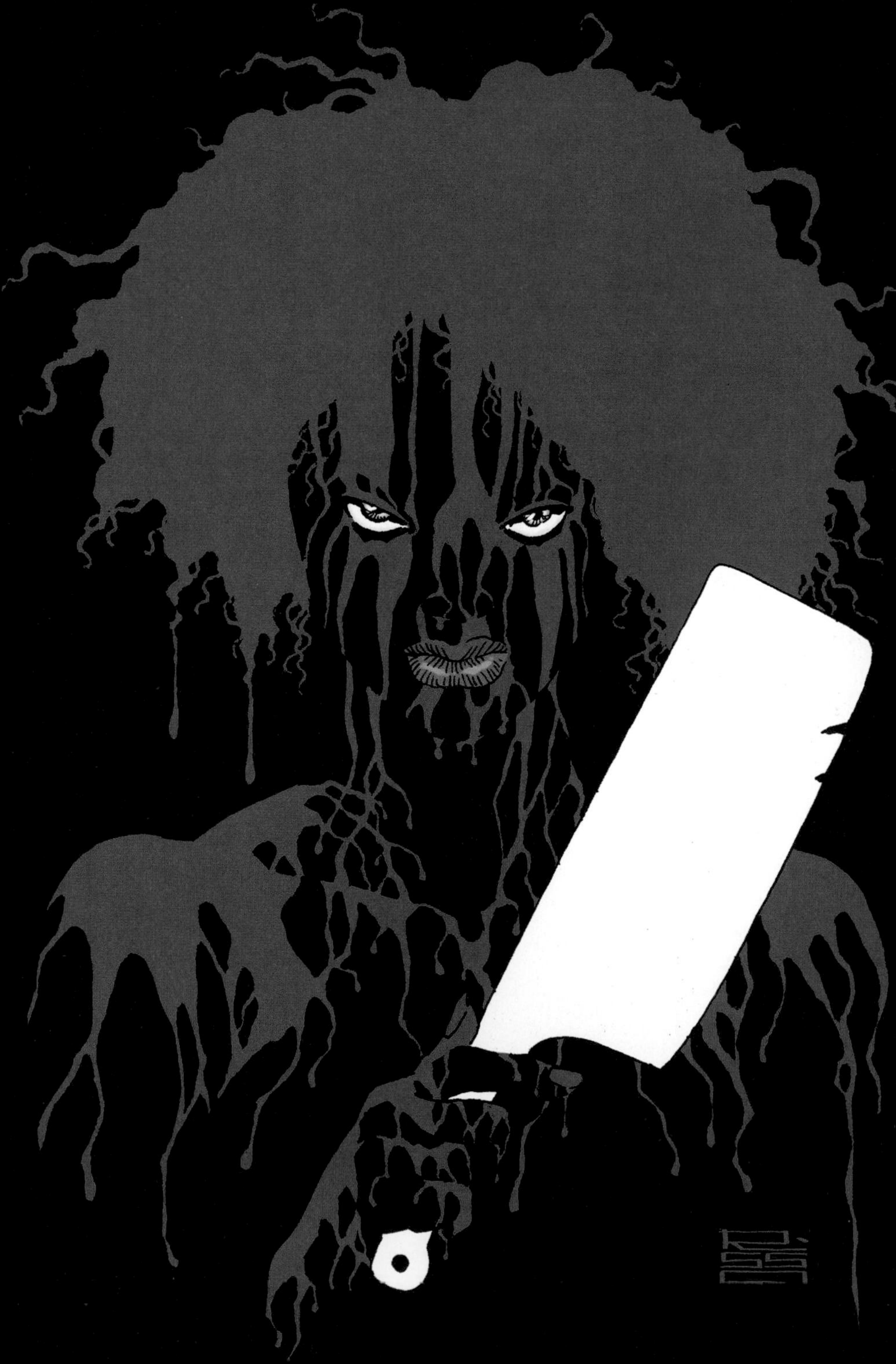

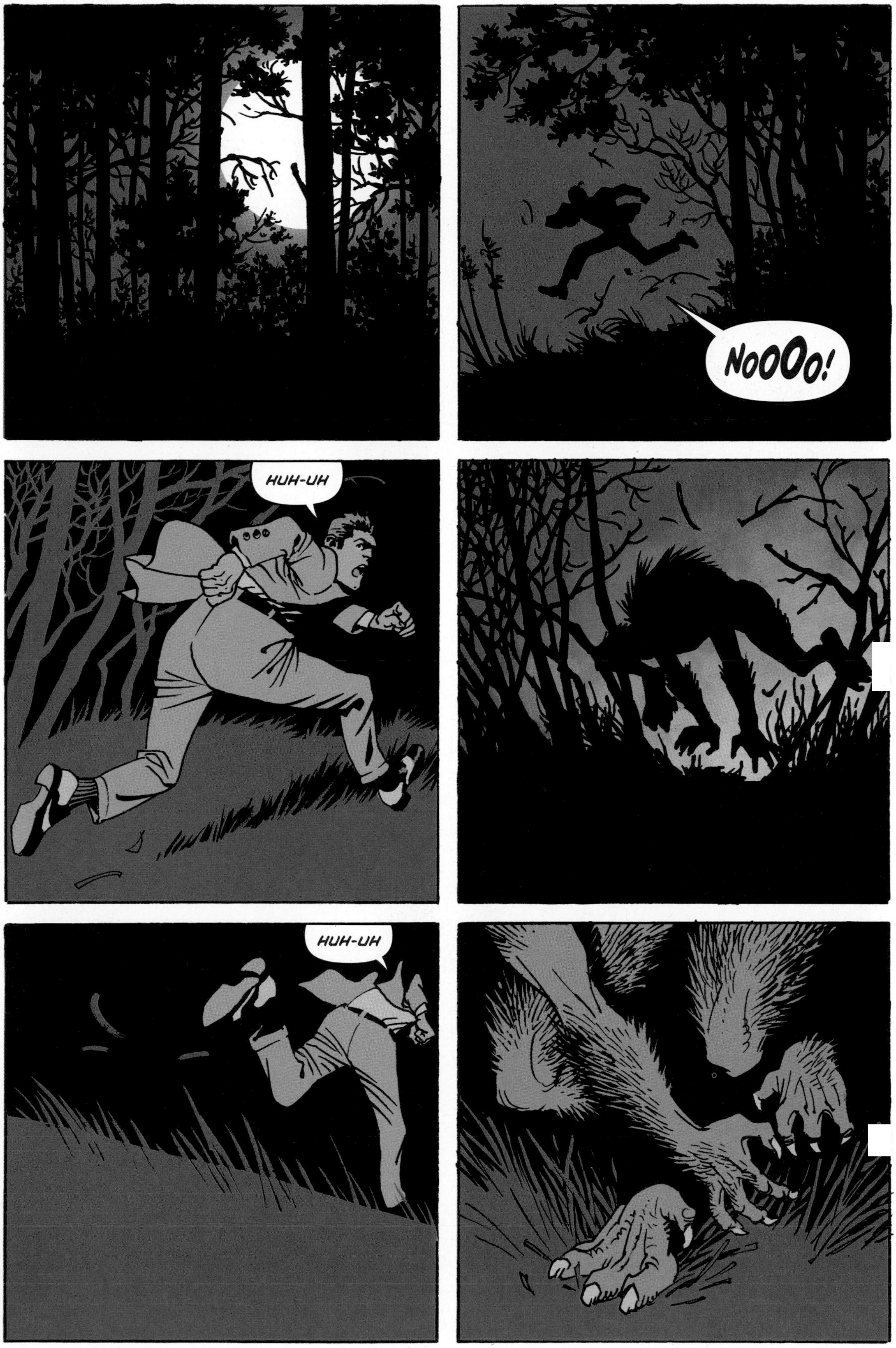
NoOOo!
HUH-UH
HUH-UH

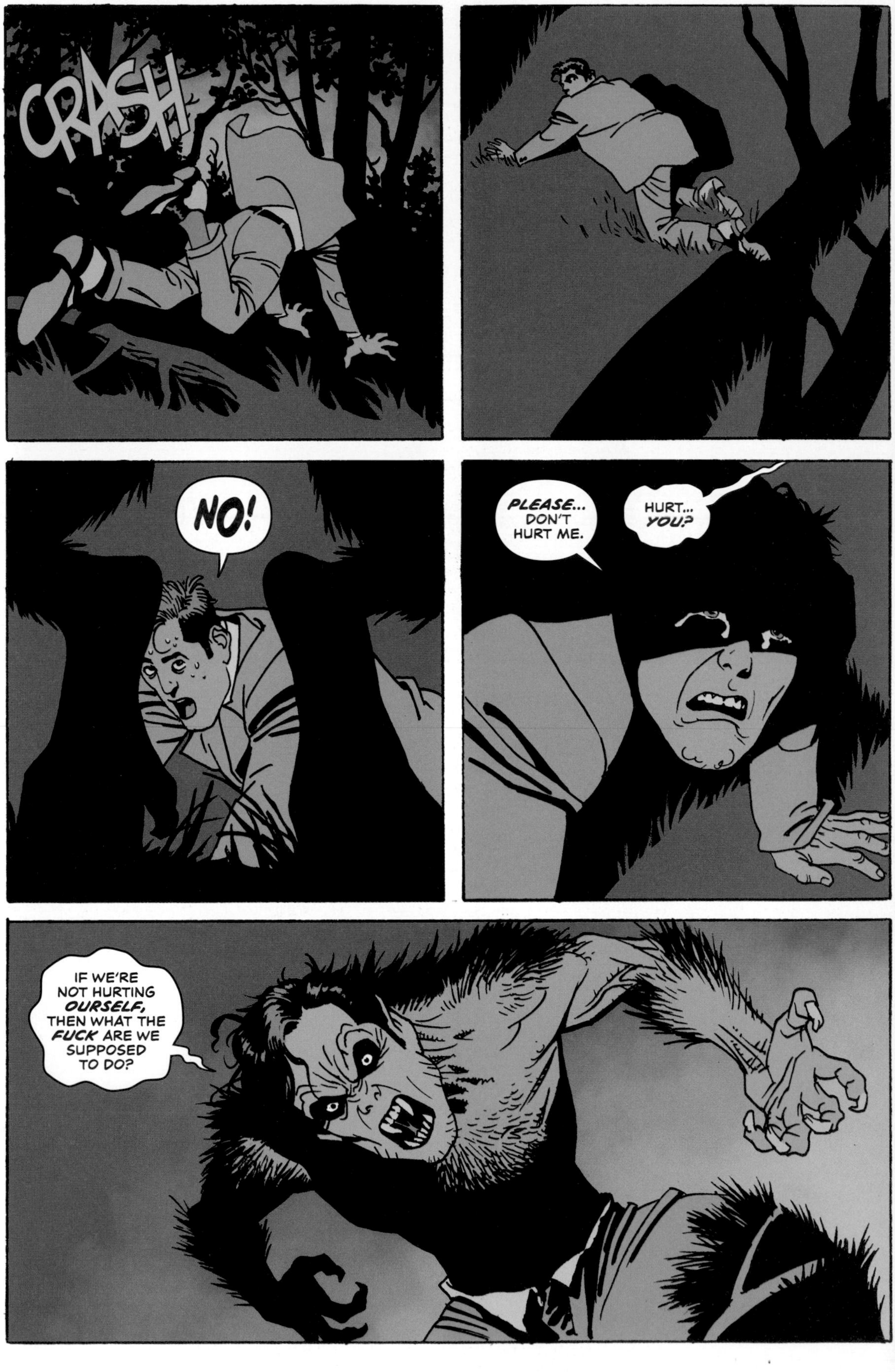
CRASH
NO!
PLEASE... DON'T HURT ME.
HURT... YOU?
IF WE'RE NOT HURTING OURSELF, THEN WHAT THE FUCK ARE WE SUPPOSED TO DO?

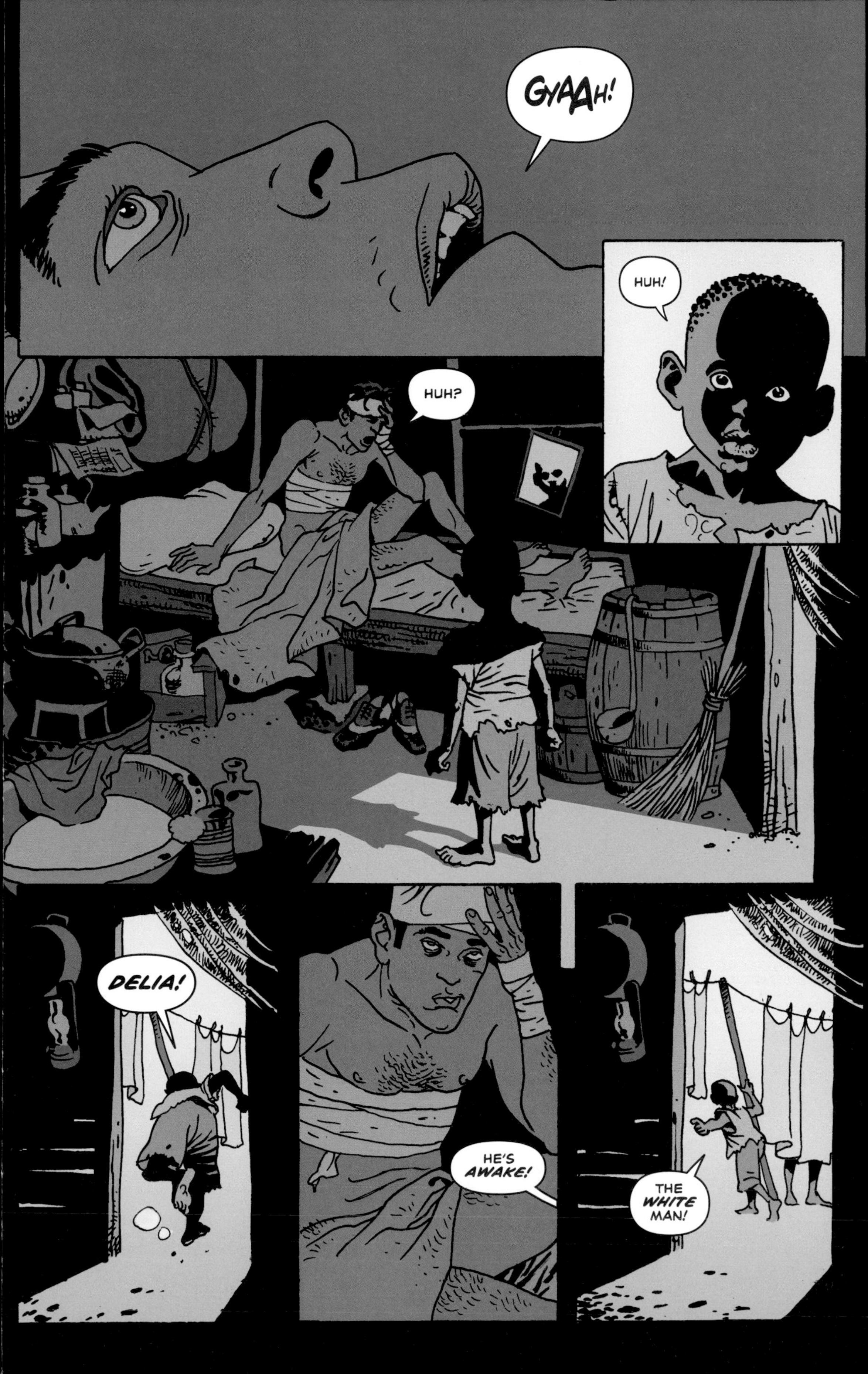
GYAAH!
HUH!
HUH?
DELIA!
HE'S AWAKE!
THE WHITE MAN!

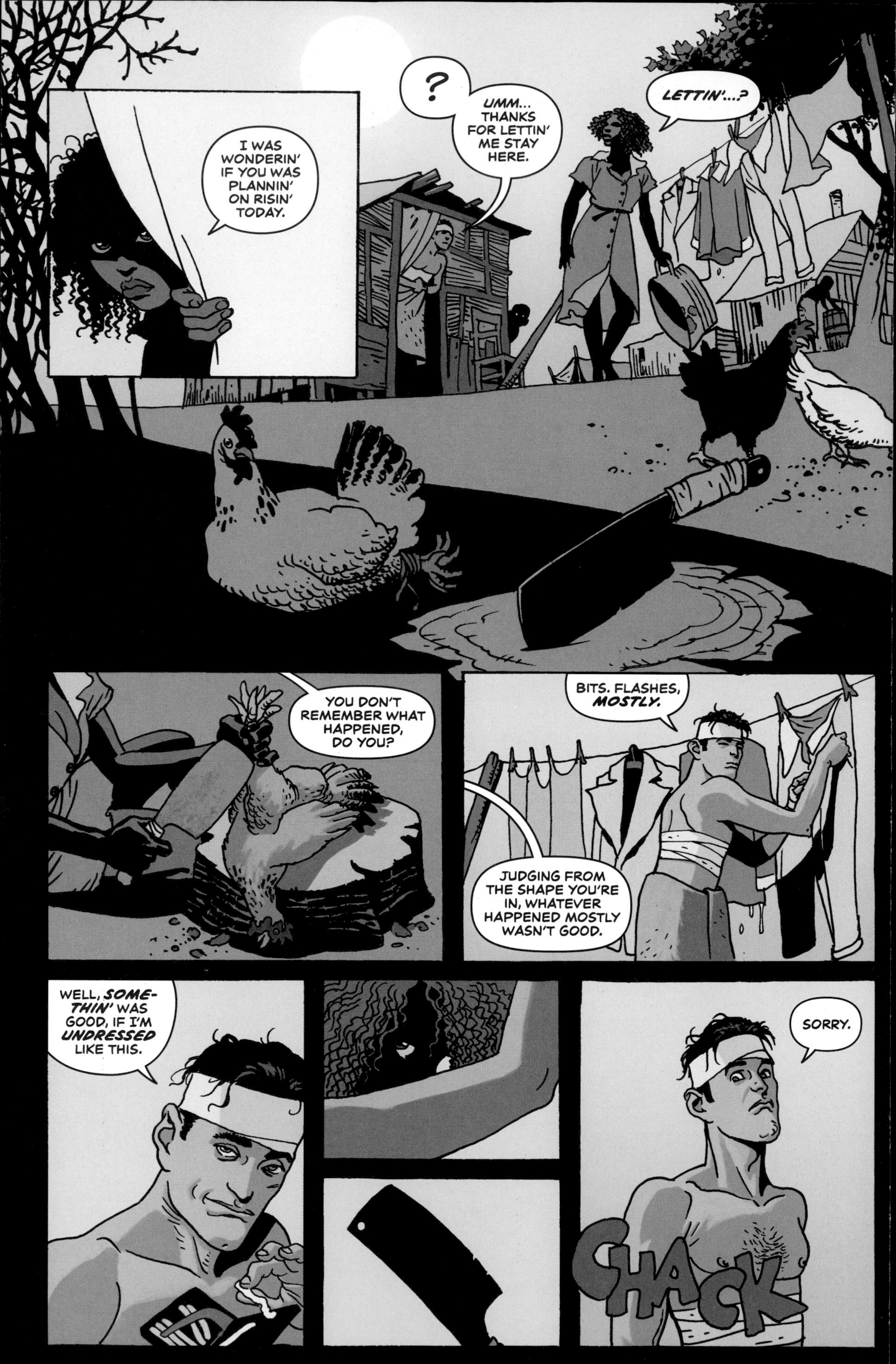
I WAS WONDERIN' IF YOU WAS PLANNIN' ON RISIN' TODAY.
?
UMM... THANKS FOR LETTIN' ME STAY HERE.
LETTIN'...?
YOU DON'T REMEMBER WHAT HAPPENED, DO YOU?
BITS. FLASHES, MOSTLY.
JUDGING FROM THE SHAPE YOU'RE IN, WHATEVER HAPPENED MOSTLY WASN'T GOOD.
WELL, SOME-THIN' WAS GOOD, IF I'M UNDRESSED LIKE THIS.
SORRY.
CHACK

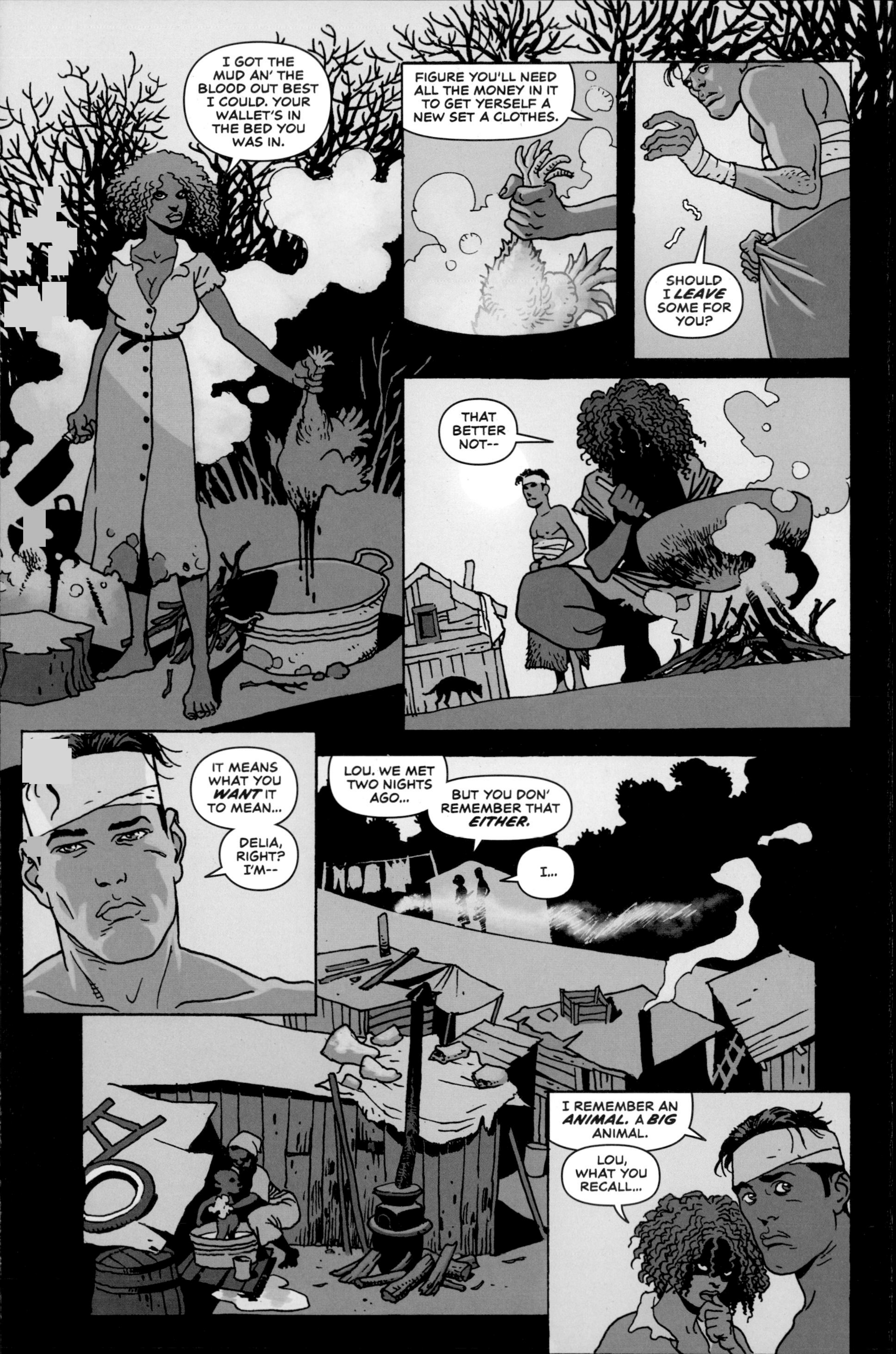
I GOT THE MUD AN' THE BLOOD OUT BEST I COULD. YOUR WALLET'S IN THE BED YOU WAS IN.
FIGURE YOU'LL NEED ALL THE MONEY IN IT TO GET YERSELF A NEW SET A CLOTHES.
SHOULD I *LEAVE* SOME FOR YOU?
THAT BETTER NOT--
IT MEANS WHAT YOU *WANT* IT TO MEAN...
DELIA, RIGHT? I'M--
LOU. WE MET TWO NIGHTS AGO...
BUT YOU DON' REMEMBER THAT *EITHER.*
I...
I REMEMBER AN *ANIMAL.* A *BIG* ANIMAL.
LOU, WHAT YOU RECALL...

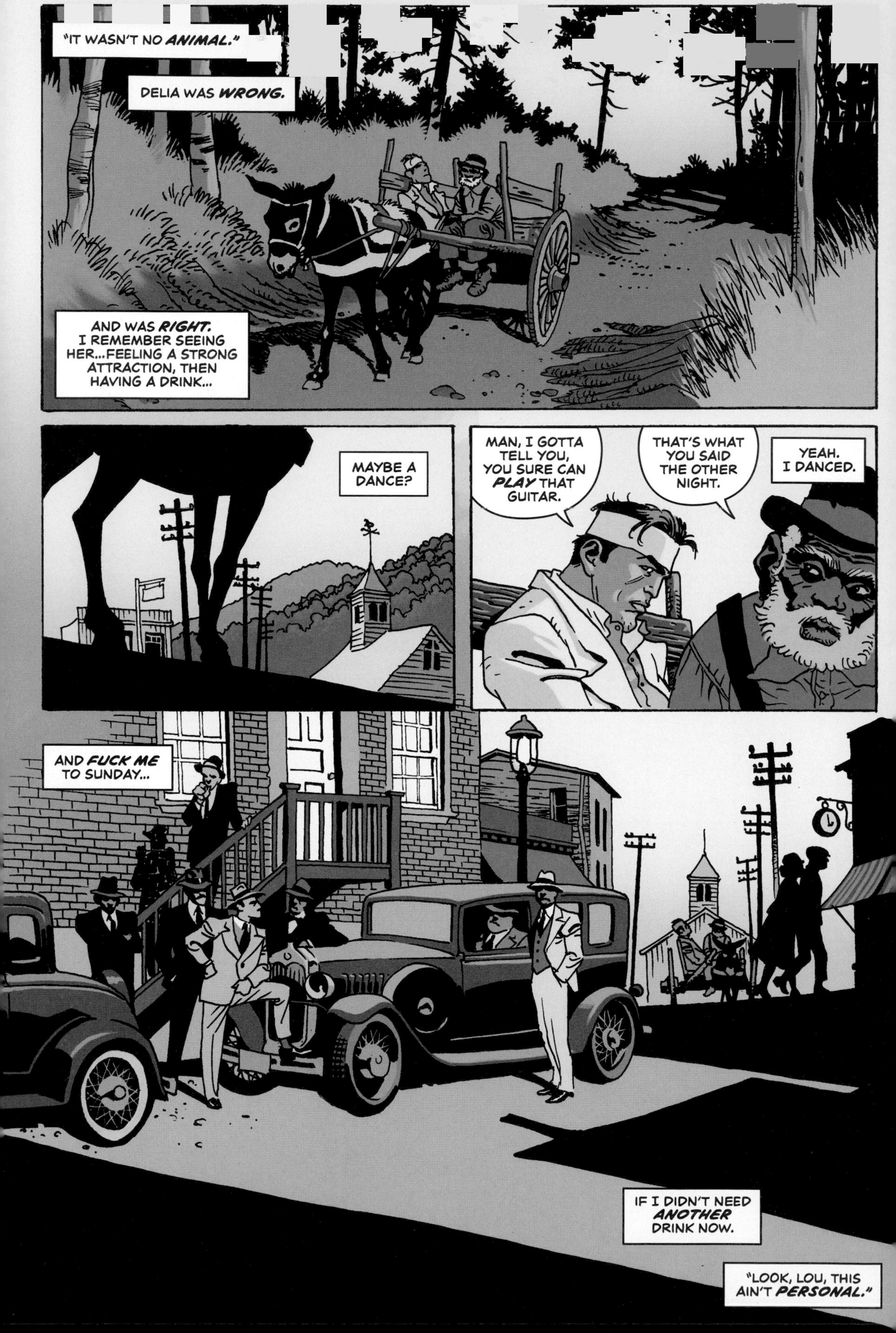
"IT WASN'T NO ANIMAL."
DELIA WAS WRONG.
AND WAS RIGHT. I REMEMBER SEEING HER...FEELING A STRONG ATTRACTION, THEN HAVING A DRINK...
MAYBE A DANCE?
MAN, I GOTTA TELL YOU, YOU SURE CAN PLAY THAT GUITAR.
THAT'S WHAT YOU SAID THE OTHER NIGHT.
YEAH. I DANCED.
AND FUCK ME TO SUNDAY...
IF I DIDN'T NEED ANOTHER DRINK NOW.
"LOOK, LOU, THIS AIN'T PERSONAL."

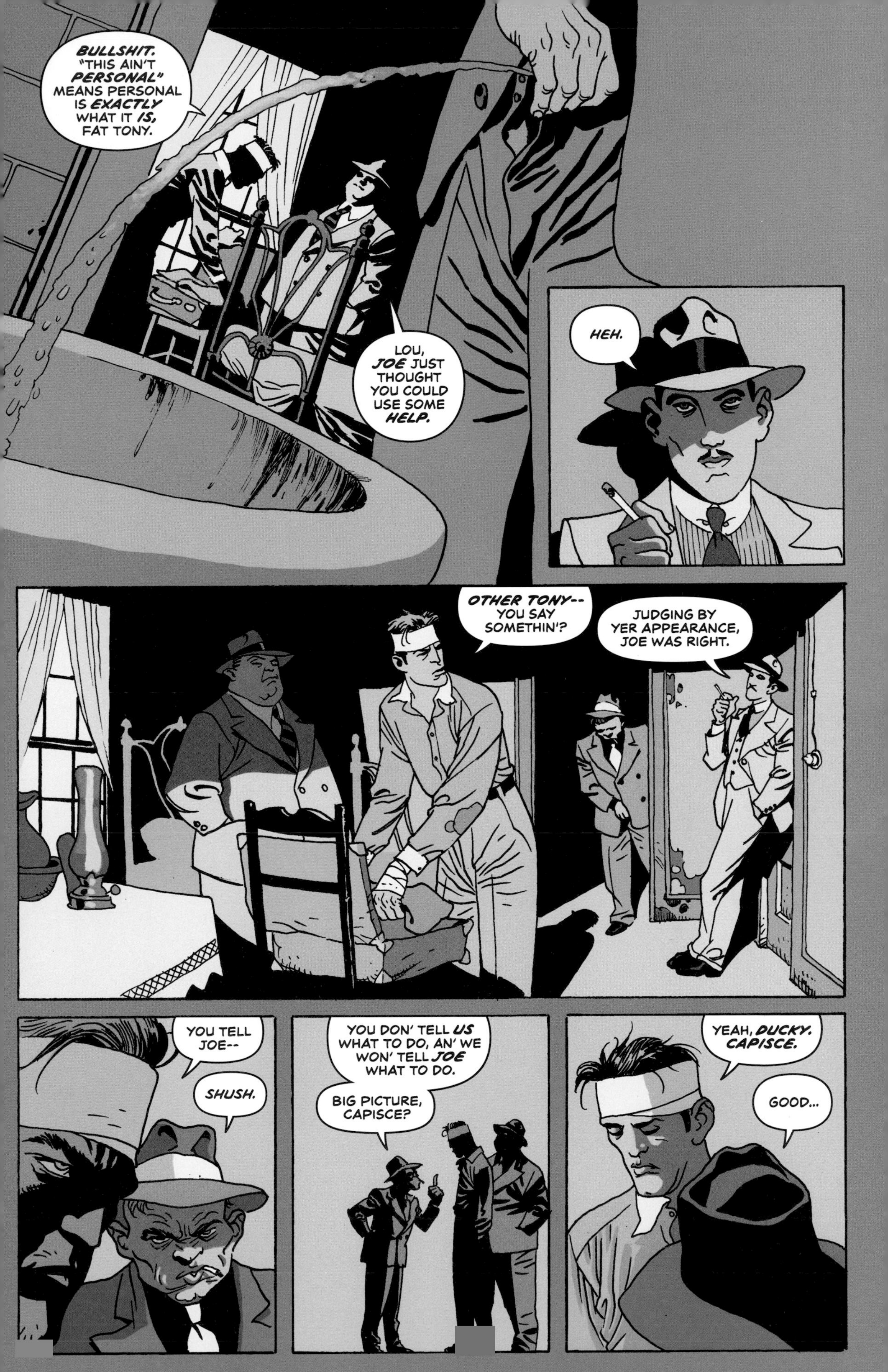
BULLSHIT. "THIS AIN'T PERSONAL" MEANS PERSONAL IS EXACTLY WHAT IT IS, FAT TONY.
LOU, JOE JUST THOUGHT YOU COULD USE SOME HELP.
HEH.
OTHER TONY-- YOU SAY SOMETHIN'?
JUDGING BY YER APPEARANCE, JOE WAS RIGHT.
YOU TELL JOE--
SHUSH.
YOU DON' TELL US WHAT TO DO, AN' WE WON' TELL JOE WHAT TO DO.
BIG PICTURE, CAPISCE?
YEAH, DUCKY. CAPISCE.
GOOD...

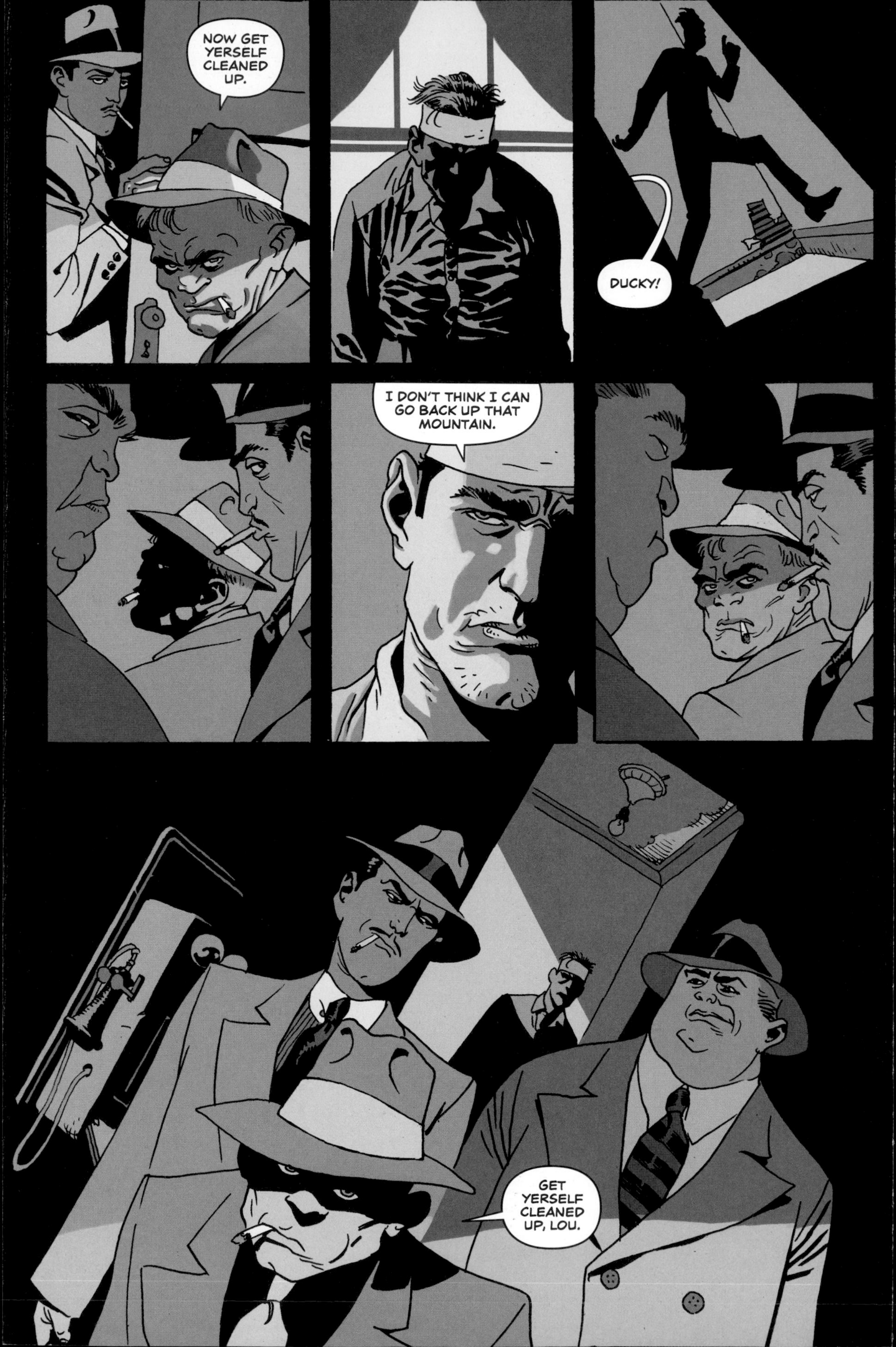
NOW GET YERSELF CLEANED UP.
DUCKY!
I DON'T THINK I CAN GO BACK UP THAT MOUNTAIN.
GET YERSELF CLEANED UP, LOU.

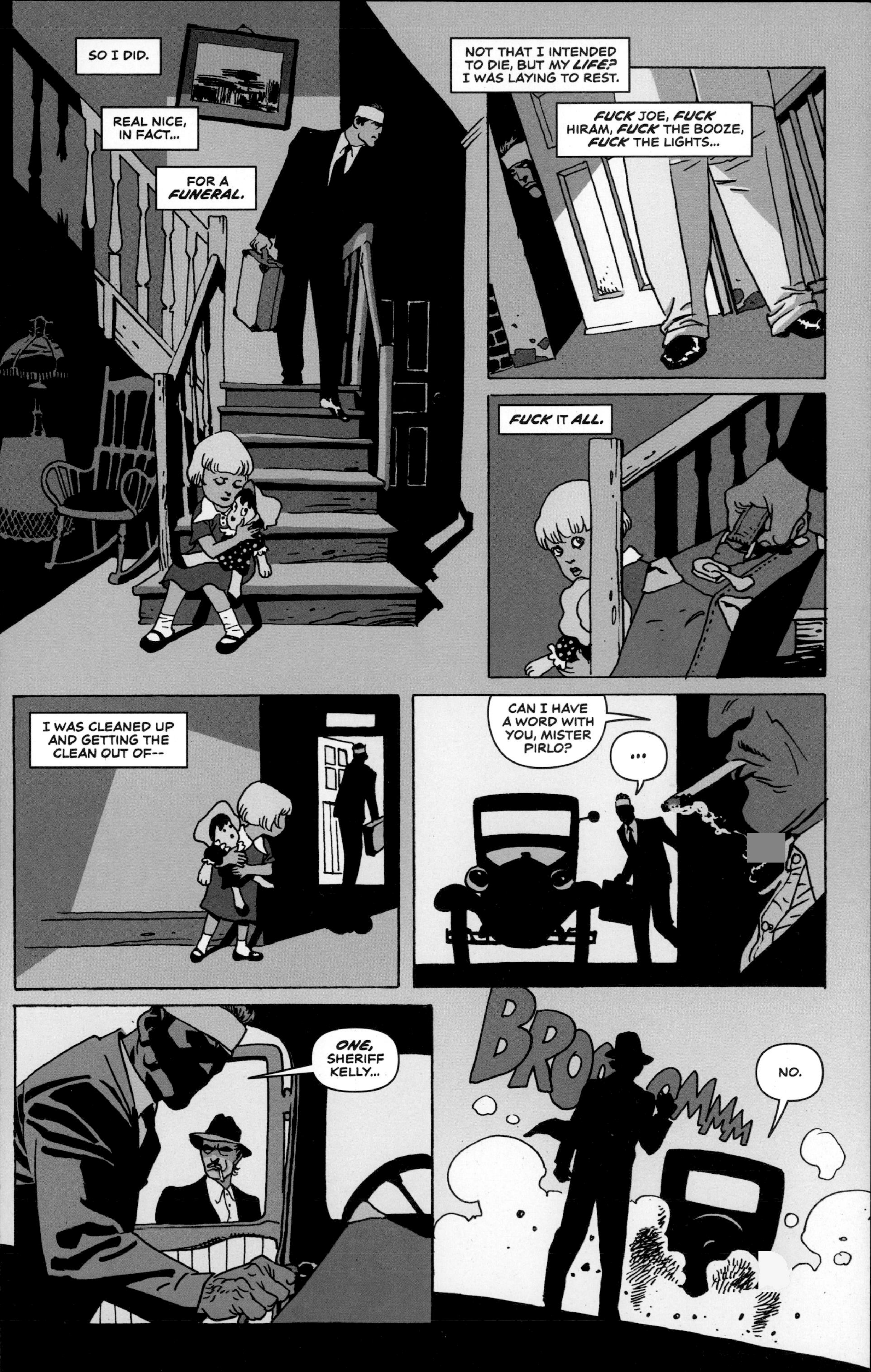
SO I DID.
REAL NICE, IN FACT...
FOR A FUNERAL.
NOT THAT I INTENDED TO DIE, BUT MY LIFE? I WAS LAYING TO REST.
FUCK JOE, FUCK HIRAM, FUCK THE BOOZE, FUCK THE LIGHTS...
FUCK IT ALL.
I WAS CLEANED UP AND GETTING THE CLEAN OUT OF--
CAN I HAVE A WORD WITH YOU, MISTER PIRLO?
...
ONE, SHERIFF KELLY...
BROOOOMMM
NO.

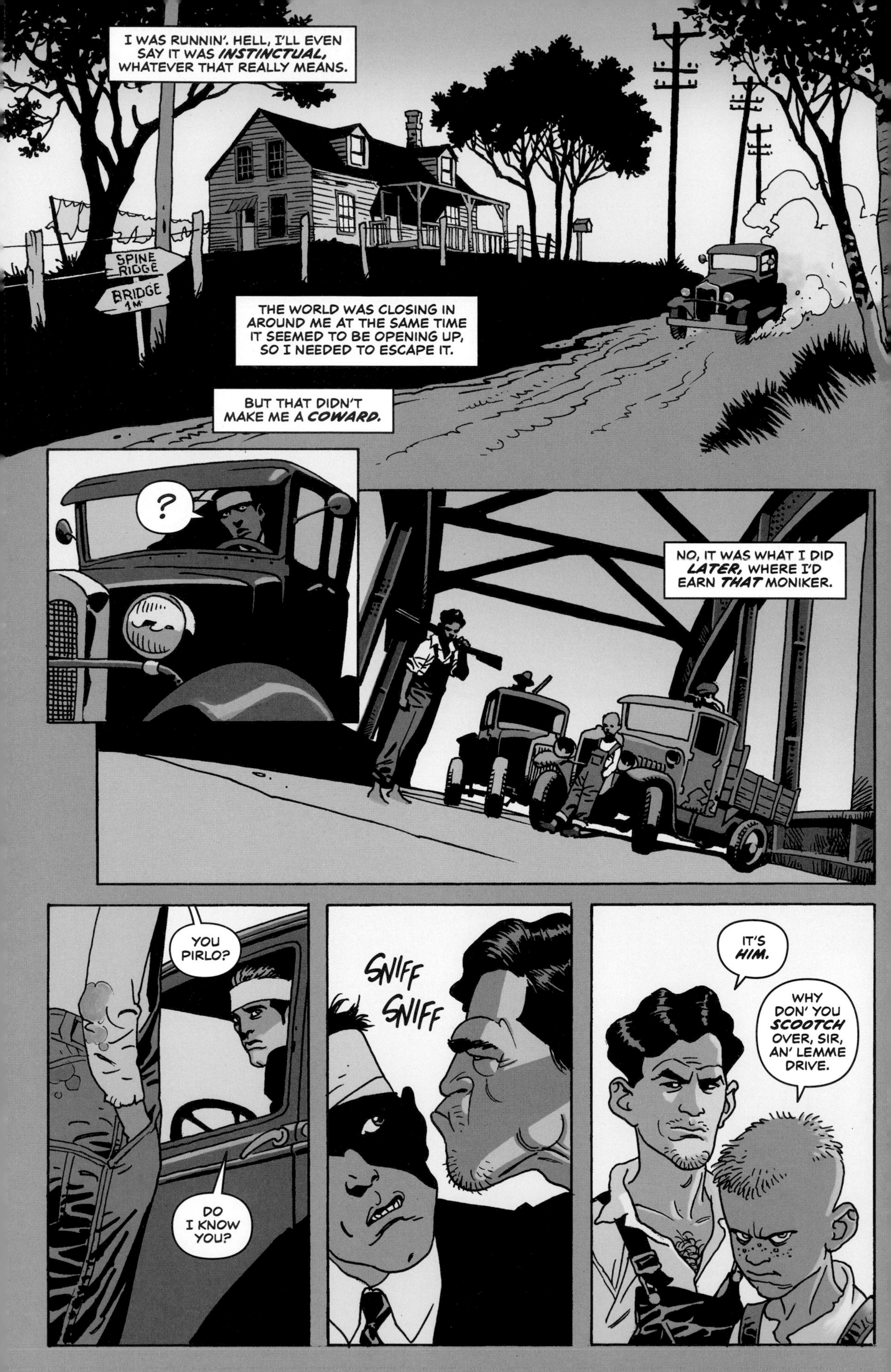
I WAS RUNNIN'. HELL, I'LL EVEN SAY IT WAS *INSTINCTUAL,* WHATEVER THAT REALLY MEANS.
SPINE RIDGE
BRIDGE 1M.
THE WORLD WAS CLOSING IN AROUND ME AT THE SAME TIME IT SEEMED TO BE OPENING UP, SO I NEEDED TO ESCAPE IT.
BUT THAT DIDN'T MAKE ME A *COWARD.*
?
NO, IT WAS WHAT I DID *LATER,* WHERE I'D EARN *THAT* MONIKER.
YOU PIRLO?
DO I KNOW YOU?
SNIFF SNIFF
IT'S *HIM.*
WHY DON' YOU *SCOOTCH* OVER, SIR, AN' LEMME DRIVE.

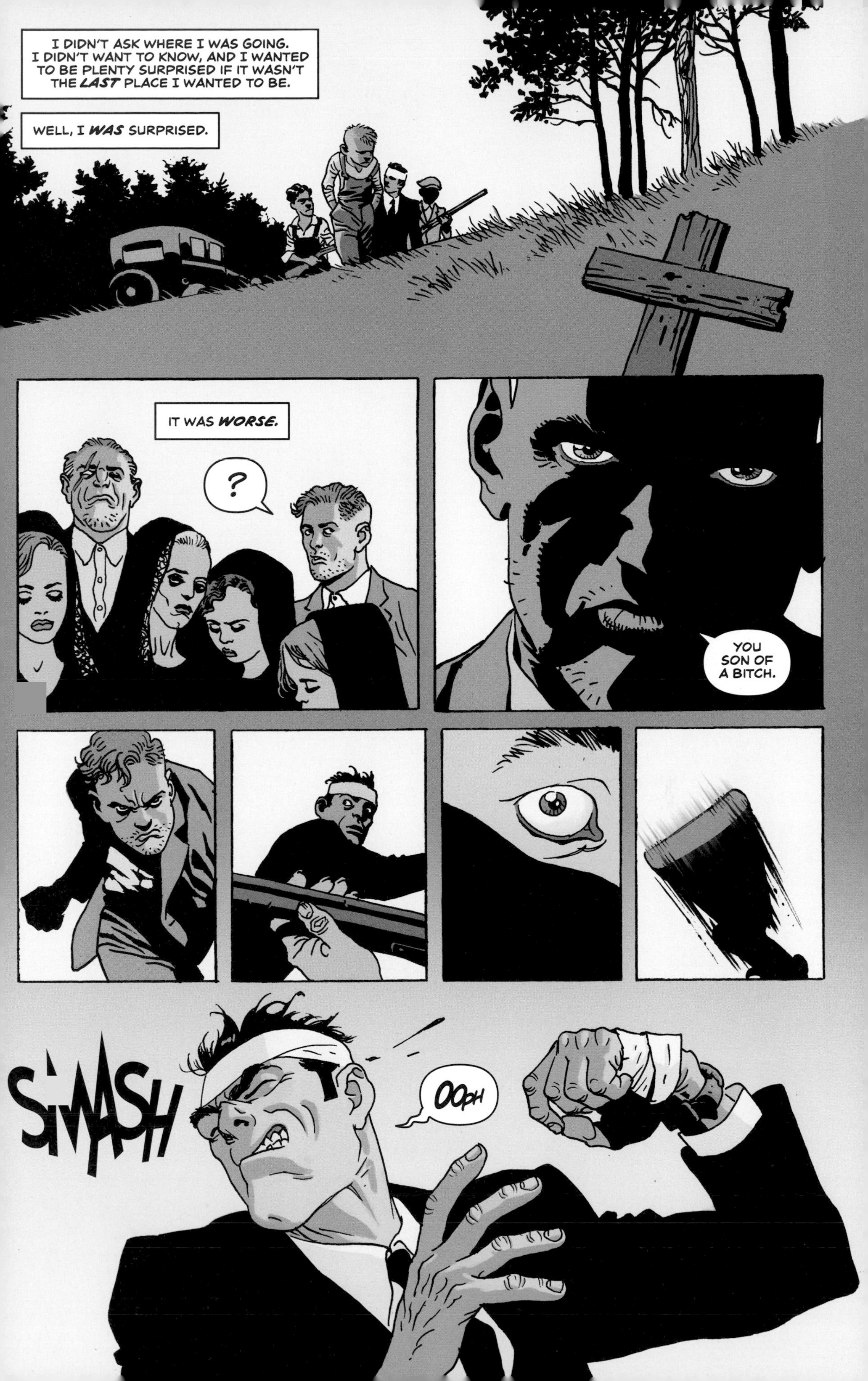
I DIDN'T ASK WHERE I WAS GOING. I DIDN'T WANT TO KNOW, AND I WANTED TO BE PLENTY SURPRISED IF IT WASN'T THE LAST PLACE I WANTED TO BE.
WELL, I WAS SURPRISED.
IT WAS WORSE.
?
YOU SON OF A BITCH.
SMASH
OOPH

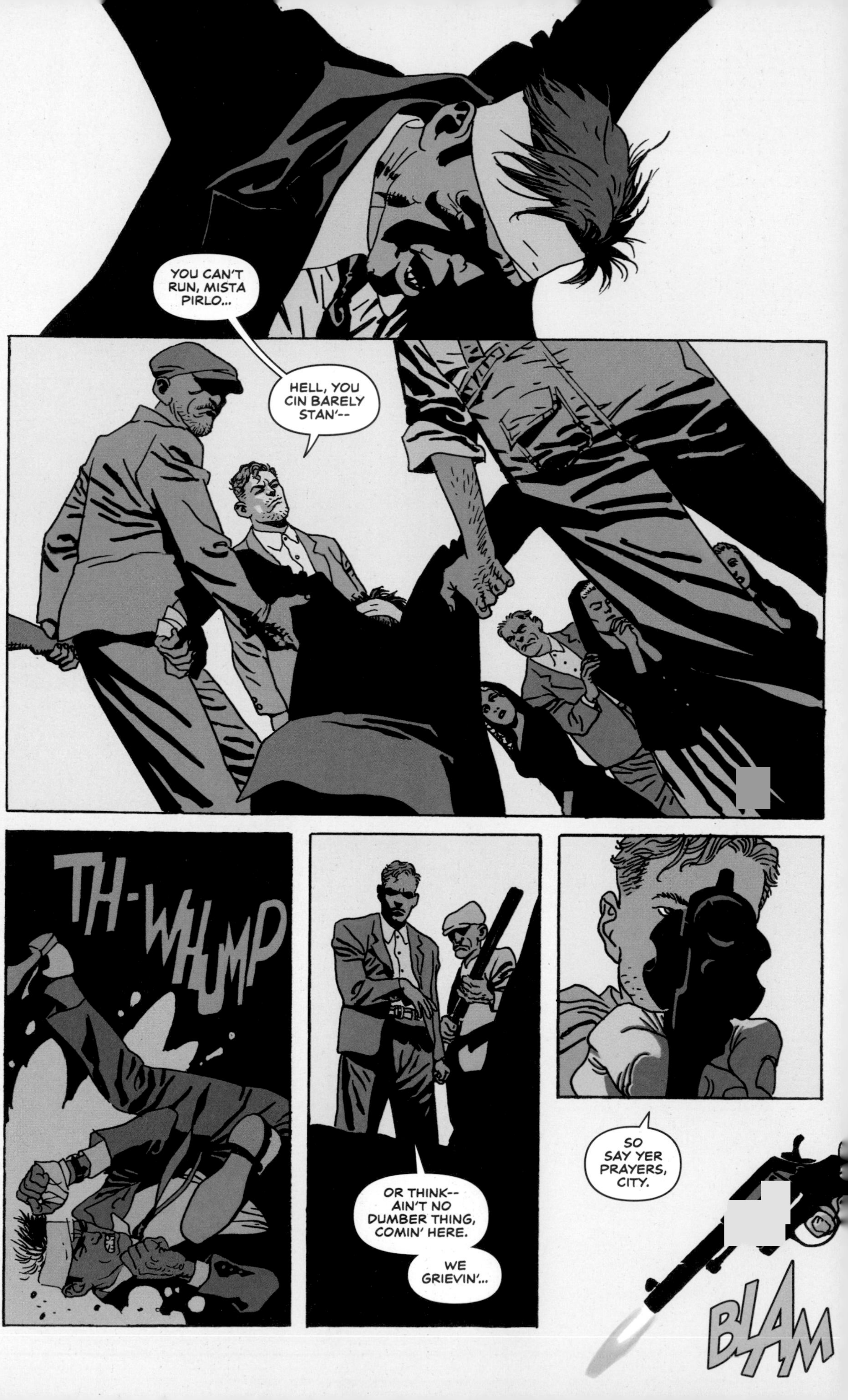
YOU CAN'T RUN, MISTA PIRLO...
HELL, YOU CIN BARELY STAN'--
TH-WHUMP
OR THINK-- AIN'T NO DUMBER THING, COMIN' HERE.
WE GRIEVIN'...
SO SAY YER PRAYERS, CITY.
BLAM

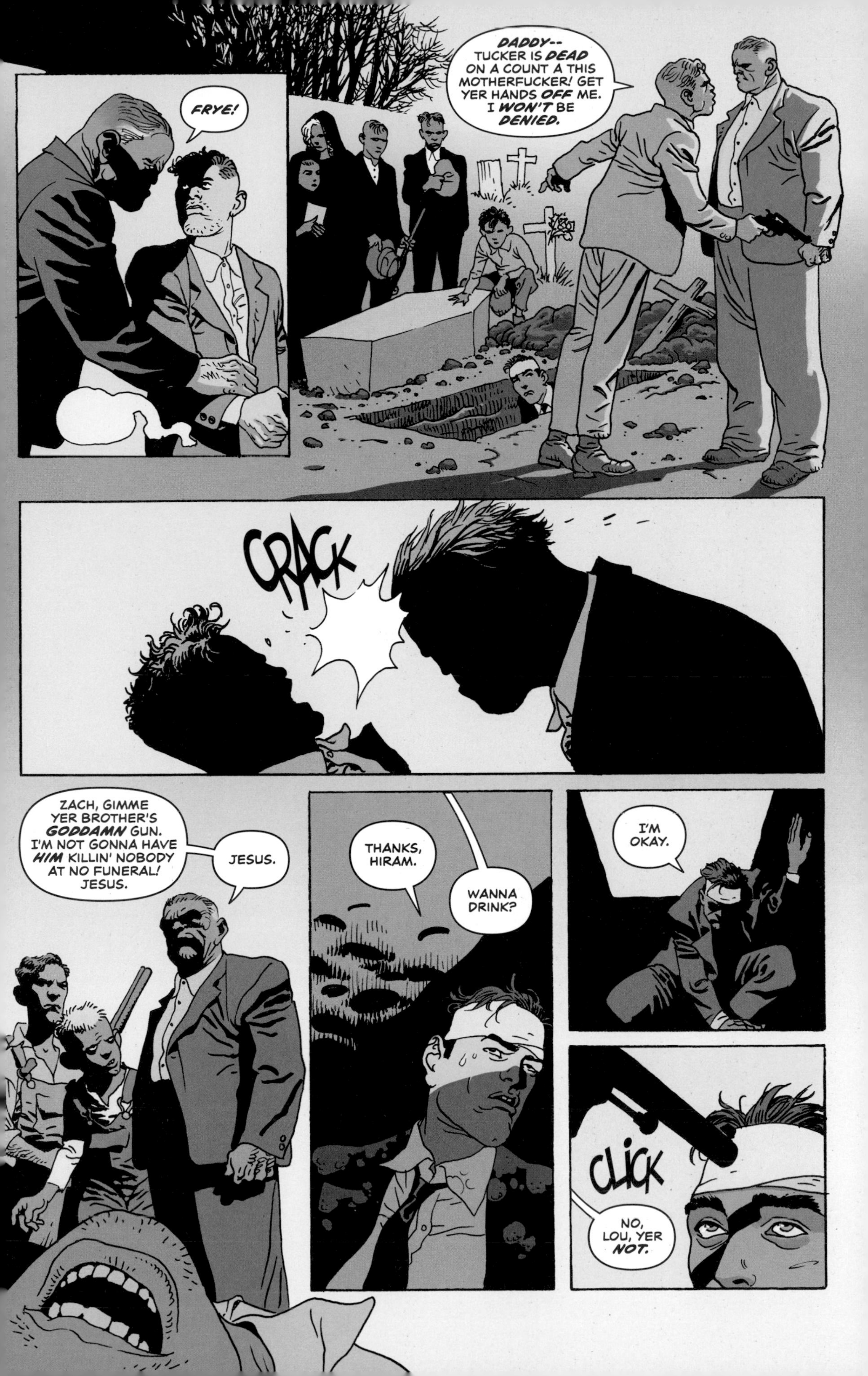
FRYE!
DADDY-- TUCKER IS DEAD ON A COUNT A THIS MOTHERFUCKER! GET YER HANDS OFF ME. I WON'T BE DENIED.
CRACK
ZACH, GIMME YER BROTHER'S GODDAMN GUN. I'M NOT GONNA HAVE HIM KILLIN' NOBODY AT NO FUNERAL! JESUS.
JESUS.
THANKS, HIRAM.
WANNA DRINK?
I'M OKAY.
CLICK
NO, LOU, YER NOT.

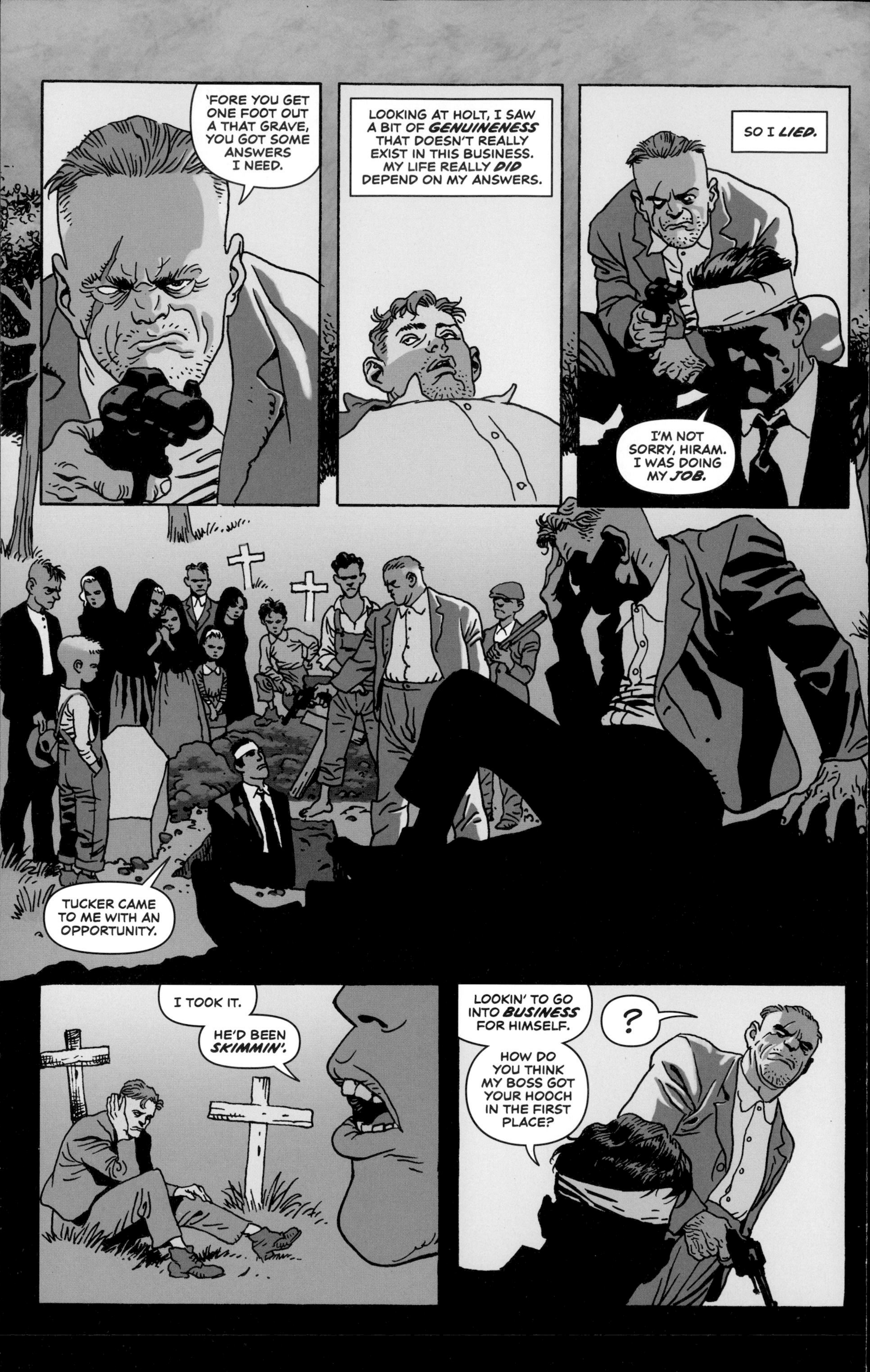
'FORE YOU GET ONE FOOT OUT A THAT GRAVE, YOU GOT SOME ANSWERS I NEED.
LOOKING AT HOLT, I SAW A BIT OF GENUINENESS THAT DOESN'T REALLY EXIST IN THIS BUSINESS. MY LIFE REALLY DID DEPEND ON MY ANSWERS.
SO I LIED.
I'M NOT SORRY, HIRAM. I WAS DOING MY JOB.
TUCKER CAME TO ME WITH AN OPPORTUNITY.
I TOOK IT.
HE'D BEEN SKIMMIN'.
LOOKIN' TO GO INTO BUSINESS FOR HIMSELF.
?
HOW DO YOU THINK MY BOSS GOT YOUR HOOCH IN THE FIRST PLACE?

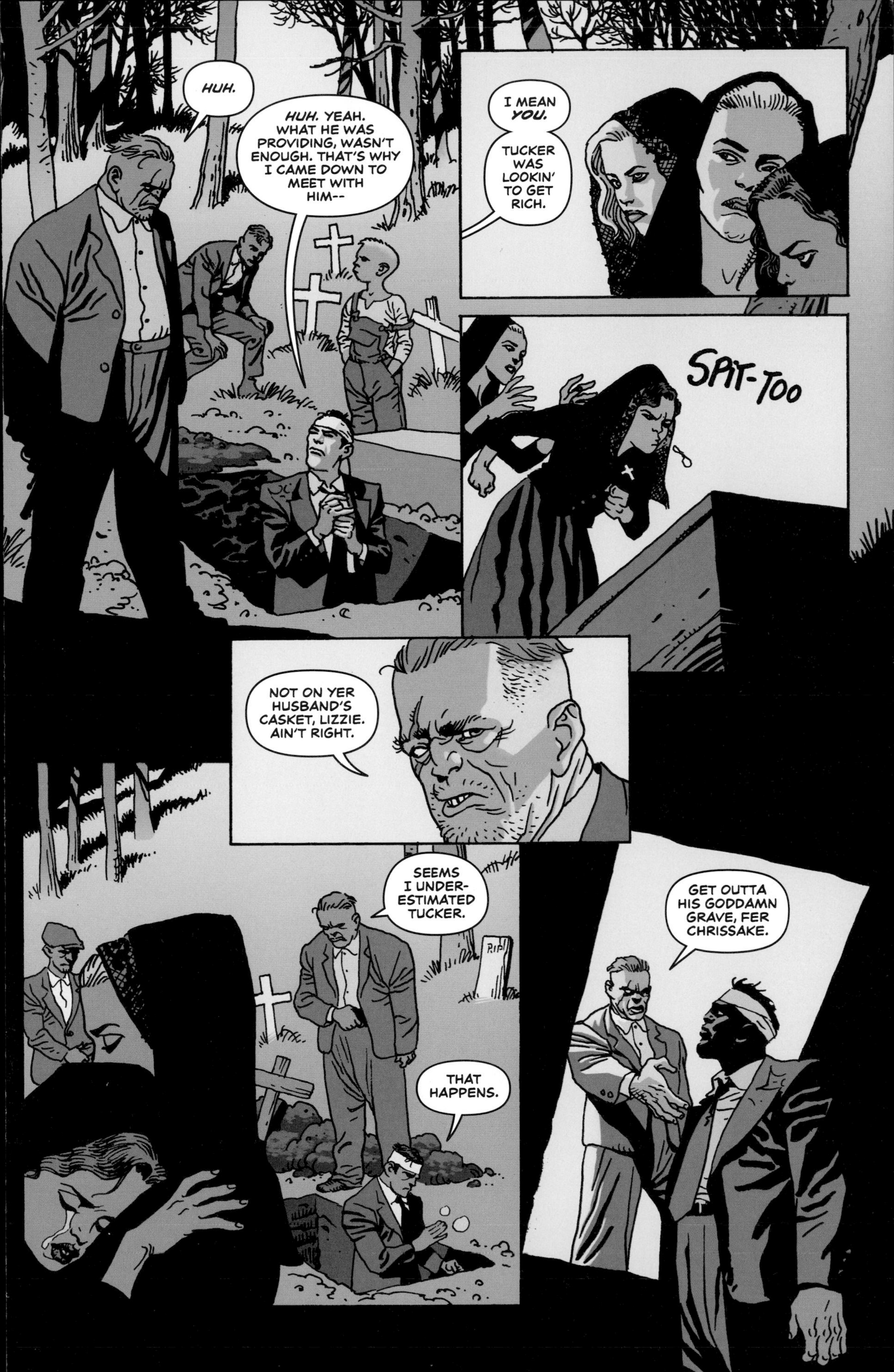
HUH.
HUH. YEAH. WHAT HE WAS PROVIDING, WASN'T ENOUGH. THAT'S WHY I CAME DOWN TO MEET WITH HIM--
I MEAN YOU.
TUCKER WAS LOOKIN' TO GET RICH.
SPIT-TOO
NOT ON YER HUSBAND'S CASKET, LIZZIE. AIN'T RIGHT.
SEEMS I UNDER-ESTIMATED TUCKER.
THAT HAPPENS.
GET OUTTA HIS GODDAMN GRAVE, FER CHRISSAKE.
RIP

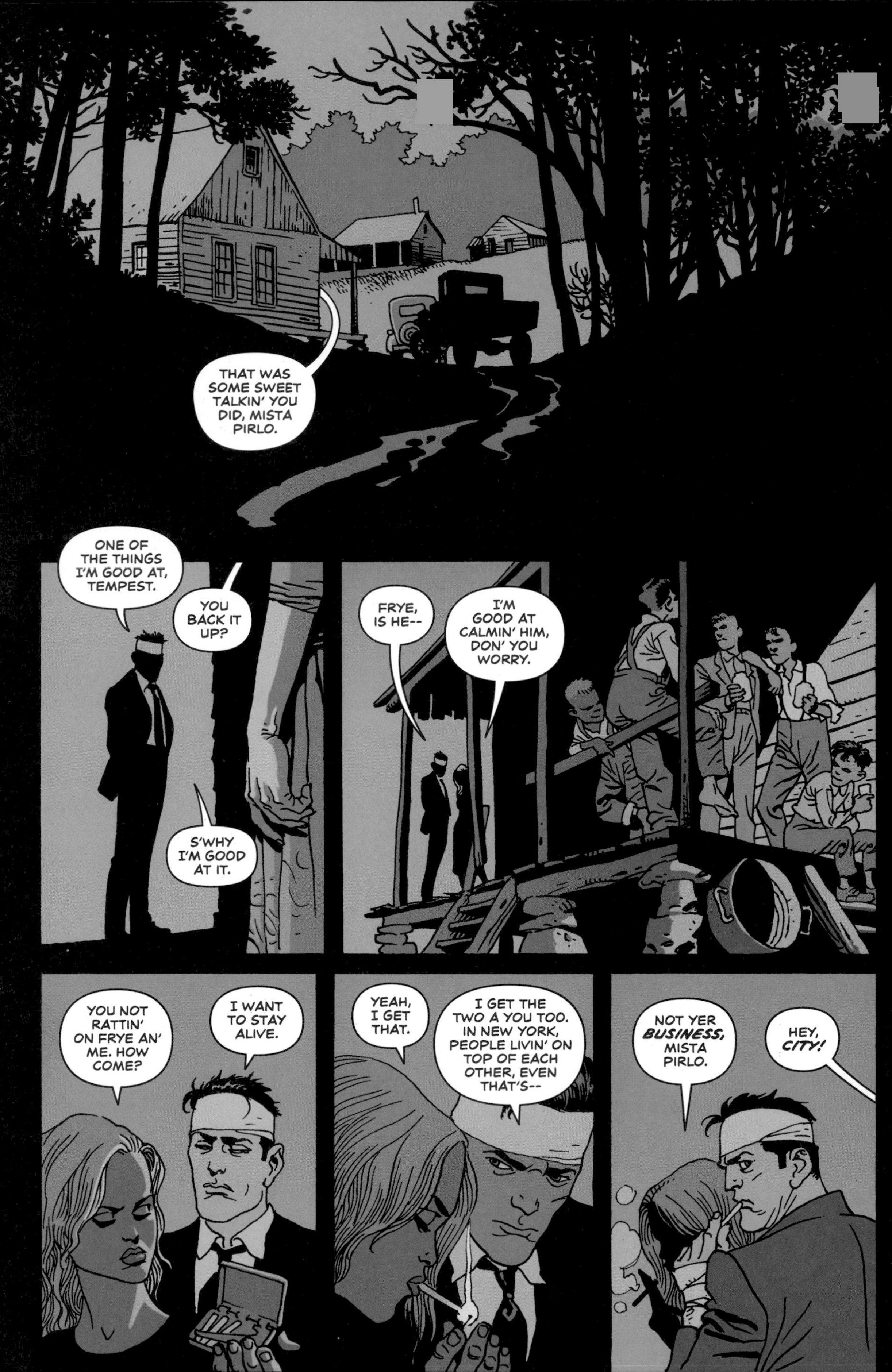
THAT WAS SOME SWEET TALKIN' YOU DID, MISTA PIRLO.
ONE OF THE THINGS I'M GOOD AT, TEMPEST.
YOU BACK IT UP?
S'WHY I'M GOOD AT IT.
FRYE, IS HE--
I'M GOOD AT CALMIN' HIM, DON' YOU WORRY.
YOU NOT RATTIN' ON FRYE AN' ME. HOW COME?
I WANT TO STAY ALIVE.
YEAH, I GET THAT.
I GET THE TWO A YOU TOO. IN NEW YORK, PEOPLE LIVIN' ON TOP OF EACH OTHER, EVEN THAT'S--
NOT YER *BUSINESS,* MISTA PIRLO.
HEY, *CITY!*

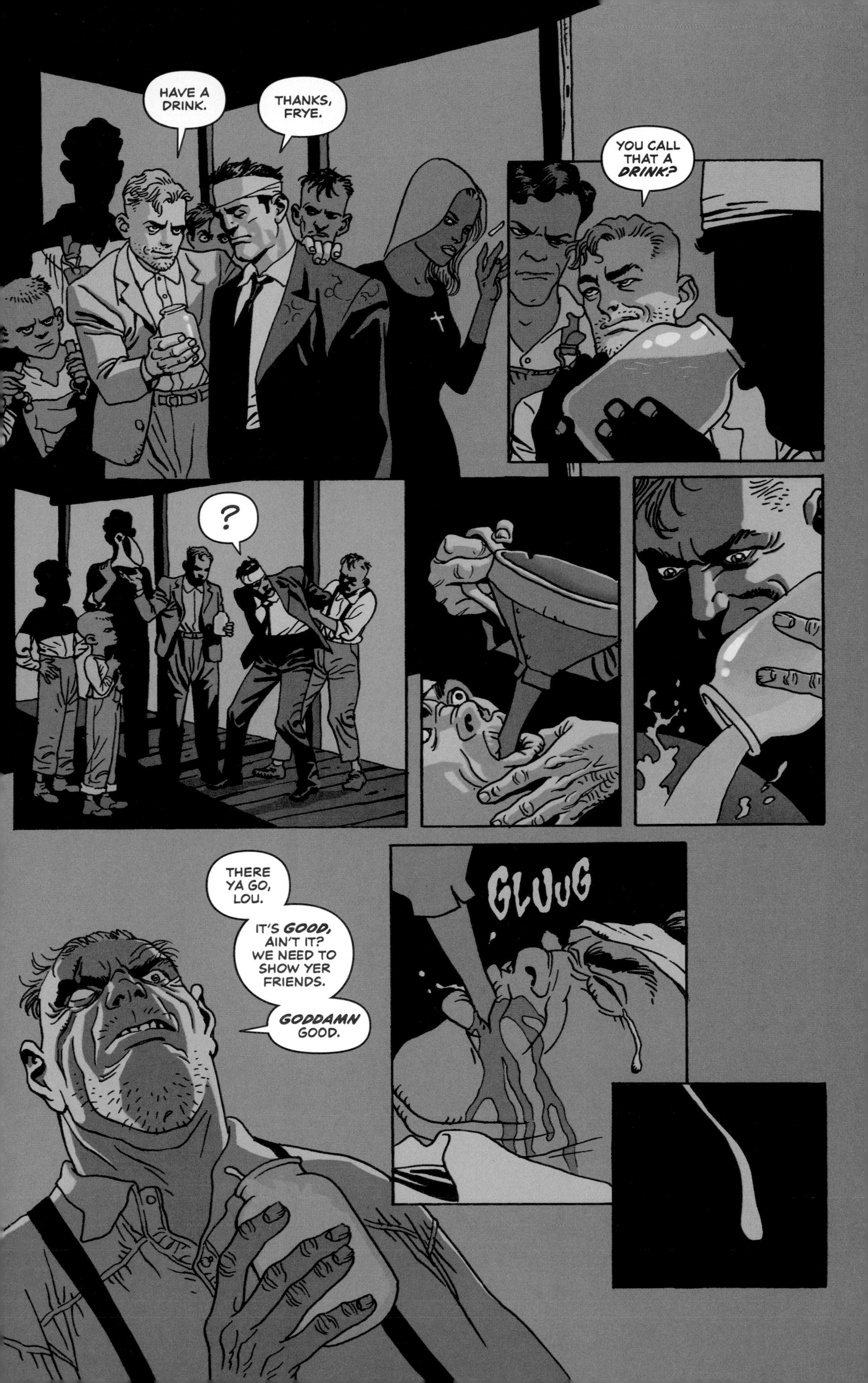
HAVE A DRINK.
THANKS, FRYE.
YOU CALL THAT A DRINK?
?
GLUUG
THERE YA GO, LOU.
IT'S GOOD, AIN'T IT? WE NEED TO SHOW YER FRIENDS.
GODDAMN GOOD.

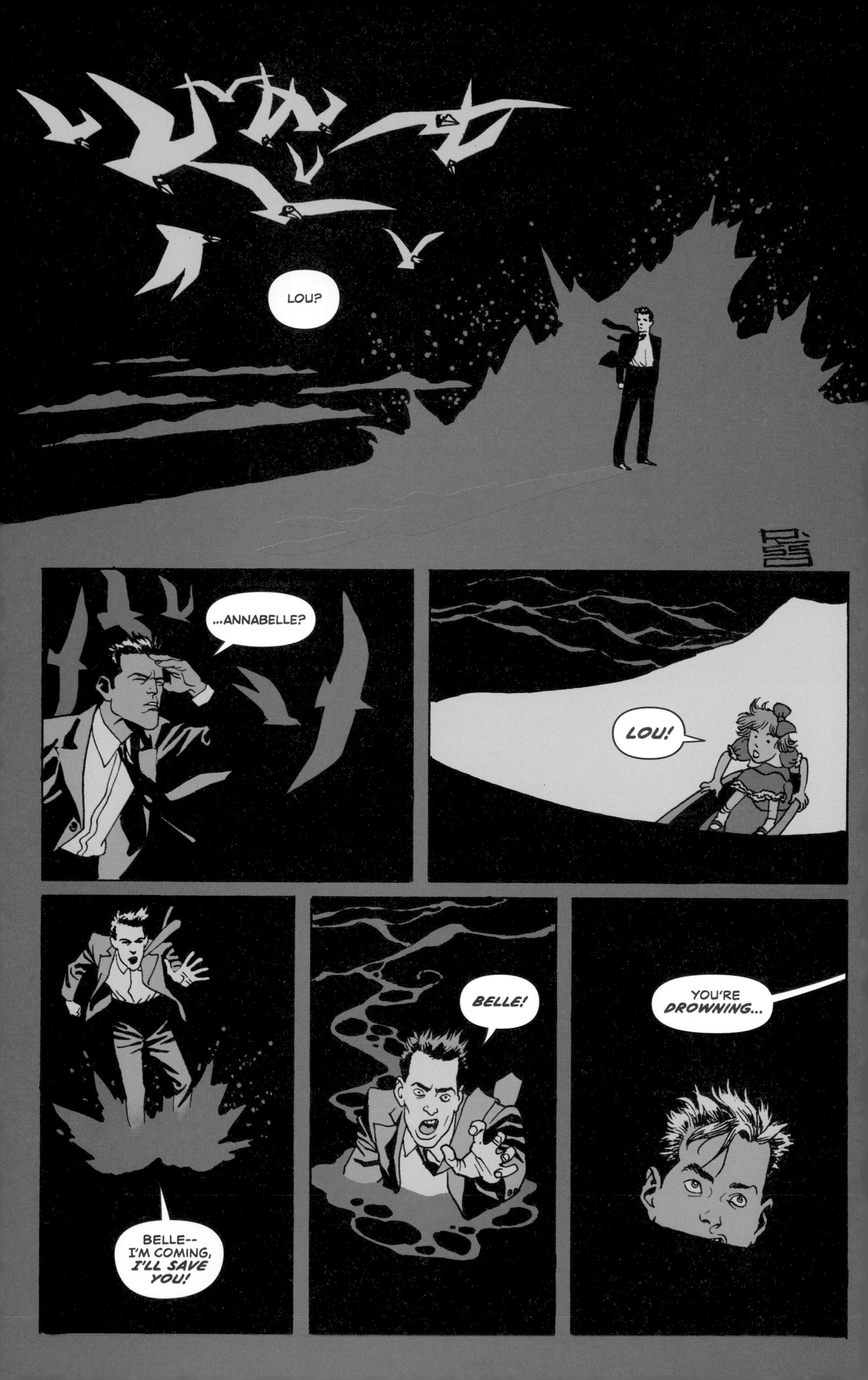
LOU?
...ANNABELLE?
LOU!
BELLE-- I'M COMING, I'LL SAVE YOU!
BELLE!
YOU'RE DROWNING...

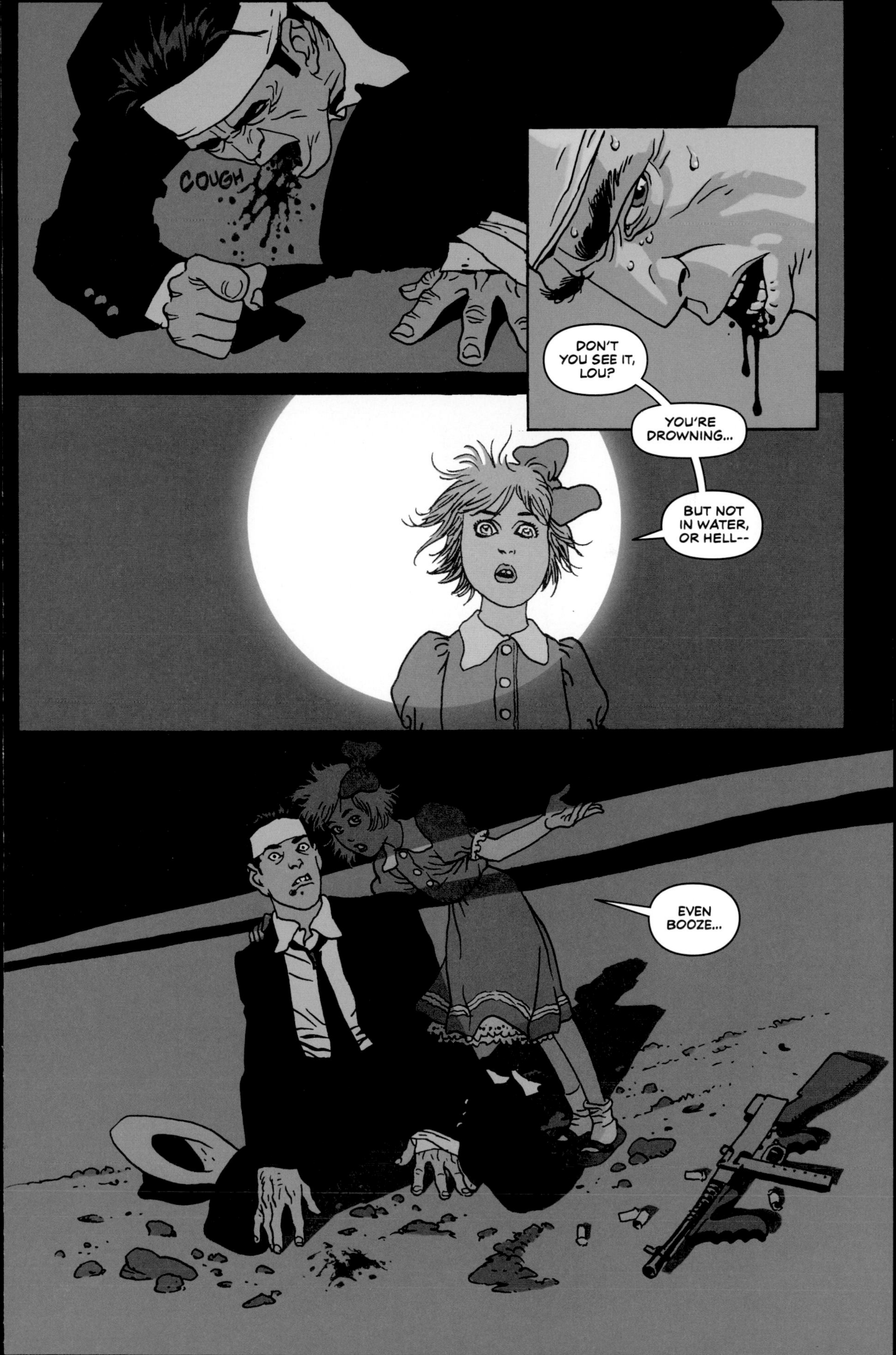
COUGH
DON'T YOU SEE IT, LOU?
YOU'RE DROWNING...
BUT NOT IN WATER, OR HELL--
EVEN BOOZE...

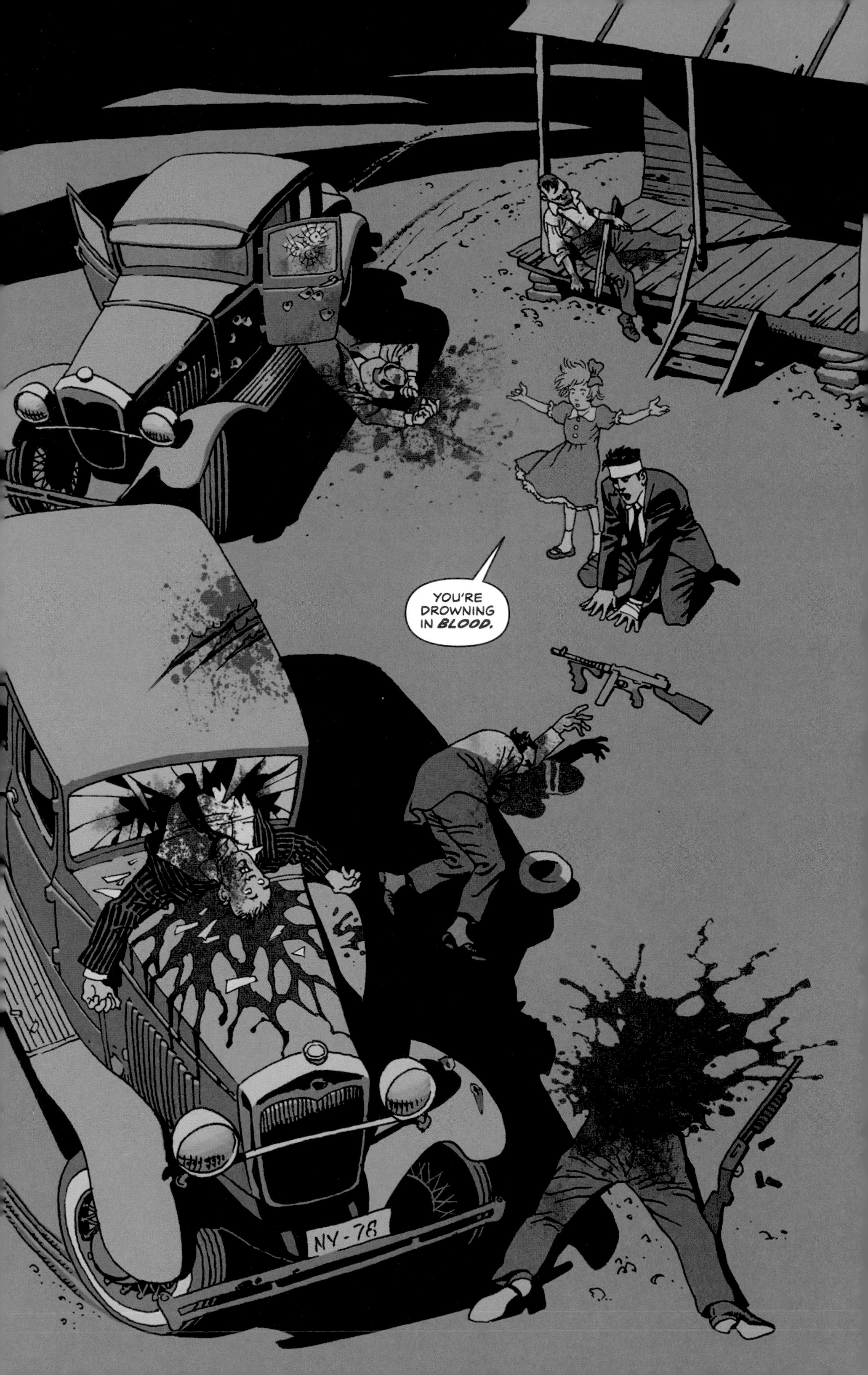
YOU'RE DROWNING IN *BLOOD.*
NY-76

Chapter FOUR

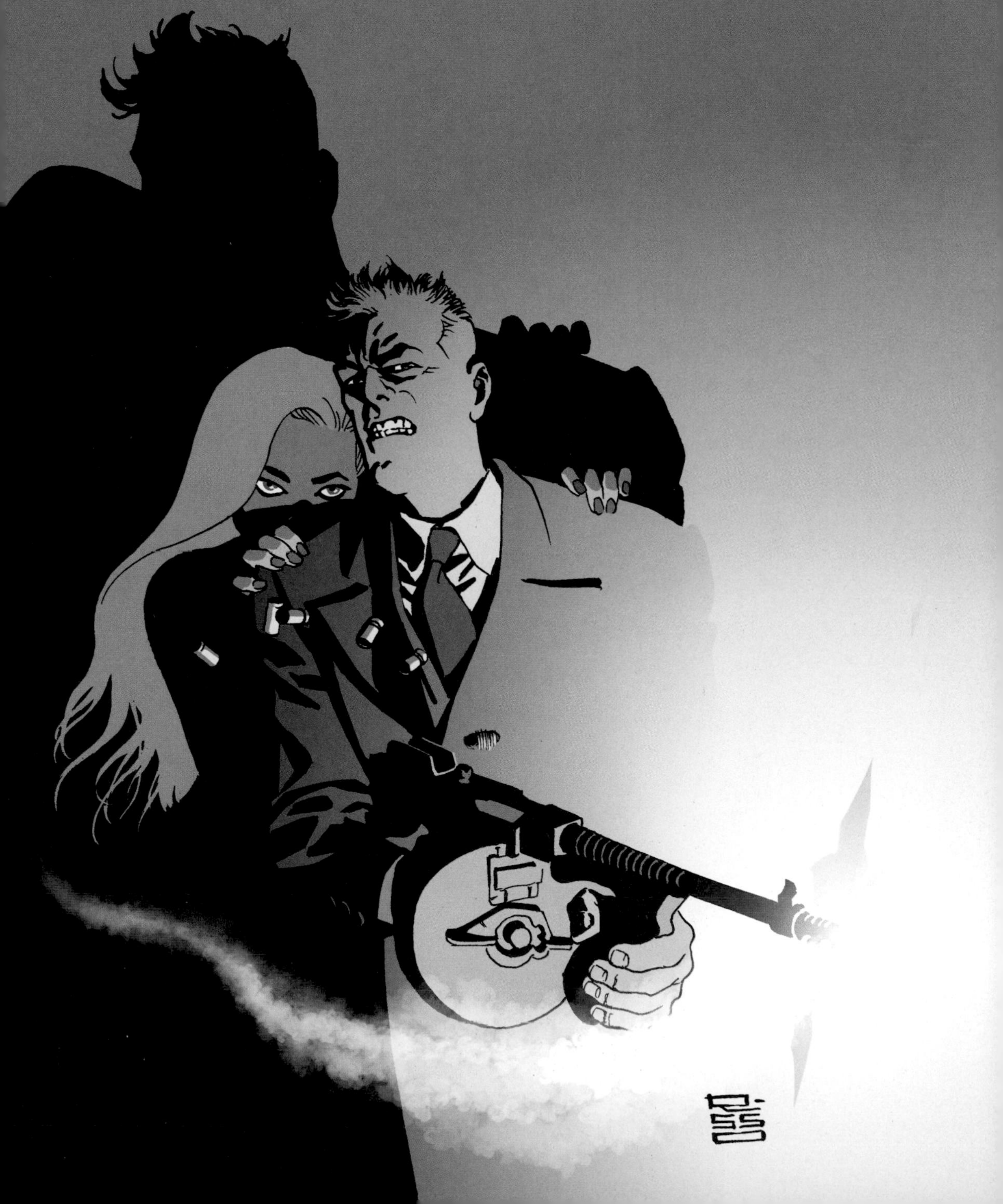

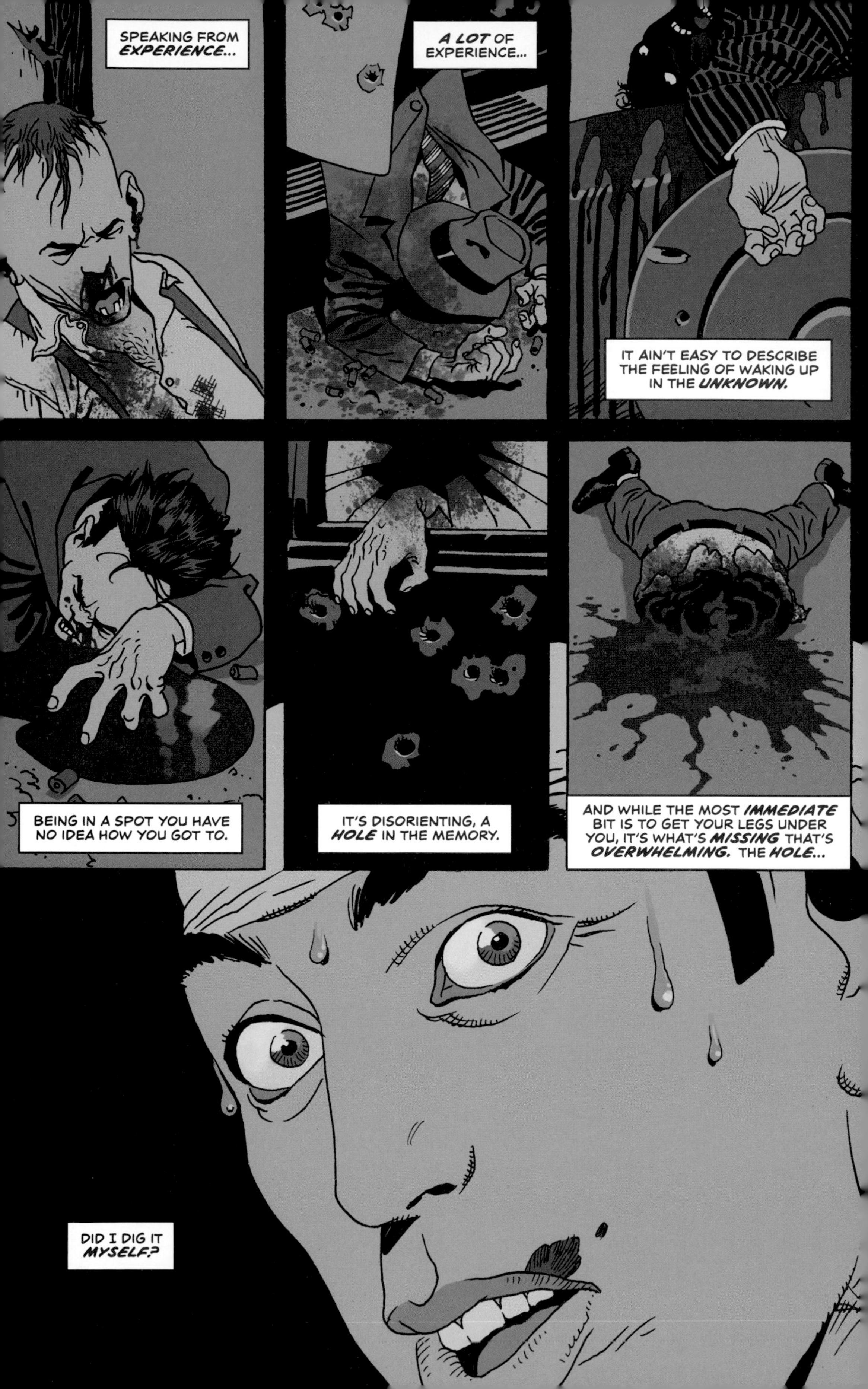
SPEAKING FROM EXPERIENCE...
A LOT OF EXPERIENCE...
IT AIN'T EASY TO DESCRIBE THE FEELING OF WAKING UP IN THE UNKNOWN.
BEING IN A SPOT YOU HAVE NO IDEA HOW YOU GOT TO.
IT'S DISORIENTING, A HOLE IN THE MEMORY.
AND WHILE THE MOST IMMEDIATE BIT IS TO GET YOUR LEGS UNDER YOU, IT'S WHAT'S MISSING THAT'S OVERWHELMING. THE HOLE...
DID I DIG IT MYSELF?

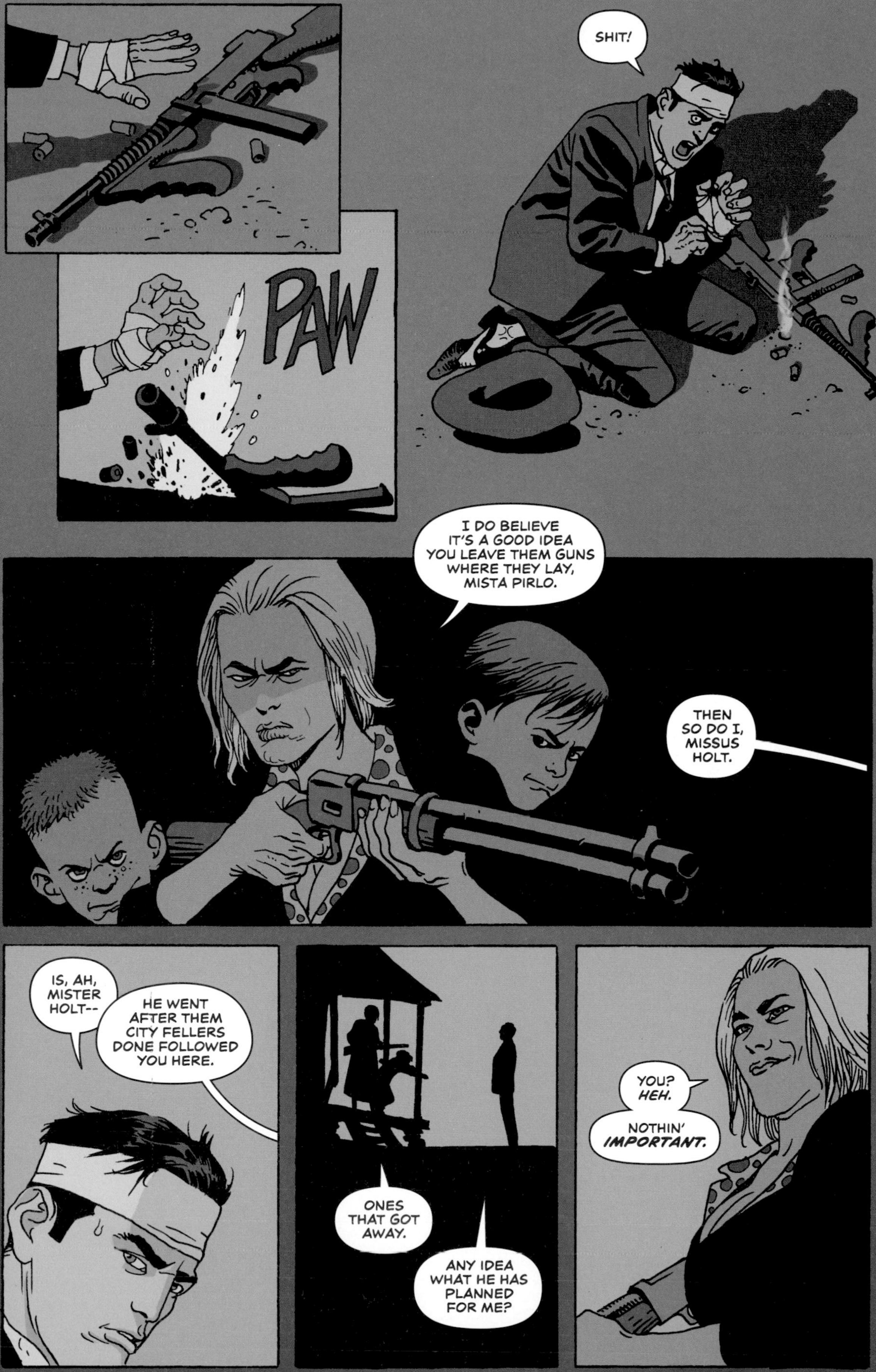
PAW
SHIT!
I DO BELIEVE IT'S A GOOD IDEA YOU LEAVE THEM GUNS WHERE THEY LAY, MISTA PIRLO.
THEN SO DO I, MISSUS HOLT.
IS, AH, MISTER HOLT--
HE WENT AFTER THEM CITY FELLERS DONE FOLLOWED YOU HERE.
ONES THAT GOT AWAY.
ANY IDEA WHAT HE HAS PLANNED FOR ME?
YOU? HEH.
NOTHIN' IMPORTANT.

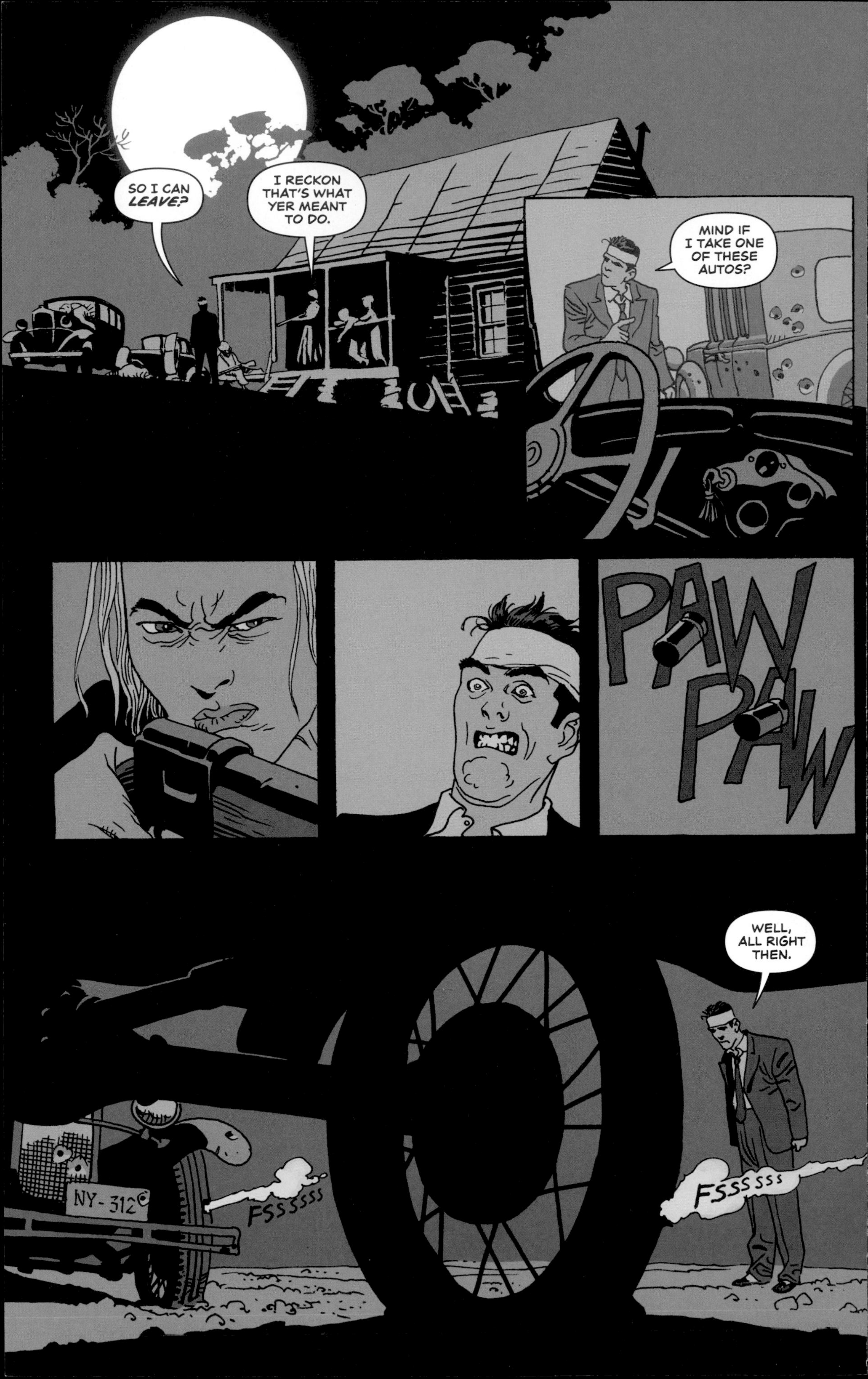
SO I CAN *LEAVE?*
I RECKON THAT'S WHAT YER MEANT TO DO.
MIND IF I TAKE ONE OF THESE AUTOS?
PAW
PAW
PAW
WELL, ALL RIGHT THEN.
NY- 312
FSSSSSS
FSSSSSS

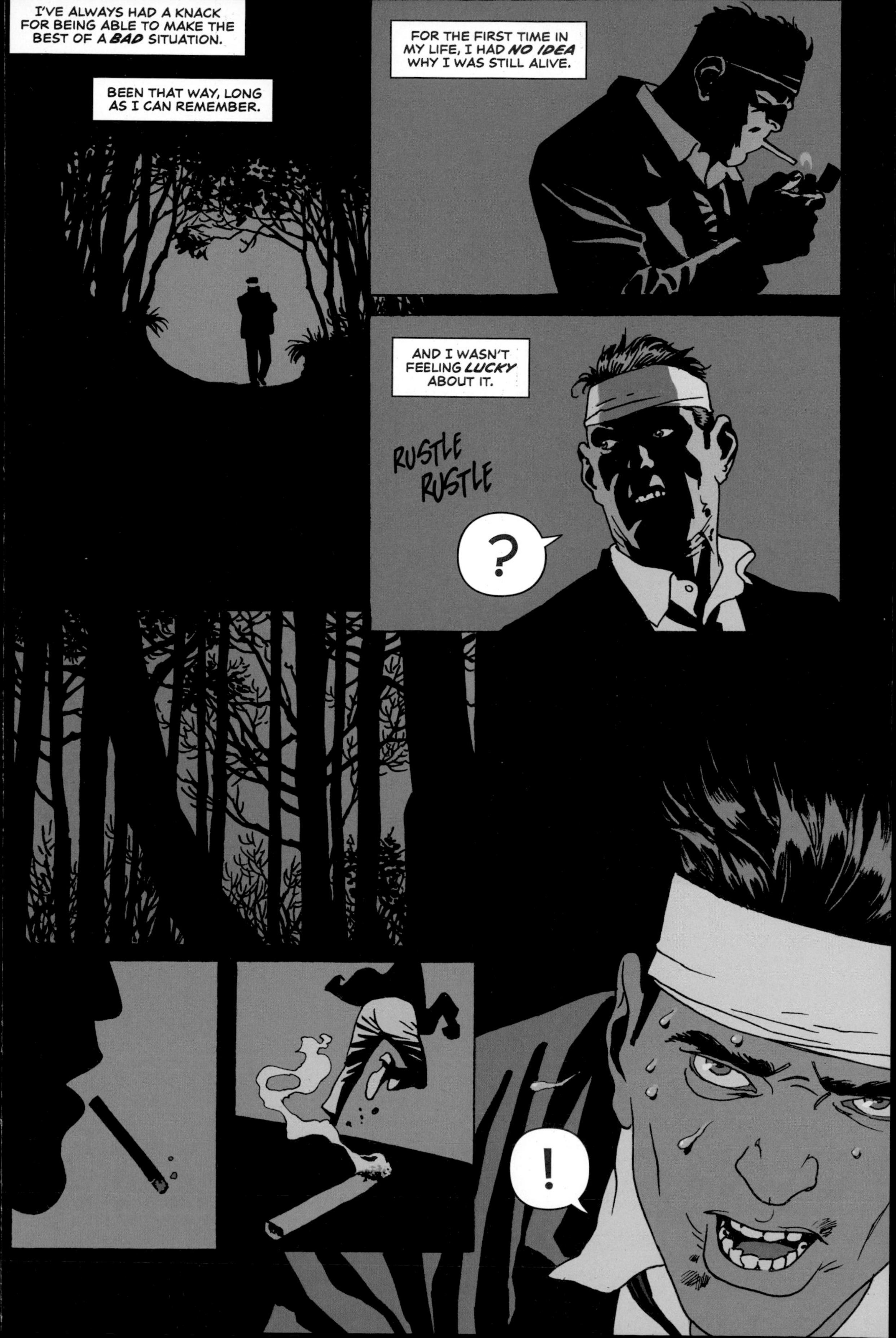

I'VE ALWAYS HAD A KNACK FOR BEING ABLE TO MAKE THE BEST OF A BAD SITUATION.
BEEN THAT WAY, LONG AS I CAN REMEMBER.
FOR THE FIRST TIME IN MY LIFE, I HAD NO IDEA WHY I WAS STILL ALIVE.
AND I WASN'T FEELING LUCKY ABOUT IT.
RUSTLE RUSTLE
?
!

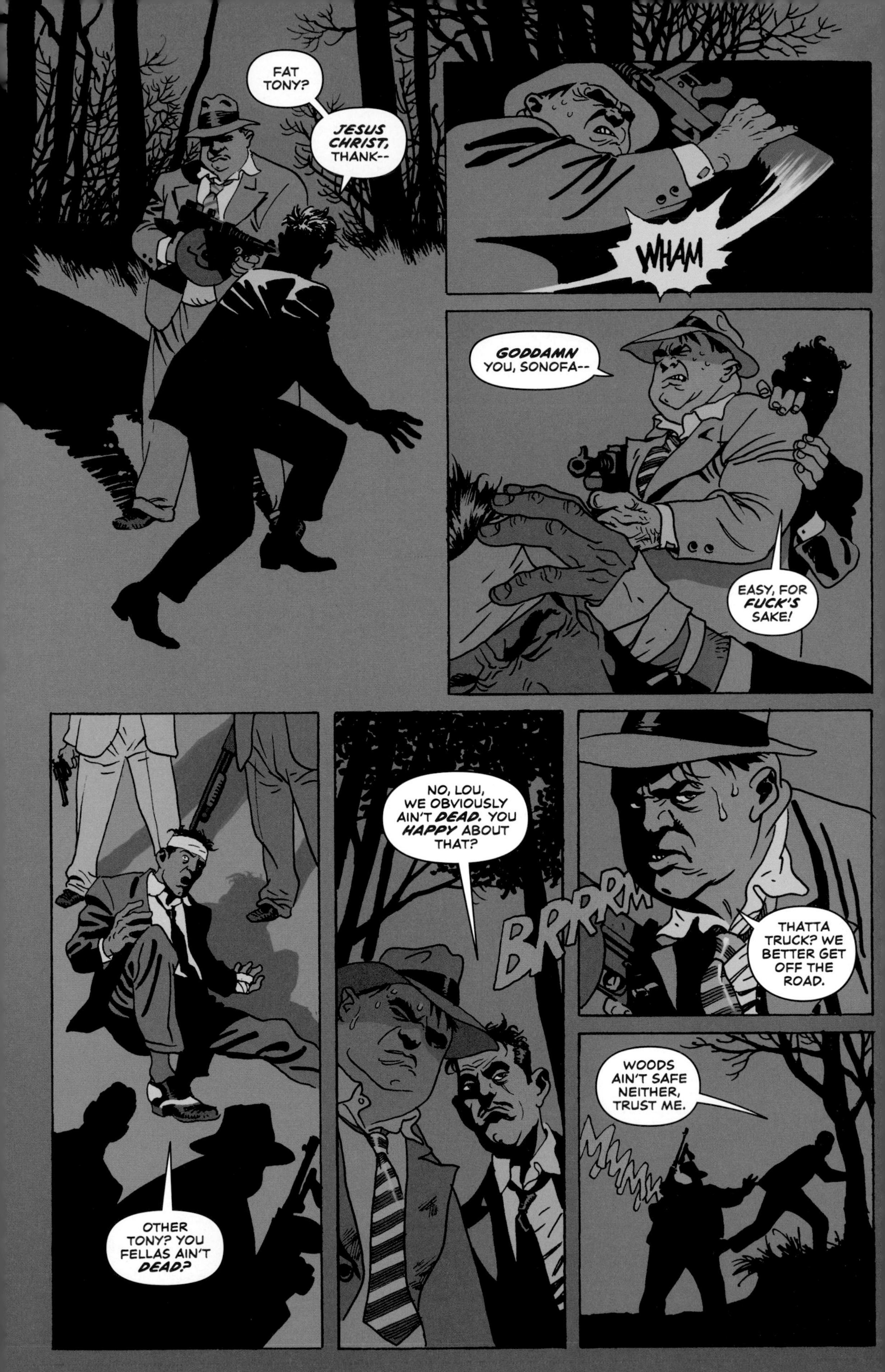
FAT TONY?
JESUS CHRIST, THANK--
WHAM
GODDAMN YOU, SONOFA--
EASY, FOR FUCK'S SAKE!
OTHER TONY? YOU FELLAS AIN'T DEAD?
NO, LOU, WE OBVIOUSLY AIN'T DEAD. YOU HAPPY ABOUT THAT?
BRRRM
THATTA TRUCK? WE BETTER GET OFF THE ROAD.
WOODS AIN'T SAFE NEITHER, TRUST ME.

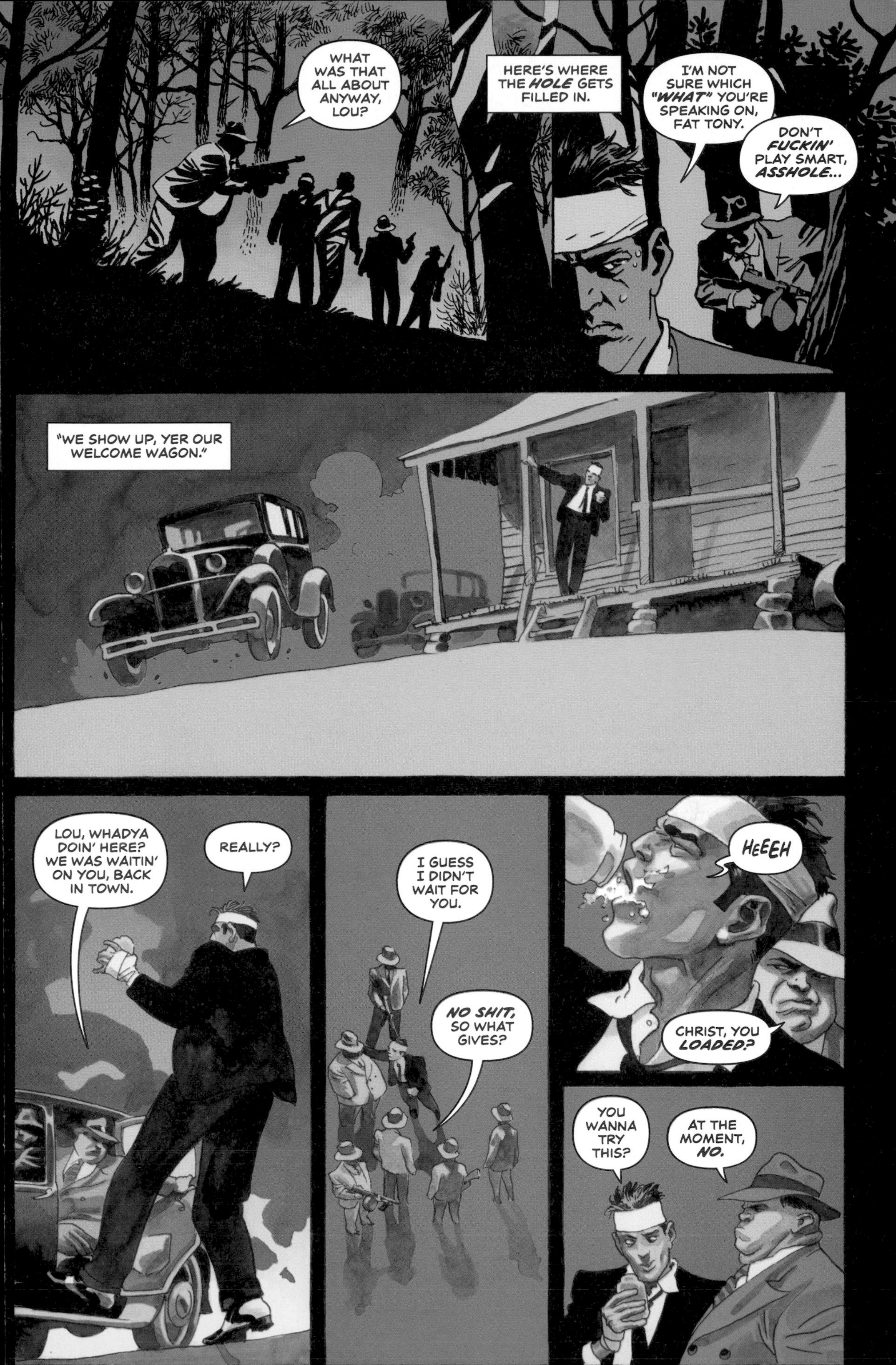

WHAT WAS THAT ALL ABOUT ANYWAY, LOU?
HERE'S WHERE THE HOLE GETS FILLED IN.
I'M NOT SURE WHICH "WHAT" YOU'RE SPEAKING ON, FAT TONY.
DON'T FUCKIN' PLAY SMART, ASSHOLE...
"WE SHOW UP, YER OUR WELCOME WAGON."
LOU, WHADYA DOIN' HERE? WE WAS WAITIN' ON YOU, BACK IN TOWN.
REALLY?
I GUESS I DIDN'T WAIT FOR YOU.
NO SHIT, SO WHAT GIVES?
HEEEH
CHRIST, YOU LOADED?
YOU WANNA TRY THIS?
AT THE MOMENT, NO.

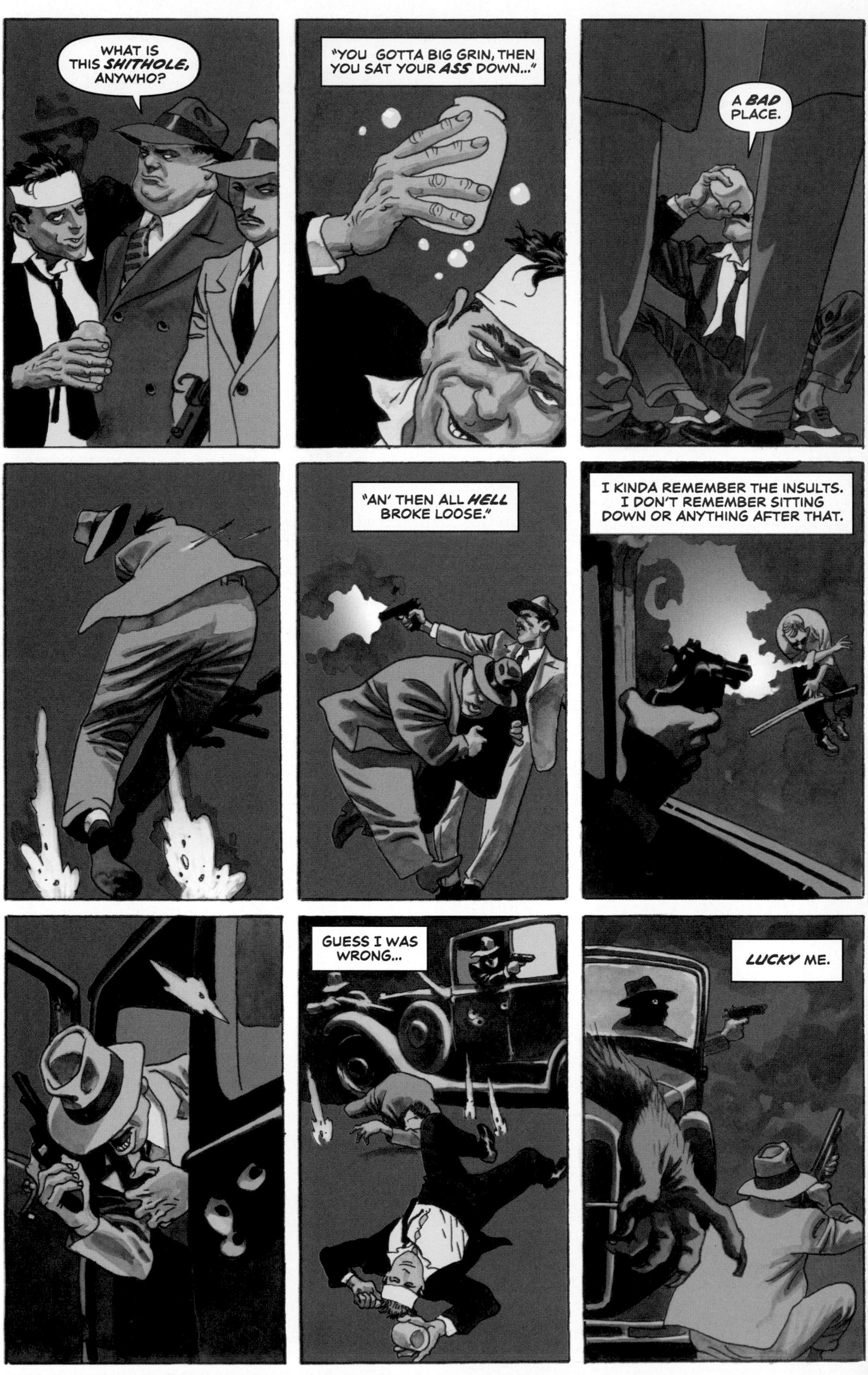
WHAT IS THIS SHITHOLE, ANYWHO?
"YOU GOTTA BIG GRIN, THEN YOU SAT YOUR ASS DOWN..."
A BAD PLACE.
"AN' THEN ALL HELL BROKE LOOSE."
I KINDA REMEMBER THE INSULTS. I DON'T REMEMBER SITTING DOWN OR ANYTHING AFTER THAT.
GUESS I WAS WRONG...
LUCKY ME.

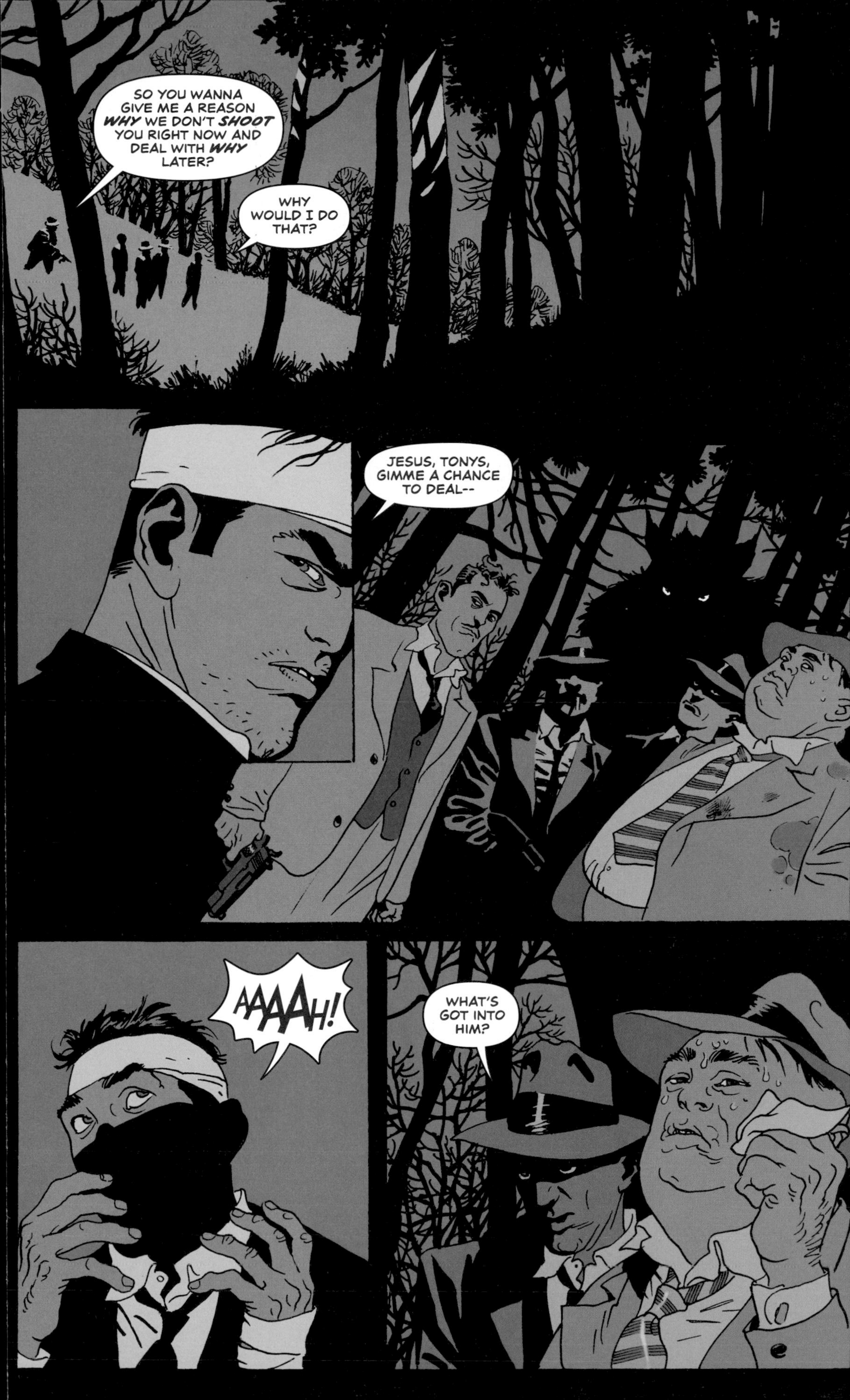
SO YOU WANNA GIVE ME A REASON WHY WE DON'T SHOOT YOU RIGHT NOW AND DEAL WITH WHY LATER?
WHY WOULD I DO THAT?
JESUS, TONYS, GIMME A CHANCE TO DEAL--
AAAAH!
WHAT'S GOT INTO HIM?

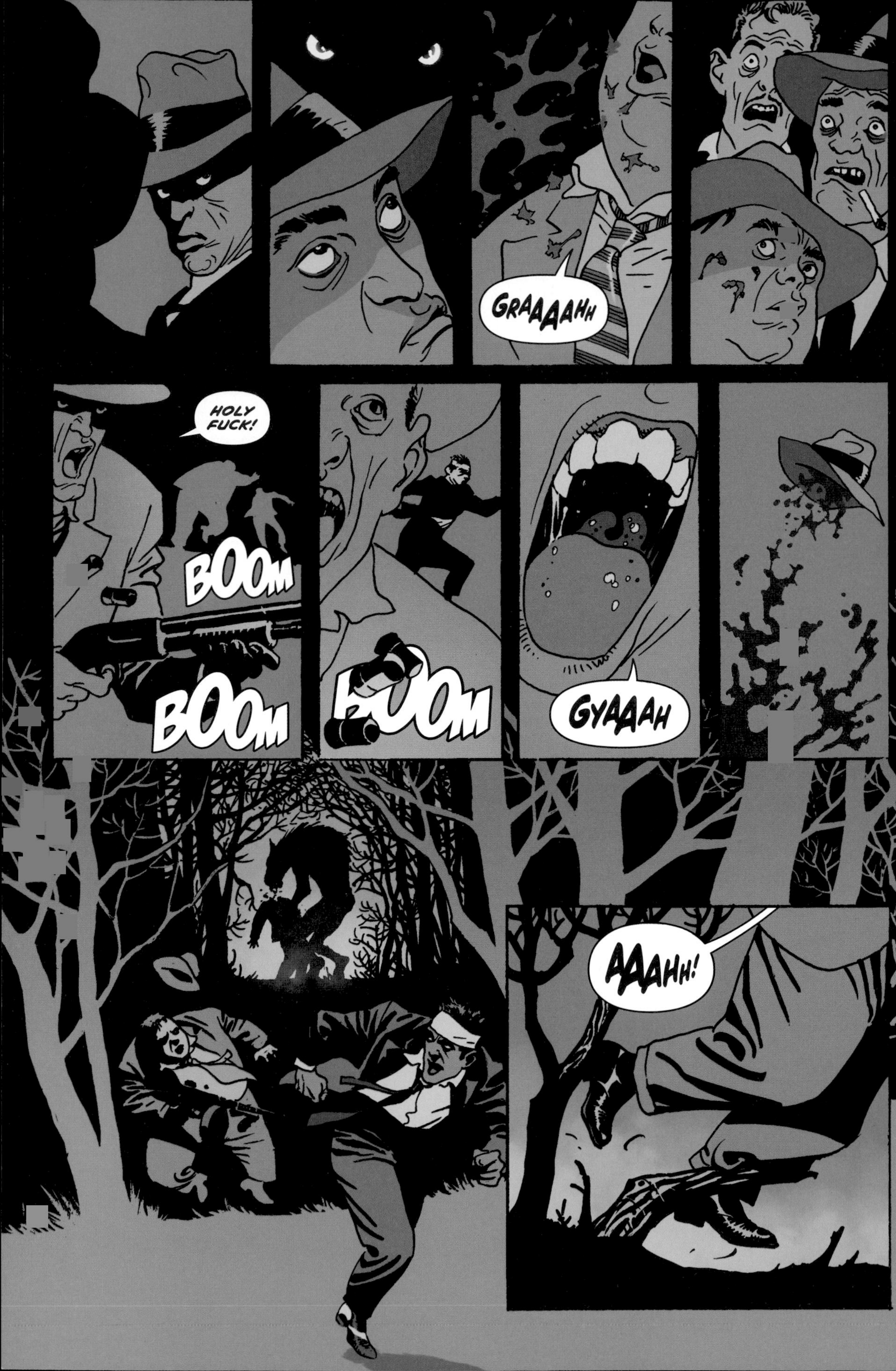
GRAAAAHH
HOLY FUCK!
BOOM
BOOM
BOOM
GYAAAH
AAAHH!

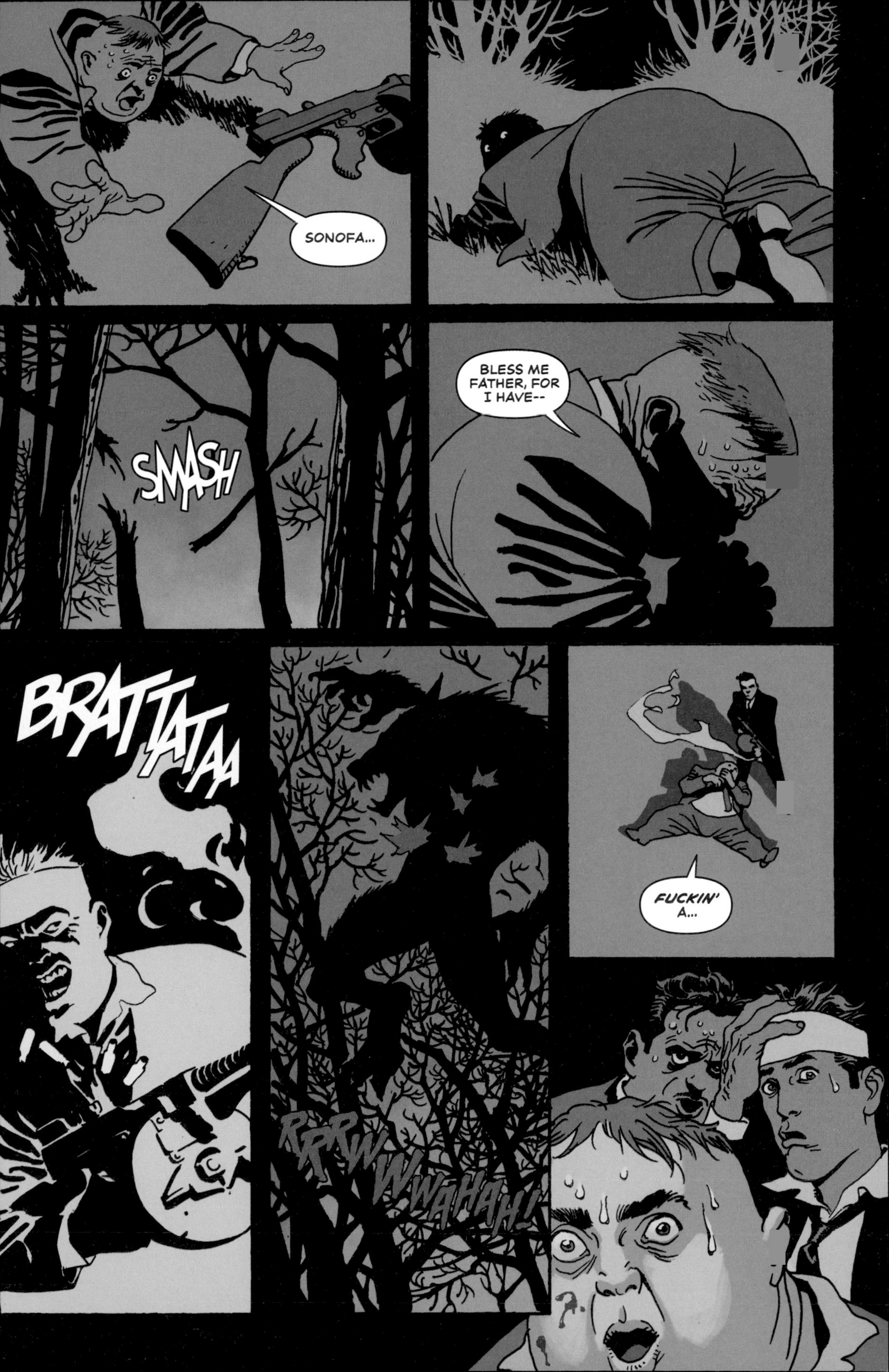
SONOFA...
SMASH
BLESS ME FATHER, FOR I HAVE--
BRATTATAA
RRRWWWAHAH!
FUCKIN' A...

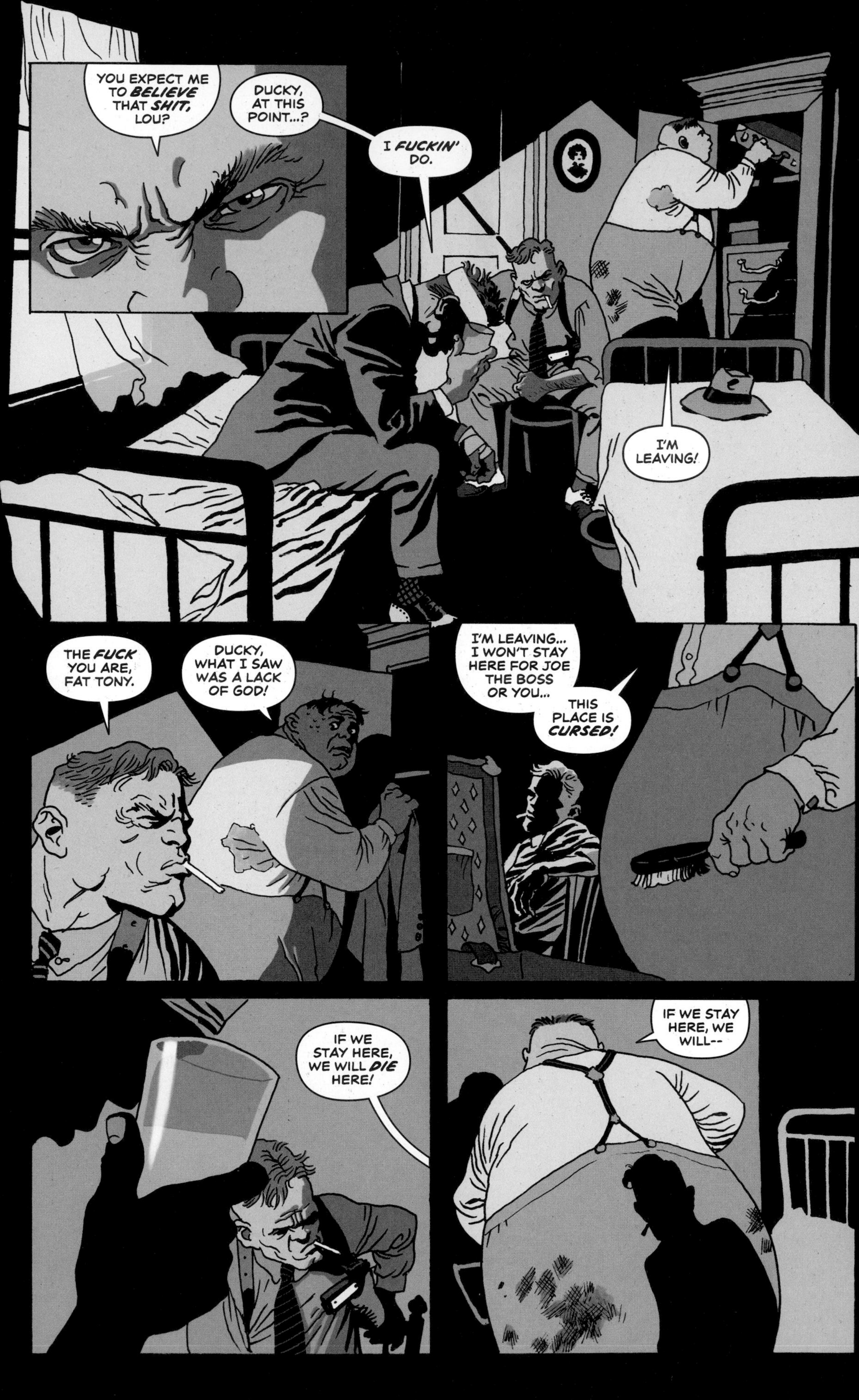
YOU EXPECT ME TO BELIEVE THAT SHIT, LOU?
DUCKY, AT THIS POINT...?
I FUCKIN' DO.
I'M LEAVING!
THE FUCK YOU ARE, FAT TONY.
DUCKY, WHAT I SAW WAS A LACK OF GOD!
I'M LEAVING... I WON'T STAY HERE FOR JOE THE BOSS OR YOU...
THIS PLACE IS CURSED!
IF WE STAY HERE, WE WILL DIE HERE!
IF WE STAY HERE, WE WILL--

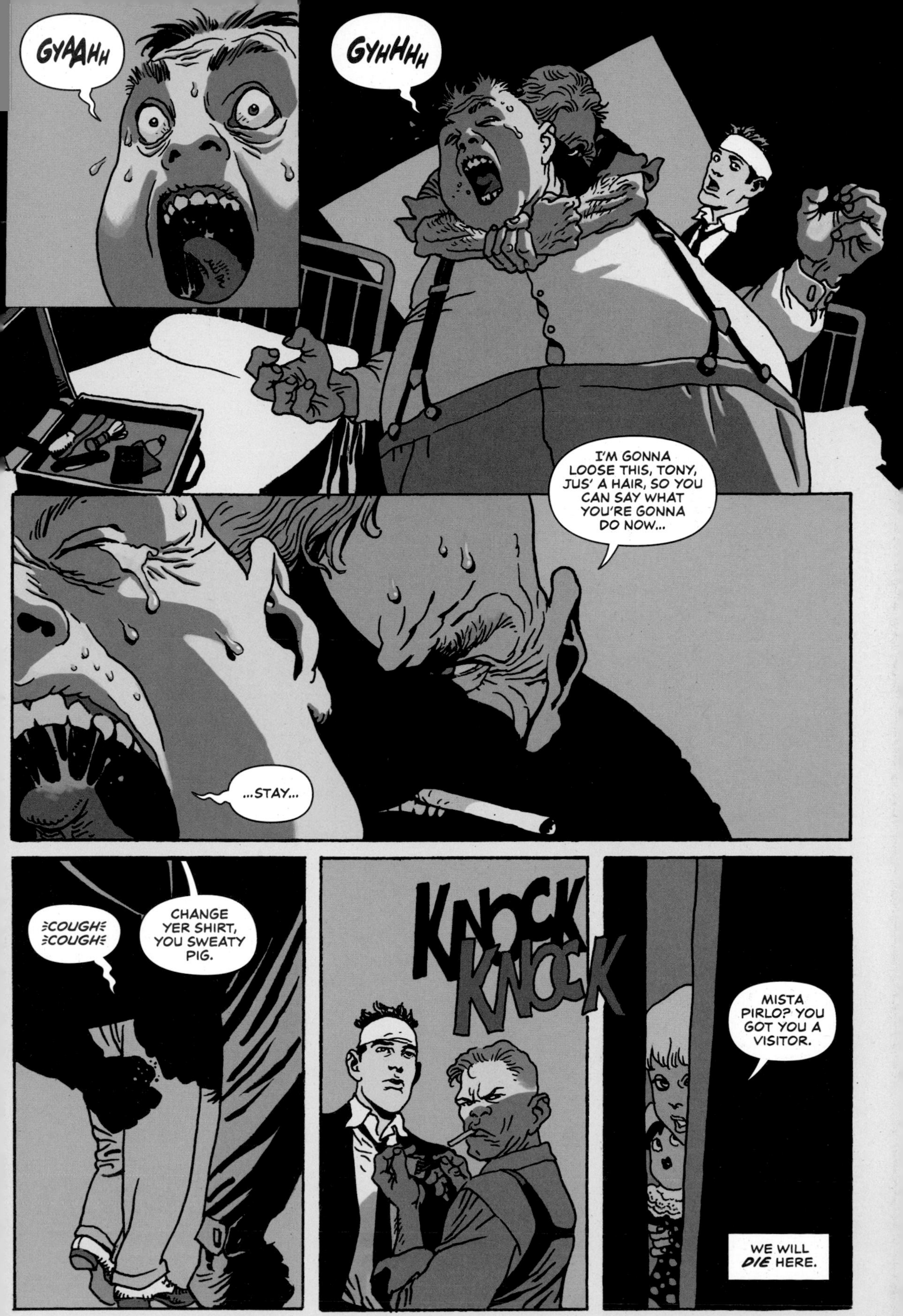
GYAAHH
GYHHHH
I'M GONNA LOOSE THIS, TONY, JUS' A HAIR, SO YOU CAN SAY WHAT YOU'RE GONNA DO NOW...
...STAY...
COUGH COUGH
CHANGE YER SHIRT, YOU SWEATY PIG.
KNOCK KNOCK
MISTA PIRLO? YOU GOT YOU A VISITOR.
WE WILL *DIE* HERE.

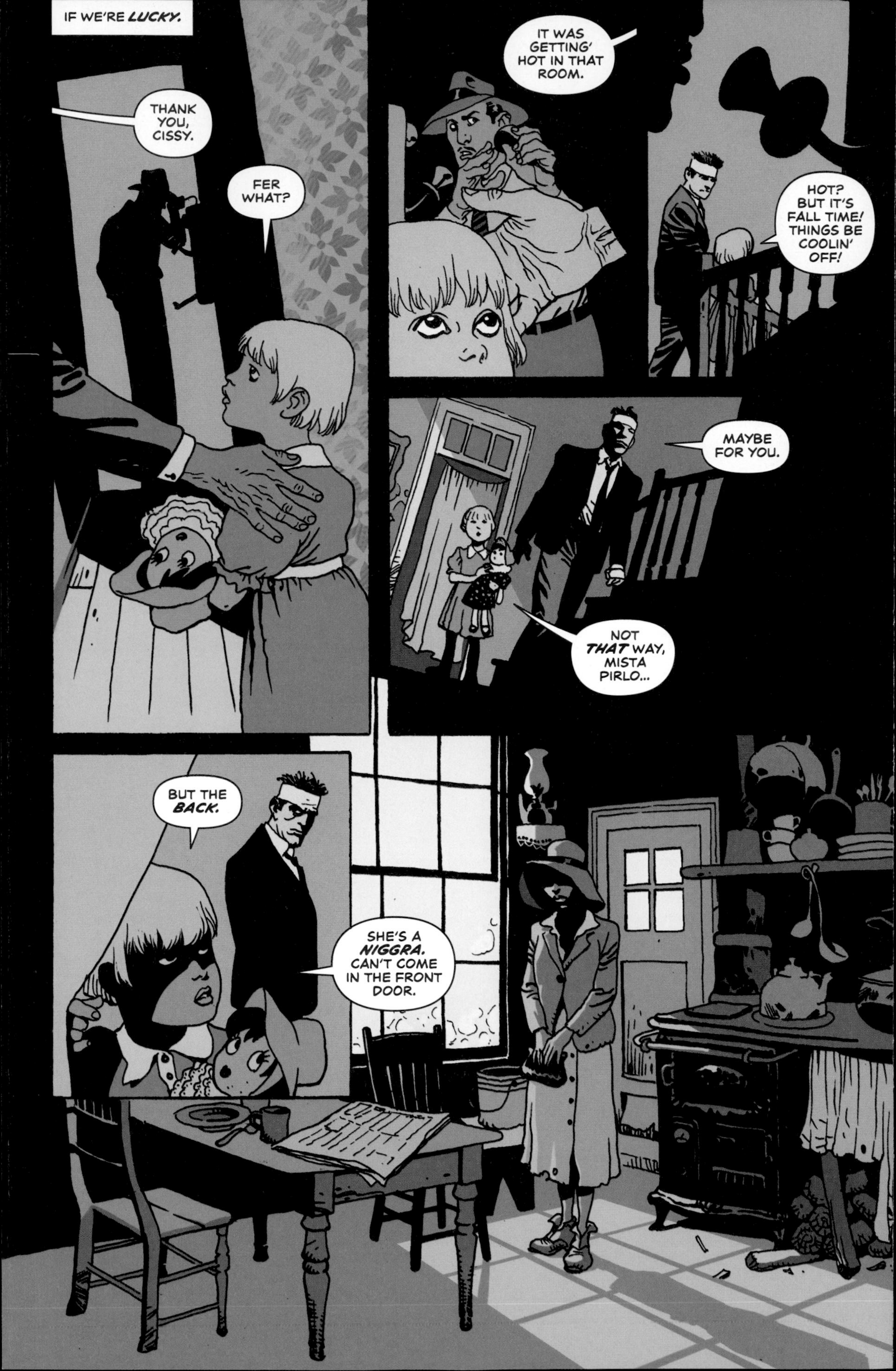
IF WE'RE LUCKY.
THANK YOU, CISSY.
FER WHAT?
IT WAS GETTING' HOT IN THAT ROOM.
HOT? BUT IT'S FALL TIME! THINGS BE COOLIN' OFF!
MAYBE FOR YOU.
NOT THAT WAY, MISTA PIRLO...
BUT THE BACK.
SHE'S A NIGGRA. CAN'T COME IN THE FRONT DOOR.

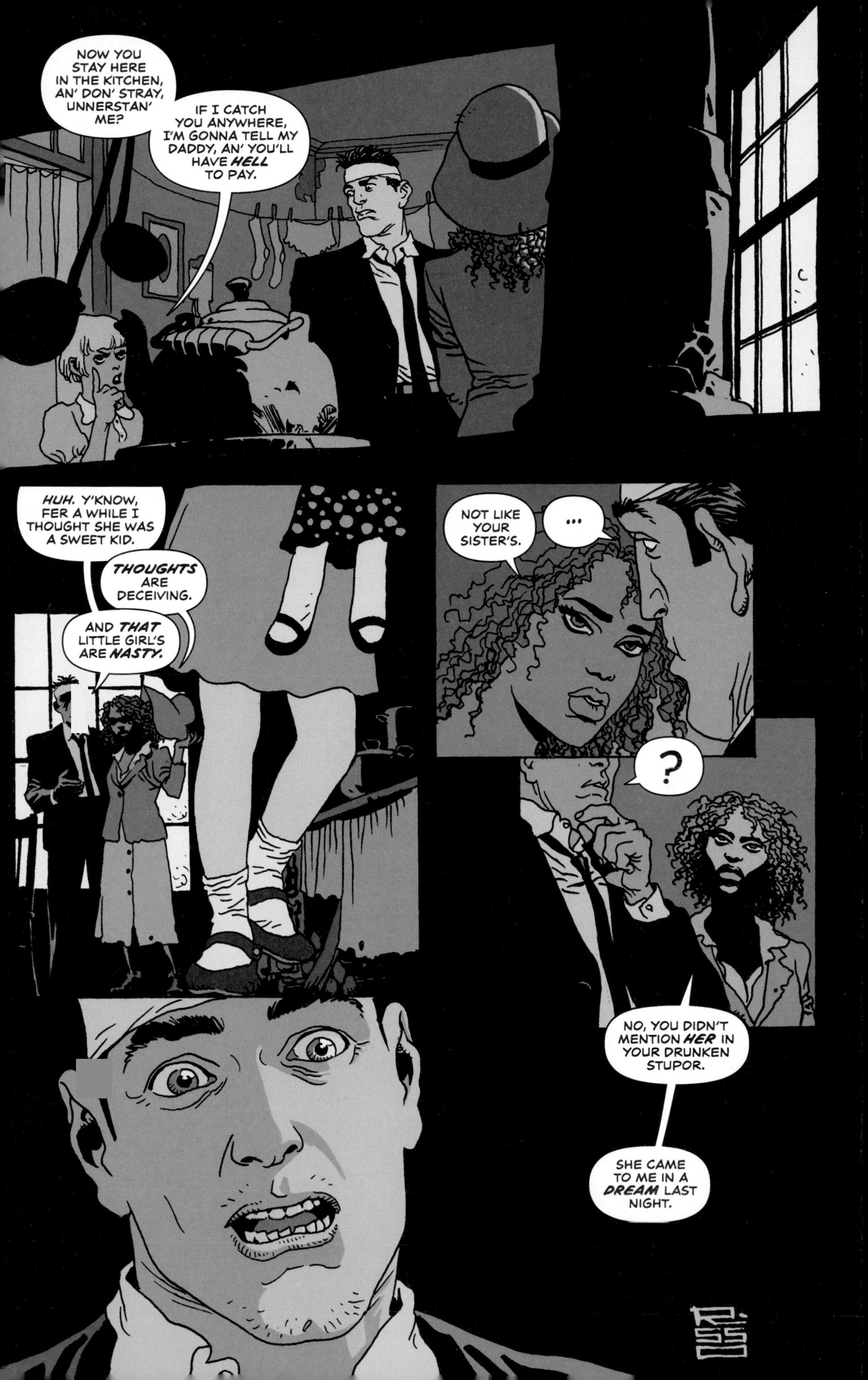
NOW YOU STAY HERE IN THE KITCHEN, AN' DON' STRAY, UNNERSTAN' ME?
IF I CATCH YOU ANYWHERE, I'M GONNA TELL MY DADDY, AN' YOU'LL HAVE HELL TO PAY.
HUH. Y'KNOW, FER A WHILE I THOUGHT SHE WAS A SWEET KID.
THOUGHTS ARE DECEIVING.
AND THAT LITTLE GIRL'S ARE NASTY.
NOT LIKE YOUR SISTER'S.
...
?
NO, YOU DIDN'T MENTION HER IN YOUR DRUNKEN STUPOR.
SHE CAME TO ME IN A DREAM LAST NIGHT.

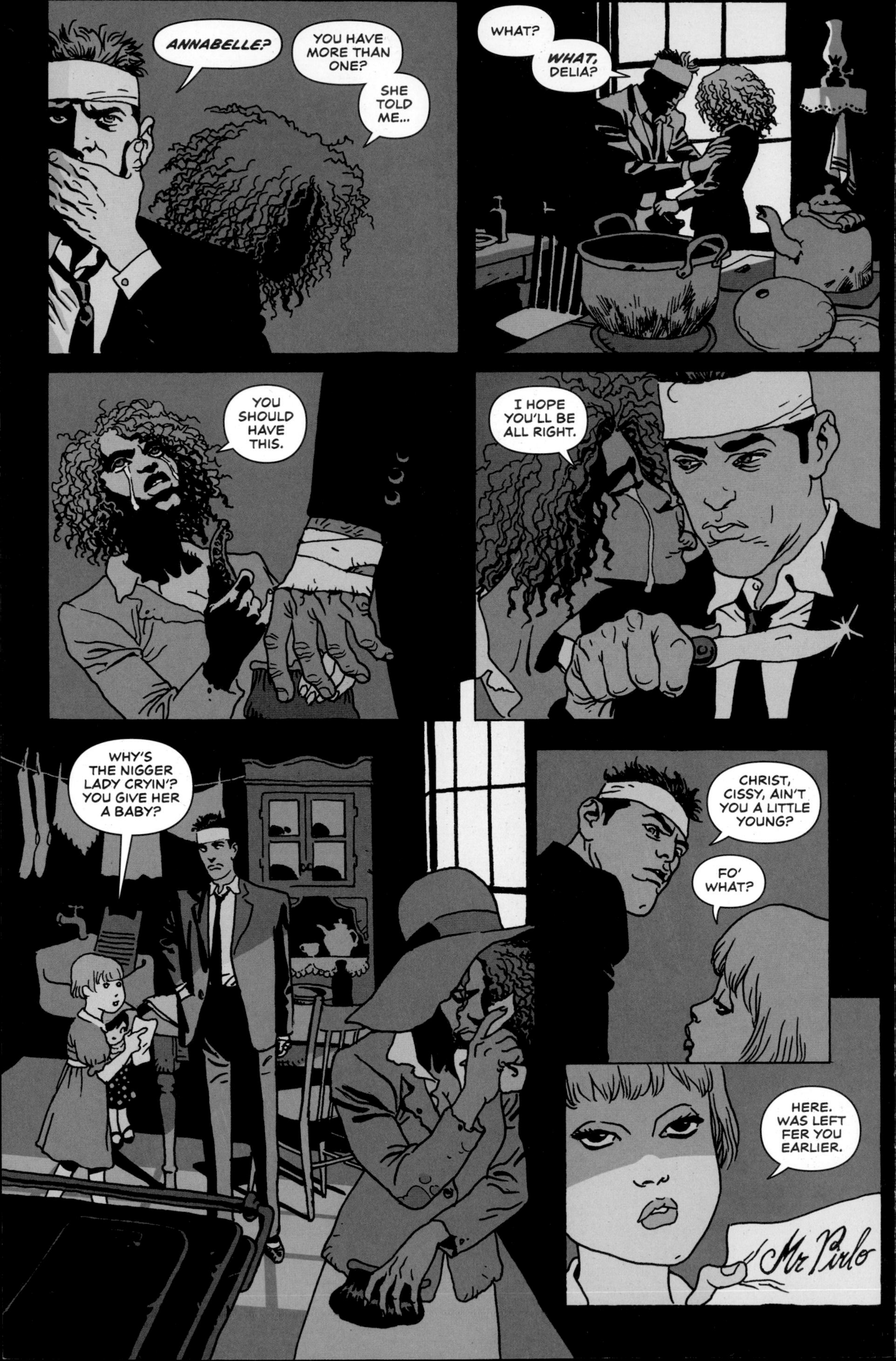
ANNABELLE?
YOU HAVE MORE THAN ONE?
SHE TOLD ME...
WHAT?
WHAT, DELIA?
YOU SHOULD HAVE THIS.
I HOPE YOU'LL BE ALL RIGHT.
WHY'S THE NIGGER LADY CRYIN'? YOU GIVE HER A BABY?
CHRIST, CISSY, AIN'T YOU A LITTLE YOUNG?
FO' WHAT?
HERE. WAS LEFT FER YOU EARLIER.
Mr Pirlo

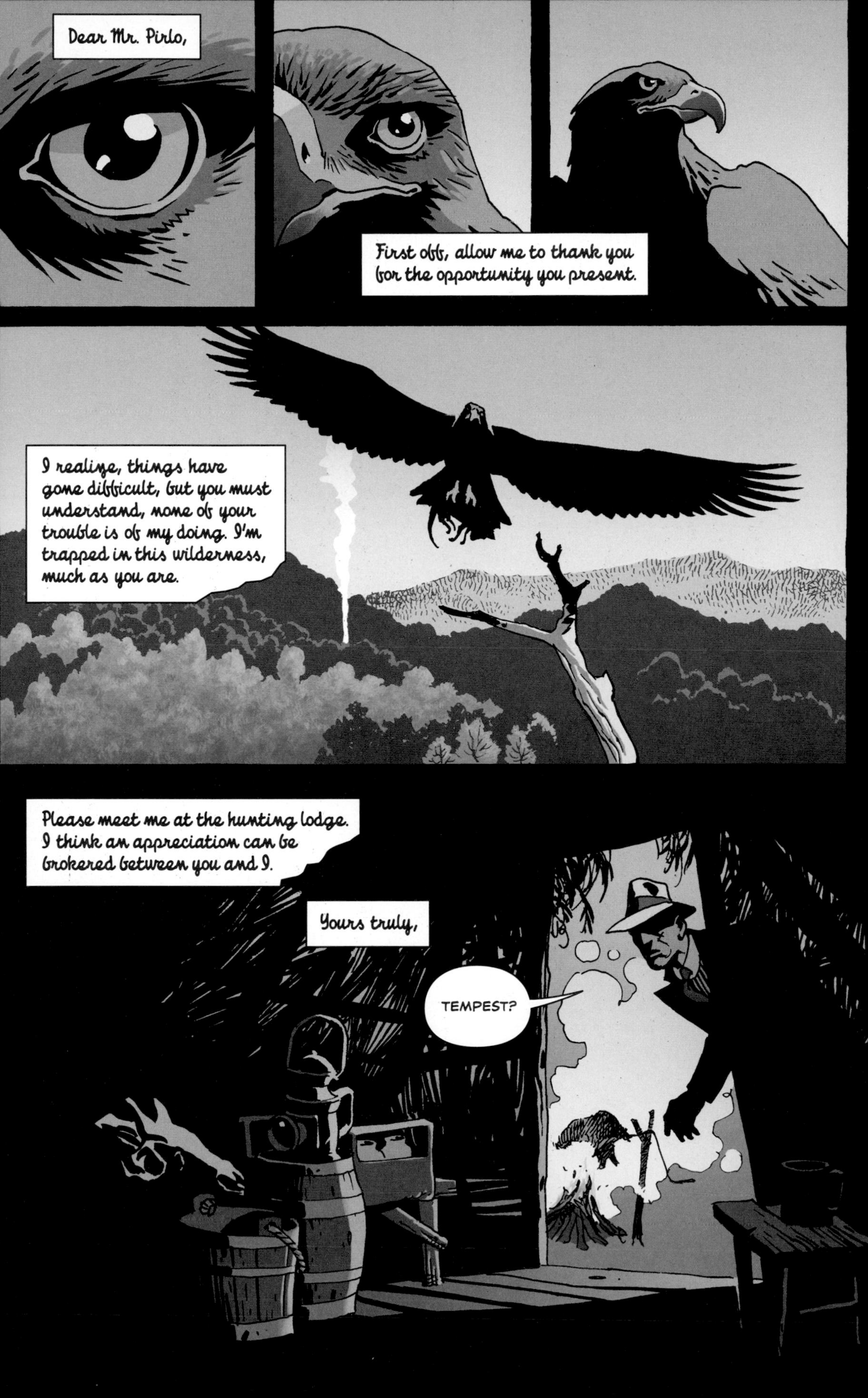
Dear Mr. Pirlo,
First off, allow me to thank you for the opportunity you present.
I realize, things have gone difficult, but you must understand, none of your trouble is of my doing. I'm trapped in this wilderness, much as you are.
Please meet me at the hunting lodge. I think an appreciation can be brokered between you and I.
Yours truly,
TEMPEST?

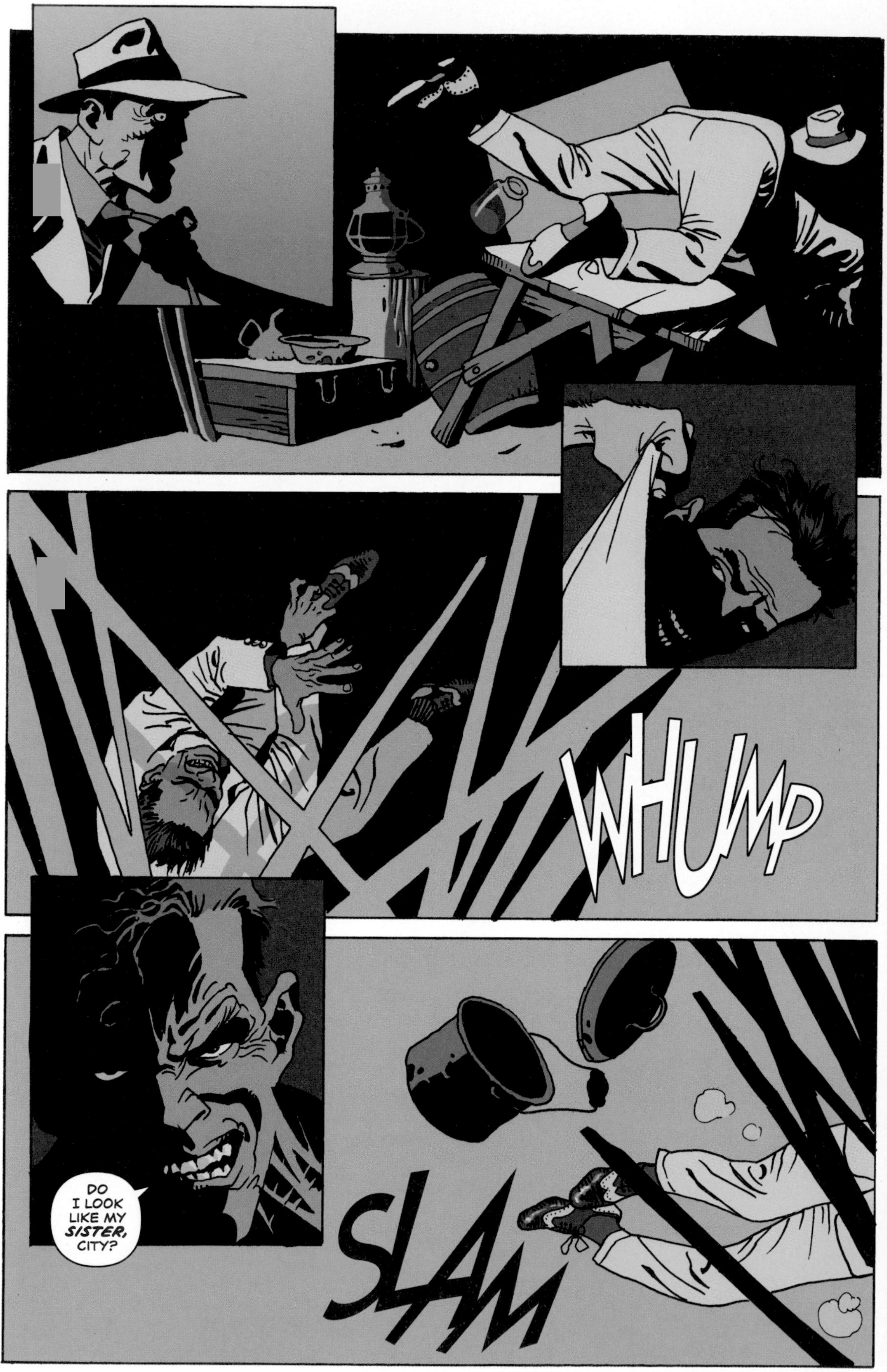
WHUMP
DO I LOOK LIKE MY *SISTER,* CITY?
SLAM

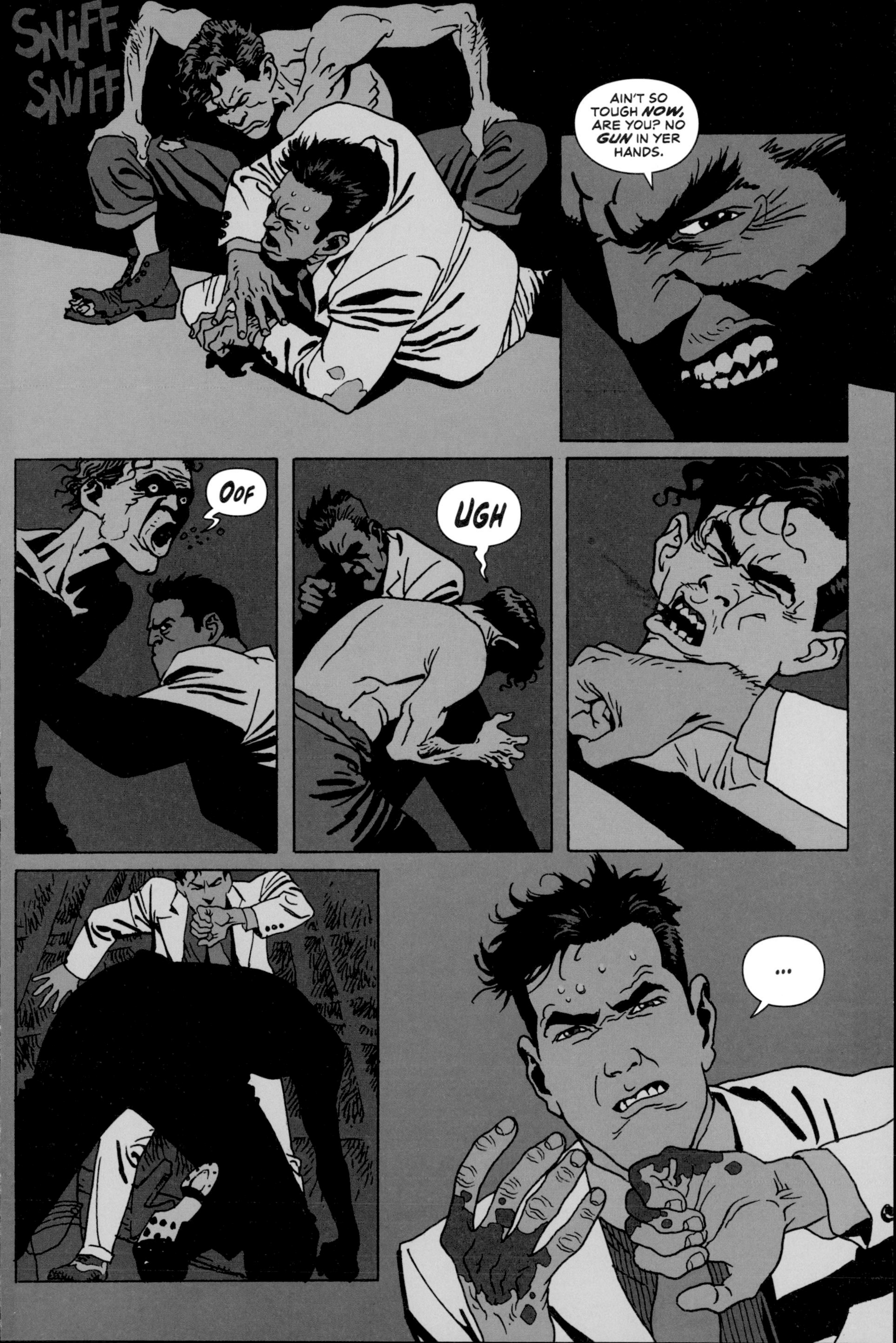
SNIFF
SNIFF
AIN'T SO TOUGH NOW, ARE YOU? NO GUN IN YER HANDS.
OOF
UGH
...

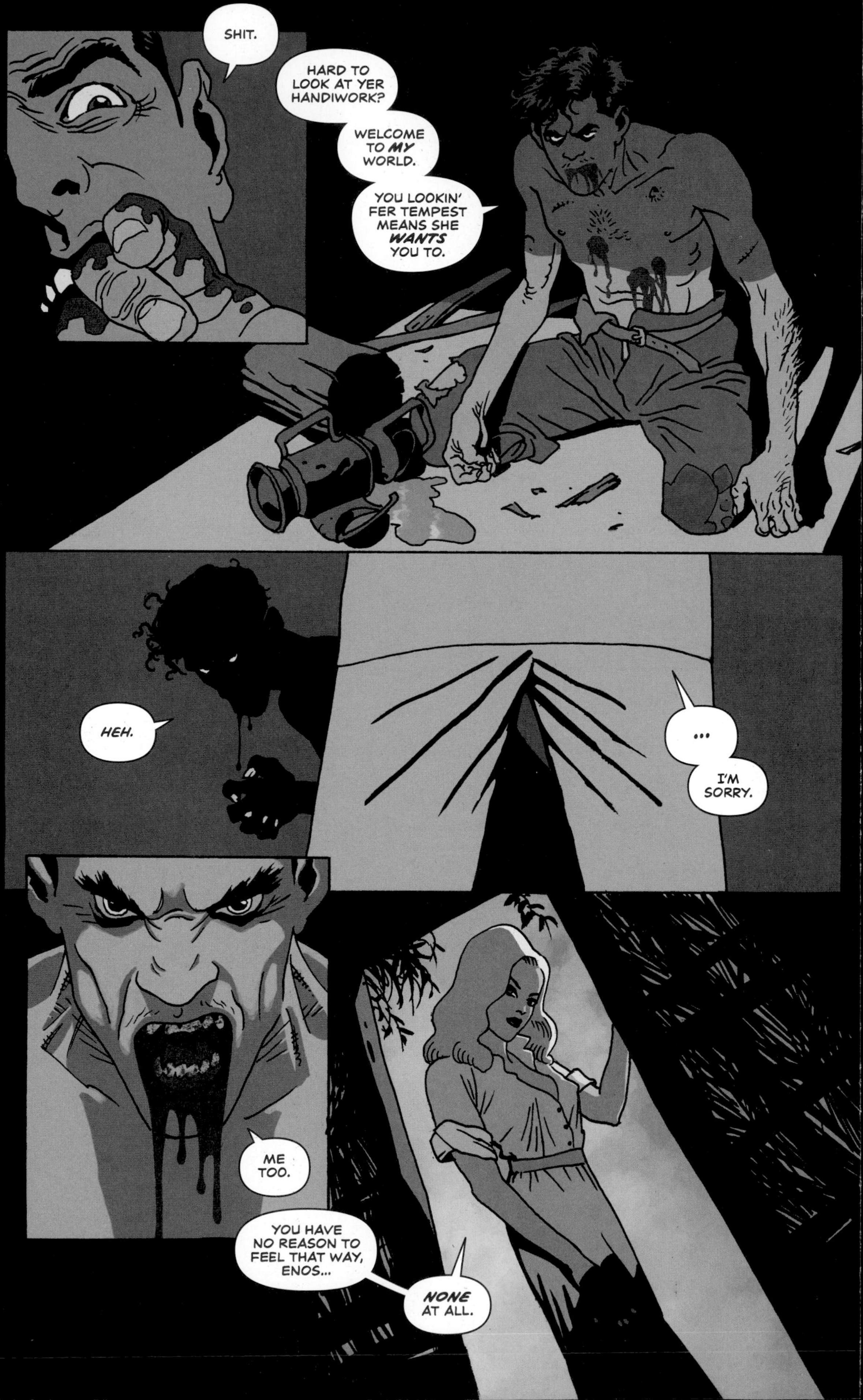
SHIT.
HARD TO LOOK AT YER HANDIWORK?
WELCOME TO MY WORLD.
YOU LOOKIN' FER TEMPEST MEANS SHE WANTS YOU TO.
HEH.
...
I'M SORRY.
ME TOO.
YOU HAVE NO REASON TO FEEL THAT WAY, ENOS...
NONE AT ALL.

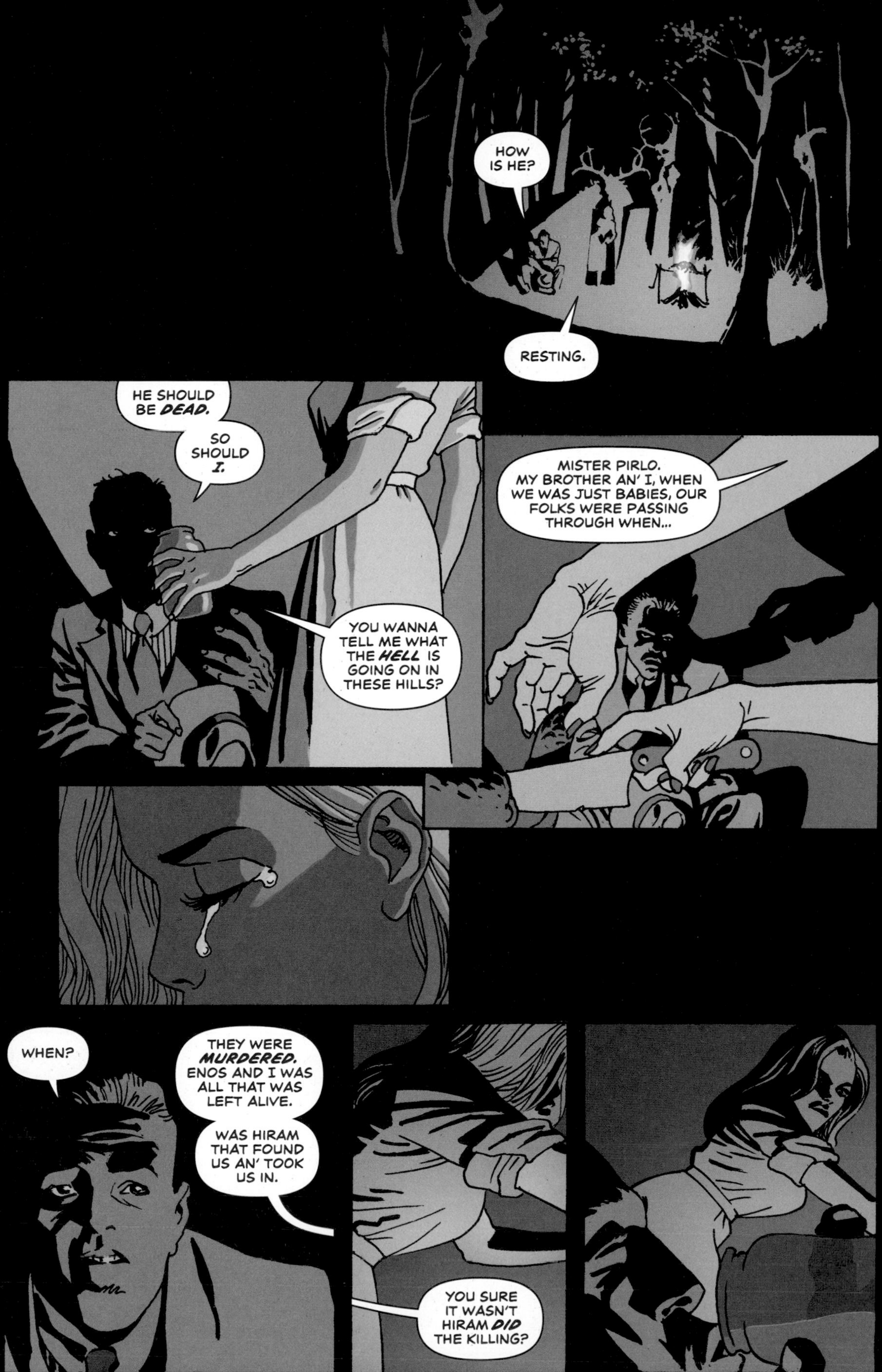
HOW IS HE?
RESTING.
HE SHOULD BE DEAD.
SO SHOULD I.
YOU WANNA TELL ME WHAT THE HELL IS GOING ON IN THESE HILLS?
MISTER PIRLO. MY BROTHER AN' I, WHEN WE WAS JUST BABIES, OUR FOLKS WERE PASSING THROUGH WHEN...
WHEN?
THEY WERE MURDERED. ENOS AND I WAS ALL THAT WAS LEFT ALIVE.
WAS HIRAM THAT FOUND US AN' TOOK US IN.
YOU SURE IT WASN'T HIRAM DID THE KILLING?

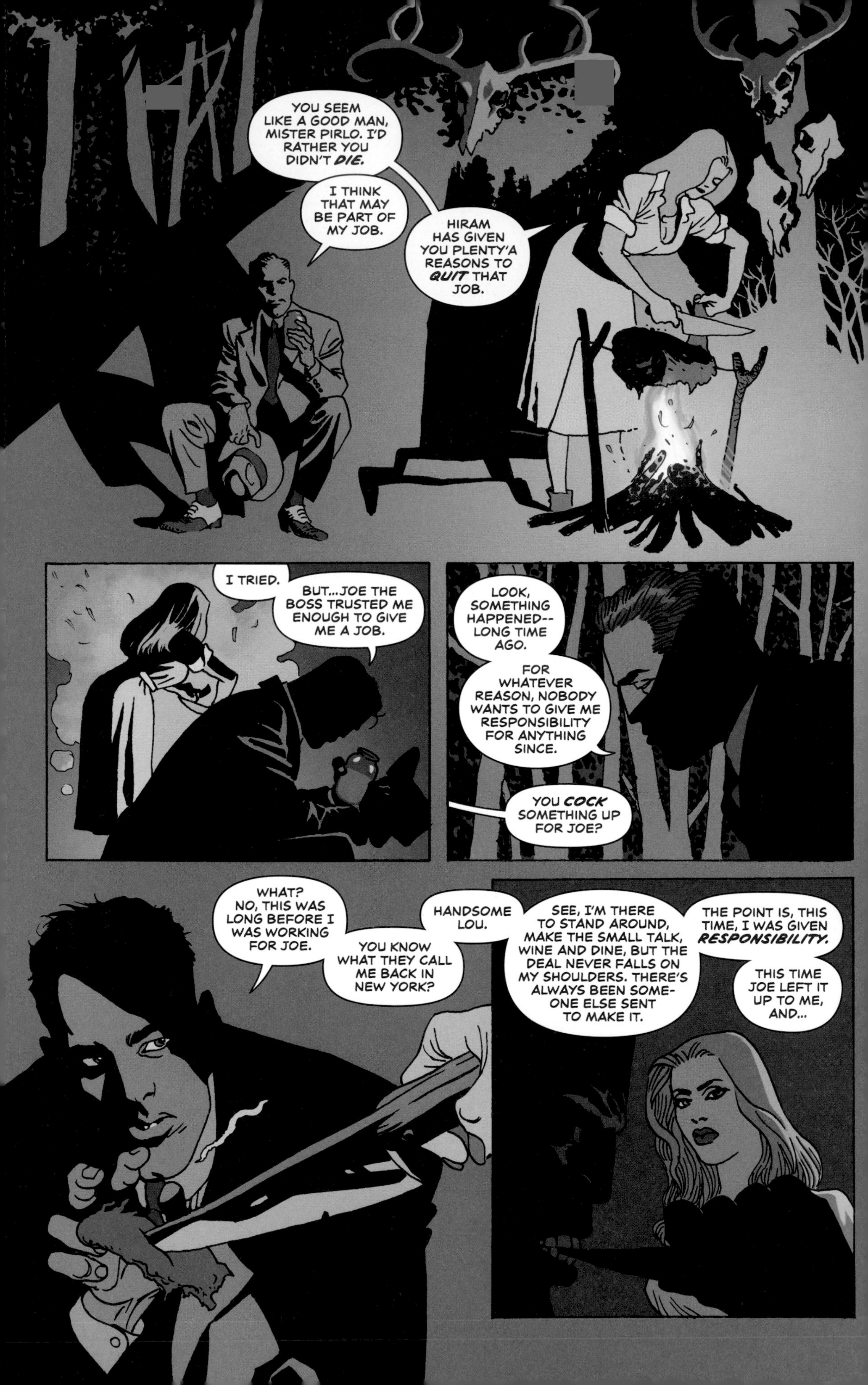

YOU SEEM LIKE A GOOD MAN, MISTER PIRLO. I'D RATHER YOU DIDN'T DIE.
I THINK THAT MAY BE PART OF MY JOB.
HIRAM HAS GIVEN YOU PLENTY'A REASONS TO QUIT THAT JOB.
I TRIED.
BUT...JOE THE BOSS TRUSTED ME ENOUGH TO GIVE ME A JOB.
LOOK, SOMETHING HAPPENED-- LONG TIME AGO.
FOR WHATEVER REASON, NOBODY WANTS TO GIVE ME RESPONSIBILITY FOR ANYTHING SINCE.
YOU COCK SOMETHING UP FOR JOE?
WHAT? NO, THIS WAS LONG BEFORE I WAS WORKING FOR JOE.
YOU KNOW WHAT THEY CALL ME BACK IN NEW YORK?
HANDSOME LOU.
SEE, I'M THERE TO STAND AROUND, MAKE THE SMALL TALK, WINE AND DINE, BUT THE DEAL NEVER FALLS ON MY SHOULDERS. THERE'S ALWAYS BEEN SOME-ONE ELSE SENT TO MAKE IT.
THE POINT IS, THIS TIME, I WAS GIVEN RESPONSIBILITY.
THIS TIME JOE LEFT IT UP TO ME, AND...

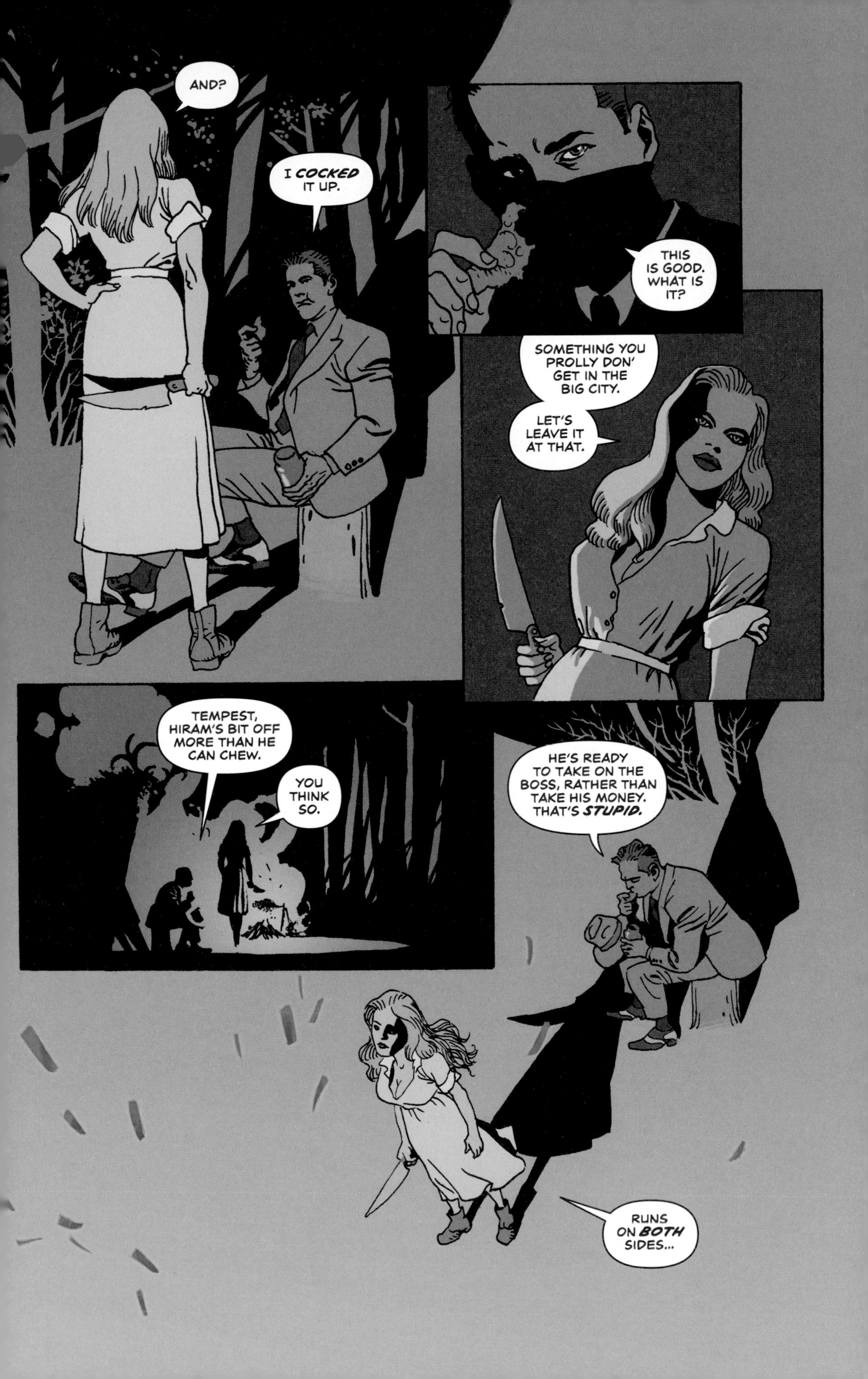
AND?
I *COCKED* IT UP.
THIS IS GOOD. WHAT IS IT?
SOMETHING YOU PROLLY DON' GET IN THE BIG CITY.
LET'S LEAVE IT AT THAT.
TEMPEST, HIRAM'S BIT OFF MORE THAN HE CAN CHEW.
YOU THINK SO.
HE'S READY TO TAKE ON THE BOSS, RATHER THAN TAKE HIS MONEY. THAT'S *STUPID.*
RUNS ON *BOTH* SIDES...

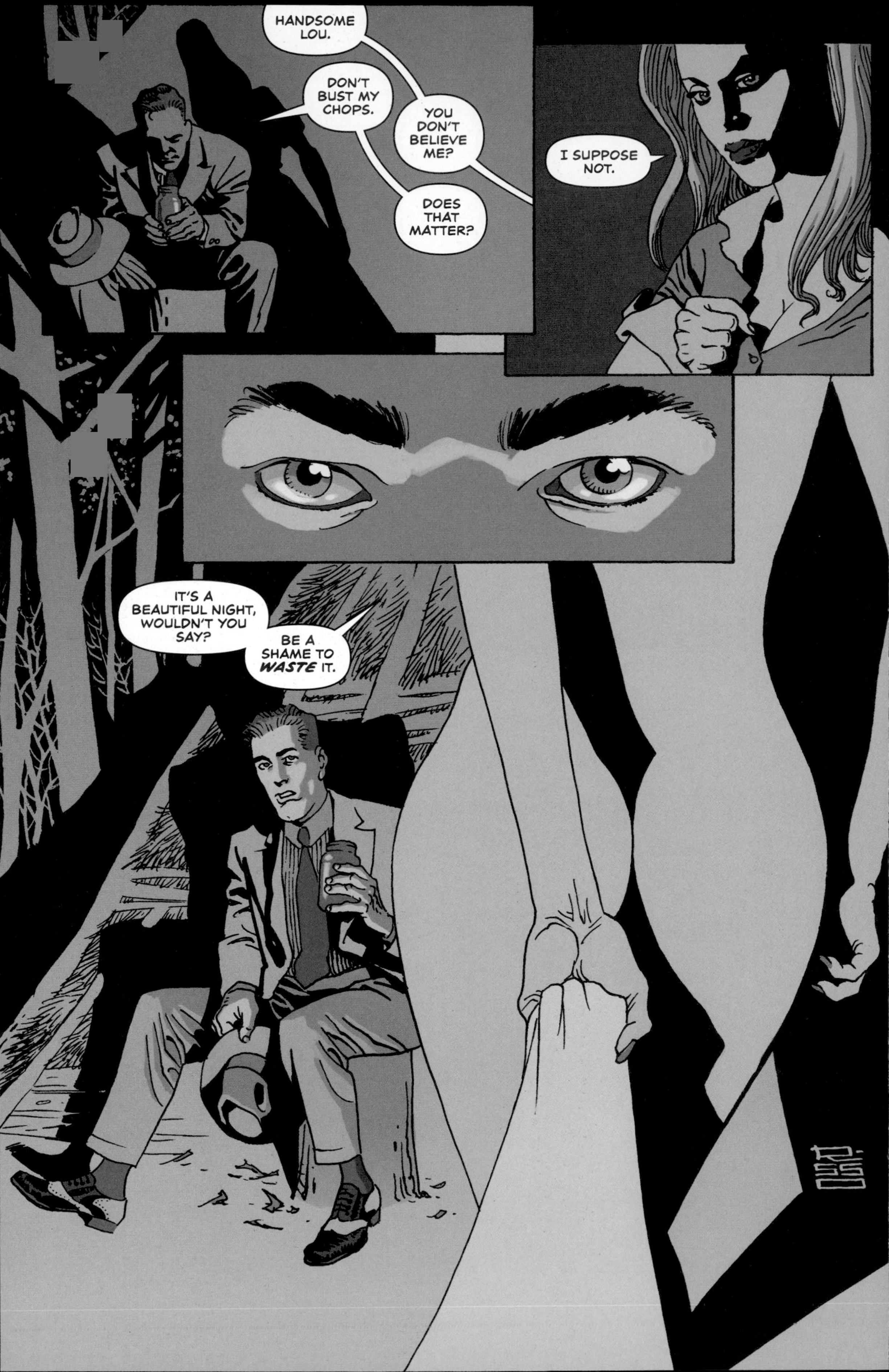
HANDSOME LOU.
DON'T BUST MY CHOPS.
YOU DON'T BELIEVE ME?
DOES THAT MATTER?
I SUPPOSE NOT.
IT'S A BEAUTIFUL NIGHT, WOULDN'T YOU SAY?
BE A SHAME TO WASTE IT.

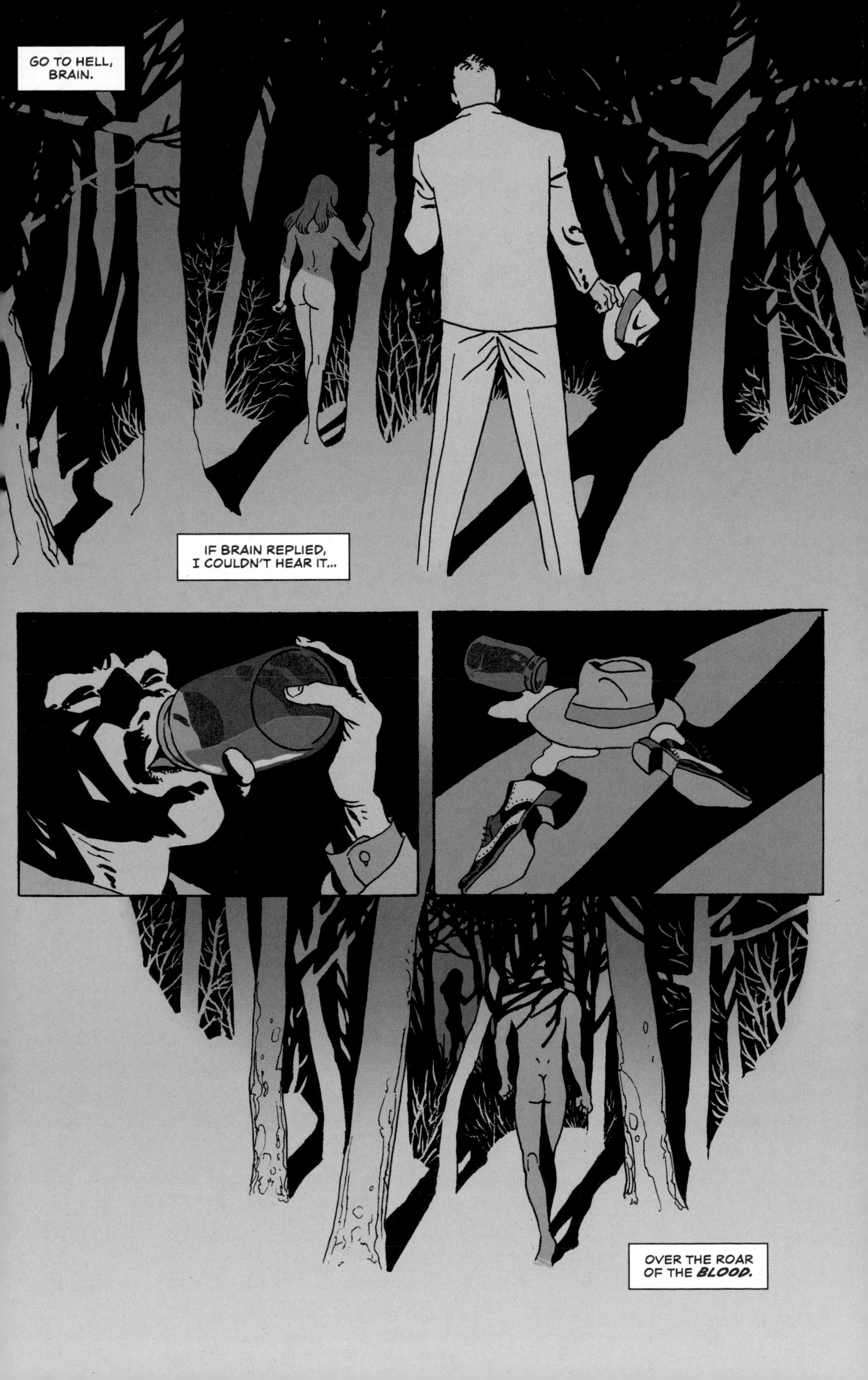
GO TO HELL, BRAIN.
IF BRAIN REPLIED, I COULDN'T HEAR IT...
OVER THE ROAR OF THE *BLOOD.*

Chapter FIVE

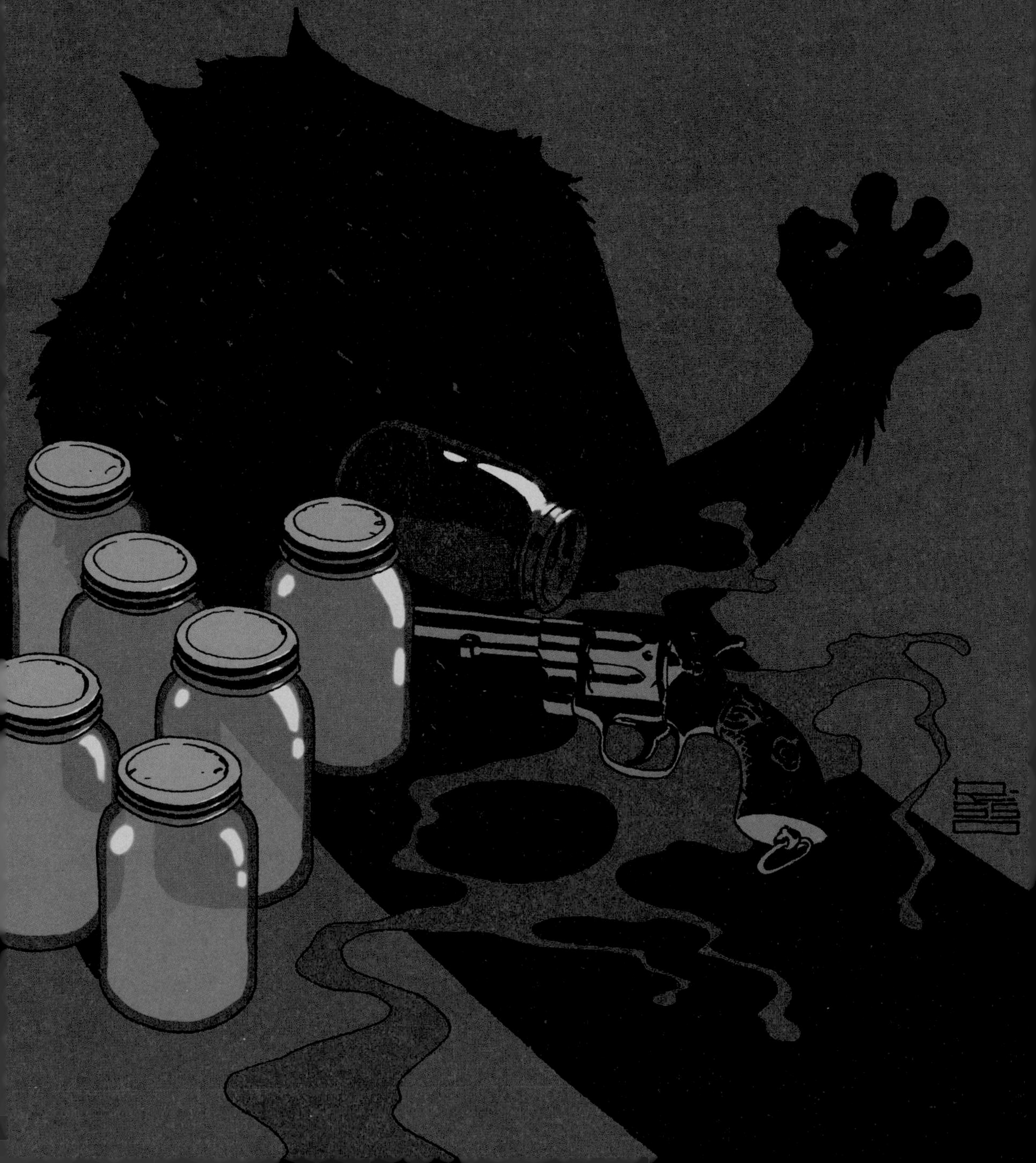

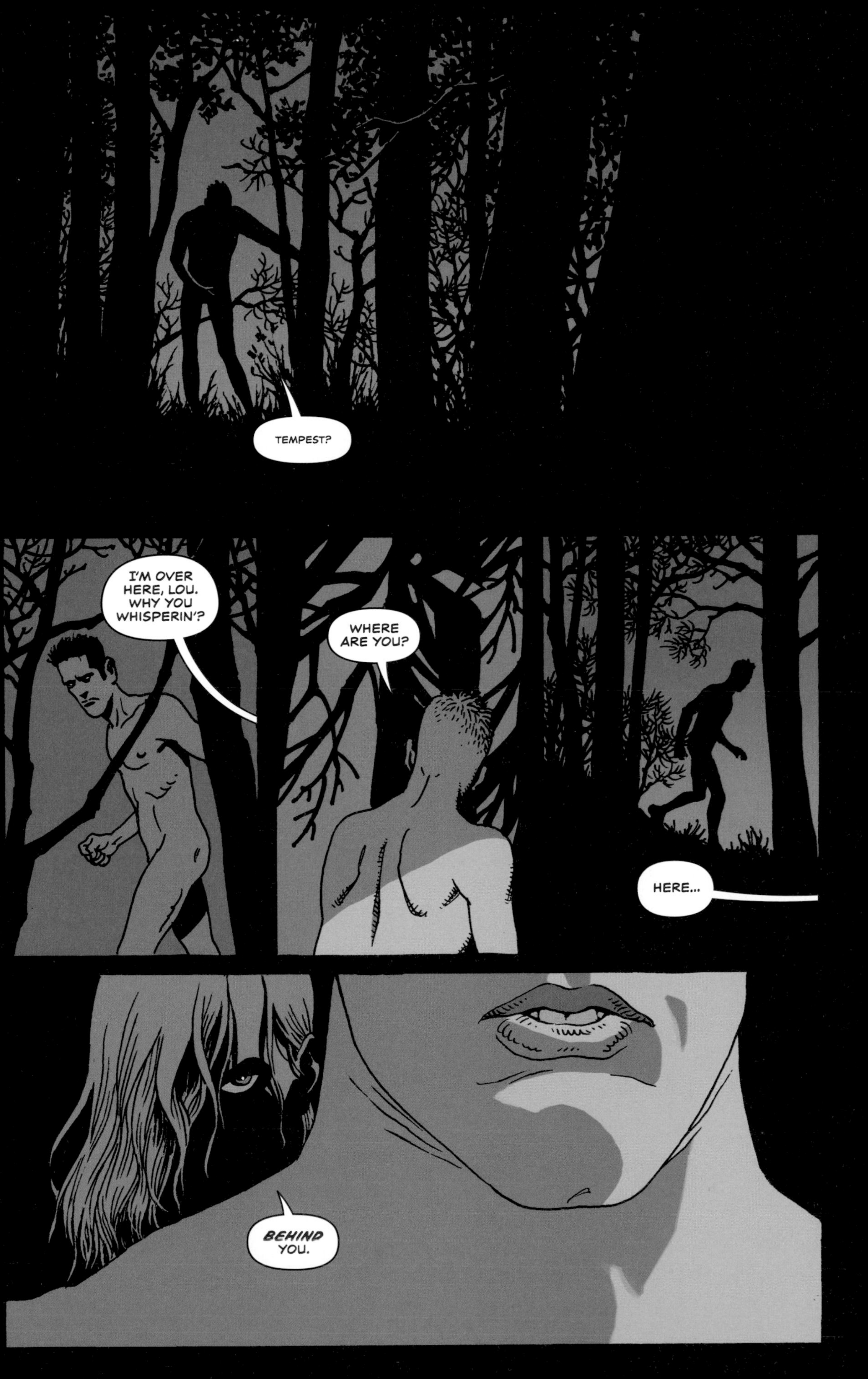
TEMPEST?
I'M OVER HERE, LOU. WHY YOU WHISPERIN'?
WHERE ARE YOU?
HERE...
BEHIND YOU.

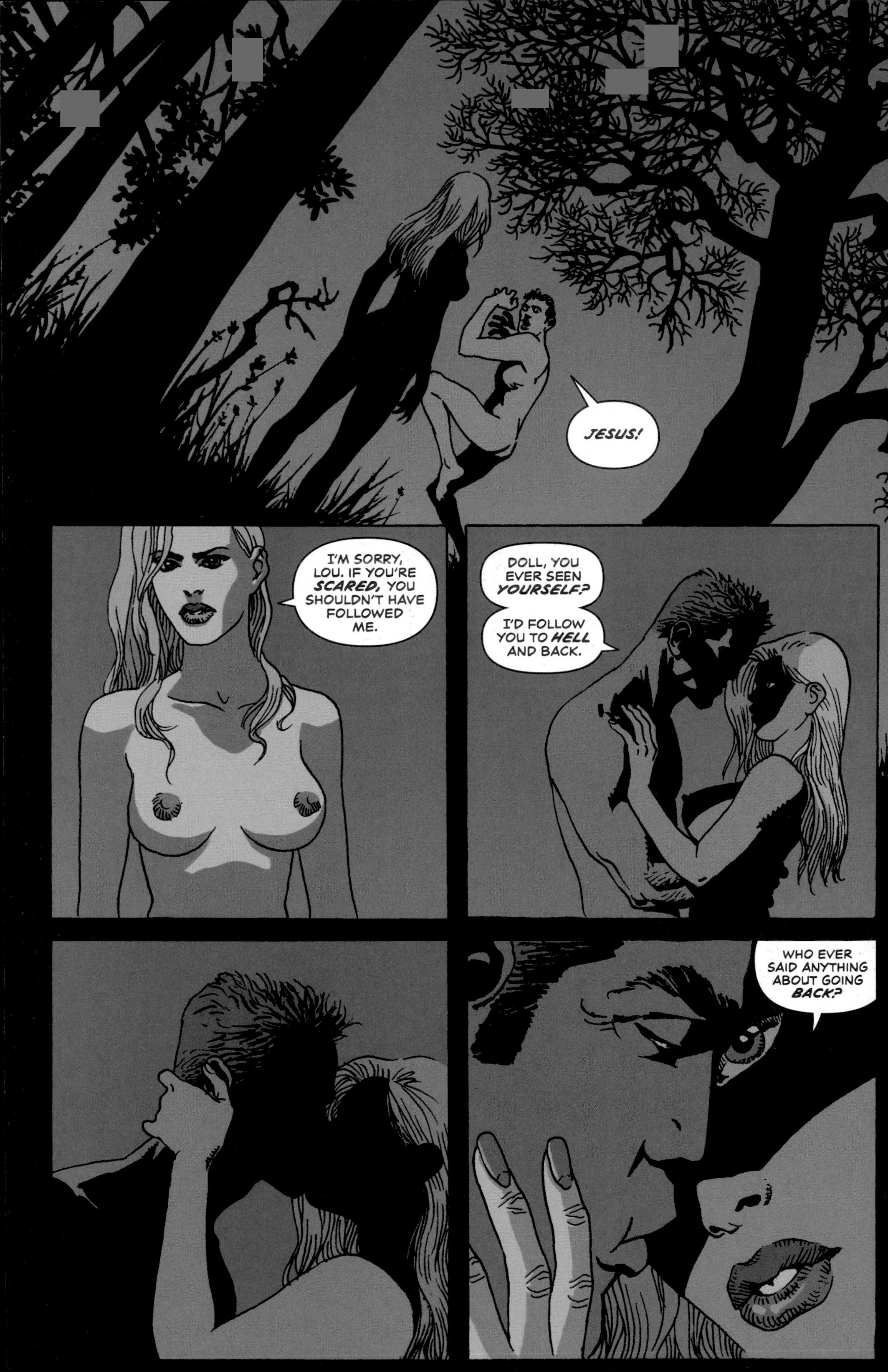
JESUS!
I'M SORRY, LOU. IF YOU'RE SCARED, YOU SHOULDN'T HAVE FOLLOWED ME.
DOLL, YOU EVER SEEN YOURSELF?
I'D FOLLOW YOU TO HELL AND BACK.
WHO EVER SAID ANYTHING ABOUT GOING BACK?

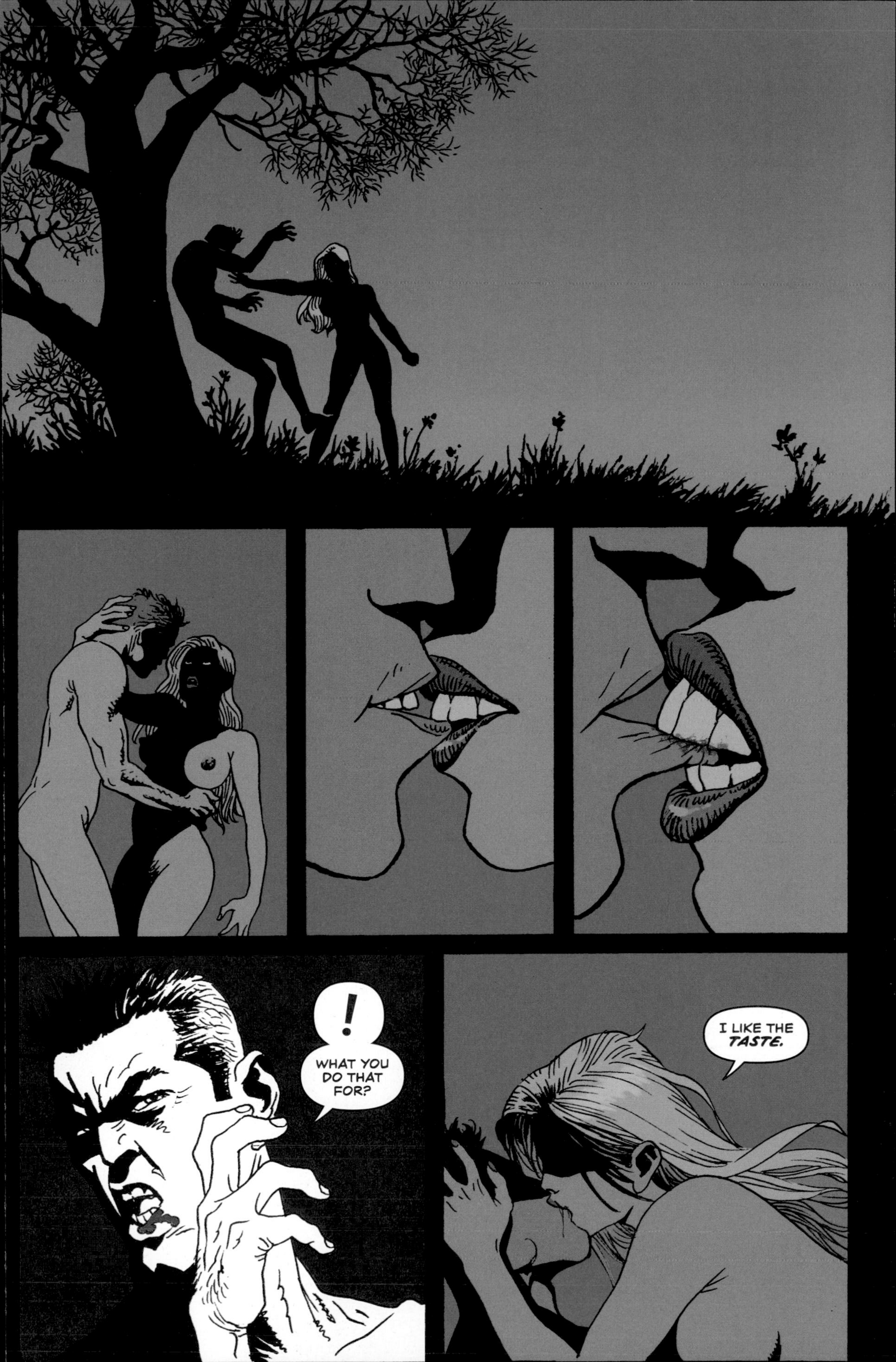
!
WHAT YOU DO THAT FOR?
I LIKE THE *TASTE.*

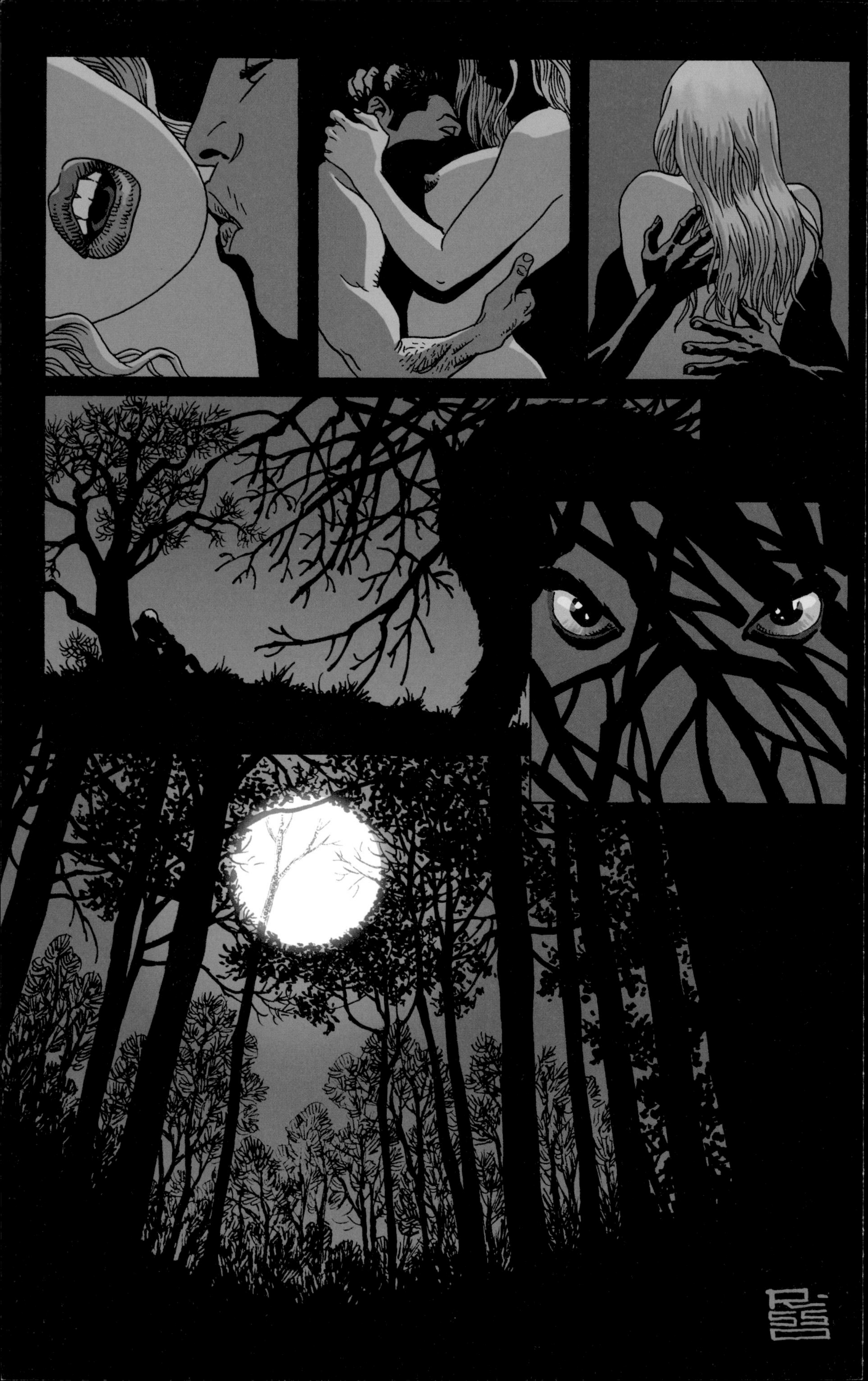

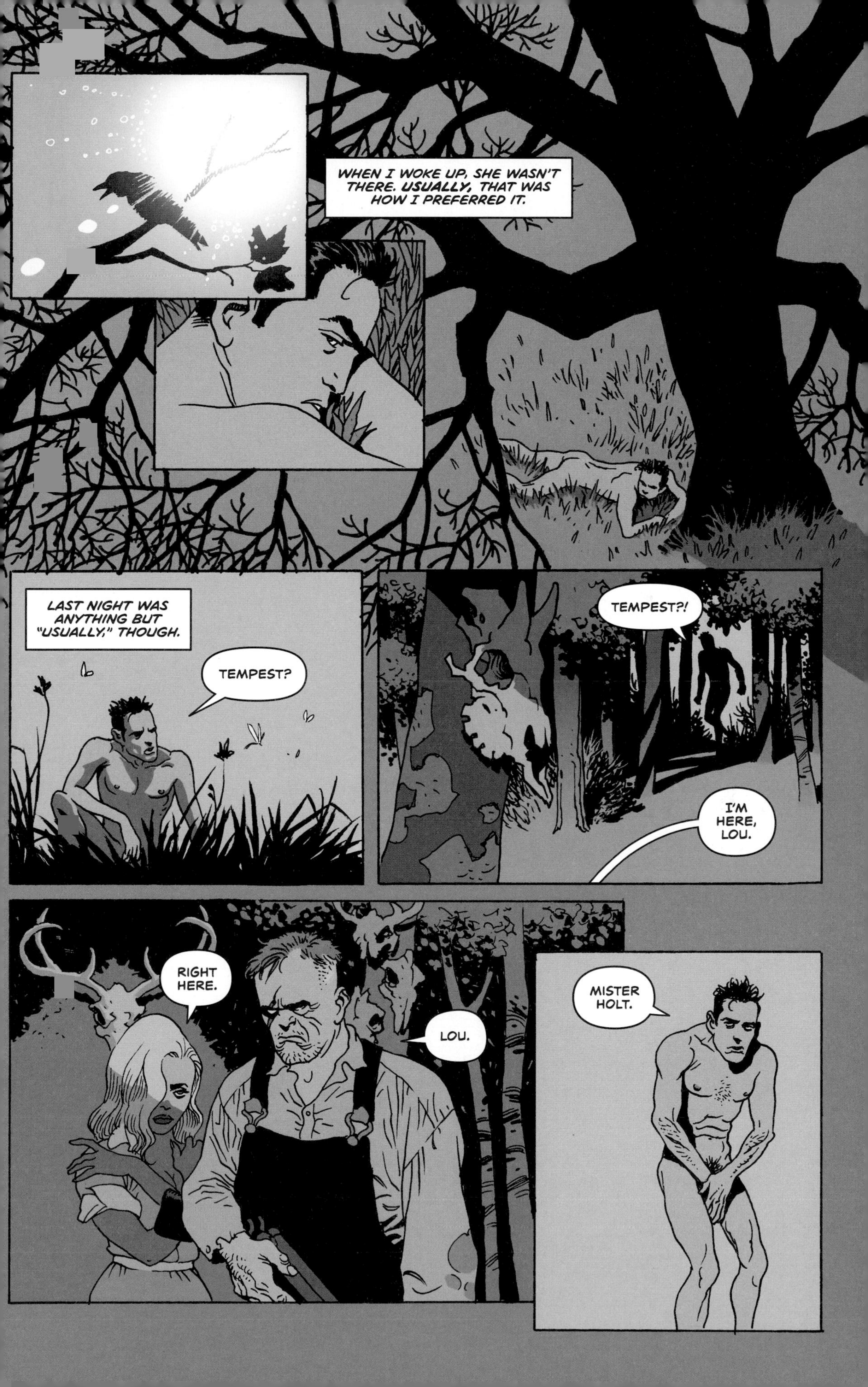
WHEN I WOKE UP, SHE WASN'T THERE. USUALLY, THAT WAS HOW I PREFERRED IT.
LAST NIGHT WAS ANYTHING BUT "USUALLY," THOUGH.
TEMPEST?
TEMPEST?!
I'M HERE, LOU.
RIGHT HERE.
LOU.
MISTER HOLT.

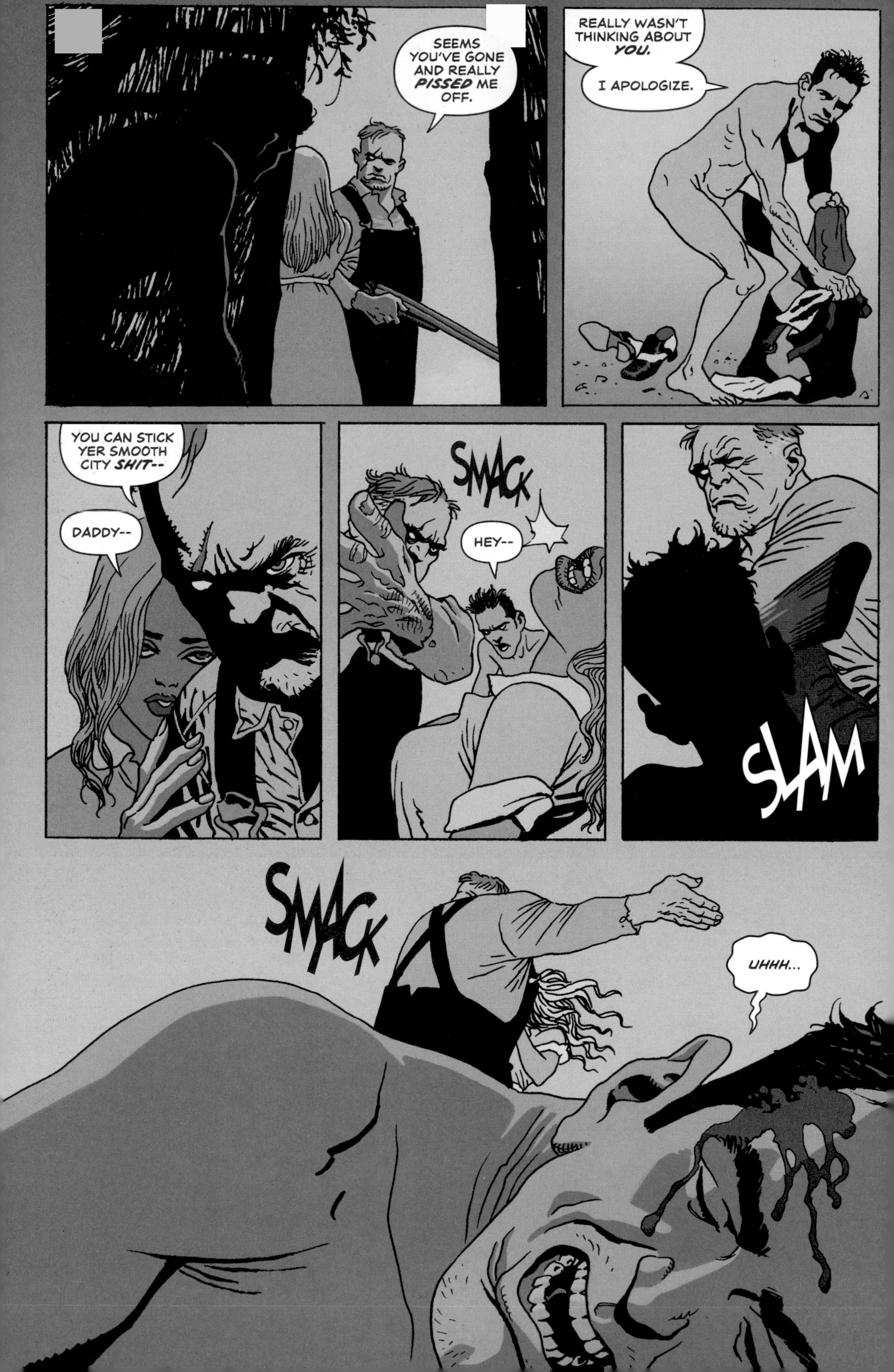
SEEMS YOU'VE GONE AND REALLY PISSED ME OFF.
REALLY WASN'T THINKING ABOUT YOU.
I APOLOGIZE.
YOU CAN STICK YER SMOOTH CITY SHIT--
DADDY--
SMACK
HEY--
SLAM
SMACK
UHHH...

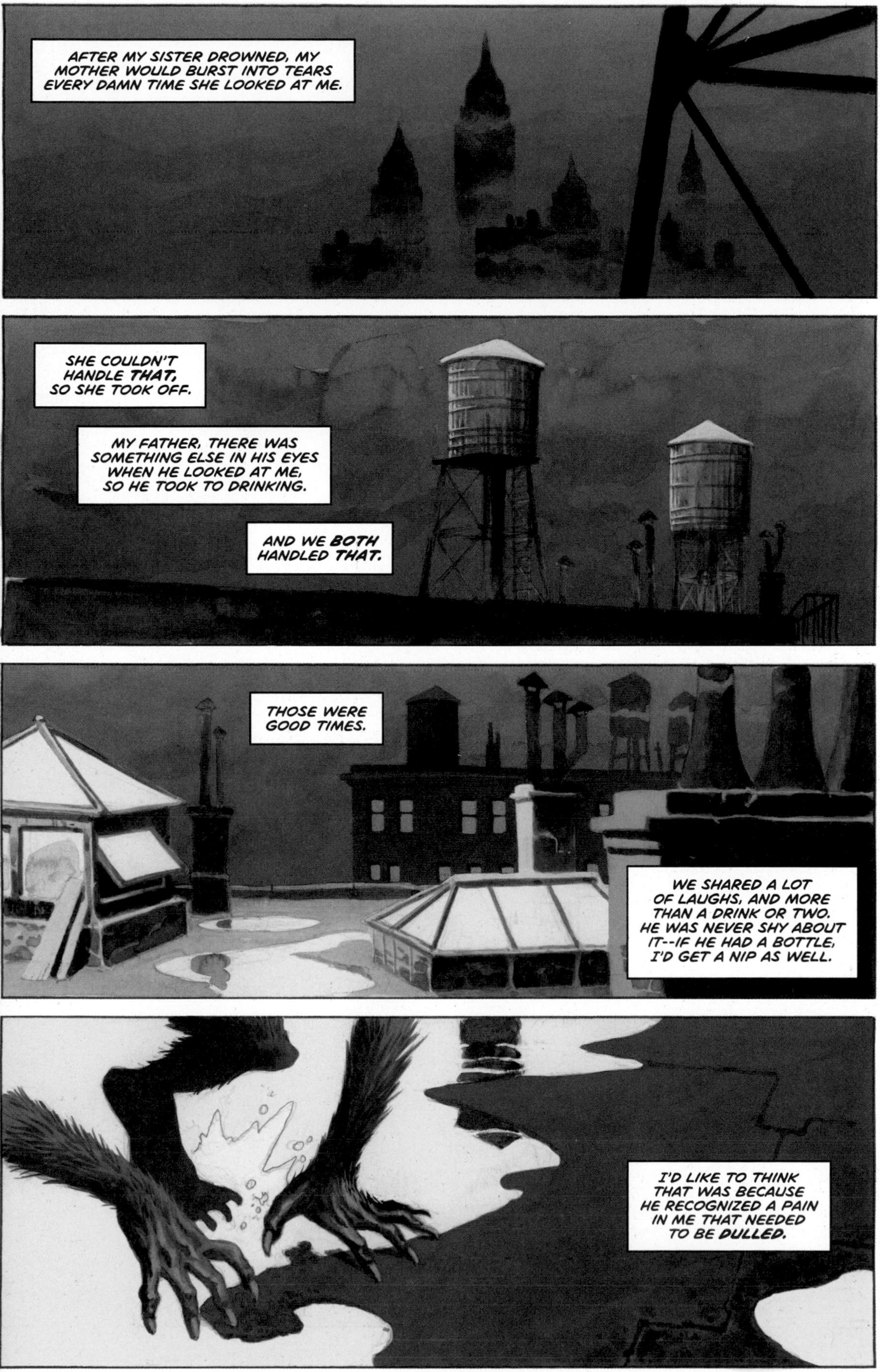
AFTER MY SISTER DROWNED, MY MOTHER WOULD BURST INTO TEARS EVERY DAMN TIME SHE LOOKED AT ME.
SHE COULDN'T HANDLE THAT, SO SHE TOOK OFF.
MY FATHER, THERE WAS SOMETHING ELSE IN HIS EYES WHEN HE LOOKED AT ME, SO HE TOOK TO DRINKING.
AND WE BOTH HANDLED THAT.
THOSE WERE GOOD TIMES.
WE SHARED A LOT OF LAUGHS, AND MORE THAN A DRINK OR TWO. HE WAS NEVER SHY ABOUT IT--IF HE HAD A BOTTLE, I'D GET A NIP AS WELL.
I'D LIKE TO THINK THAT WAS BECAUSE HE RECOGNIZED A PAIN IN ME THAT NEEDED TO BE DULLED.

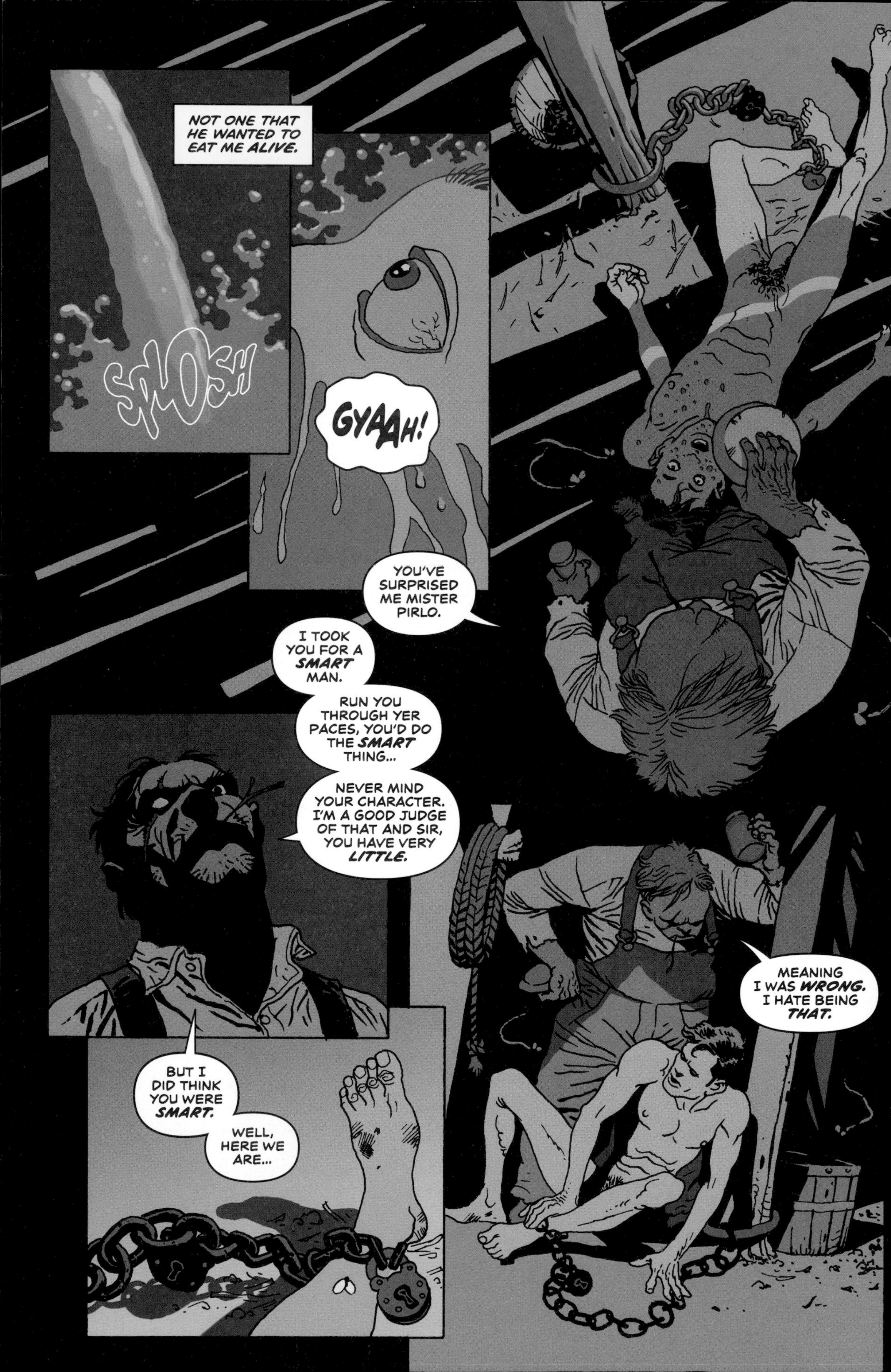

NOT ONE THAT HE WANTED TO EAT ME ALIVE.
SPLOSH
GYAAAH!
YOU'VE SURPRISED ME MISTER PIRLO.
I TOOK YOU FOR A SMART MAN.
RUN YOU THROUGH YER PACES, YOU'D DO THE SMART THING...
NEVER MIND YOUR CHARACTER. I'M A GOOD JUDGE OF THAT AND SIR, YOU HAVE VERY LITTLE.
MEANING I WAS WRONG. I HATE BEING THAT.
BUT I DID THINK YOU WERE SMART.
WELL, HERE WE ARE...

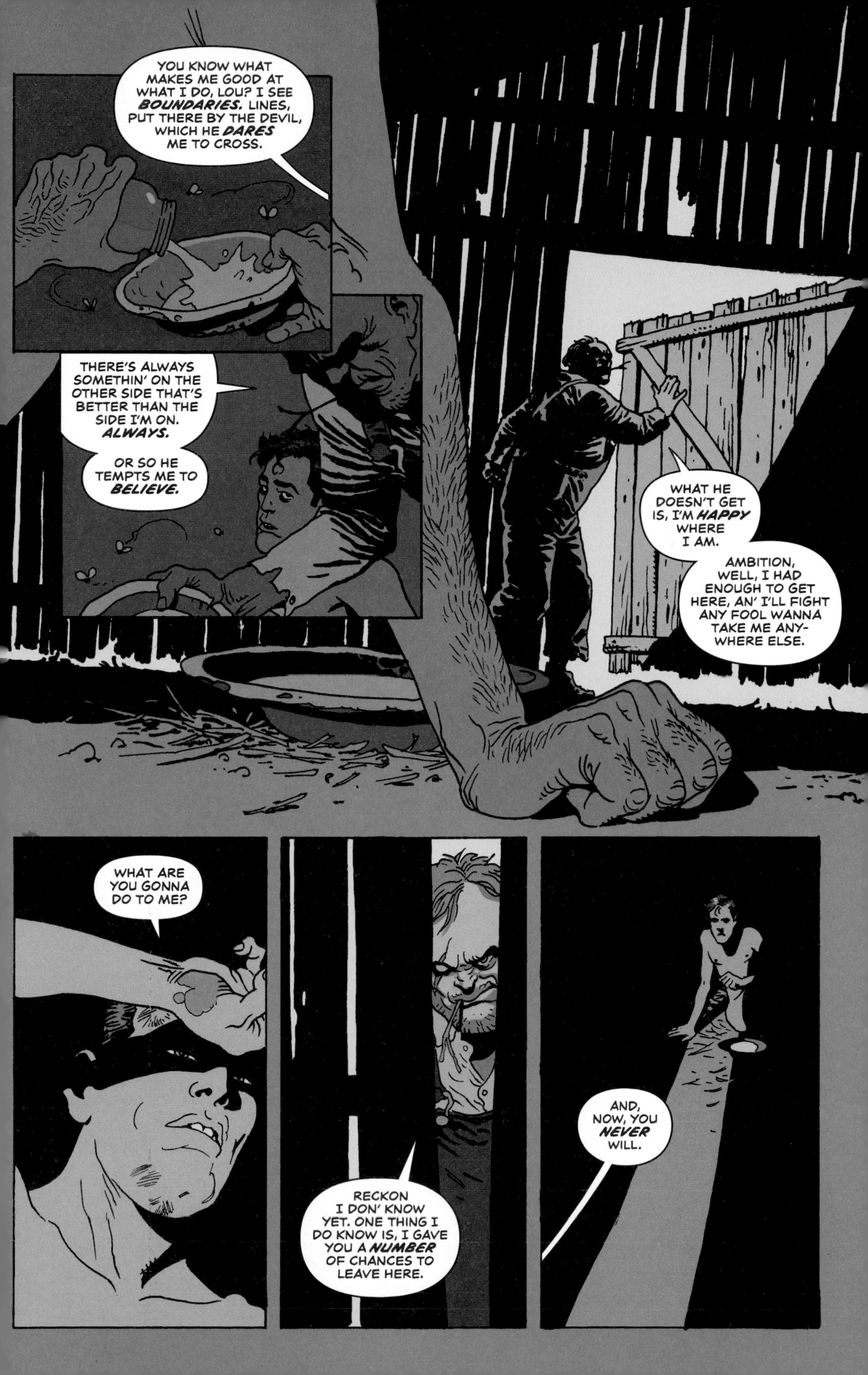
YOU KNOW WHAT MAKES ME GOOD AT WHAT I DO, LOU? I SEE BOUNDARIES. LINES, PUT THERE BY THE DEVIL, WHICH HE DARES ME TO CROSS.
THERE'S ALWAYS SOMETHIN' ON THE OTHER SIDE THAT'S BETTER THAN THE SIDE I'M ON. ALWAYS.
OR SO HE TEMPTS ME TO BELIEVE.
WHAT HE DOESN'T GET IS, I'M HAPPY WHERE I AM.
AMBITION, WELL, I HAD ENOUGH TO GET HERE, AN' I'LL FIGHT ANY FOOL WANNA TAKE ME ANY-WHERE ELSE.
WHAT ARE YOU GONNA DO TO ME?
RECKON I DON' KNOW YET. ONE THING I DO KNOW IS, I GAVE YOU A NUMBER OF CHANCES TO LEAVE HERE.
AND, NOW, YOU NEVER WILL.

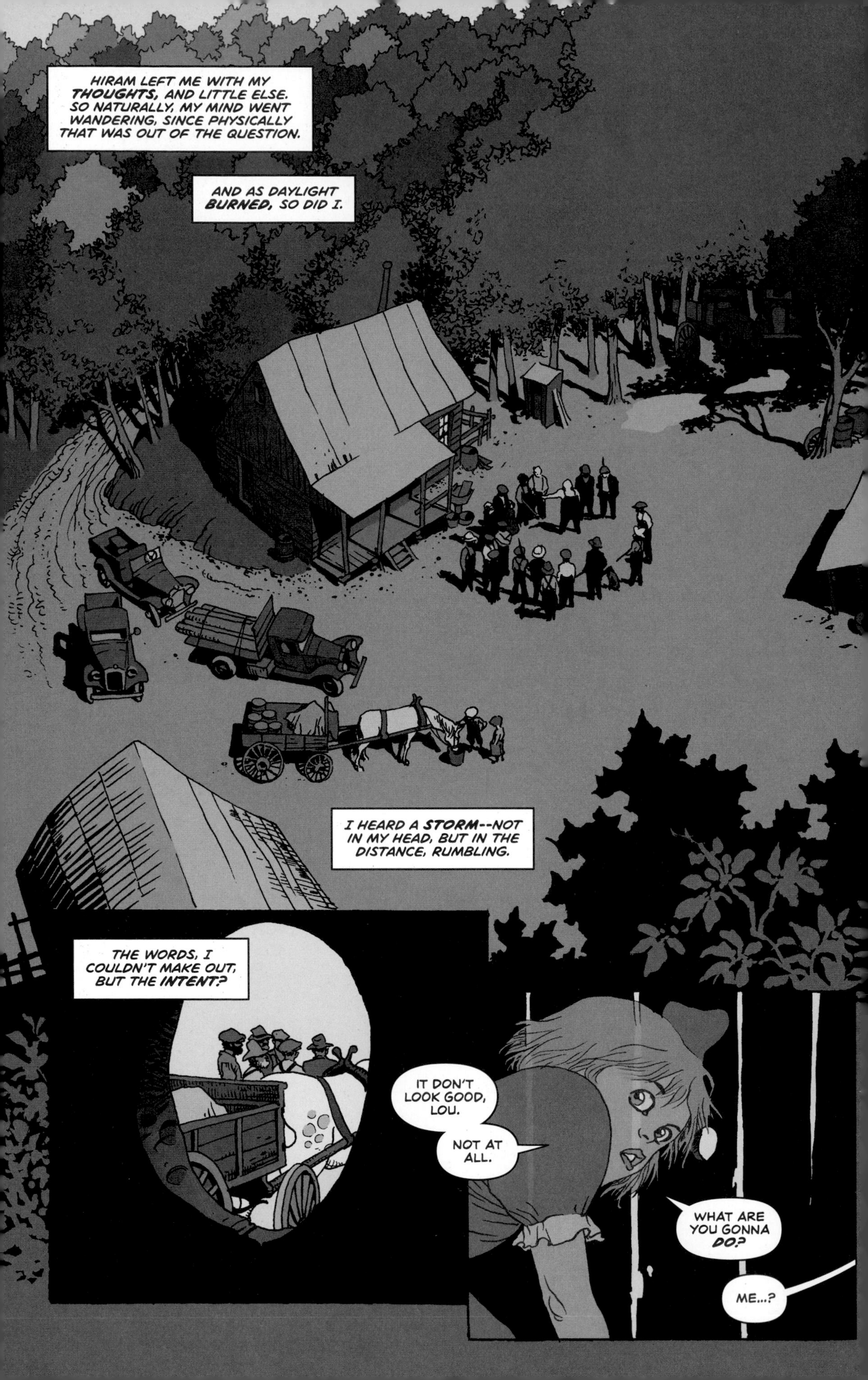
HIRAM LEFT ME WITH MY THOUGHTS, AND LITTLE ELSE. SO NATURALLY, MY MIND WENT WANDERING, SINCE PHYSICALLY THAT WAS OUT OF THE QUESTION.
AND AS DAYLIGHT BURNED, SO DID I.
I HEARD A STORM--NOT IN MY HEAD, BUT IN THE DISTANCE, RUMBLING.
THE WORDS, I COULDN'T MAKE OUT, BUT THE INTENT?
IT DON'T LOOK GOOD, LOU.
NOT AT ALL.
WHAT ARE YOU GONNA DO?
ME...?

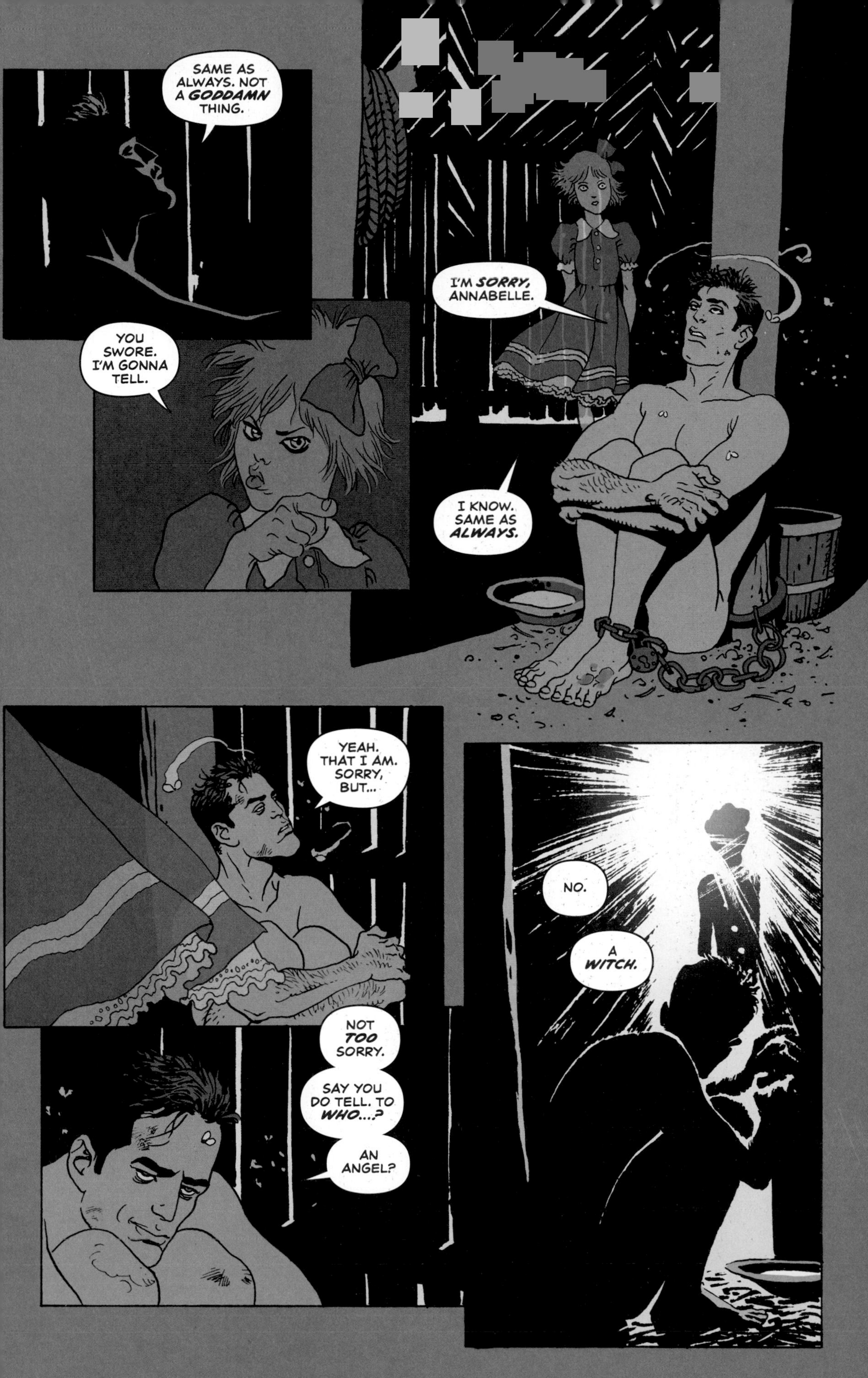
SAME AS ALWAYS. NOT A *GODDAMN* THING.
YOU SWORE. I'M GONNA TELL.
I'M *SORRY,* ANNABELLE.
I KNOW. SAME AS *ALWAYS.*
YEAH. THAT I AM. SORRY, BUT...
NOT *TOO* SORRY.
SAY YOU DO TELL. TO *WHO...?*
AN ANGEL?
NO.
A *WITCH.*

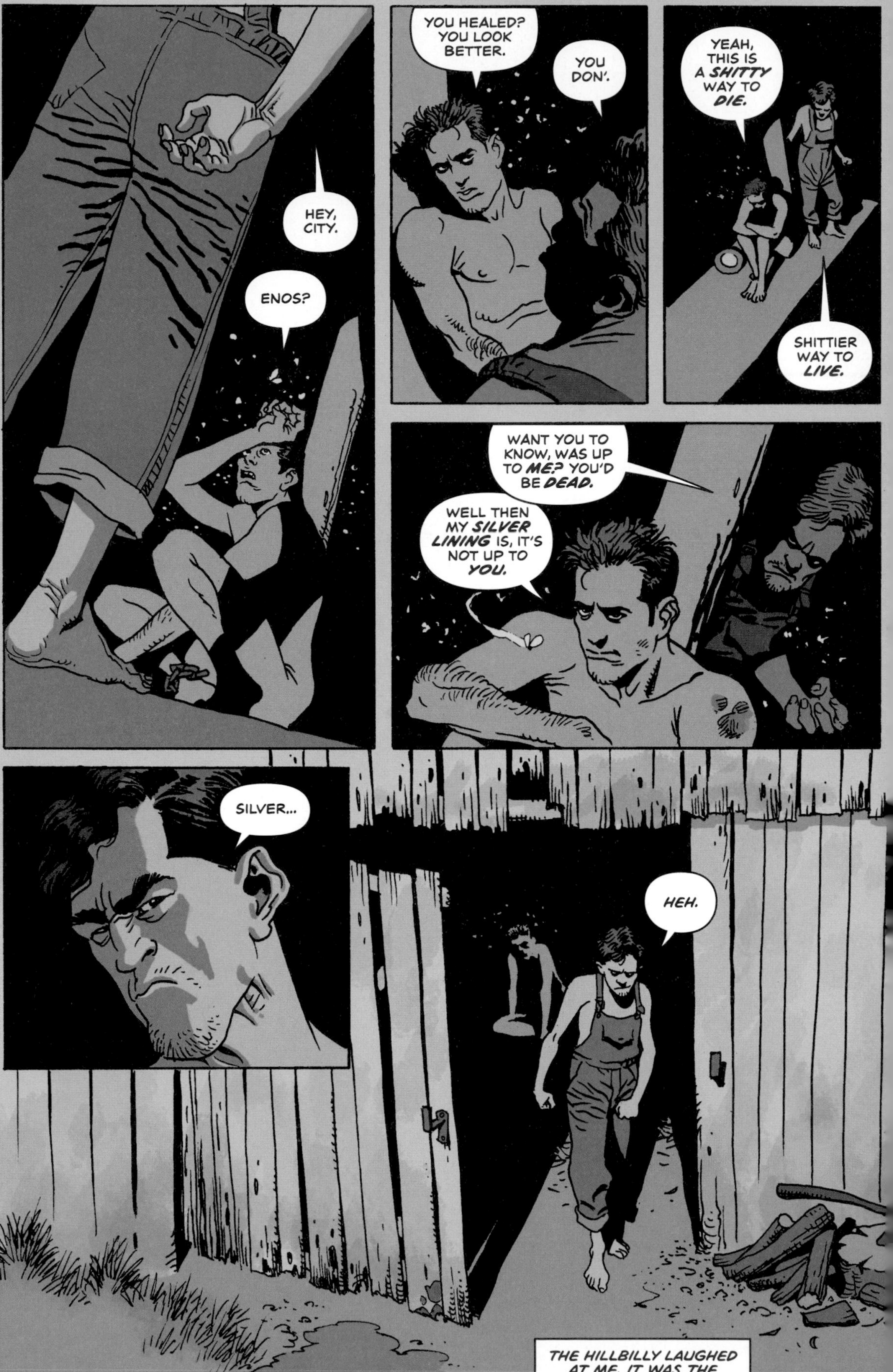
HEY, CITY.
ENOS?
YOU HEALED? YOU LOOK BETTER.
YOU DON'.
YEAH, THIS IS A SHITTY WAY TO DIE.
SHITTIER WAY TO LIVE.
WANT YOU TO KNOW, WAS UP TO ME? YOU'D BE DEAD.
WELL THEN MY SILVER LINING IS, IT'S NOT UP TO YOU.
SILVER...
HEH.
THE HILLBILLY LAUGHED AT ME. IT WAS THE KINDA LAUGH I HATED.

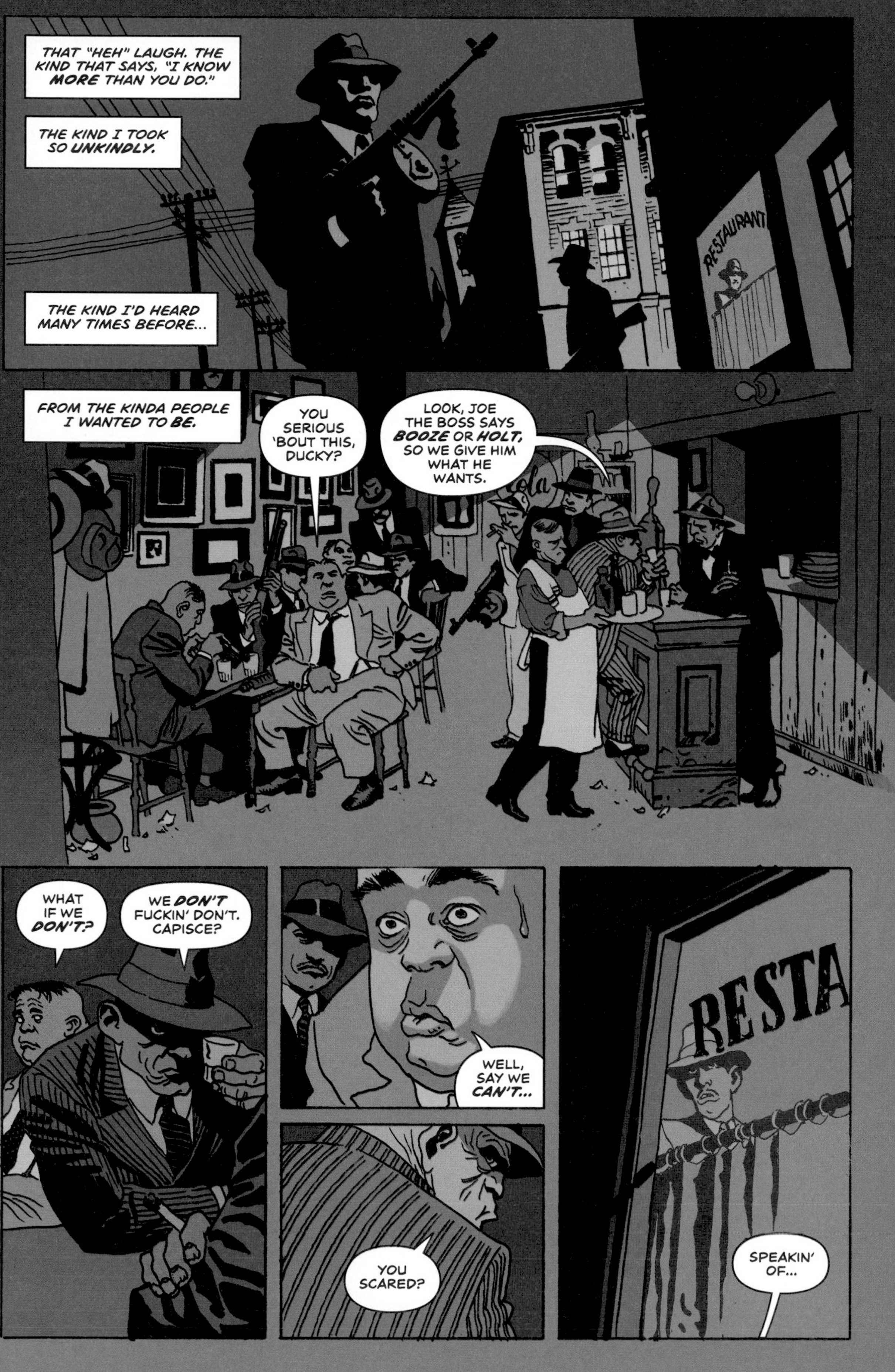
THAT "HEH" LAUGH. THE KIND THAT SAYS, "I KNOW MORE THAN YOU DO."
THE KIND I TOOK SO UNKINDLY.
RESTAURANT
THE KIND I'D HEARD MANY TIMES BEFORE...
FROM THE KINDA PEOPLE I WANTED TO BE.
YOU SERIOUS 'BOUT THIS, DUCKY?
LOOK, JOE THE BOSS SAYS BOOZE OR HOLT, SO WE GIVE HIM WHAT HE WANTS.
WHAT IF WE DON'T?
WE DON'T FUCKIN' DON'T. CAPISCE?
WELL, SAY WE CAN'T...
YOU SCARED?
RESTA
SPEAKIN' OF...

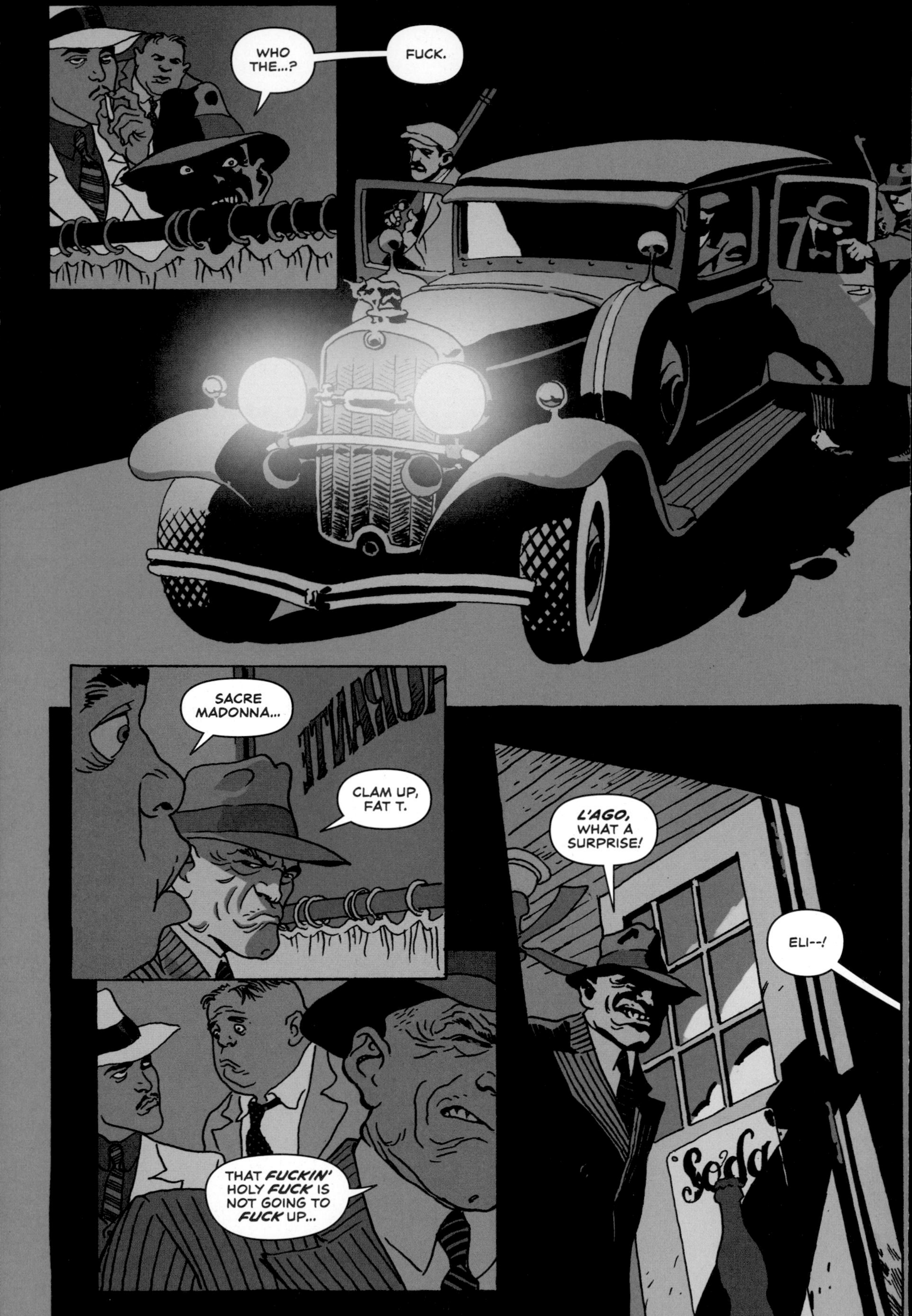
WHO THE...?
FUCK.
SACRE MADONNA...
CLAM UP, FAT T.
THAT FUCKIN' HOLY FUCK IS NOT GOING TO FUCK UP...
L'AGO, WHAT A SURPRISE!
ELI--!

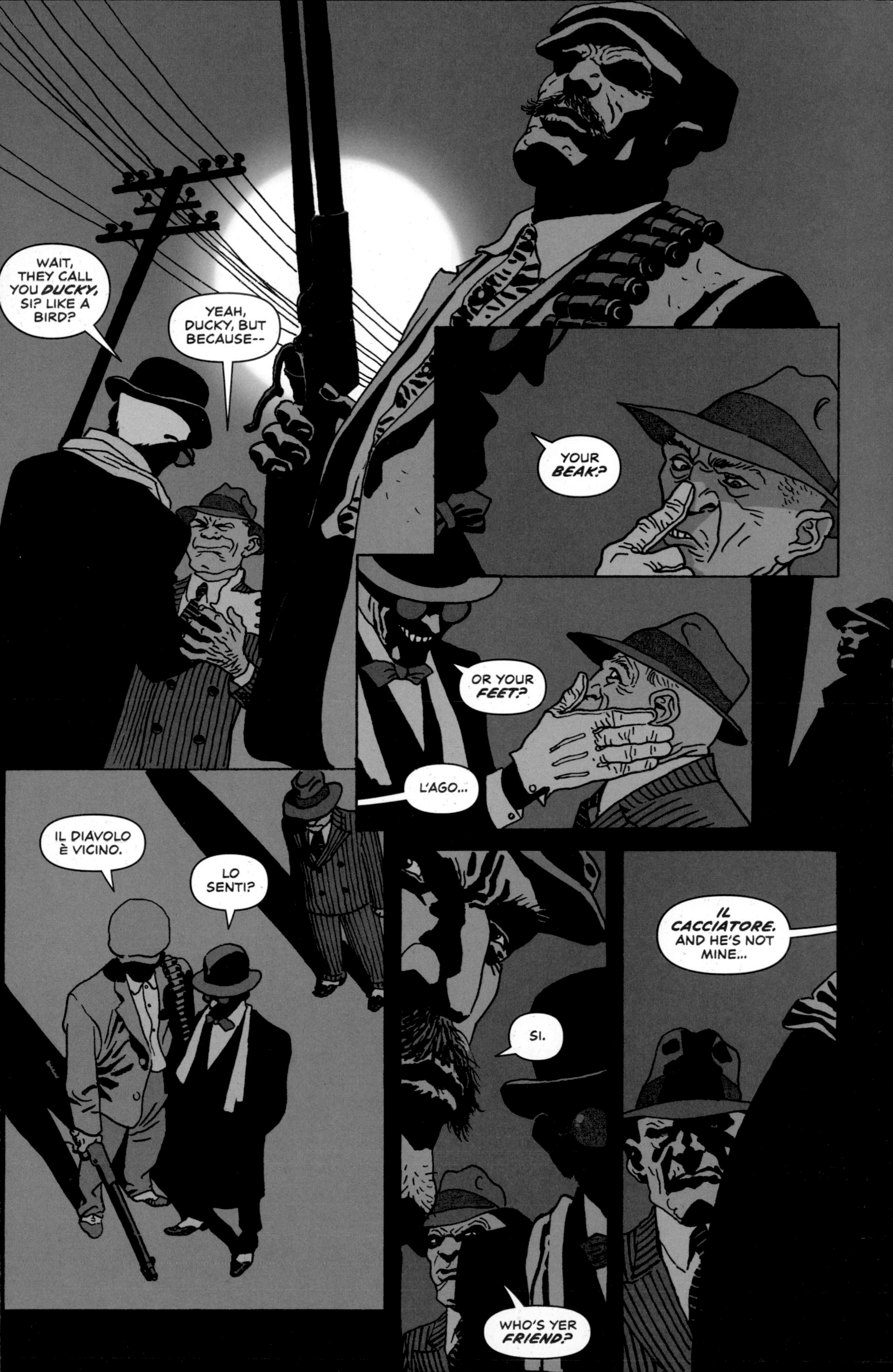
WAIT, THEY CALL YOU *DUCKY,* SI? LIKE A BIRD?
YEAH, DUCKY, BUT BECAUSE--
YOUR *BEAK?*
OR YOUR *FEET?*
L'AGO...
IL DIAVOLO È VICINO.
LO SENTI?
IL CACCIATORE. AND HE'S NOT MINE...
SI.
WHO'S YER *FRIEND?*

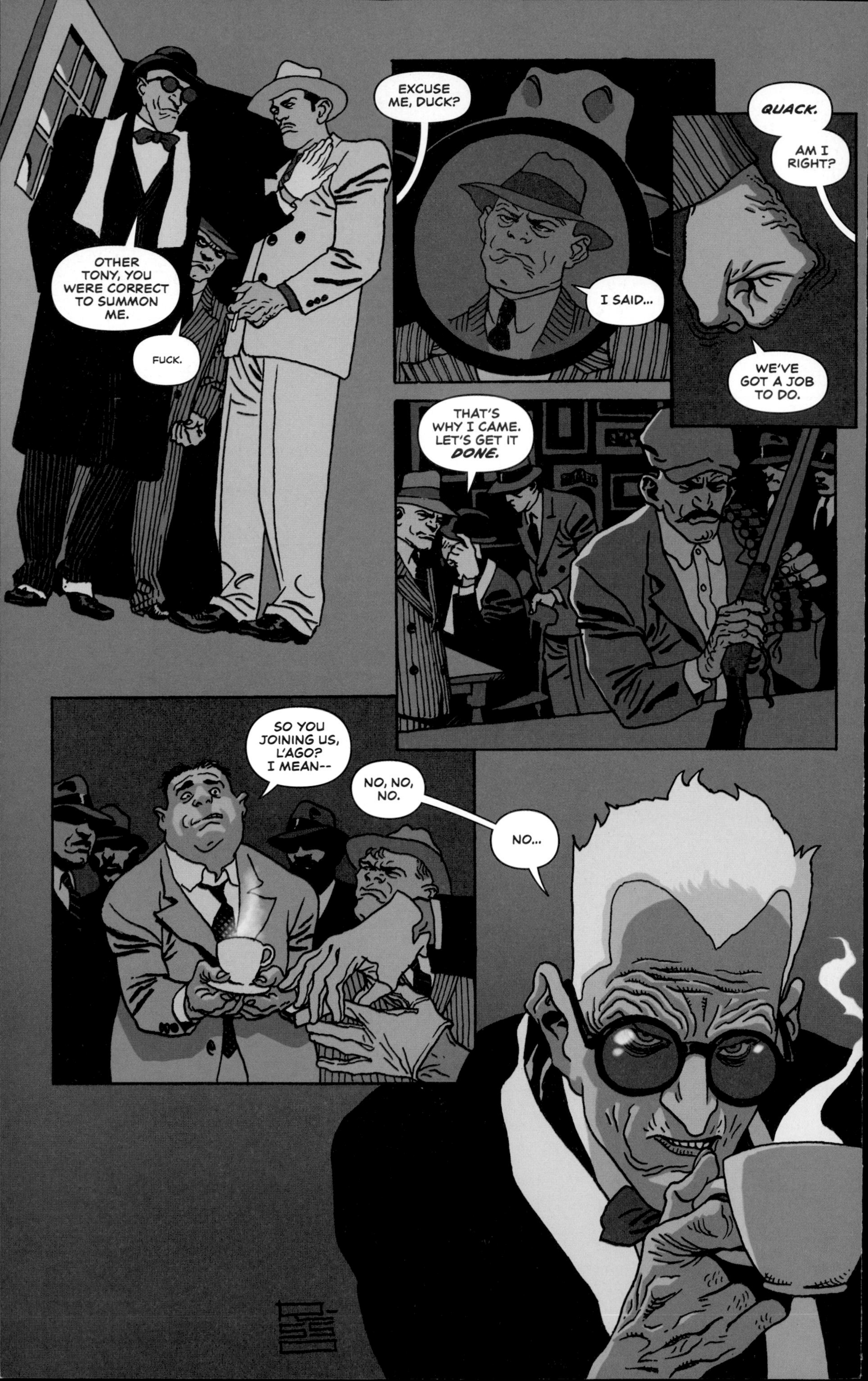
OTHER TONY, YOU WERE CORRECT TO SUMMON ME.
FUCK.
EXCUSE ME, DUCK?
I SAID...
QUACK.
AM I RIGHT?
WE'VE GOT A JOB TO DO.
THAT'S WHY I CAME. LET'S GET IT DONE.
SO YOU JOINING US, L'AGO? I MEAN--
NO, NO, NO.
NO...

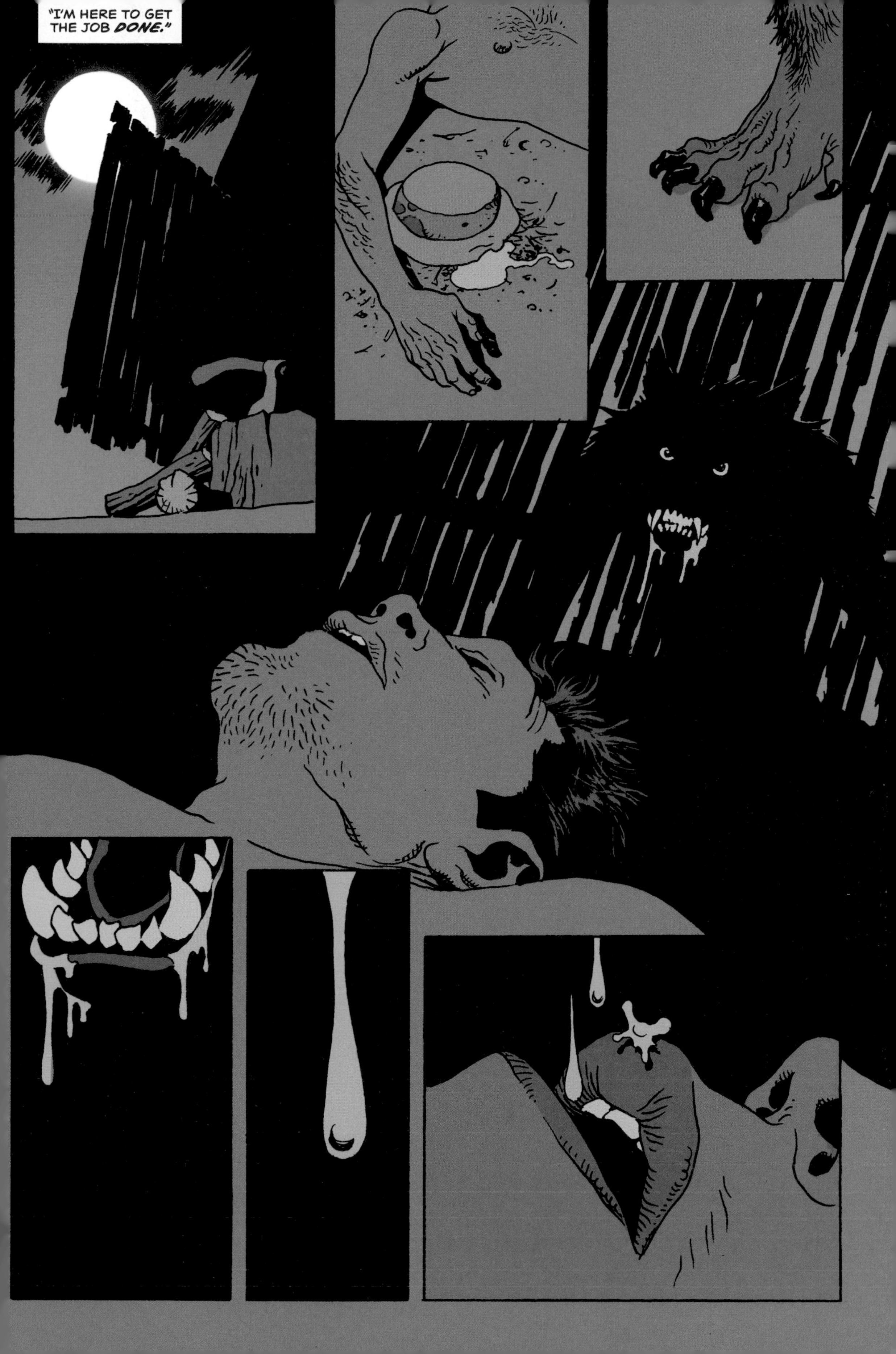
"I'M HERE TO GET THE JOB DONE."

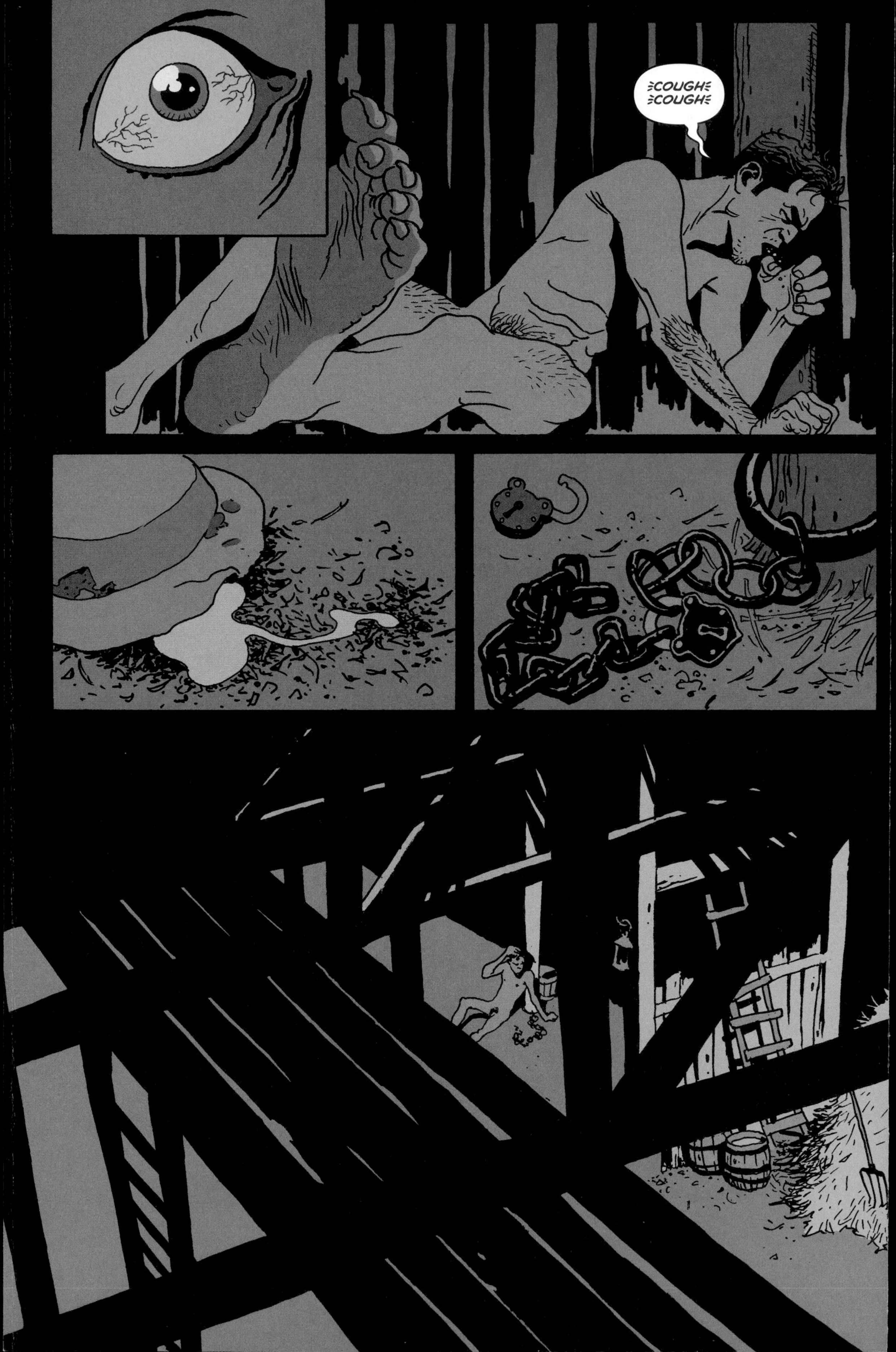
COUGH COUGH

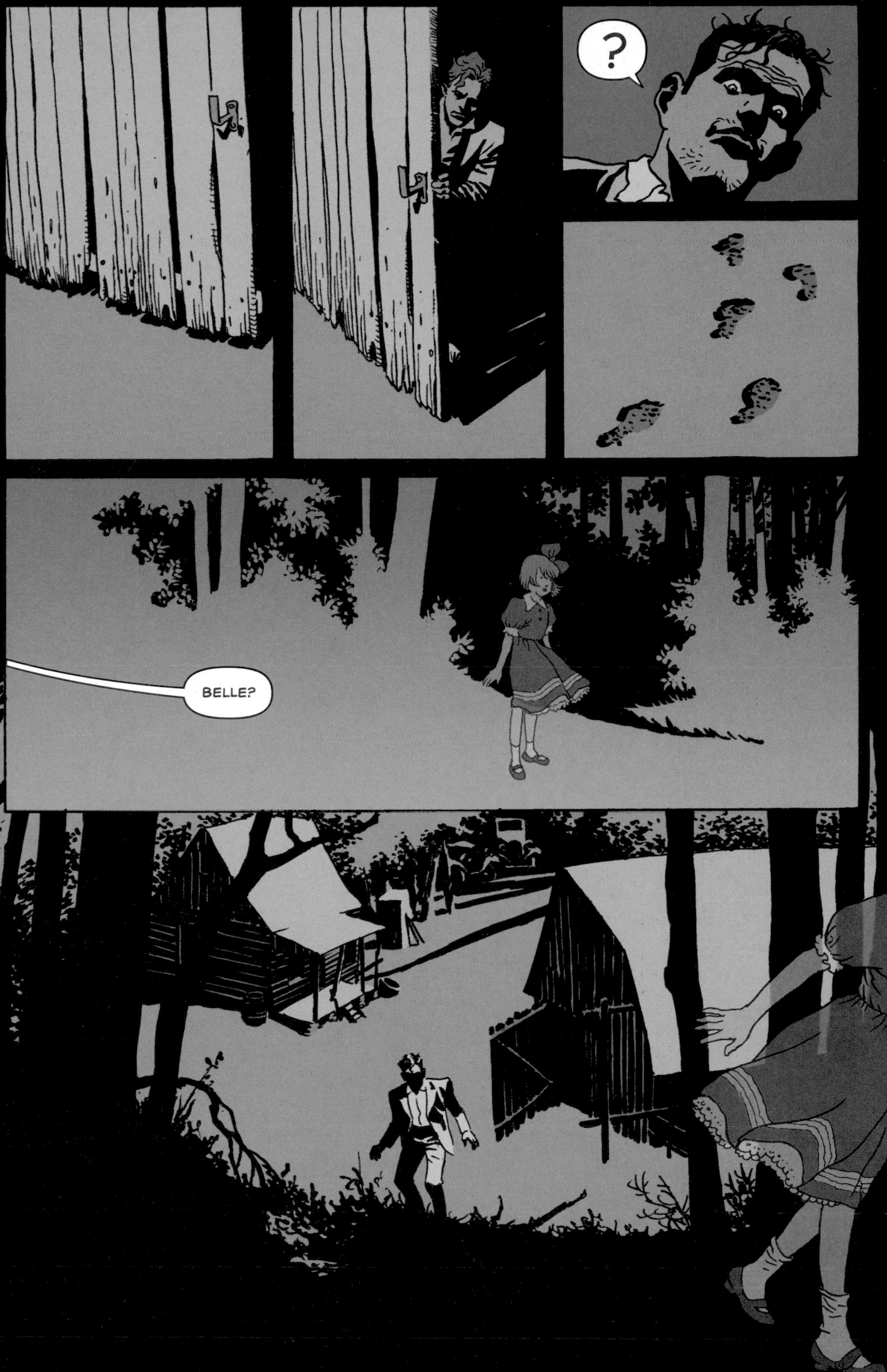
?
BELLE?

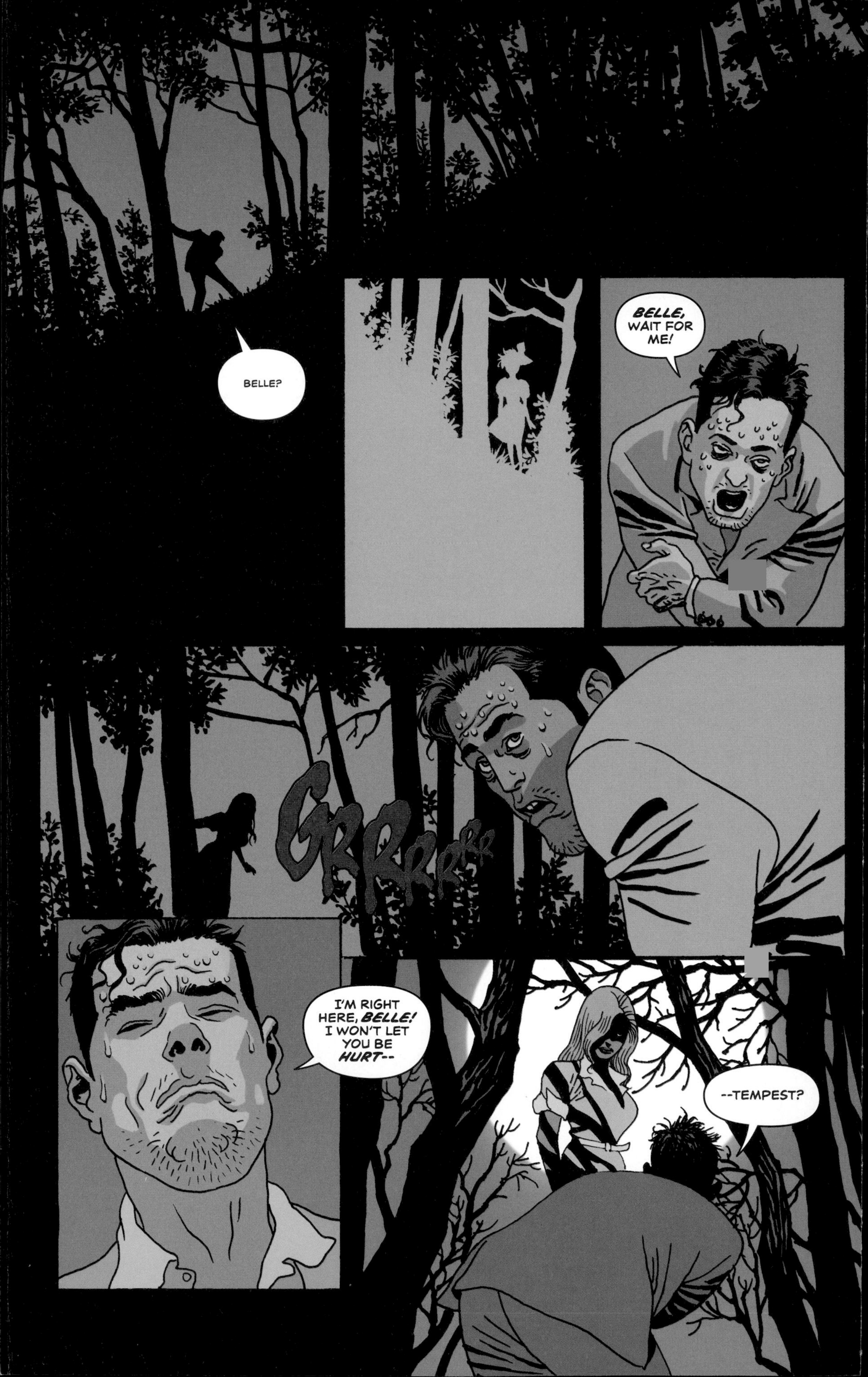
BELLE?
BELLE, WAIT FOR ME!
GRRRRRR
I'M RIGHT HERE, BELLE! I WON'T LET YOU BE HURT--
--TEMPEST?

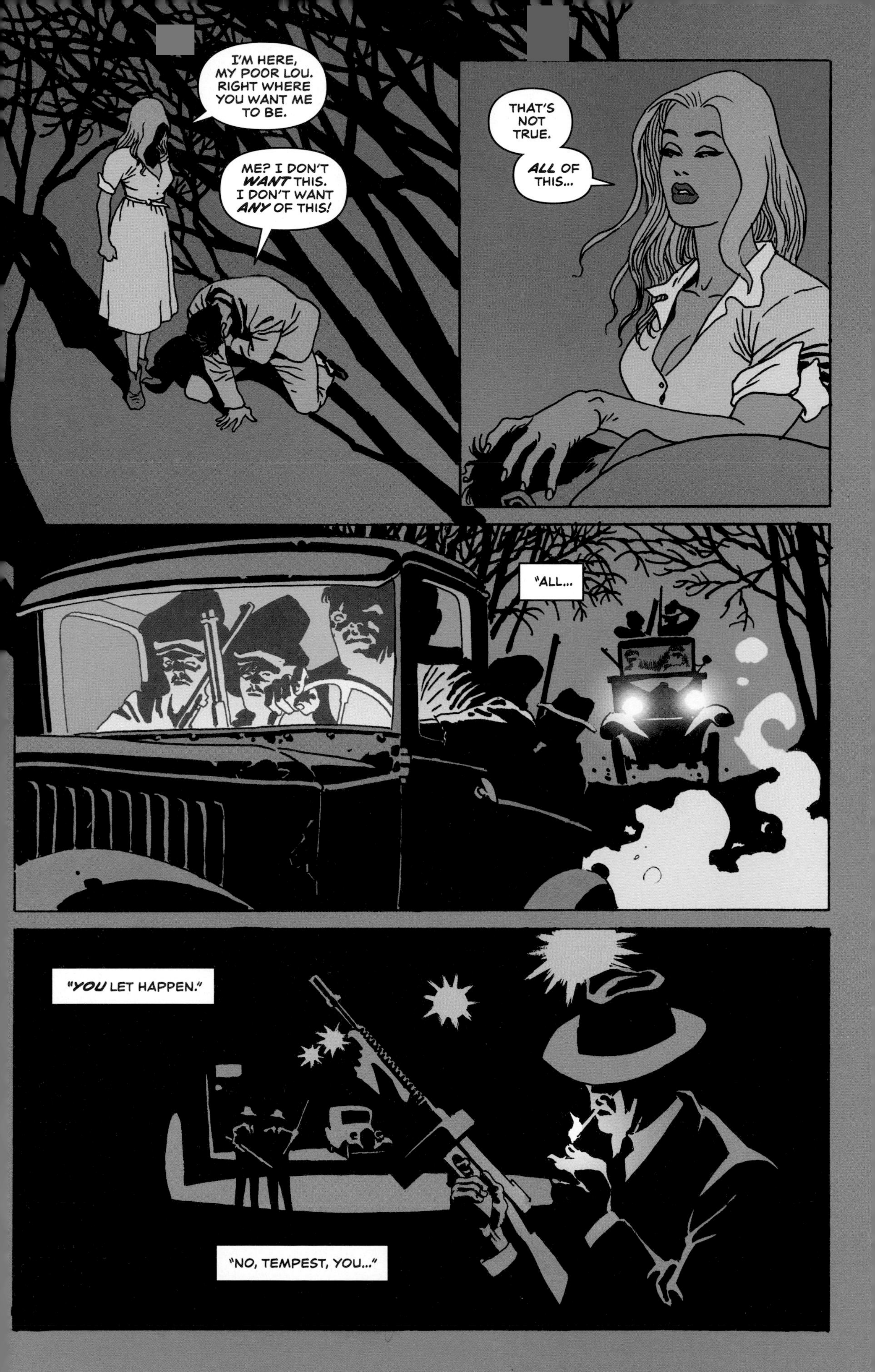
I'M HERE, MY POOR LOU. RIGHT WHERE YOU WANT ME TO BE.
ME? I DON'T WANT THIS. I DON'T WANT ANY OF THIS!
THAT'S NOT TRUE.
ALL OF THIS...
"ALL...
"YOU LET HAPPEN."
"NO, TEMPEST, YOU..."

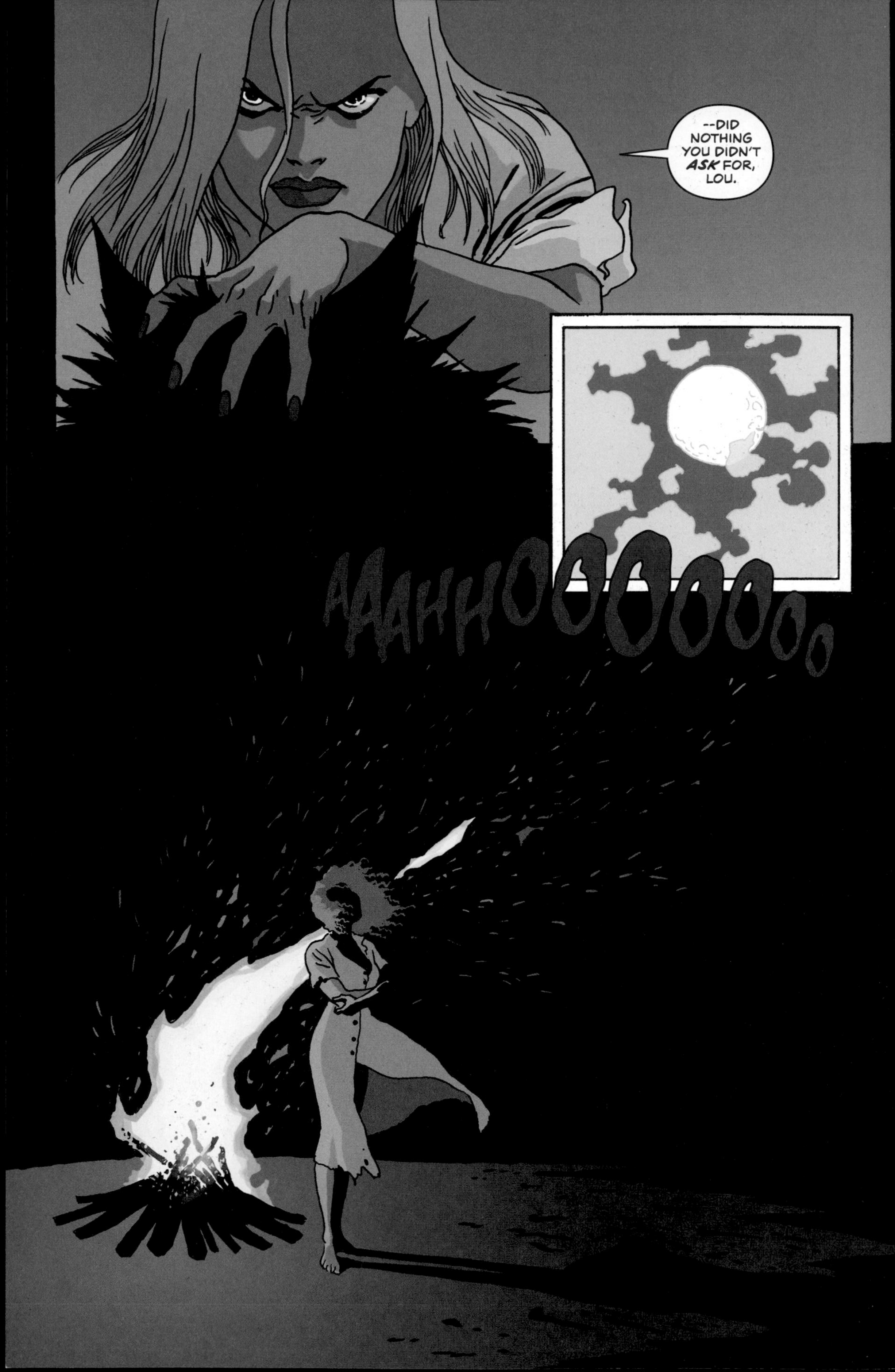
--DID NOTHING YOU DIDN'T ASK FOR, LOU.
AAAHHOOOOOOOo

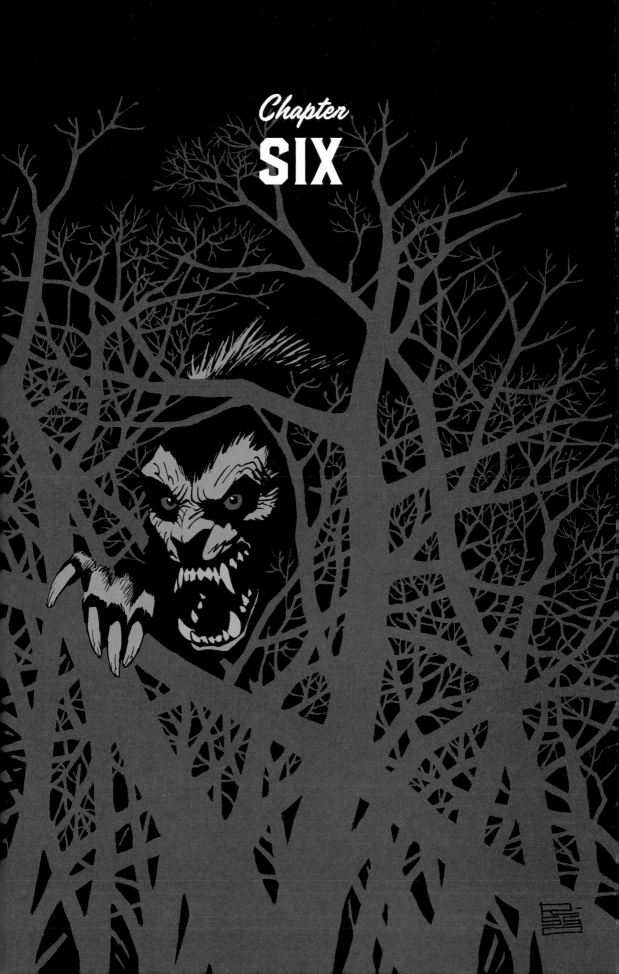

Chapter
SIX

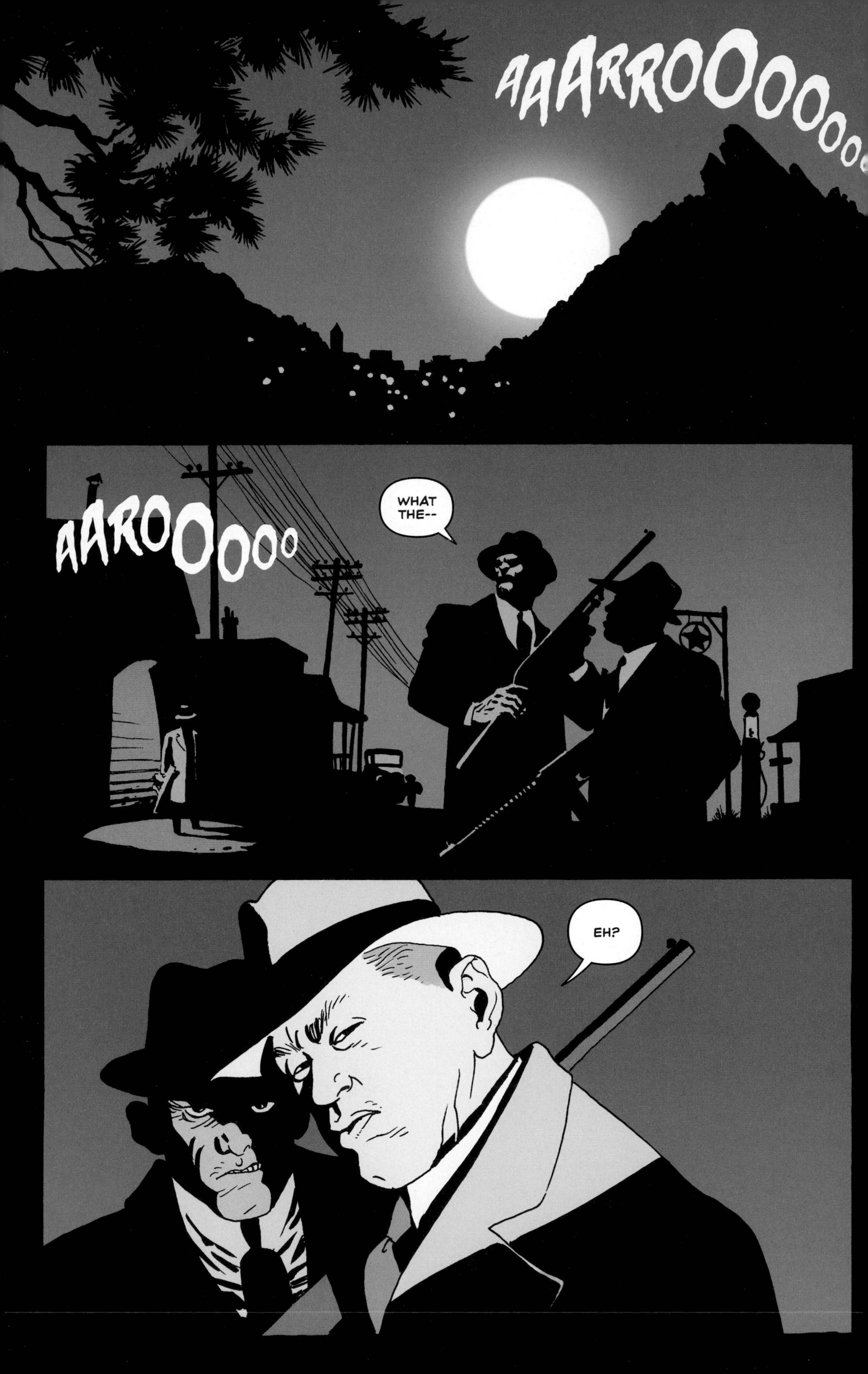
AAARROOOOOO
AAROOOOO
WHAT THE--
EH?

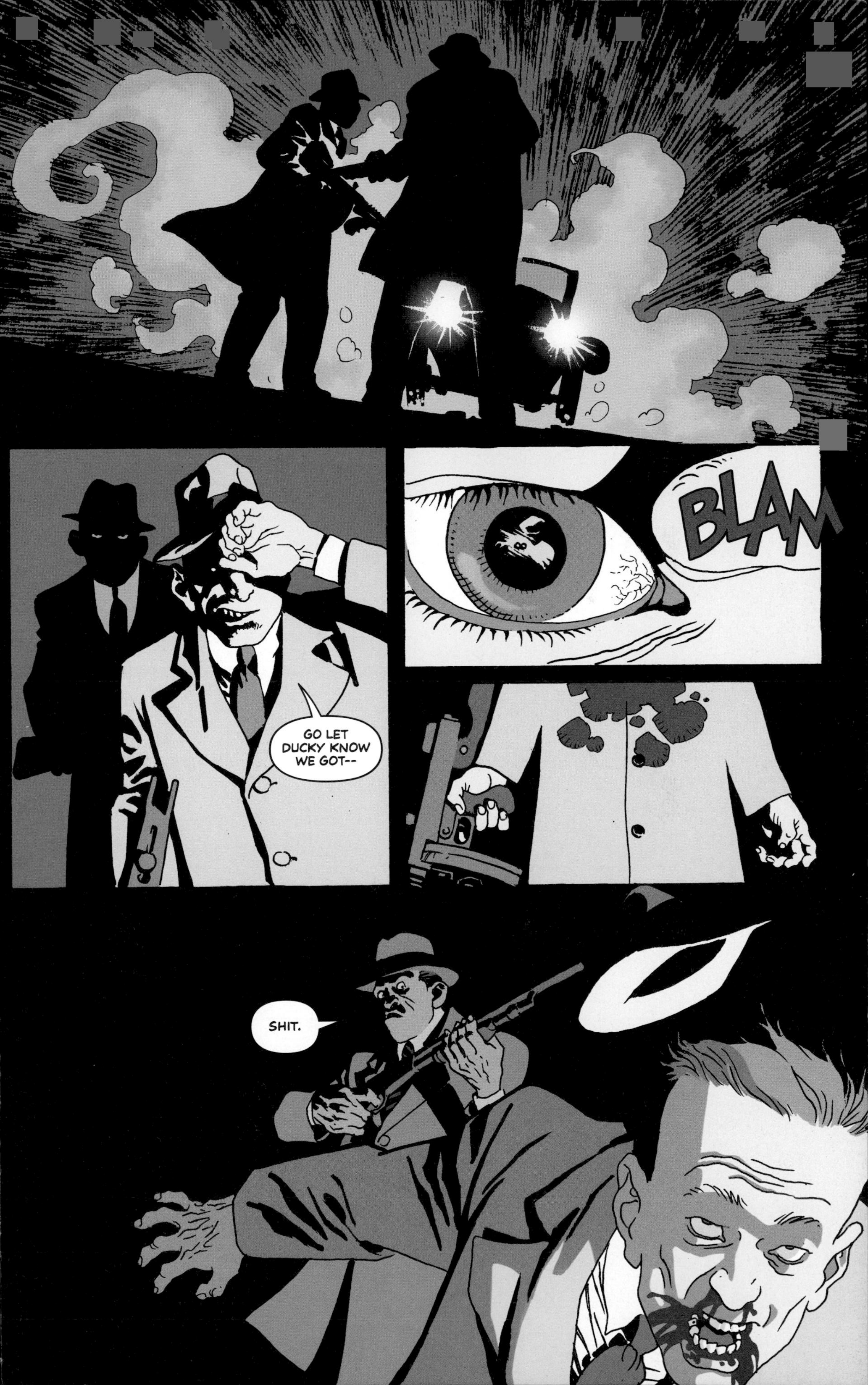

BLAM
GO LET DUCKY KNOW WE GOT--
SHIT.

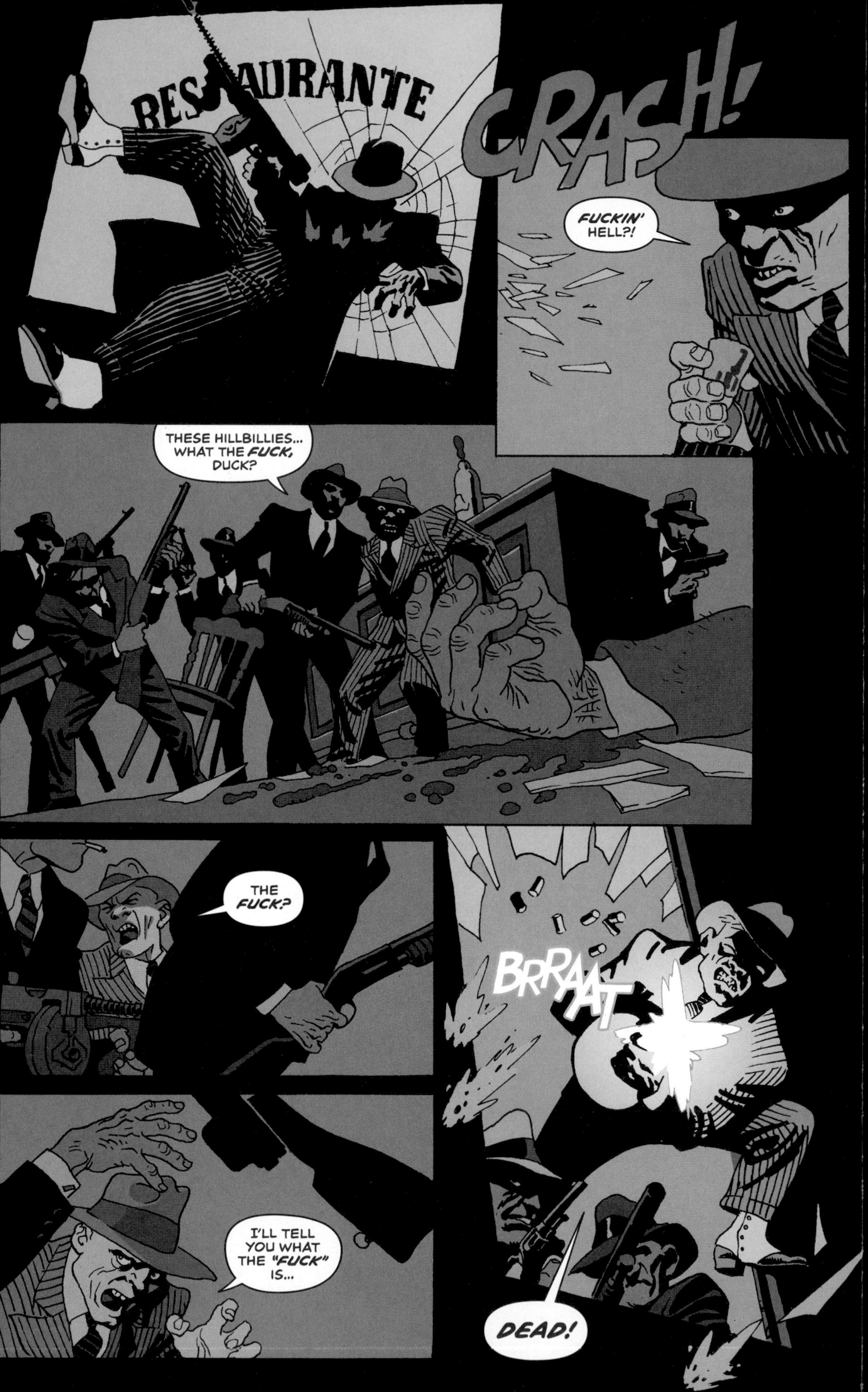
RESTAURANTE
CRASH!
FUCKIN' HELL?!
THESE HILLBILLIES... WHAT THE FUCK, DUCK?
THE FUCK?
BRRAAT
I'LL TELL YOU WHAT THE "FUCK" IS...
DEAD!

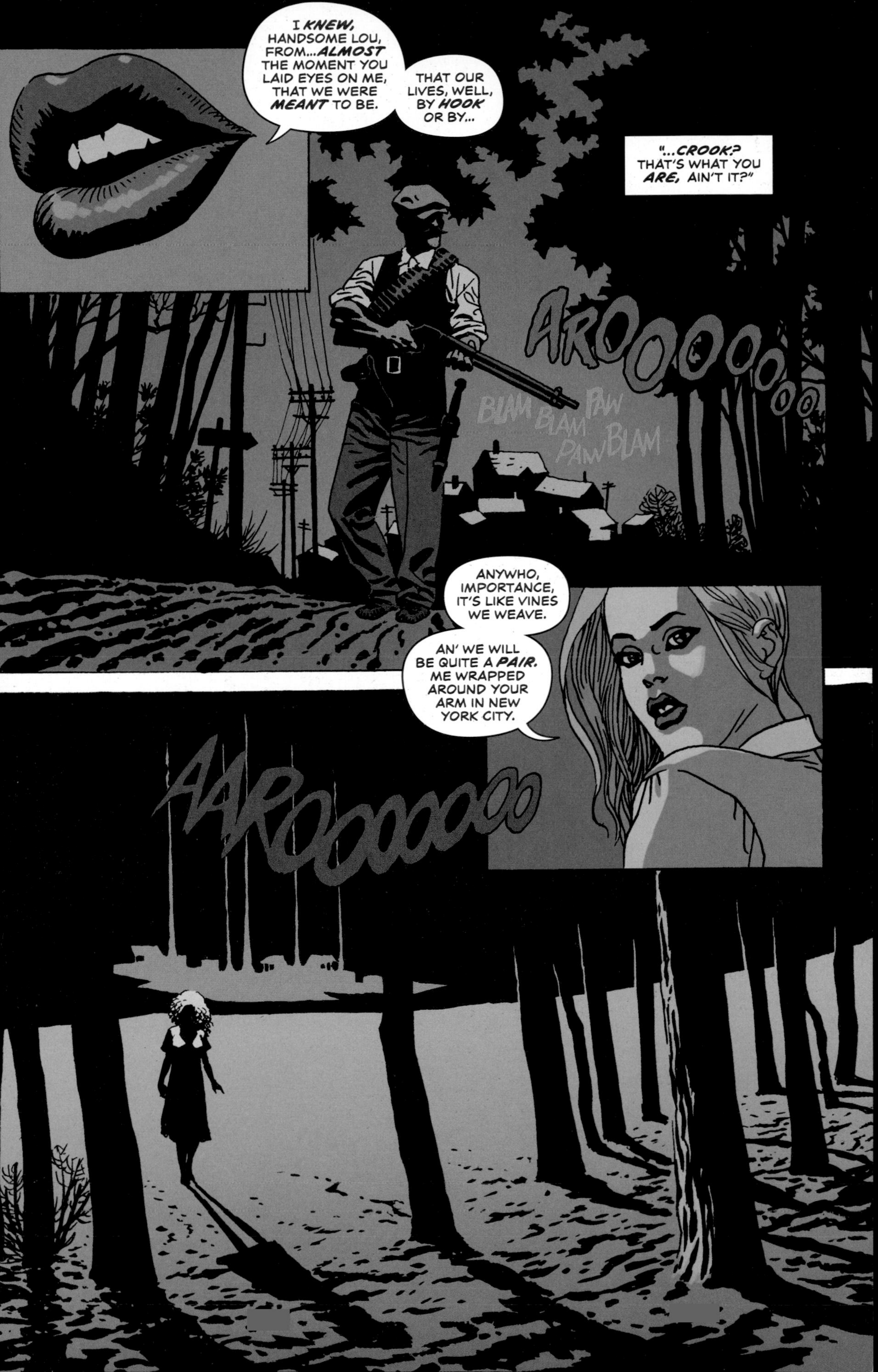
I KNEW, HANDSOME LOU, FROM...ALMOST THE MOMENT YOU LAID EYES ON ME, THAT WE WERE MEANT TO BE.
THAT OUR LIVES, WELL, BY HOOK OR BY...
"...CROOK? THAT'S WHAT YOU ARE, AIN'T IT?"
AROOOOOOOO
BLAM BLAM PAW PAW BLAM
ANYWHO, IMPORTANCE, IT'S LIKE VINES WE WEAVE.
AN' WE WILL BE QUITE A PAIR. ME WRAPPED AROUND YOUR ARM IN NEW YORK CITY.
AAROOOOOOO

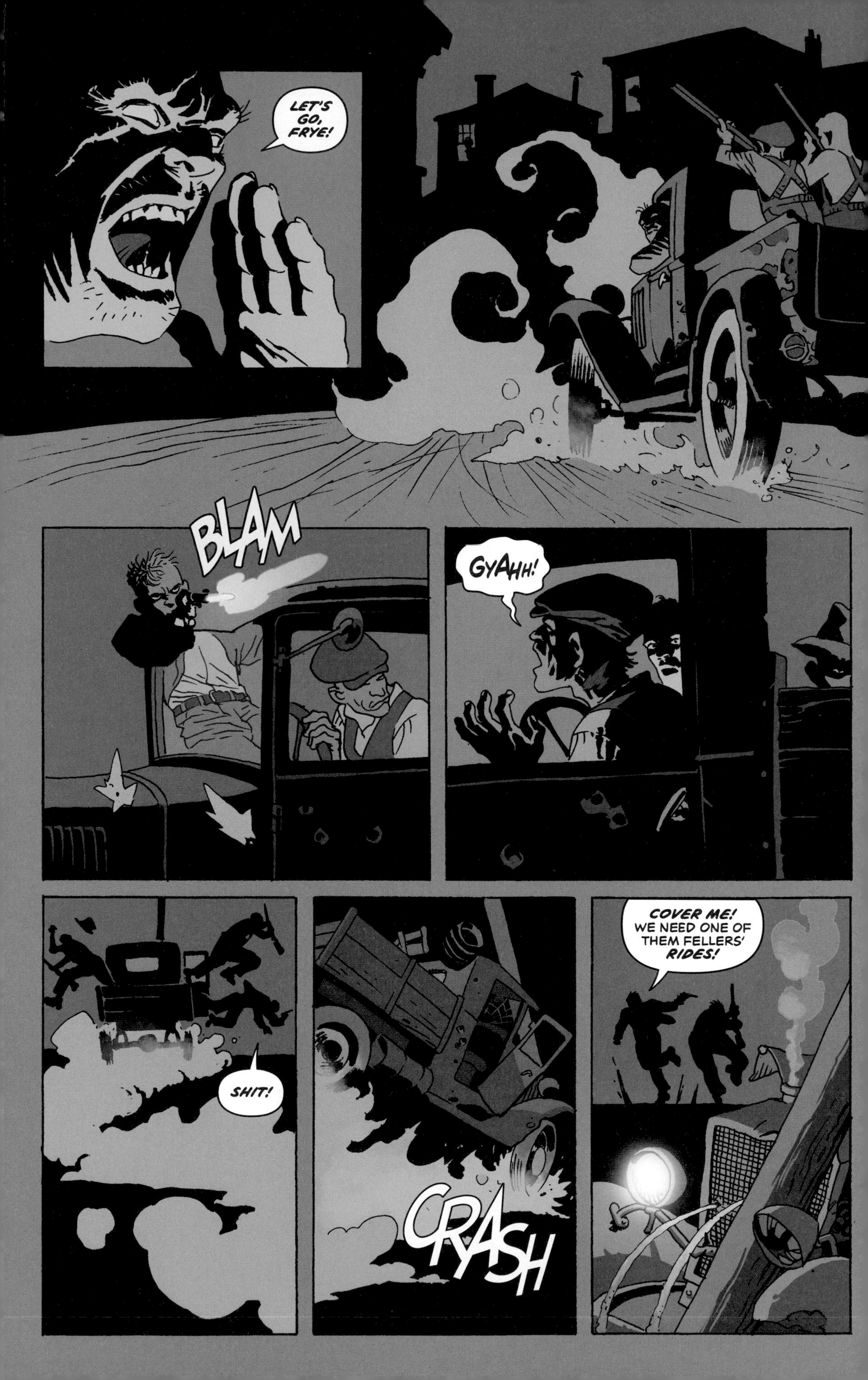
LET'S GO, FRYE!
BLAM
GYAHH!
SHIT!
CRASH
COVER ME! WE NEED ONE OF THEM FELLERS' RIDES!

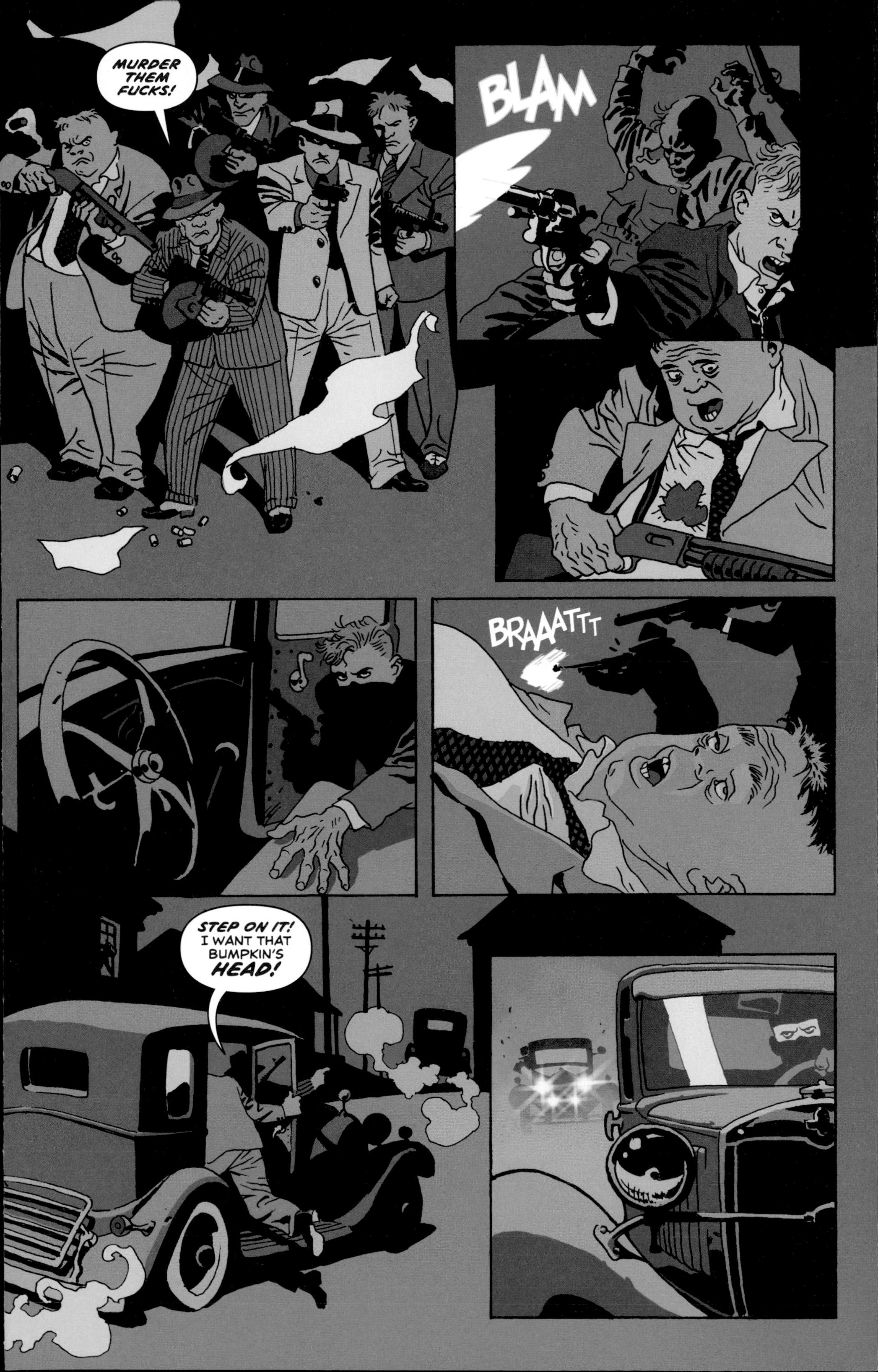
MURDER THEM FUCKS!
BLAM
BRAAATTT
STEP ON IT! I WANT THAT BUMPKIN'S HEAD!

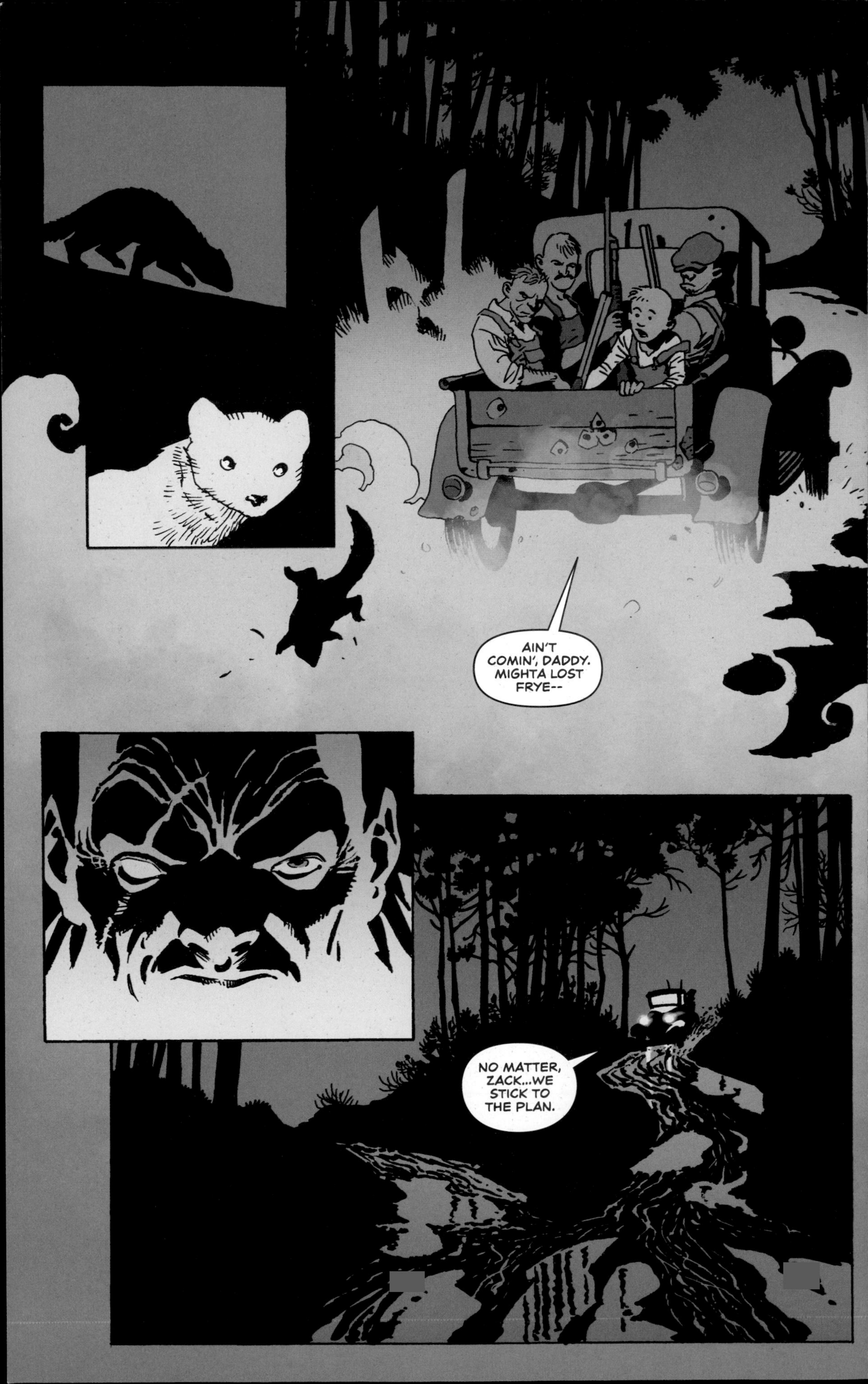
AIN'T COMIN', DADDY. MIGHTA LOST FRYE--
NO MATTER, ZACK...WE STICK TO THE PLAN.

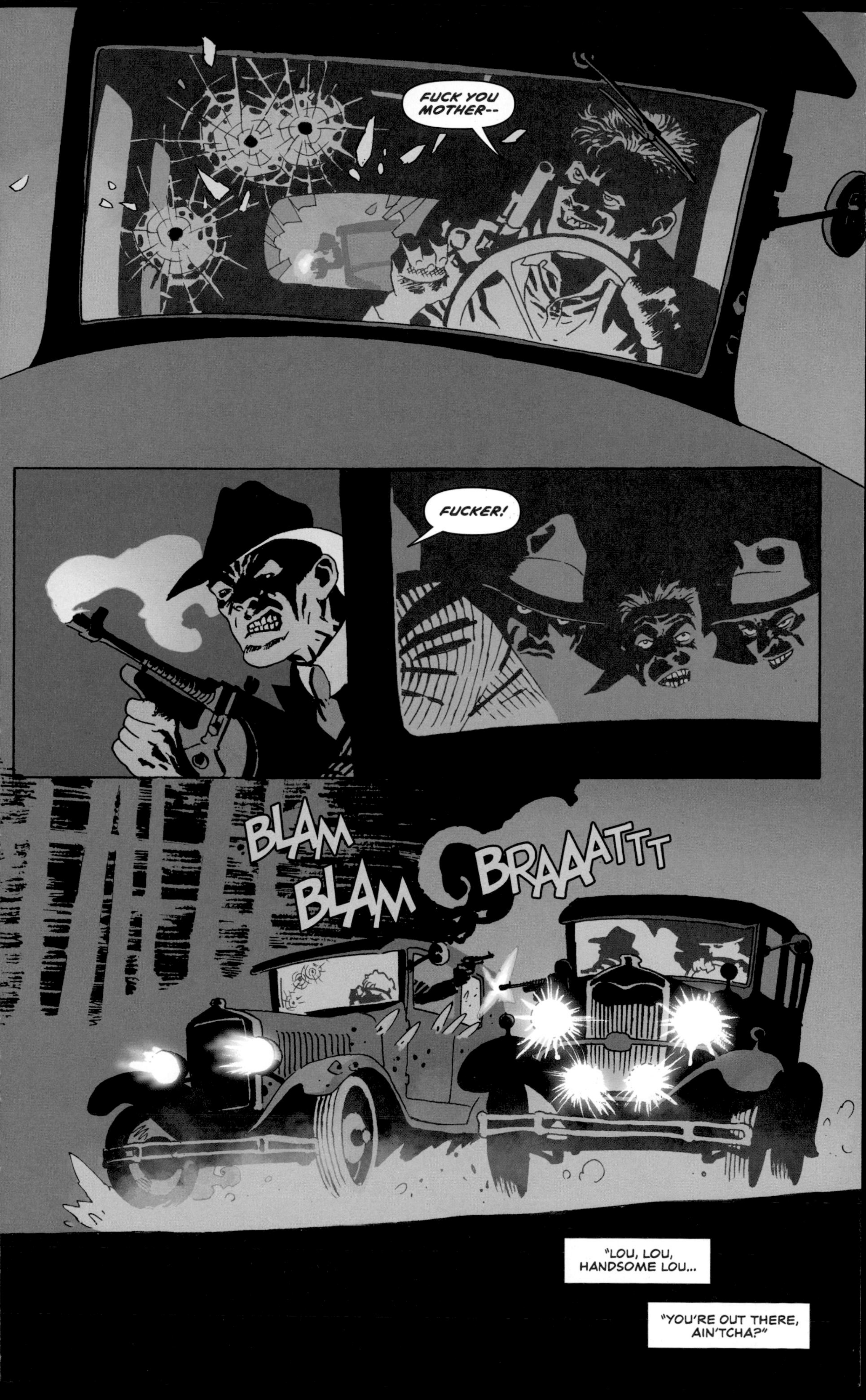
FUCK YOU MOTHER--
FUCKER!
BLAM
BLAM
BRAAATTT
"LOU, LOU, HANDSOME LOU...
"YOU'RE OUT THERE, AIN'TCHA?"

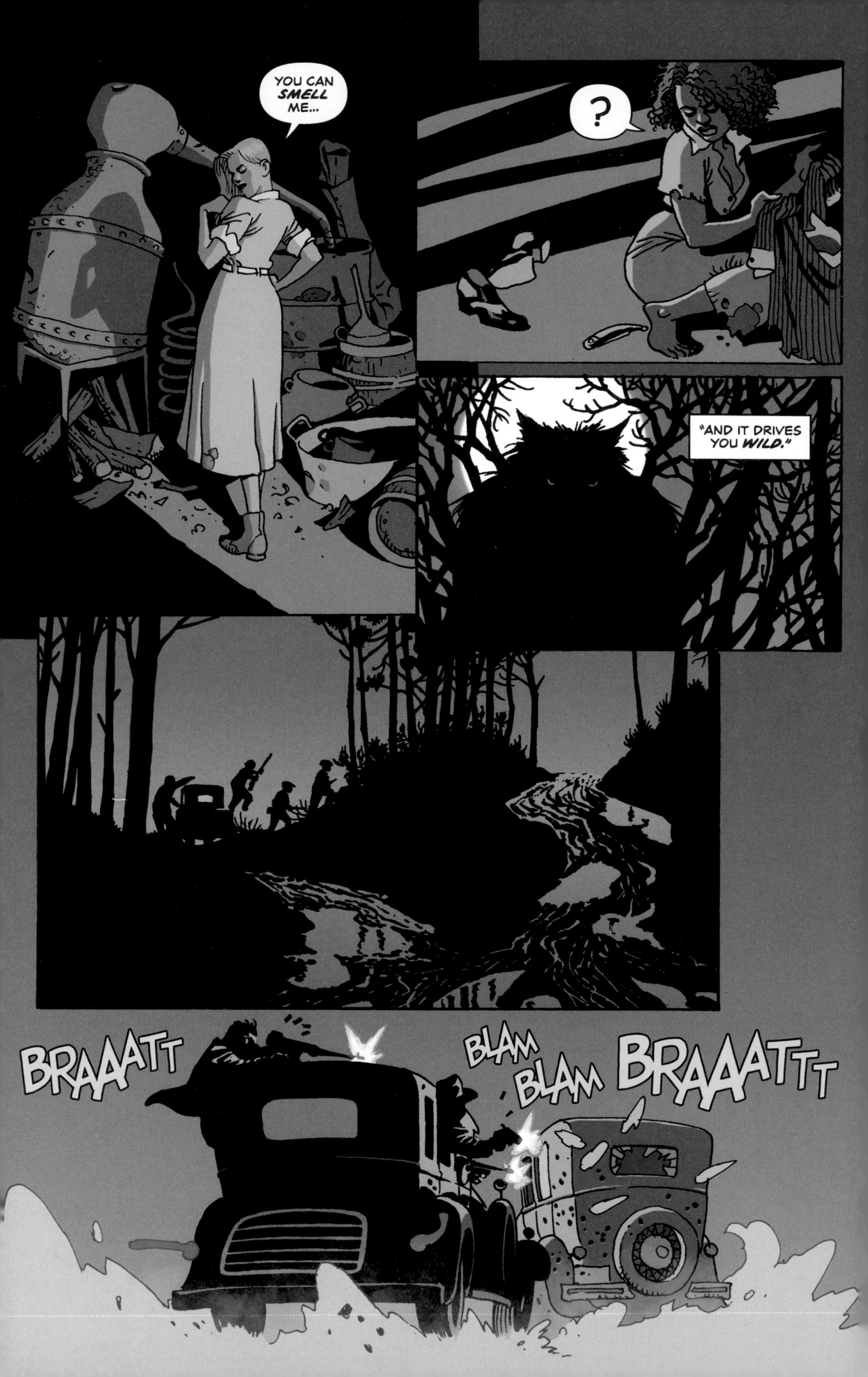
YOU CAN SMELL ME...
?
"AND IT DRIVES YOU WILD."
BRAAATT
BLAM
BLAM
BRAAATTTT

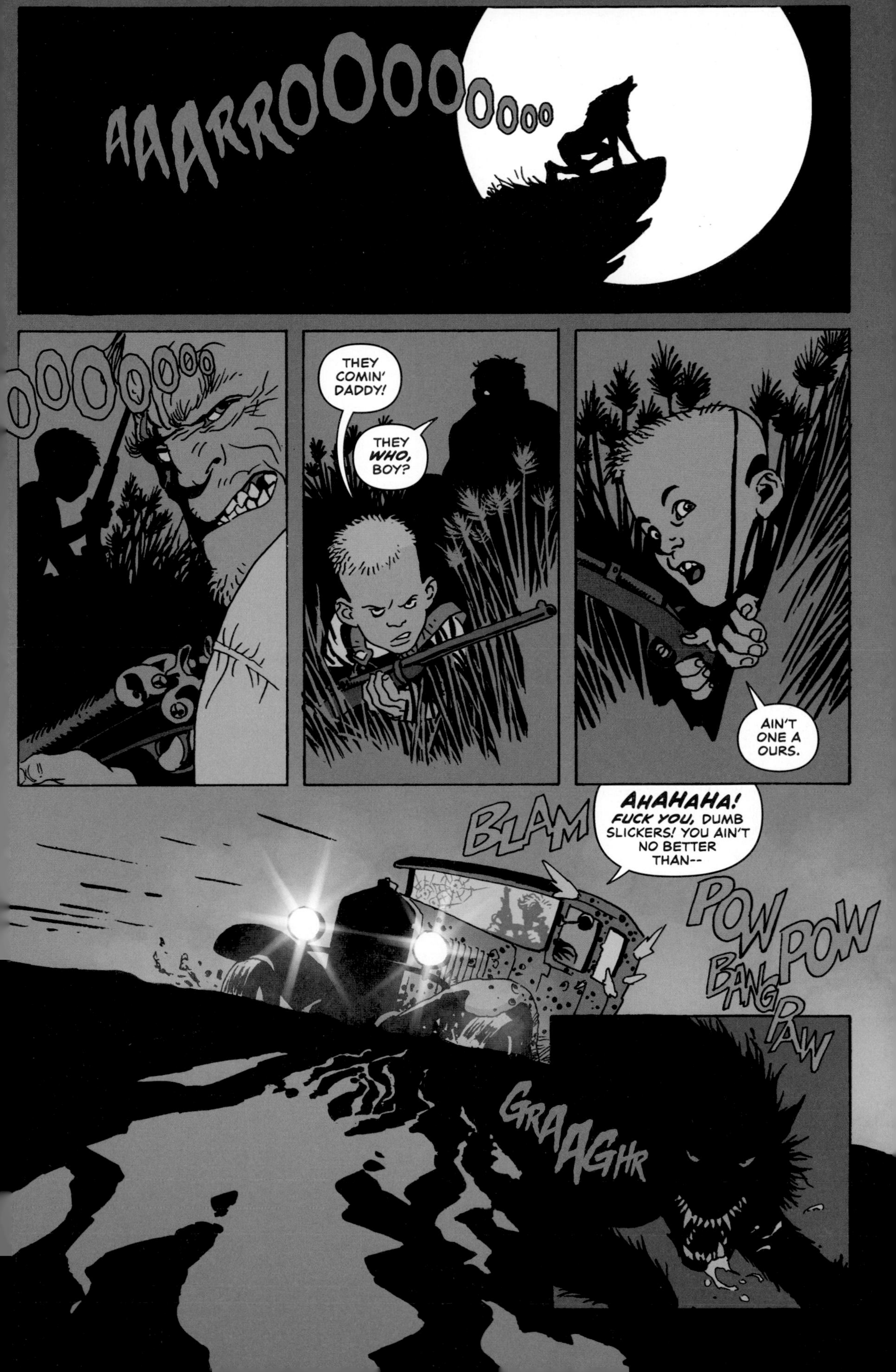
AAARROOOOOOoooo
OOOOOOOo
THEY COMIN' DADDY!
THEY WHO, BOY?
AIN'T ONE A OURS.
BLAM
AHAHAHA! FUCK YOU, DUMB SLICKERS! YOU AIN'T NO BETTER THAN--
POW POW POW
BANG PAW
GRAAGHR

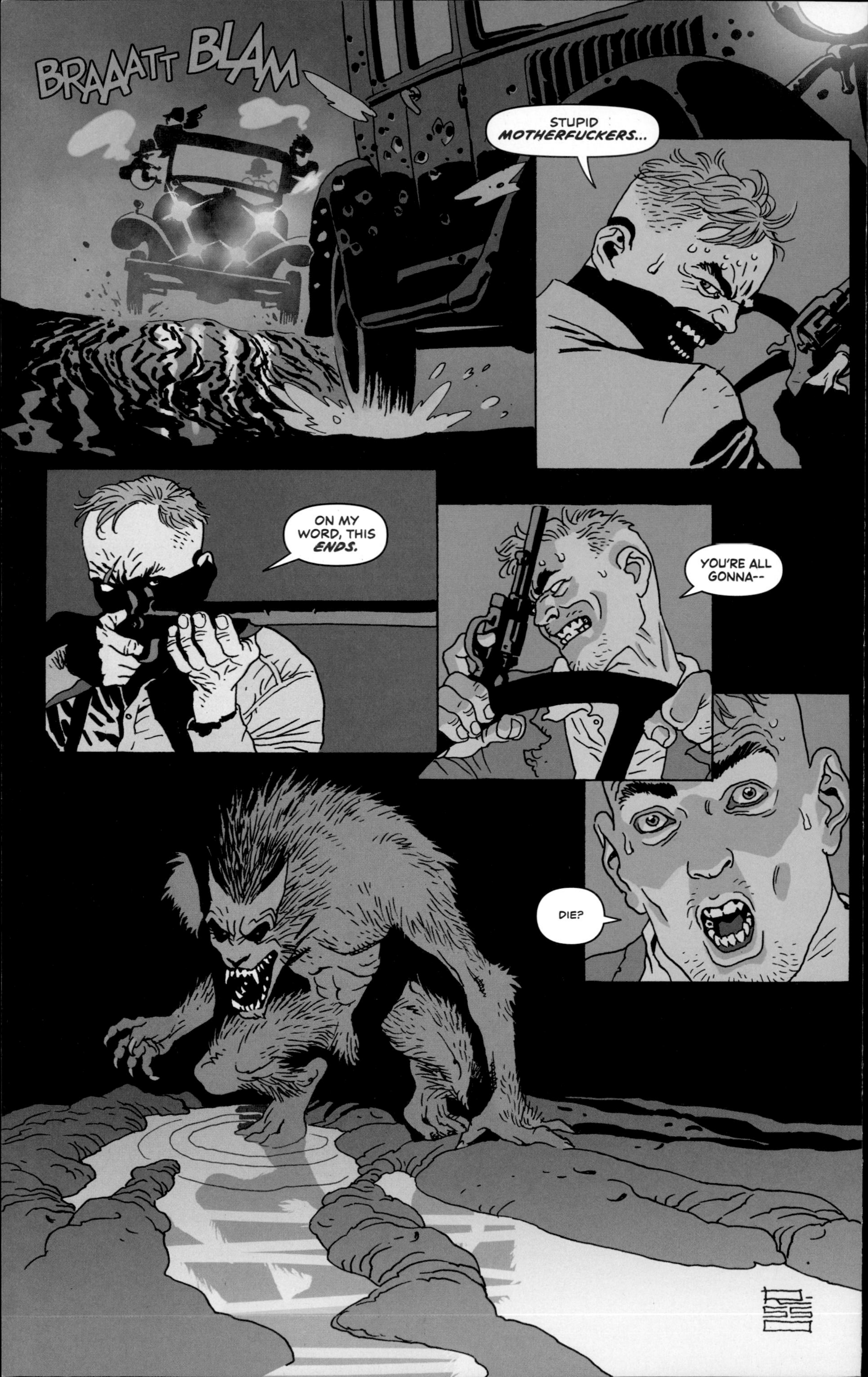
BRAAATT BLAM
STUPID MOTHERFUCKERS...
ON MY WORD, THIS ENDS.
YOU'RE ALL GONNA--
DIE?

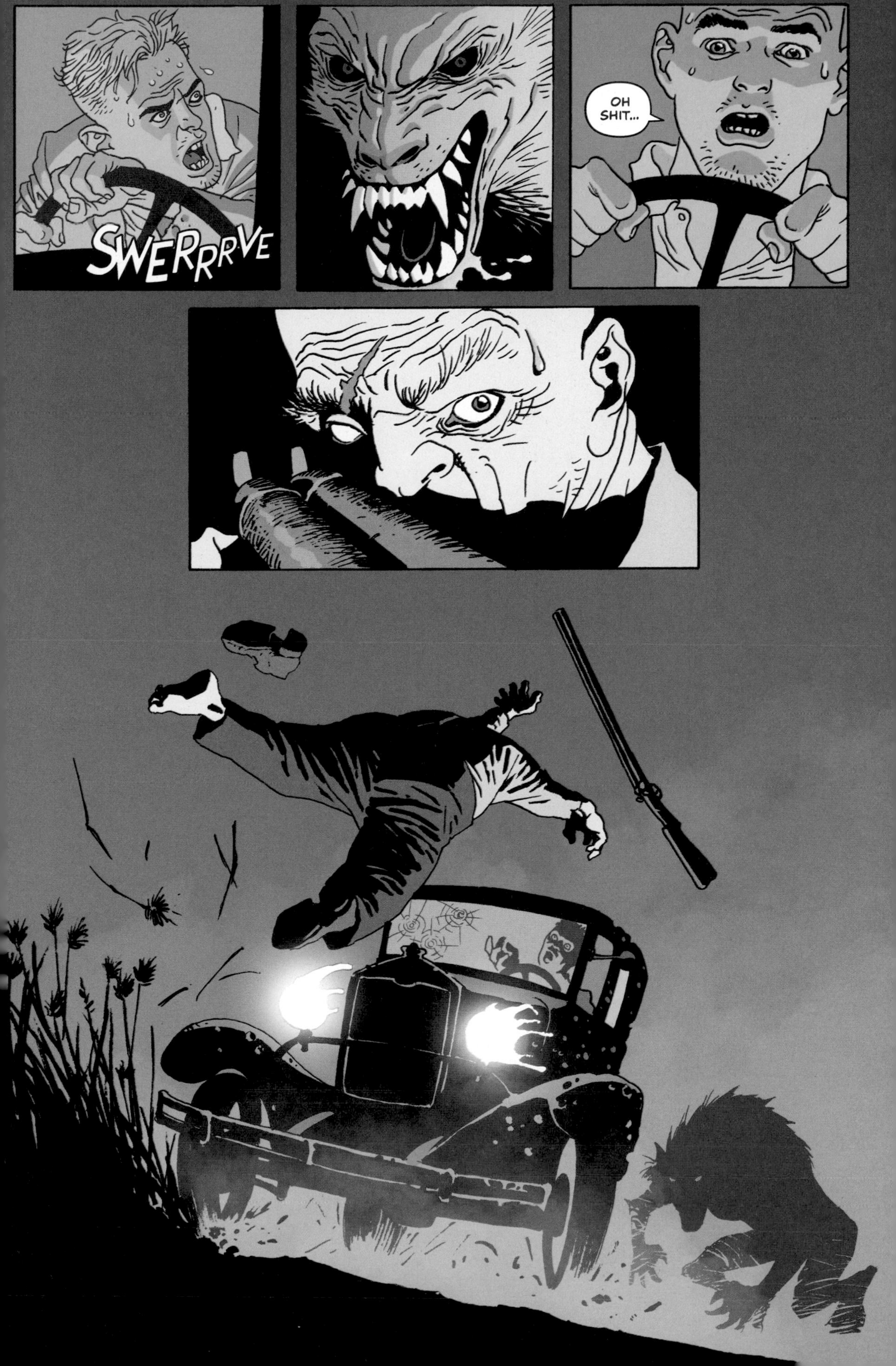
SWERRRVE
OH SHIT...

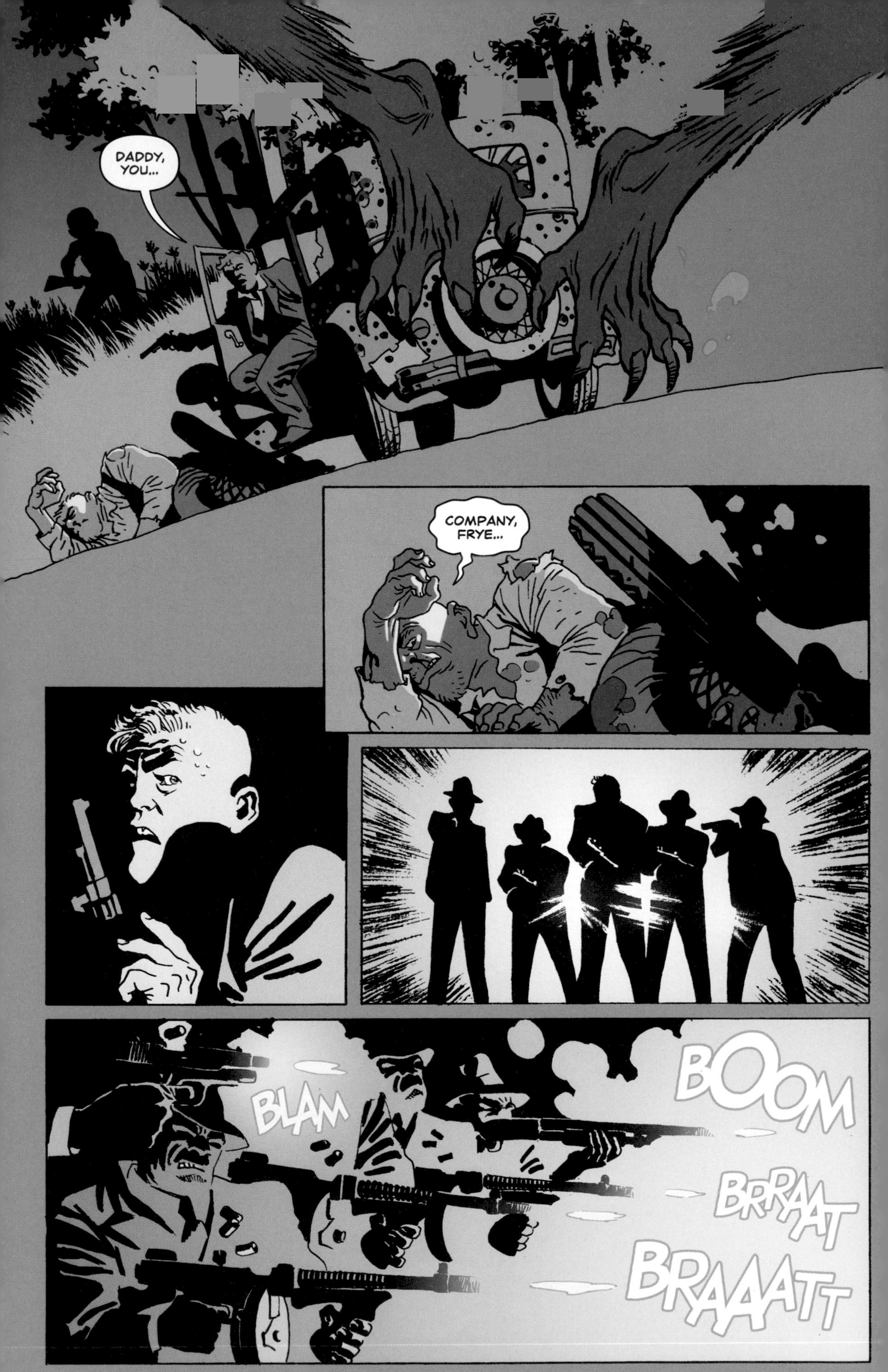
DADDY, YOU...
COMPANY, FRYE...
BLAM
BOOM
BRRAAT
BRAAATT

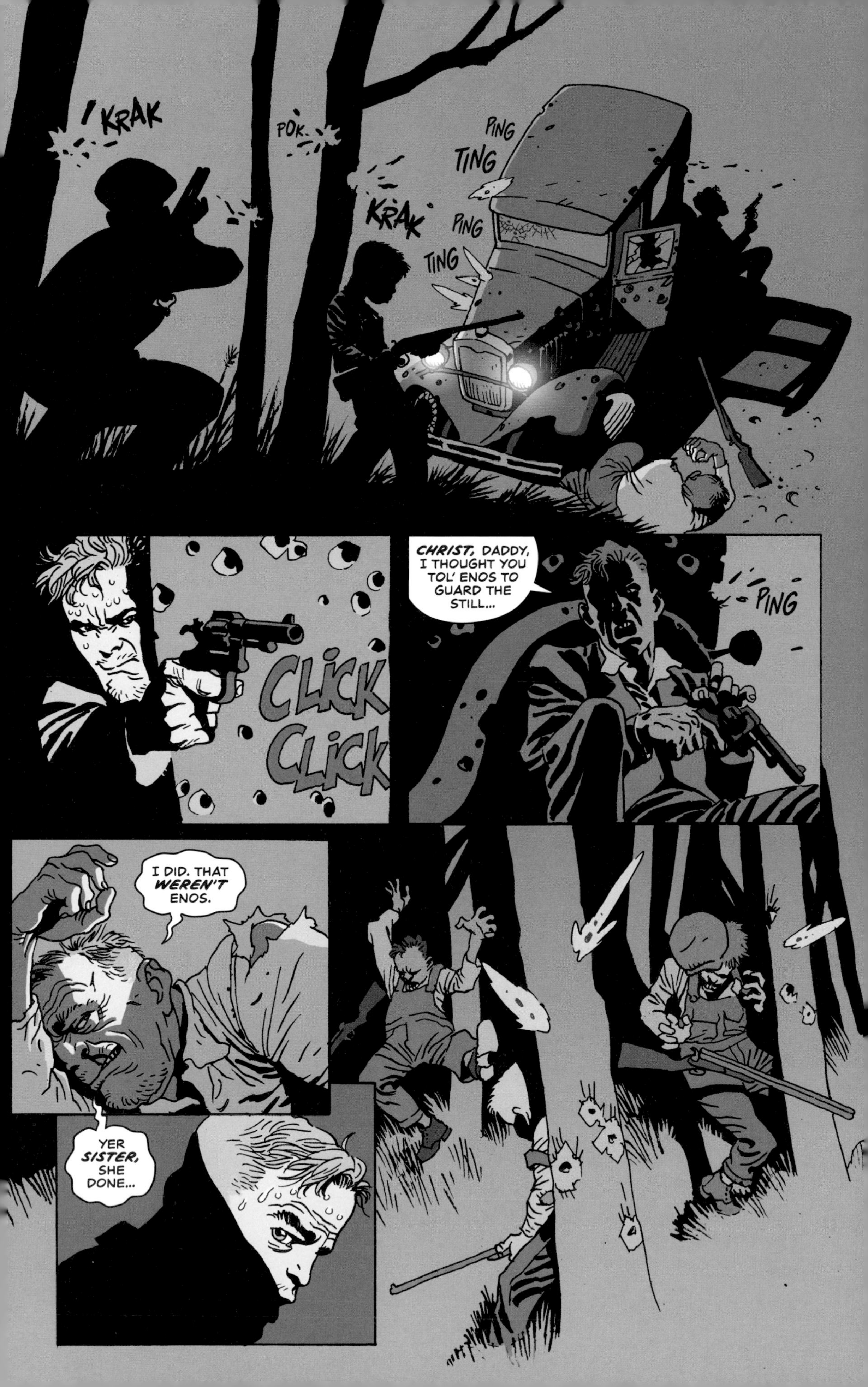
KRAK
POK
KRAK
PING
TING
PING
TING
CLICK
CLICK
CHRIST, DADDY, I THOUGHT YOU TOL' ENOS TO GUARD THE STILL...
PING
I DID. THAT WEREN'T ENOS.
YER SISTER, SHE DONE...

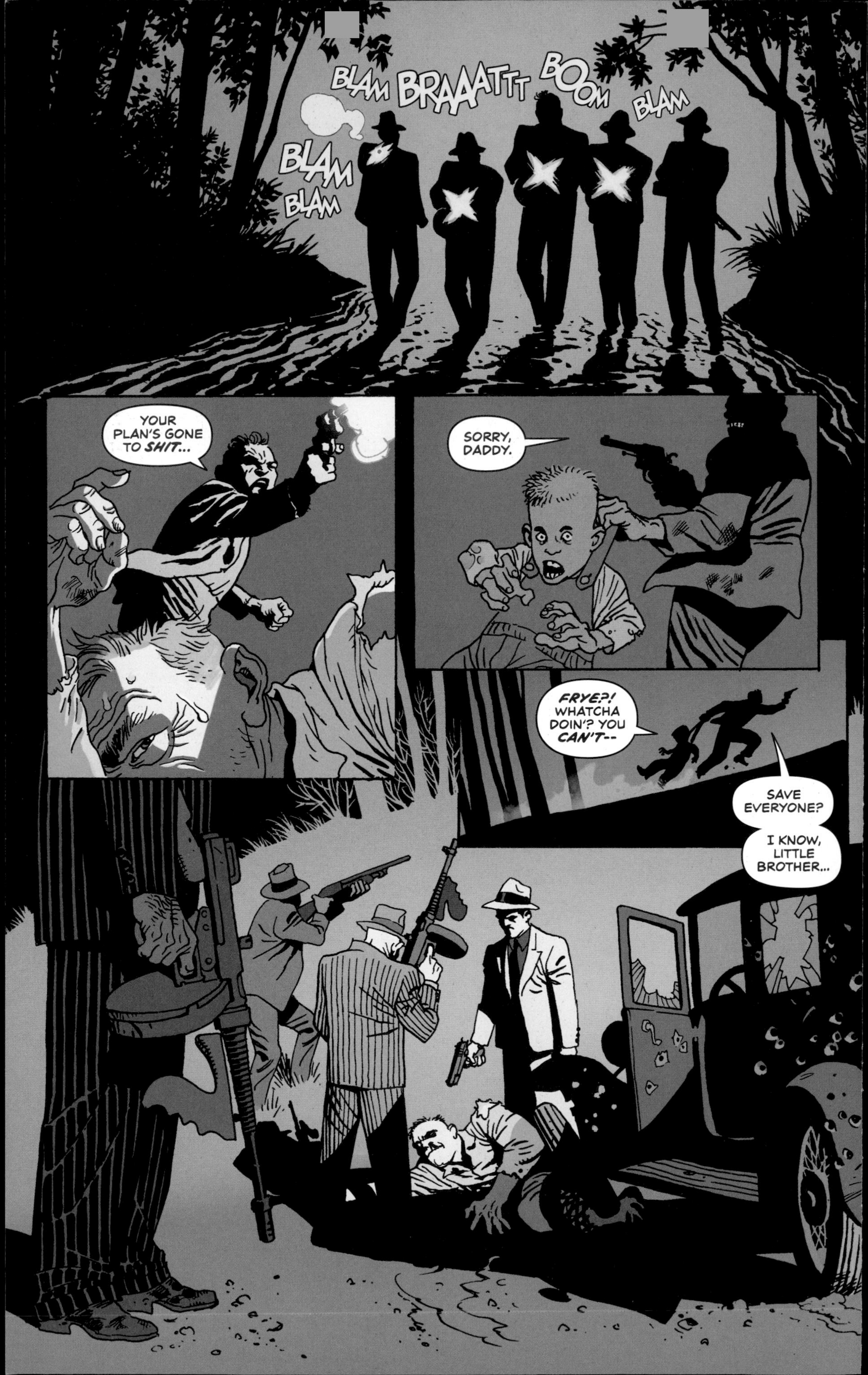
BLAM BRAAATTT BOOM
BLAM
BLAM
BLAM
YOUR PLAN'S GONE TO *SHIT*...
SORRY, DADDY.
FRYE?! WHATCHA DOIN'? YOU *CAN'T*--
SAVE EVERYONE?
I KNOW, LITTLE BROTHER...

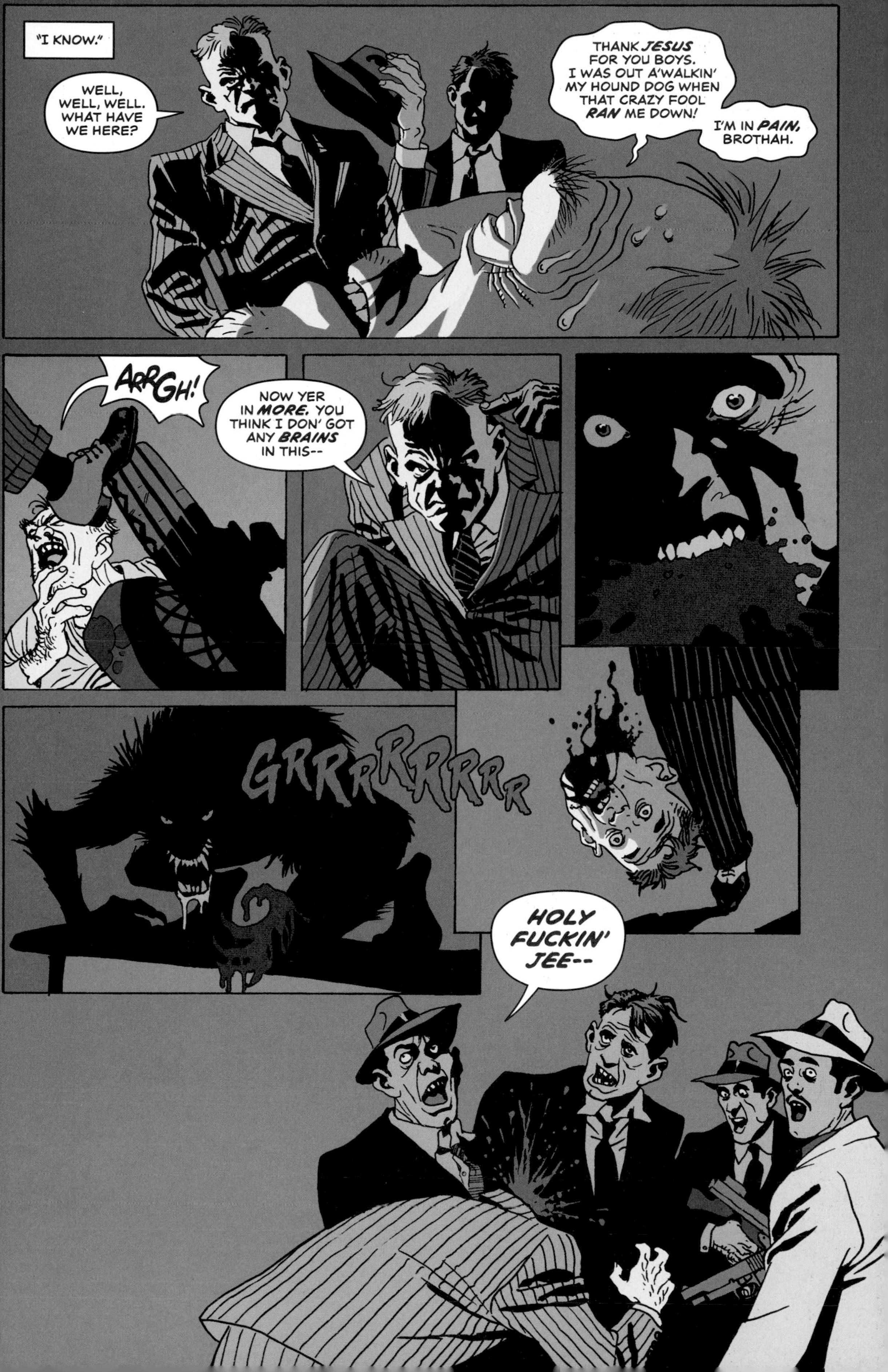
"I KNOW."
WELL, WELL, WELL. WHAT HAVE WE HERE?
THANK JESUS FOR YOU BOYS. I WAS OUT A'WALKIN' MY HOUND DOG WHEN THAT CRAZY FOOL RAN ME DOWN!
I'M IN PAIN, BROTHAH.
ARRGH!
NOW YER IN MORE. YOU THINK I DON' GOT ANY BRAINS IN THIS--
GRRRRRRRRR
HOLY FUCKIN' JEE--

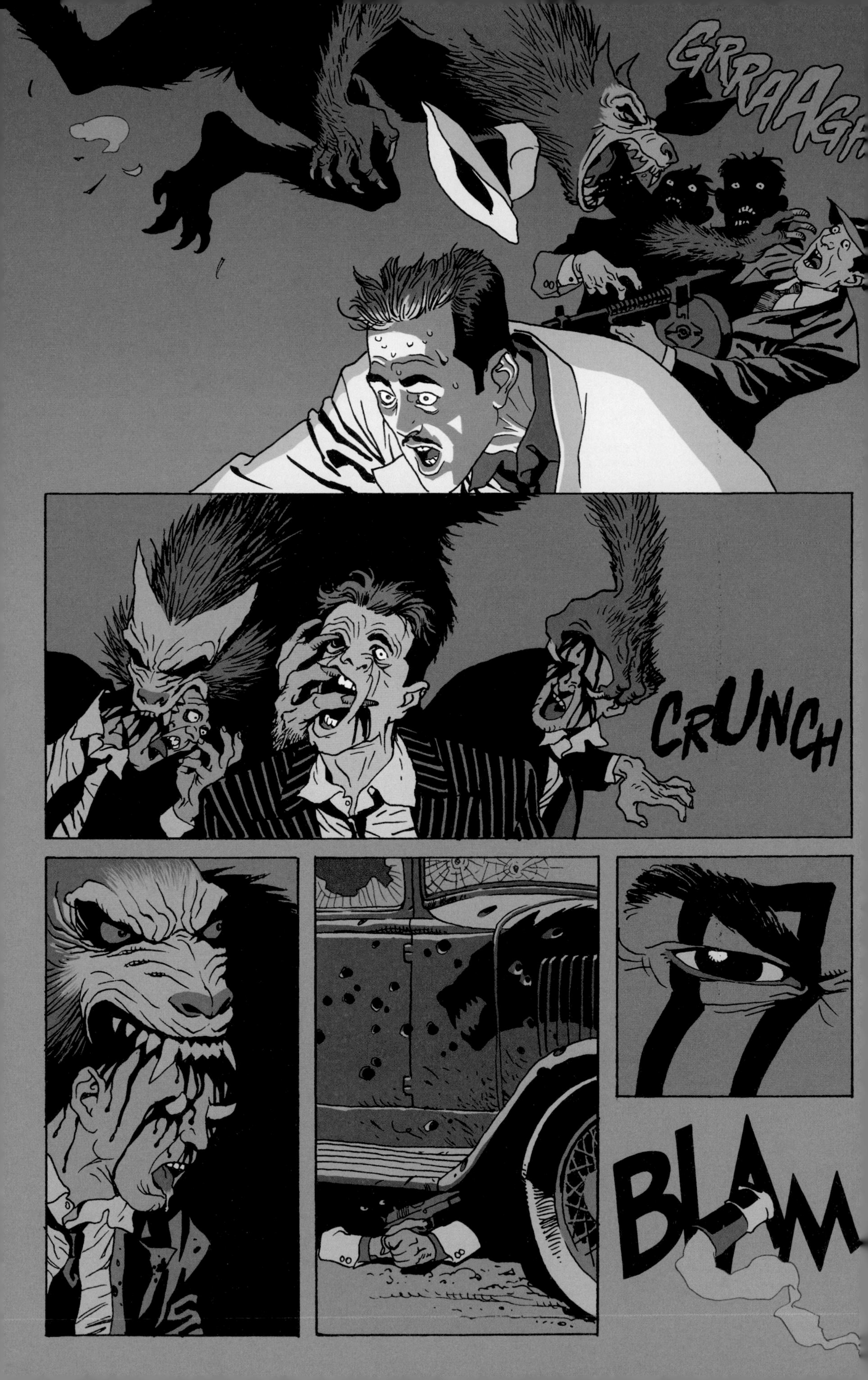
GRRAAAGH
CRUNCH
BLAM

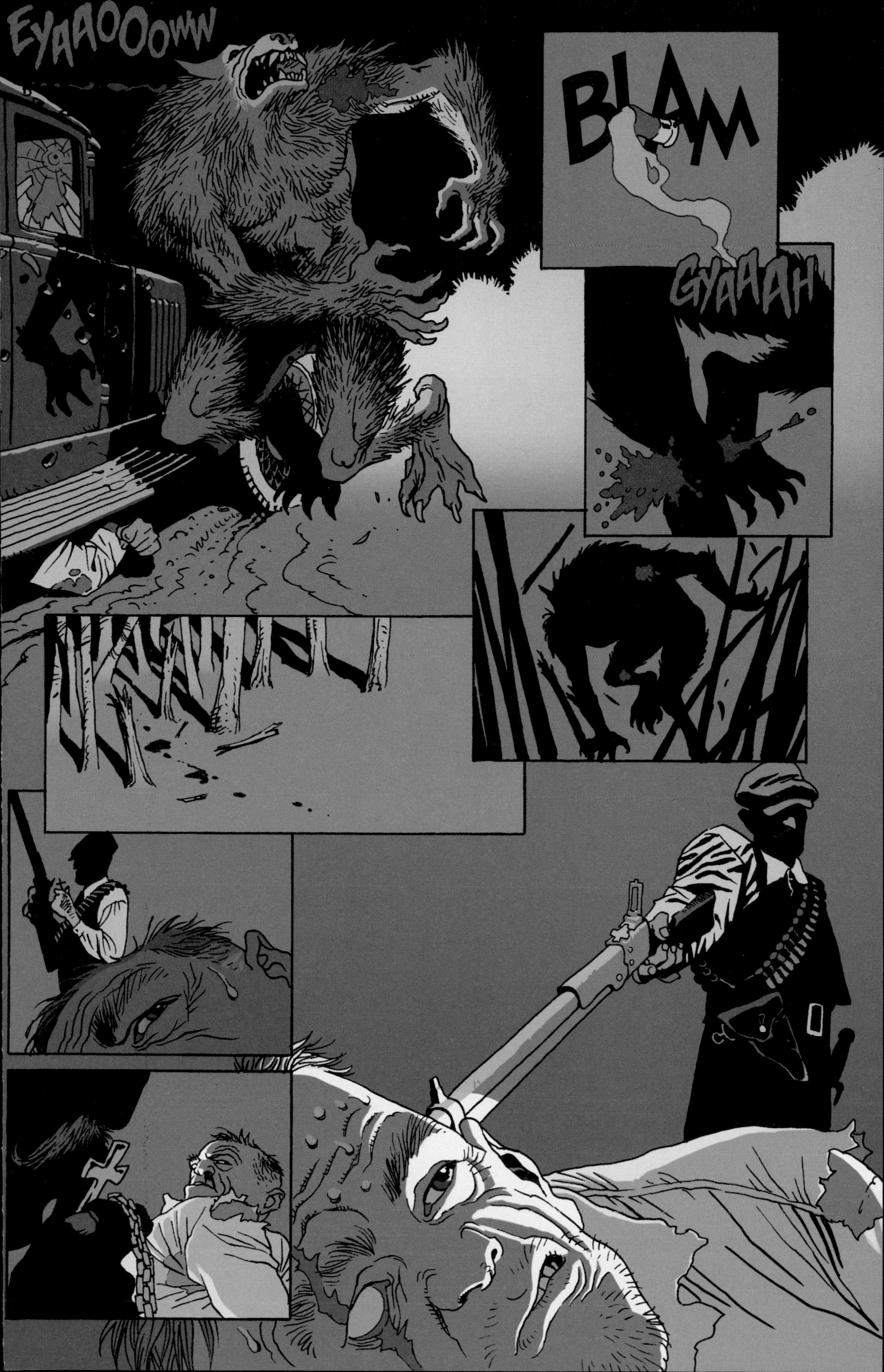
EYAAOOOWW
BLAM
GYAAAH

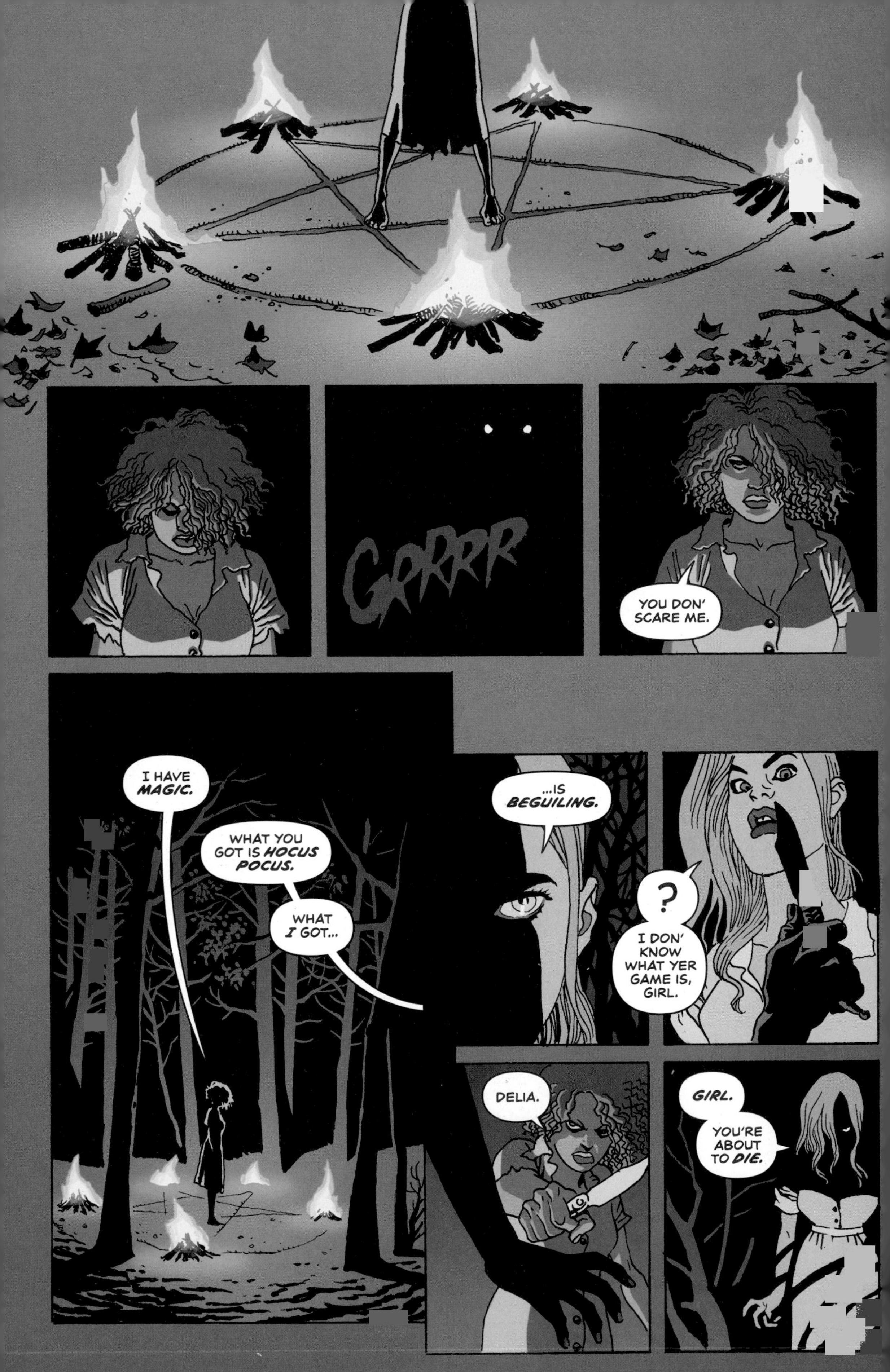
GRRRR
YOU DON' SCARE ME.
I HAVE MAGIC.
WHAT YOU GOT IS HOCUS POCUS.
WHAT I GOT...
...IS BEGUILING.
?
I DON' KNOW WHAT YER GAME IS, GIRL.
DELIA.
GIRL.
YOU'RE ABOUT TO DIE.

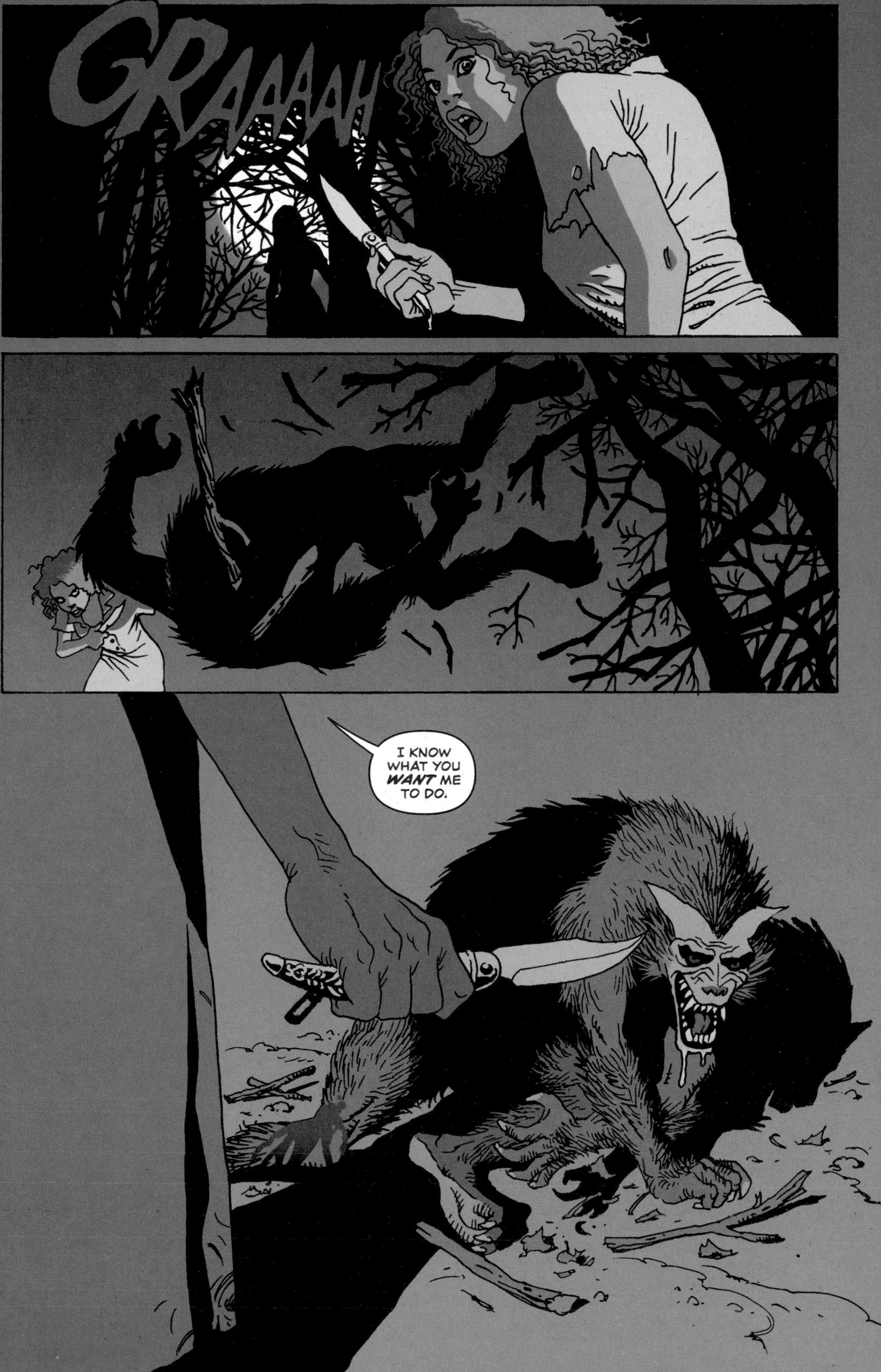
GRAAAAH
I KNOW WHAT YOU WANT ME TO DO.

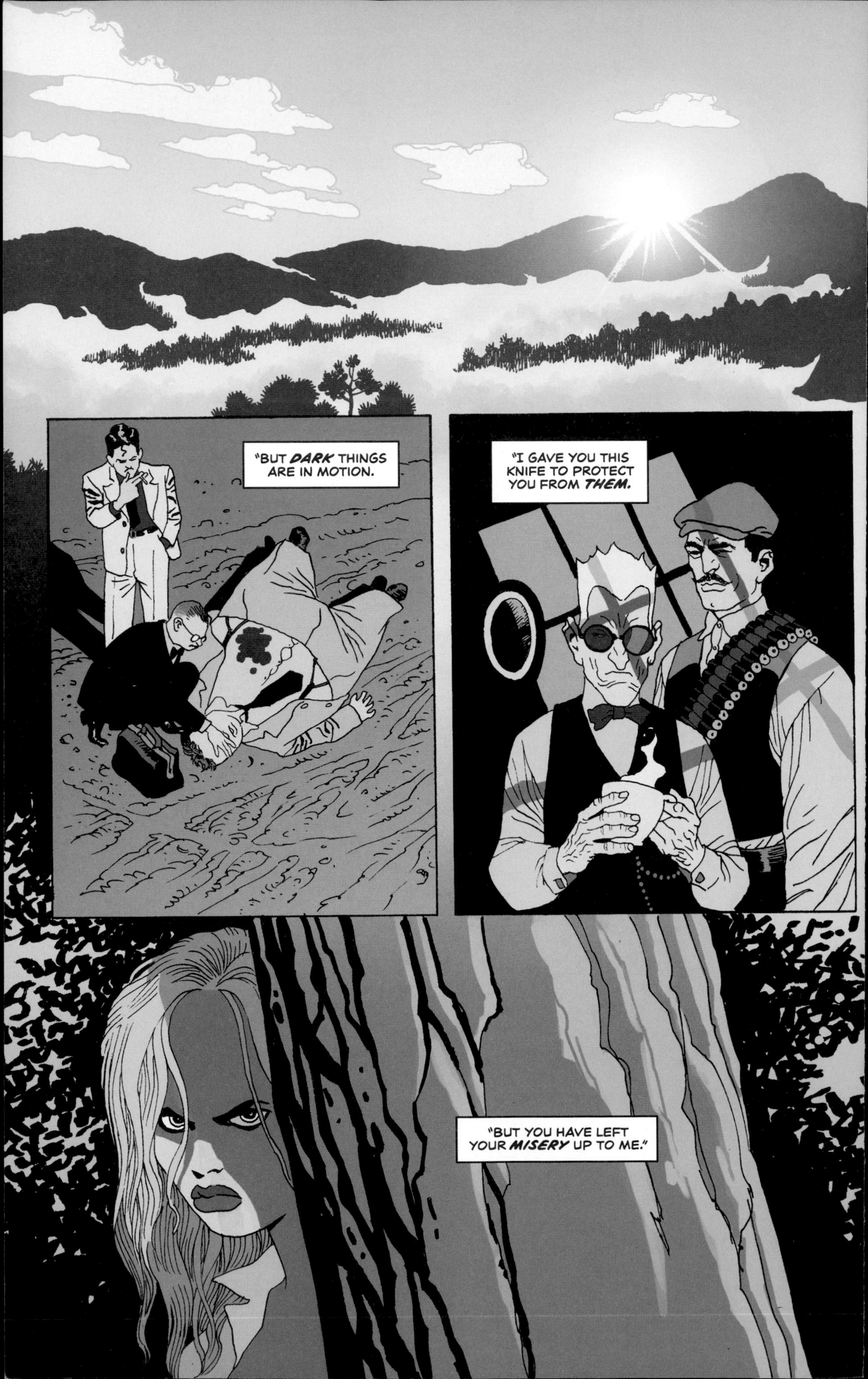
"BUT DARK THINGS ARE IN MOTION.
"I GAVE YOU THIS KNIFE TO PROTECT YOU FROM THEM.
"BUT YOU HAVE LEFT YOUR MISERY UP TO ME."

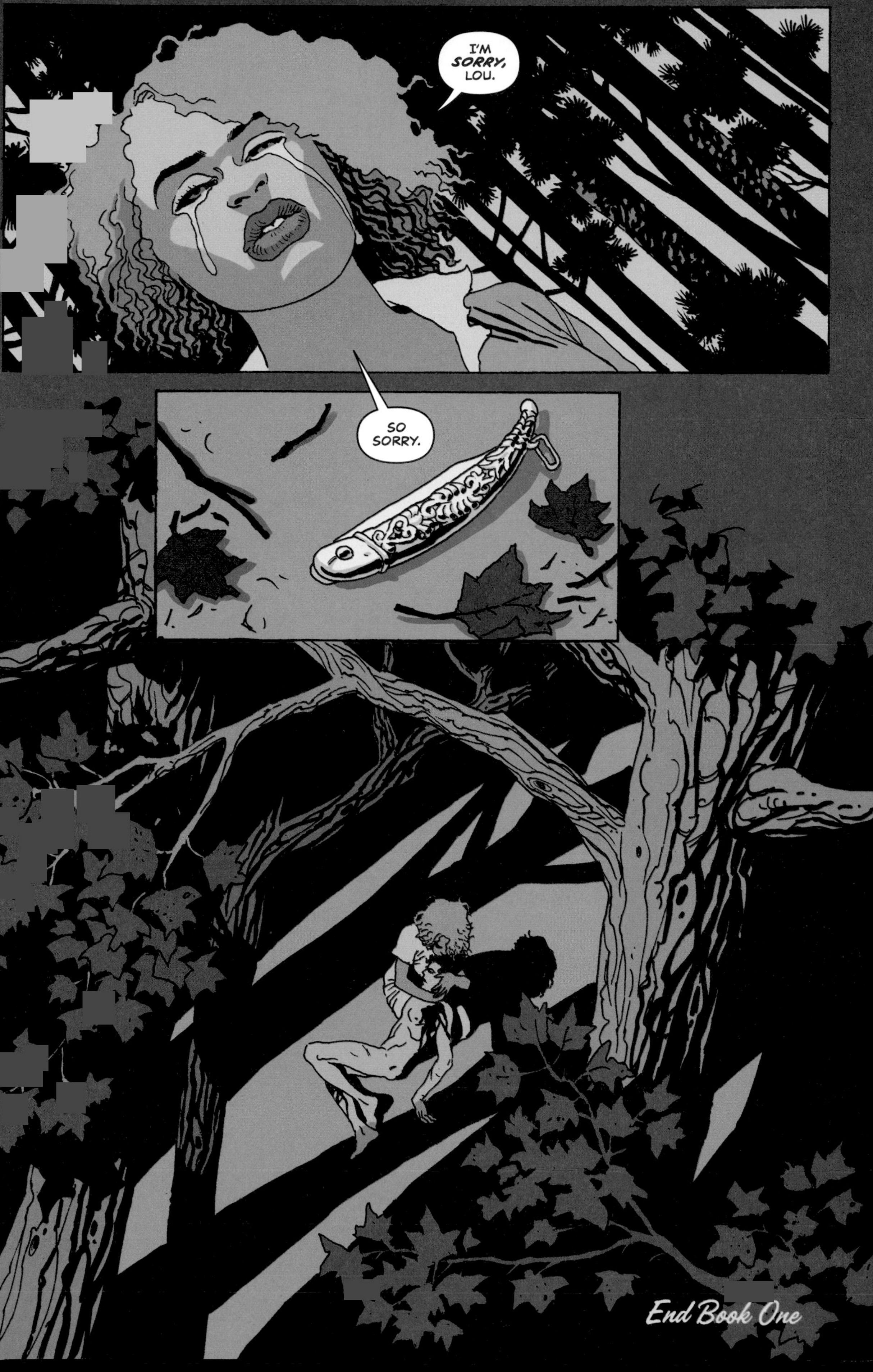
I'M SORRY, LOU.
SO SORRY.
End Book One

MOONSHINE

Variant Cover Gallery

FRANK MILLER

DAVE JOHNSON

JOCK

LEE BERMEJO

JUAN DOE

JILL THOMPSON

CLIFF CHIANG

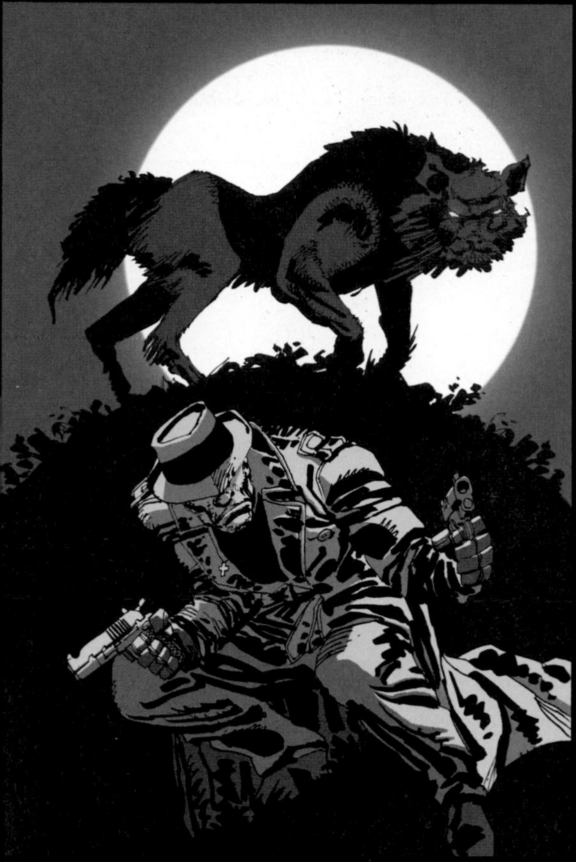

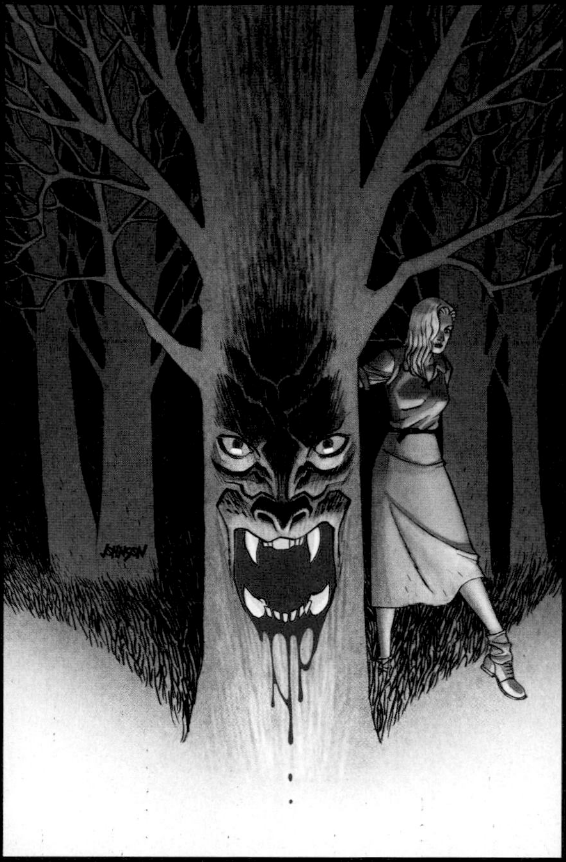

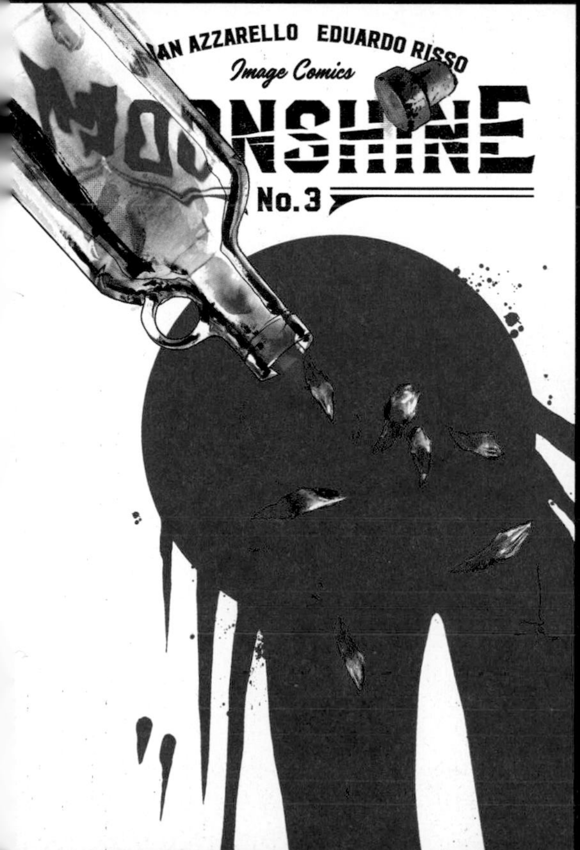
AN AZZARELLO EDUARDO RISSO
Image Comics
ONSHINE
No. 3

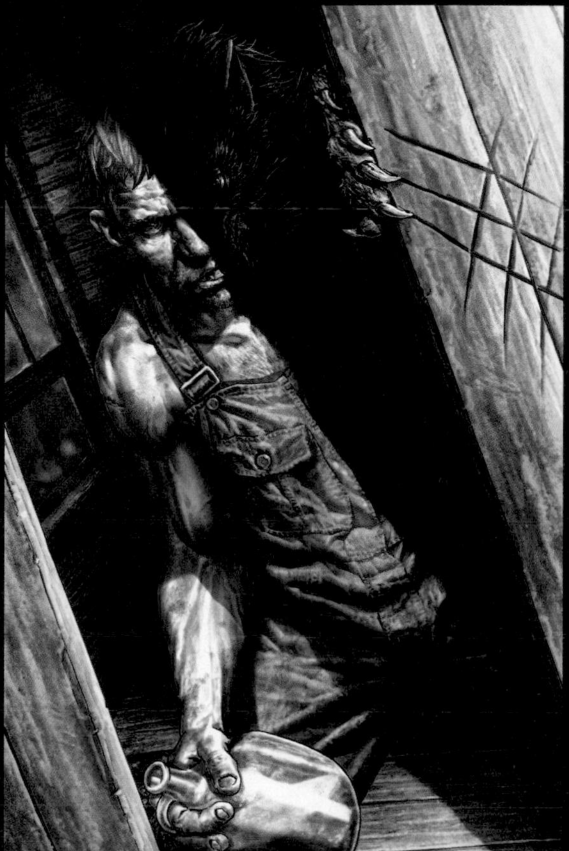

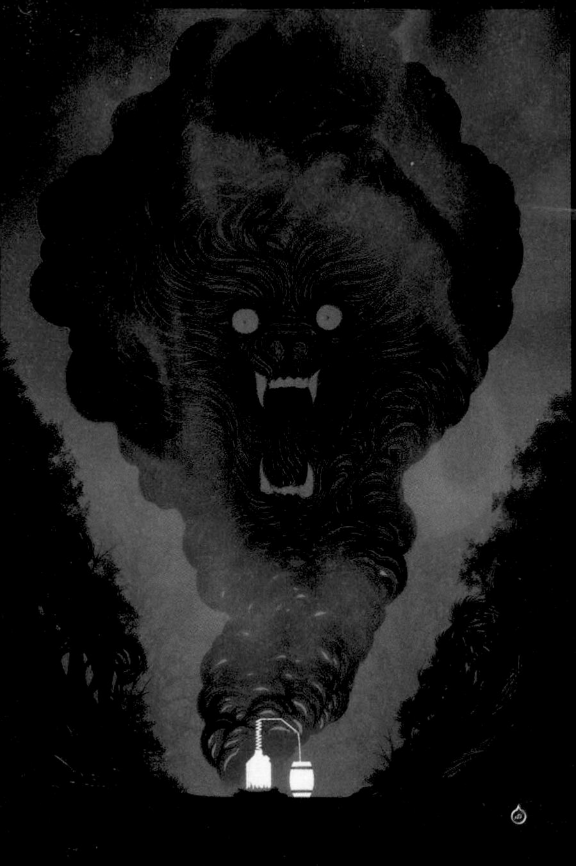

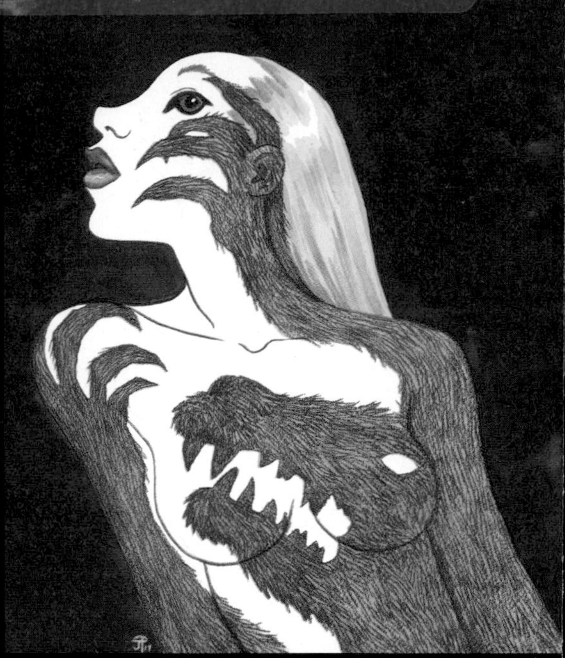

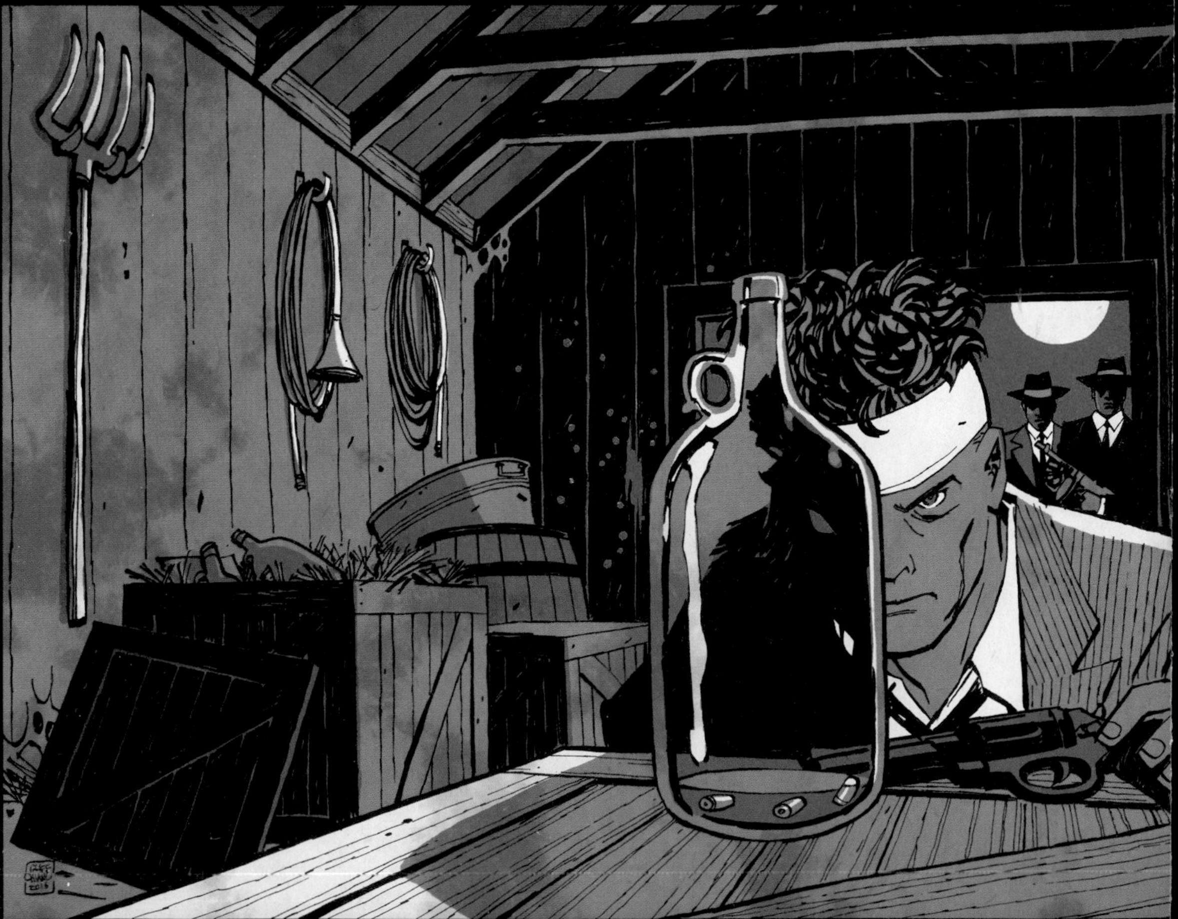